"What's it like to fly, Cody?"

"When you're flying you're fully alive. When you're in the air, every minute seems like an hour. You'll never forget any of it."

He turned her slowly in his arms. "I will always remember every moment, just like now." He kissed her forehead lightly. "You are so beautiful." Brushing her lips with his own, he whispered, "I don't think I've ever been so attracted to a woman. When I turned and saw you in the crowd it was as though lightning had struck only a few feet from me."

Cody lowered his lips to hers, and Katherine gave no resistance. His lips were gentle at first, then grew more demanding. Running her fingers into his sandy hair, she touched his windblown curls—the same curls that had touched the clouds. . . .

Praise for Jodi Thomas's previous novels:

PRAIRIE SONG

"A THOROUGHLY ENTERTAINING ROMANCE."
—*Gothic Journal*

THE TENDER TEXAN

Winner of the Romance Writers of America
Best Historical Series Romance in 1991 Award

"EXCELLENT! . . . HAVE THE TISSUES READY;
THIS TENDER LOVE STORY . . . WILL
TUG AT YOUR HEART. MEMORABLE READING."
—*Rend*

CHERISH THE DREAM

JODI THOMAS

DIAMOND BOOKS, NEW YORK

This book is a Diamond original edition,
and has never been previously published.

CHERISH THE DREAM

A Diamond Book / published by arrangement with
the author

PRINTING HISTORY
Diamond edition / April 1993

ISBN: 1-55773-881-5

Diamond Books are published by The Berkley Publishing Group,
200 Madison Avenue, New York, NY 10016.
The name "DIAMOND" and its logo
are trademarks belonging to Charter Communications, Inc.

PRINTED IN THE UNITED STATES OF AMERICA

10 9 8 7 6 5 4 3 2 1

*I dedicate this book to one of the true
heroes in my life, my brother,
Philip Clifton Price,
and to the best cheerleader in the world,
my sister-in-law,
Victoria Price*

Prologue

1900

"I CAN'T CUT myself!" eight-year-old Sarah Anderson whispered, trying not to sound like a baby.

"You have to or it won't work," Katherine McMiller insisted, pulling the stolen knife from her smock pocket.

Sarah lifted her tiny hand up to her friend. "You do it for me, Kat."

Raising her head above the hay fortress they were hiding in, Katherine agreed. "All right, Sarah, but we have to hurry. The wagon will be coming back from town any minute." She gripped the old pocket knife in her fist and ran the blade over Sarah's open palm.

Sarah blinked hard but didn't pull away or cry out as a line of crimson followed the blade across her flesh. She stared at her chubby hand as if it were someone else's. Her nails were dirty and ragged, as were those of most of the children at the farm. Calluses lined her palms like war ribbons as evidence of her hard labor. Slowly her blood dripped between her fingers and onto the barn floor.

Katherine opened her own hand and ran the knife across her palm. Watching, Sarah felt Katherine's pain as deeply as she felt her own. The two girls tenderly pressed their bleeding hands together. Katherine pulled a tattered blue ribbon from Sarah's ebony hair and bound their wrists together. "Now," she whispered, "we're blood sisters, just as the Indians were blood brothers."

"Forever and ever. No matter what." Sarah nodded.

"Forever and ever. No matter what," Katherine echoed.

That night the girls lay on their cots in a cold windowless room that was little more than a closet. After forcing themselves not to cry while being whipped by Mrs. McFail, the farm manager, they now let their tears flow in the darkness. The iodine had stung their hands even worse than the knife. The cuts would heal and the welts from the belt would fade, but both girls knew nothing would ever break the bond they had forged.

"Sarah," Katherine whispered between sobs, "you should have told her I did it; then she would have only whipped me."

"I couldn't; we're blood sisters, remember?"

Katherine tried to answer, but the fear that always overtook her at night choked her words before they could leave her throat. She could face anything in daylight, but not in the darkness.

"Sarah, hold my hand?" Katherine's brave young voice shook slightly.

"Sure," Sarah answered, stretching her bandaged hand across the open space to Katherine. "When we're grown, we'll live in a house somewhere nice and we'll leave the lamp burning all night long. Your room will have windows from floor to ceiling, and if the night's too cloudy for stars, I'll put Chinese lanterns up in the trees so you can always see out no matter how dark it gets."

Katherine drifted off to sleep as Sarah spoke in her gentle voice of years to come. Neither one of them had any family, but they had each other.

We're really sisters now, Sarah thought. She smiled as she covered Katherine's hand with her blanket. Katherine was the only person on this earth who cared about her, and Sarah knew that one was a long way from none.

One

1910

KATHERINE PULLED SARAH up the grassy hill just outside Dayton, Ohio. The late autumn wind whipped at Katherine's long navy skirt and pulled strands of her red hair away from her white cap. "Come on, Sarah, or we'll miss seeing the flight."

At age eighteen, Sarah was fully grown, but with her short legs, she could not keep up with Katherine's long strides. "Go on without me. I'll see this great flying machine when it lands."

"No, we want to see it take off."

Sarah mumbled, "*We*," under her breath and tried to keep up with her long-legged friend. Everything about Katherine was like the wind of a summer storm. She was tall and willowy with hair that seemed to battle itself in different lights to be first red, then auburn. She could explode with laughter one minute and with anger the next as easily as a breeze whirls into a tornado. She was straightforward, unafraid to take gulps of life, be they swallows of joy or pain. Katherine's only fear lay hidden in the hours of darkness, but the night seemed far away on this chilly morning. No, Sarah thought, Katherine never backed away from anything, but fought with both fury and warmth for her right to survive.

"You're going to love what we see, Sarah. One of the nurses told me this is a test site for new Wright Company planes and pilots. She said the machines just lift off the ground and fly through the air like birds. A man sits smack in the middle of each one's breast, telling it where to go.''

"Katherine!" Sarah scolded and laughed as her friend acted shocked at having said the word "breast" aloud. Sarah shook her finger as she climbed. "Proper young ladies at the Mamie Willingham School of Nursing don't use the names of parts of the body lightly.''

Katherine whirled in front of Sarah, holding her hand to her forehead in a mock faint. "Heaven help me if I ever have to treat a man who's been injured in what Miss Willingham calls 'the privates.' He'll probably die before I find the wound.''

Something about being eighteen and a month away from graduating from nursing school made everything seem funny and bright. Sarah knew she worried more than Katherine did about the upcoming year of working at the county mental hospital to pay off their tuition, but then, she worried about everything more than Katherine did.

They reached the top of the hill just as the roar of an engine filled the crisp air.

"Look, Sarah, there are the biplanes. Folks say the Wright pilots make fifty dollars a day for flying.''

Sarah watched as men moved away from a plane that looked like a huge toy kite. The wheels began to roll down the field as another man, looking quite fragile, crouched low inside the plane to face the wind. Two men ran beside each wing, steadying the flimsy boxlike bird. The wheels moved faster and faster over the grassy earth.

Suddenly the whirling wheels slackened their speed, but the vehicle advanced even faster. The two men on the wings fell away as if running backward. Sarah blinked, trying to make her mind accept what her eyes beheld. In a moment of miracles the craft was airborne. She felt her heart jump. The plane climbed, and her pulse quickened as if a part of her had also risen up over the countryside. She could understand why people paid to see air shows. Every person watching felt like a passenger on the flight, experiencing a tiny fraction of the miracle, a tiny taste of the fear.

Katherine whispered, afraid her voice would somehow endanger the pilot's safety. "Isn't it wonderful? I feel I may explode just watching."

The plane took a sudden dip, and both girls caught their breath in terror. It leveled and turned, bumping against a gray bank of clouds, and began its journey back to the field.

The marvelous man-made bird flew over them while they waved frantically, caught up in the excitement of flight. As the machine descended to the ground, a sudden gust of wind bounced it up, then flung it hard against the earth. Sarah cried out as the pilot rolled out of the flimsy machine. His body seemed to be made of rags as he sprawled on the ground like a doll tossed hastily aside.

Both girls started down the hill toward the injured man, and the group of men beside the other plane all broke into a run.

The pilot raised his head, then pulled himself slowly to his feet. He removed his cap and waved toward the others as if to signal that he was fine, then limped toward the plane.

Sarah pulled Katherine to a stop. "He's going to be all right, Kat. He's lucky."

"We need to go closer. We're too far away to tell if he's broken a leg."

Sarah stood her ground. "No, Kat. He'd hardly walk away with a broken leg. Besides, I don't think two women would be welcome. Nobody's supposed to know about this place."

"You're right," Katherine answered as she watched the men reach the plane and begin pushing it back up the meadow.

Katherine sighed. "I'm going to go flying someday, Sarah. I've got to see what it's like to be that high above the earth."

"You can't be serious. A woman would never get into one of those things!" But Sarah knew her friend too well. Nothing excited Katherine more than a new adventure, even if it held the risk of danger.

Katherine fell into step with Sarah, but her mind seemed to be somewhere in the future. "I'd do anything to fly, and one of these days I'll prove it."

"The Wright brothers don't take women in their school," Sarah reasoned.

Excitement sparkled in Katherine's emerald-green eyes. "I don't care. I'll find someone to take me flying."

"But how? One of those machines must cost more than we could save in a year. You can't just walk down there and say, 'Pardon me, Mr. Birdman, I'd like to fly in your plane.'"

"Maybe not." Katherine bit her full bottom lip in thought. "But if we went to where the pilots were . . . and if we met them . . ."

"Stop right there, Katherine McMiller. I'm not going with you to any place where men crazy enough to go up in a machine like that might be and that's final."

Katherine linked her arm in Sarah's. "You could wear your mist-blue dress. I just know you'd dance ever so grandly in those new suede shoes." Katherine lifted her cotton apron as though it were fine silk and twirled around. "I'm sure I can talk Miss Willingham into giving us Saturday night off if we promise to work Sunday night instead. One of the other girls said a lot of the birdmen go to O'Grady's on Saturday nights."

"No, Kat! I'm not going. That place is only one step above a saloon. Some of the girls may go there, but not me."

"But who'll keep me out of trouble if I go alone?"

"You'd go alone?"

"If I have to."

Sarah sighed, trying to decide whether to give in now or

later. She knew if Kat had her mind set on going, nothing would change it. Sarah also knew she would never let her go alone. The night they'd run away from the children's farm together flashed through Sarah's mind. Katherine was the one who'd been brave enough to plan the escape, but it was Sarah who'd dreamed of going to the Mamie Willingham School of Nursing and saved enough money to get them there. No matter how hard things got, they always had each other. "You're right. I'll wear my blue dress." Sarah tried to sound excited. "But I'm having nothing to do with any man who has a death wish so huge he must try flying. I want to heal people, not watch them splatter themselves over a field when that funny machine decides not to stay in the air."

Katherine hugged her friend wildly and laughed. "We'll have fun, Sarah, just wait and see."

Sarah wasn't worried about having fun. She'd watched Katherine do some pretty wild things over the years and had always gone along for the ride. But this time Sarah's sensible mind feared the ride might just get one of them killed.

Two

KATHERINE PUSHED A rebellious strand of hair back into her cap and straightened her apron as she walked toward Miss Willingham's office. It would never do to be caught shabbily dressed by the hawk-eyed dean.

The office door was open, and Katherine approached with determination and entered. Immediately the room sent a chill over her, even though a stove clanked feverishly in one corner. The stately dean of the nursing school looked like an aging queen behind the massive desk. Her blouse was as starched and crisp as her manner; and though most nurses now wore the more fashionable soft collars on their uniforms, Miss Willingham's collar remained high, with thin ribs of boning to ensure stiffness.

As Katherine neared, the elderly woman looked up and smiled a tight-lipped greeting that altered her face for only an instant.

"Come in, Katherine."

"I need to talk with you, ma'am. If you have the time?"

The woman nodded. "I was just stopping for a cup of tea. Won't you join me?"

Katherine moved to the seating area by the windows and waited for Miss Willingham. One thing she had always admired about the dean was her sense of equality. No student was too lowly to join her for tea, as long as her hands were clean. And no man was so high she wouldn't correct him if he stepped out of line. This one trait endeared the older nurse to doctors and grounds workers alike.

Miss Willingham seated herself and began to pour. Her porcelain was fine Scottish china, and her tea silver was worn thin from polishing. "I remember the day you and Sarah came to my office pleading to attend this school. The two of you had not a dollar between you and couldn't have been more than twelve years old. Runaways, but from the looks of you, the life you left couldn't have been easy."

"We'll never forget how kind you were to take us in and let us work for our keep until we could go to nursing school."

"Kindness was not the reason, my dear," Miss Willingham replied as she handed Katherine a cup of tea. "It is my duty to ease the pain of others, just as it will be yours in the future. Now, child, what brings you to my office?"

"Two questions," Katherine said, noticing that Miss Willingham raised an eyebrow in interest. Nothing made the dean happier than to be asked advice. "First, may Sarah and I work Sunday night instead of Saturday so we can put up the Thanksgiving decorations while all is quiet?" Katherine knew better than to ask for a Saturday off to go to a place like O'Grady's.

"Certainly." Miss Willingham sipped her tea. "Now, what else?"

"Well . . ." Katherine hesitated. "Because I have no mother to go to, I feel I must turn to the only wise woman I know."

Miss Willingham wasn't easily taken in by flattery. "Go on, child."

"Would you please tell me what to do to discourage . . . men?" Katherine had it all figured out. Whatever the old spinster told her, she'd do the opposite. For if nothing else Miss Willingham was an expert at discouraging men. She was reported to have been a beauty in her youth and with her father's fortune must have had many a caller. But

Mamie Willingham had remained unmarried and used her wealth to establish the nursing school as well as the Willingham Clinic and Hospital.

"Well, well, what a question!" Miss Willingham pressed her lips so tightly together they disappeared. Her gray eyes stared out the window as if she could see the past just beyond the pane. Her silence lasted so long Katherine decided she wasn't going to answer.

When Miss Willingham turned back, a coldness iced her eyes, a frost of scarred-over pain long ago buried. "I'll tell you the truth, dear. Men are respectful for the most part, but when they're young and hot-blooded, watch your step. They want only one thing, and they'll promise you anything to get it."

Katherine would have liked to ask more, but Miss Willingham drained her cup, indicating tea was at an end and so was the conversation. All the way back to the women's dormitory, Katherine tried to figure out how she could make use of what Miss Willingham had said to help her interest a man enough to take her up in an airplane. Finally, she decided she'd try to reverse that technique: *she* would promise the *man* anything to get what she wanted.

Sarah was waiting when Katherine reached their tiny room. She sat by the window in the only chair. The girls had chosen the room not for its size but because it had the dorm's largest window. Rising, Sarah placed her book on the dresser. "Did Miss Willingham give us Saturday night off?"

"Yes!" Katherine's excitement was so contagious that even Sarah grinned.

The girls spent the next day planning what they would wear and making up a code system so that they could talk to each other secretly with men around. Patting your forehead with a scarf meant, Help me get away from this man. Coughing three times within a minute meant, I'm ready to go if you are. And most important, saying "It's a lovely night'' meant, See you back at the dorm; I want to be alone with this man.

They made up a few more but kept getting them mixed up and decided after an hour of laughter to limit their code to three.

When Saturday night finally arrived, they strolled along the street just at dusk still rehearsing their code. The evening was warm for fall with little wind, but each girl carried her wool cape for the walk home. Sarah's dress of heavy satin was far more practical for the cool later hours of the evening. Close-fitting, with a princess line and a narrow skirt, the garment was slightly shorter in front to show her new suede shoes. The girls had spent hours sewing to make her dress look like a picture Sarah had seen in *Vanity Fair* magazine.

Luxuriant auburn hair cascaded over Katherine's shoulders, setting off her cream-colored silk dress. She'd designed its elegant overskirt, which was higher on the left than on the right. Though the neckline was square and the bodice plainly cut, creamy heliotrope chiffon and embroidery ornamented the sleeves and hem. The rich reddish color gave the dress a stylish quality and made Katherine feel rich and important, even though this was her only dress other than her uniforms.

Several girls from the school walked in front of them. Katherine didn't miss the stares from passing men, first at the other student nurses, then more lingeringly toward her. She knew hers was a bolder beauty than Sarah's. Katherine had been catching men's glances since her tall frame had rounded out when she was fifteen. Sarah, with her black hair and petite figure, had a quieter beauty that grew with each meeting.

''Now, remember,'' Katherine coached, ''we're going to meet a birdman tonight.''

''I know, I know, Kat. And when you meet one, I'm to go home with the other girls so you'll be alone and he'll walk you back to the dorm.'' Sarah shook her head. ''I don't like this plan much, having some strange man walk you home.''

"What could happen? We only live a mile away, and all the streets are well lit. I'll be fine.''

They turned the corner onto Market Street and moved excitedly toward the music and noise. "Look, Sarah, O'Grady's is only another block.''

Everyone this side of the Ohio seemed to be dancing at O'Grady's tonight. The building was little more than a barn with a dance floor almost a hundred feet wide. An orchestra of sorts played from a bandstand on one side. A bar opened up off the other end. Sarah had been harsh to call the place a saloon. In the summer months families brought picnics and sat on the grass next to the open doors near the bandstand. Couples young and old twirled around the polished wooden floor while lovers strolled out back by the creek to watch the moon and sway to a waltz.

Single men stood along the bar, with few women in their midst. Occasional laughter rumbled from the gaming tables in the back, but for the most part everyone listened to the music. Katherine and Sarah had walked by the place many a night, but this would be their first time to venture inside. Yet even the building seemed to welcome them with its wide open doors and intoxicating blend of sawdust and ladies' perfume.

As they entered, Katherine grabbed Sarah's hand for an instant. "With me?''

"Together,'' Sarah whispered.

Katherine barely heard Sarah's words. She became lost in the magic before her. A huge chandelier twirled above them, spilling light like tiny liquid diamonds on the dancers. Everyone was laughing happily as if the room were enchanted and blessed with only joy.

Finding a small table near the band, Katherine sized up each man's potential. Some were too fat to be birdmen; others were too old or too young. She'd never seen a pilot up close, but something told her she'd know one by his stance or maybe by the wild look of adventure in his eyes.

Soon men were asking both girls to dance. Whenever they returned to the table Katherine would shake her head at Sarah, indicating she hadn't found her pilot yet. The young men usually asked Sarah to dance next. When a man returned for another dance with Katherine, she always declined as she waited for a new partner and her pilot.

Finally the band took a break and Katherine jumped to her feet with nervous energy. "Let's go outside, Sarah. The dancing has made me warm."

Sarah nodded and followed. "Maybe the nurse was wrong when she said the pilots come here. We've danced with half the men in the hall and haven't talked to a birdman yet."

"Well, we'll have to dance with the other half, too, because I'm not leaving until I've asked every man in the place if he's a pilot," Katherine insisted.

"It's a shame we're not looking for a dancer. They are surely just as rare. I haven't come across one tonight." Sarah laughed. "My feet are killing me. If one more farmer steps on my toes I'll . . ."

"You'll what?" Katherine giggled just at the thought of gentle little Sarah taking a swing at one of these Ohio farmers.

Sarah couldn't keep from laughing as Katherine painted a picture of Sarah's revenge on her next partner.

The crisp night air and the laughter were refreshing as the girls strolled around to the side of O'Grady's and joined a small crowd of people.

"What's going on?" Katherine asked a boy in plaid knickers at the edge of the group. "Is it a fight?"

"No, ma'am, it's a group of them birdmen. They're betting on who can balance on a wheel axle longest with chickens dangling off a board on his shoulders. I heard one say he'd give a hundred dollars to the winner."

At last, she thought as she circled the group of spectators

until she found a place where she could see. A young man
stood, his legs wide apart, on a long narrow beam balanced
over a wheel axle. Across his shoulders he carried another
thin board with a live chicken tied from either end. The
youth rocked back and forth, trying to keep his balance as
the crowd encouraged him and the chickens flapped. An
older man with a cigar clenched between his teeth sat on a
stump staring at his pocket watch and counting out the
seconds.

The youth fell, sprawling into the dirt. A huge man with
a bushy black mustache grabbed the board with the chickens
and yelled, "Good try, Taylor! Twenty-seven seconds just
may be the record. Who'll be next?" He looked at a lean
fellow with his cap set far back atop sandy hair. "How
about you, Masters? You feel up to a little ride or are you
still nursing that ankle from the last landing you made?"

"Me leg be fine, Bart, but I'm not really interested in ye
games." The tall man's speech carried a flavoring of a
Scottish heritage. As he turned to leave the circle, his
mahogany-brown gaze caught Katherine's stare. He stopped
and studied her as if trying to place her in time. A slow easy
smile spread across his tan face, and she knew he was the
one she'd seen tumble from the plane two mornings ago.

Within this tall man's eyes Katherine saw adventure,
excitement, and a wildness unlike any she'd seen in another.
He was a fighter, by the muscular grace of his movements,
and maybe a lover, by the rakish tilt of his hat, but never a
bystander. Even with his back to the man he'd called Bart,
Katherine could tell that Masters was eager to test his skill
in any game. To her shock he winked at her boldly. She
smiled suddenly, knowing he was baiting Bart.

"All right, Cody!" Bart yelled above the noise of the
crowd. "Would you be interested if we doubled the bet?"

Cody Masters turned slowly back to the huge man. "I
might be."

Bart laughed. "I thought two hundred might get your

eyes off the redhead.'' Bart raised his hand to his forehead as if tipping an invisible hat to Katherine. ''Though you are a looker, Red.''

Katherine felt the blood rise to her cheeks. If there was one thing she hated, it was being called Red. She pushed her way through the crowd and stepped in front of the rock-hard mountain called Bart. Though his expression was cold and hard, the man looked no more than thirty at the most. He smiled, lifting only one side of his mustache and reminding Katherine of a barn cat that had just spied a nest of mice. ''My name's Katherine McMiller, sir. Not Red.''

Bart stepped back and made a wide sweep with his large hand in silent apology. His stance seemed to tell Katherine he'd seen a great deal of life and found little worth remembering.

Katherine pointed a slender finger at his face. ''Is this contest open to anyone or only half-witted birdmen?''

Bart's mouth dropped open in shock. He tried to collect himself. ''This ain't a game for girls, little lady.''

Cody moved beside Katherine. He towered a head over her, as few men did. ''Now wait a wee minute, Bart. I heard ye say a hundred dollars to anyone who can balance the beam. You made no mention of male or female.''

Bart turned to Katherine. ''Look, miss, I don't want to hurt your feelings, but this isn't a place for a lady. Why don't you run along and bat those green eyes at some young pup on the dance floor and leave the betting to the men?''

Katherine didn't budge and Cody put his arm around her waist. ''I'll tell ye what, Bart. I'll bet we can both stand on the beam for more than thirty seconds, but it will cost ye three hundred dollars.''

''I'll take that fool's bet.'' Bart laughed, his mustache spreading across his face.

Before Katherine could say a word, Cody swung her up onto the center of the beam that crossed the axle. ''All you have to do is stand perfectly still and hold on to me. I'll do the balancing. Are you game?'' The slight Scottish burr seemed to vanish when he whispered.

Katherine smiled down at his handsome face as she planted her feet solidly on the board. She loved the thrill of the game almost as much as she loved the look in his eyes. Excitement throbbed through her, and she knew standing still would probably be impossible. But this was the pilot she'd been looking for all evening, and she wouldn't give up her dream easily.

Lifting the board with a chicken tied to either end onto his broad shoulders, Cody spread his arms out to balance himself. Slowly he climbed up onto the beam with Katherine. Two men held the beam steady as he faced her, his feet on either side of hers. His lean body was molded against her as he whispered in her ear, ''Put your arms around my neck and sway with me. Remember, don't try to balance, just bend when I bend.''

Katherine nodded, too frightened and excited to speak. His slender body was pressed against her from leg to shoulder. She nestled her head into his chest and tried to stand perfectly still. She'd never been so close to a man. His touch blended with the masculine smell of soap and tweed. She turned her head ever so slightly so her cheek brushed his jawline. The chill of the night air had vanished, and Katherine felt suddenly warm.

''Ready. Start the clock,'' Cody yelled as the men let go of the beam's ends.

Closing her eyes, Katherine concentrated on the man counting off the seconds. She could feel Cody swaying first one direction, then another, as the beam rolled along the axle and the chickens squawked from each end of the board over his shoulders. Though the ground was only a few feet below, it seemed distant as the beam underneath her feet rolled back and forth.

''Twenty-eight, twenty-nine, thirty!'' yelled the time-keeper.

She felt Cody take a long breath and throw the board off his shoulders. He stepped off the beam and he swung her around to the ground. "You can let go now, lassie, and open your eyes to being a hundred and fifty dollars richer." He gave her a promising look that had nothing to do with money.

Staring up at Cody's expression, she was fascinated by the twinkle of fire she saw in his eyes. Though he was merely standing beside her now, the feel of his lean body remained imprinted upon her senses.

Bart moved forward, digging in his pocket. "Well, Red, you cost me a week's pay." The ease with which he handed her the money told her that he placed little value on wealth or women.

"Maybe that will teach you never to call people by their hair color."

Bart laughed. "Got a fiery temper to go with that fiery hair, do you?"

She started to reply, but people rushed forward to congratulate them on their winnings.

Searching the crowd for Sarah, Katherine found her near the back, talking to the young man who had first tried the balancing game. Sarah waved to Katherine and took the young man's arm, then moved with him toward the dance floor as the band began to play.

Cody pulled Katherine in the opposite direction. "Why don't we take a walk by the creek and cool off before dancing?"

The music, the excitement, the look in his eyes, swirled together in her mind, making the night suddenly magic. "And what makes you think I'll dance with you, sir? I don't even know you."

Cody bowed before her. "My name's Cody Masters. And I think you'll dance with me because we've already held each other very close. So close"—his whispered words brushed her ear—"I felt your heart beating against my chest.'' He slid his arm around her waist and pulled her against his side. ''Tell me, my beautiful lady, does it always pound so madly, or am I the first to know that the fire in those smoldering green eyes of yours also burns passionately between your breasts?''

Katherine felt her cheeks flush and was thankful for the shadows. Never in her life had anyone talked to her like this, and she had known him for only a few minutes. She decided to change the subject before she ventured too deep into unknown waters. ''Tell me, Cody Masters, why does your Scottish burr grow so thick for the crowd and vanish so easily when you whisper?''

''Would you believe the passion in me is from my English mother and the gambler in me is from my Scottish father?''

Katherine laughed. ''No. Try again.''

Cody shrugged and threaded his fingers through hers. His casual action sent a warm tingle up Katherine's arm as they walked farther and farther from O'Grady's lights. ''In truth, the crowds like to have a means of identifying each pilot. We've all picked up a few accents to use when we hit a town. The more people feel they know us, the more they'll care enough to pay a dollar to see us fly. Bart has a huge frame anyone in a crowd can recognize and a French accent he can use that'll make you believe he's never before been more than a hundred miles from Paris in his life. Cal Rodgers, the timekeeper tonight, has that cigar that never leaves his mouth, even when he's in the air. I needed something, and the accents come easy because my parents really were English and Scottish. How about your folks? I'll bet one was Irish.''

''I wouldn't know.'' Katherine could feel her muscles tightening, but she forced indifference into her tone. ''I never knew my mother, and I think I was about four when my father gave me to some people called the Wards. They ran a cannery upstate.'' She wanted to stop, but once the story started it always seemed to flow to the present.

''The Wards were horrible people who only cared about making money,'' she continued. ''I hated them and their filthy cannery, so when I was six, I ran away. After I'd spent months on the streets, the authorities caught me and sent me to an orphans' farm. I ran away from there when I was twelve and made it here to the Mamie Willingham School of Nursing. I'll graduate just before Christmas.''

Pulling away from Cody, she hugged herself as she walked by the stream. The music was now a waltz and seemed to float far into the velvet darkness. ''Now you know my life story.'' She was angry at herself for having told him so much about her past. Why hadn't she just said she grew up on a farm? She'd probably never see him again once he took her flying, so there was no reason for him to know that much about her.

Suddenly she felt Cody's jacket slide gently over her shoulders. ''It's cold out here by the water this time of year.'' He placed his arm around her, and they were both silent as they listened to the sounds of evening. The moonlight rippled over the water and touched the far bank in a thin silver ribbon.

Katherine relaxed and thought how much she could like this man, with his outrageous way of life. ''What's it like to fly, Cody?''

He moved closer behind her before he spoke. His voice brushed her hair lightly; his words excited her soul. ''It's like nothing else in the world. You're a bird flying higher and higher. The earth grows smaller beneath you, and so does the reality of it. All the problems—hunger, war, unhappiness, loneliness—disappear as you float toward the clouds.'' His arms encircled her waist, and he drew her against his lean frame.

''An old woman came up to me in the last town and offered me a hundred dollars to fly her directly to heaven so she wouldn't have to die. Everyone around us laughed, but when you're up there with the clouds, you swear you really are closer to the pearly gates." His hands moved slowly over the silk of her dress.

"What about the danger?" Katherine was totally lost in his ramblings.

"When you're flying, you're fully alive. I know men who go all day, all week, without remembering anything that happened to them or how they felt. When you're in the air, every minute seems like an hour. You'll never forget any of it. If I die tomorrow, I will have lived more lifetimes than most old men, because for a while every part of me, every cell, has been alive."

He turned her slowly in his arms. "I will always remember every moment, just like now." He kissed her forehead lightly. "You are so beautiful." Brushing her lips with his own, he whispered, "I don't think I've ever been so attracted to a woman. When I turned and saw you in the crowd I almost forgot what I was doing. It was as though lightning had struck only a few feet from me. When I saw you standing in the field the other morning I was too far away to truly appreciate your beauty."

Cody lowered his lips to hers, and Katherine gave no resistance. Tossing Miss Willingham's teachings aside, she allowed herself to follow her natural instincts. His lips were gentle at first, then grew more demanding. Katherine loved the feel of his arms encircling her. Running her fingers into his sandy hair, she touched his windblown curls—the same curls that had touched the clouds.

A warmth soared silently from deep inside her, spreading outward, heating every part of her body. His strong hands moved in wide circles over her back, pulling her not only into the kiss but into his very soul.

When she inched closer, pressing against him, she felt his low moan against her mouth and loved the way it tickled her lips. He was all she'd ever dreamed her pilot would be and more, far more. Even as she thought his kiss had reached perfection, it took her higher into the pure air of passion.

When finally Cody broke the kiss he was short of breath. Slowly he moved his lips to just below her ear. She could feel his words warm and low as he whispered, "Come with me, lovely lady, and I'll show you another way to feel totally alive."

The light touch of his lips along her throat sent a shiver of molten fire through her, but his words cooled her first taste of passion. Katherine pushed away, wanting to see his face when he answered her question. "What are you asking?"

Cupping her chin with his palm, he kissed her eyes. "I'm asking the same question these green eyes of yours have been answering since we met: Will you spend the night with me and feel totally alive?"

Surprise shot through her as though her body were a whip that had suddenly been violently cracked. She'd been kissed a few times by boys and asked to dine with them once or twice, but never, never had a man been so bold.

"How dare you! " Katherine pushed away from him, too angry to say more. Cody looked surprised as she threw his jacket at him and stormed back toward the dance hall.

Tears burned Katherine's eyes, but she refused to let them fall. This wasn't going at all as she had planned. She couldn't believe a man would say such a thing so soon after meeting her. What must he think of her to talk that way? Katherine pushed a hint of guilt from her thoughts. Had she led him in the wrong direction? No, he'd started this. Still furious, she marched toward the lights, wishing she'd slapped him.

A strong hand grabbed her arm suddenly and swung her around violently. "How dare I?" Cody shouted. "How dare *I*?"

Even in the shadows she could see that his anger matched her own, and for an instant she was afraid.

"Excuse me, Miss Katherine High-and-Mighty, but I

thought you were flirting with me back there. I saw no
hesitation when I touched you. I heard no protest when I
kissed you. So just what kind of game are you playing with
me?''

"None," Katherine lied.

"Oh, do you stare so boldly at every man you meet in a
crowd?'' Cody's fingers were bruising her arm. "Do you go
walking out by the creek with every man so soon after
meeting? Do you mold yourself so easily to any other? Do
you melt with enough softness in his arms to drive him
mad?''

"No, not every man. Not any man . . . just you,"
Katherine answered as she tried to pull away.

"And why was I the lucky one you chose to torture? Was
it the money we won or did you just pick me at random to
tease and then discard as if I had insulted you when I
suggested what was on both our minds?''

"Bedding you was not on my mind!" Katherine resented
his accusation and denied the truth that was beginning to
throb at her temples and eat at her principles.

"And what *was* on your mind, my lovely lady?'' Cody
lowered his voice but did not slacken his grip.

Katherine spoke the words before she could stop. "I want
to go flying.''

The anger in Cody seemed to mount with her confession,
but he held himself in tight control. "So it was not me you
were attracted to. If I hadn't suggested the walk, you would
have picked another pilot. Bart, Cal, or even young Taylor,
it would have made no difference.'' He dropped his hand
from her arm as if her flesh had burned him. "Do you have
any idea how that makes me feel? You were planning on
using me to fly, weren't you? Just pick one of the dumb
boys and play with his emotions until you get what you
want, right?''

"No . . . well, yes.'' Katherine hated hearing her

thoughts coming from him. It sounded so awful. "I would have done anything to get to fly in an airplane."

"Anything?" Cody's voice was emotionless.

"Anything," Katherine answered, wishing she'd taken Sarah's advice and stayed home.

Cody stepped into the shadows so she could no longer see his face. "Meet me tomorrow morning at the same field I saw you watching me from the other day. Wear trousers, and tie a scarf over all that hair." His voice was colder than an icy breeze before a winter storm. "Be there at eight sharp, and be willing to pay anything for your ride or don't show up."

She heard disdain in his tone. The same voice that had whispered words of love so easily only minutes before. Had she hurt him so deeply? The echo of his footsteps left her with a feeling of bitter aloneness, and Katherine felt the darkness closing in around her as it had when she was a child. She wanted to call Cody back, but she couldn't face his anger again. She hated the darkness because even in the open air she could almost feel creatures moving toward her in the dancing shadows of night, as they had when the Wards used to lock her in the cannery for punishment. Any minute she would feel the animals of the night biting at her flesh, trying to devour her even while she was still breathing.

She had to find Sarah. Sarah could always chase the nightmare away. Lifting her skirt, she ran as fast as she could back toward the lights. When she reached the dance hall her hair was windblown and her skin felt clammy with fear. She searched the room for Sarah, but her friend was nowhere to be seen.

"Looking for your little dark-haired friend?" a voice asked from behind her.

Katherine turned to face the man who'd been the time-keeper. He had an honest face and a polite manner that seemed to say his wife was watching. "Have you seen her?"

"She left a little while ago with one of them pilots. Said to say, if I saw you, that it was a real nice night."

Katherine smiled, remembering their code. Sarah had found someone she liked. The evening wasn't a complete disaster, after all. "She must have left with that nice Taylor boy who asked her to dance," Katherine said, thinking how quiet and earnest Taylor had seemed. Just Sarah's type.

"No, miss," Cal answered. "It was Bart Rome at her side. You remember him—big guy with a mustache. The one who called you Red."

Katherine shook her head in disbelief. Sarah couldn't have left with Bart. He was loud, and his eyes were hard with indifference. He hadn't seemed to care when he hurt Katherine's feelings at all. How could Sarah have left with such a man?

"It's not a nice night," Katherine said to herself. "Not a nice night at all."

Three

BART ROME GUIDED his sleek Palmer-Singer automobile through the sleeping streets of Dayton as Sarah sat quietly beside him. She'd never ridden in a roadster before, even though they'd been in use for several years. The noisy open-air automobile was almost as thrilling as the man at her side. The moonlight outlined his strong masculine hands as they gripped the steering wheel in a continuing battle for control.

The car was traveling as fast as a horse could run. But it wasn't just the speed that excited Sarah and made her blood race. Never in her life had she dared to do such an outragcous thing. Leaving a public place with a man! But Bart was different from any other man she'd ever known. He had a way about him that told everyone he always did as he pleased. Sarah, who'd spent her life as a follower, admired his spirit and dreamed of having such a character trait. She knew his independence wouldn't rub off on her any more than Katherine's outgoing manner had. But secretly she hoped it might.

Bart pulled a scarf from under his seat. "Better put this around those beautiful black curls of yours. Traveling this fast can make your ears cold even on a nice night."

"Thank you." Sarah wrapped the colorful woolen scarf around her hair after pushing her own blue silk scarf down around her neck. She shoved her ebony curls into the new warmth. The wool smelled of pipe tobacco and campfires. For a moment she wished the scarf were a blanket she could curl up in and spend hours remembering this night and the man beside her. He was so intriguing, with his dark hair and mustache. The strong set of his square jaw and Roman nose might have seemed hard to most people, but Sarah saw a depth of caring hidden behind his smoky gray eyes. Once he loved someone, she decided he would care deeply and forever.

The car hit a rut in the road, jostling them like marbles in a matchbox. Bart slowed his speed and regained control of the wheel. "You all right, little lady?" he asked. His large hand reached over and patted Sarah's fingers, now gripping the edge of her seat.

"Yes," she answered, very much aware of his touch. She remembered Kat's disapproving glare at the big pilot. How could a man with hands like Bart's be anything but honest? How could he not be worth knowing?

"We're almost to the test sight." Bart drew his hand away slowly. "This is a good field, with a hill and trees blocking the wind from the north, and open fields on three sides for takeoffs and landings. We're coming in on the north side. It'll mean climbing down the hill, but it will be shorter than driving around."

Sarah didn't mention that she and Katherine had climbed the hill two mornings ago. She smiled, thinking of how shocked Katherine would be when she found out Sarah was with Bart. The few times they'd gone to parties or church socials, Katherine had always been the one to come back with exciting stories. Well, tonight Sarah would have an adventure of her own to tell.

Bart was the first man she'd ever met who interested her enough to allow her to overcome her shyness. The fact that he was a pilot had nothing to do with her interest. The moment she'd first looked into his eyes she had seen the sadness behind his rough exterior, and she couldn't look away. He was like the silent patients who watched her care for them. Though they said nothing, their stares were always a cry for relief from pain. Bart's unspoken pain was deep inside, and Sarah felt both fascinated and helpless. She sensed that trying to comfort him would somehow only deepen the wound, unless she was very careful, but she felt compelled to try.

Bart stopped the car at the top of the small hill overlooking the test field. "I'd hate to think of these rocks ruining that lovely dress of yours. Would you like me to carry you down?"

Sarah nodded, lifting her arms with the open trust of a child. Bart swept her up in his powerful arms as if she were weightless. His chest was rock-hard against her, but his grip was gentle as if he held a treasure. She wrapped one arm around his neck and spread her fingers over his shoulder, trying to memorize his touch, the fresh smell of smoking tobacco and leather that surrounded him, and the pounding of his heart next to her side.

"You're not much bigger than a half minute. You sure you're old enough to stay out this late?"

"I was eighteen last month," Sarah answered and blushed as she realized her breast was pressed against his chest. She looked into his face and knew from the sudden darkening of his gray eyes that he was very much aware of her as a woman.

When they reached the bottom of the rocky hill, Bart didn't lower her to the ground. The stars glittered behind his head, and the moon provided all the light she needed to see the longing in his face.

"What are you thinking?" she asked.

"I'm thinking you may be the most beautiful woman I've ever seen." His words came slowly, for compliments seemed rusty on his tongue. "If I were halfway good-looking and ten years younger, I'd give every buck in this county a race for your time."

Sarah smiled at him. In truth, he was not what even a mother could call handsome. His forehead was a bit too high and his nose a fraction too long. His hair was a muddy mix of black and brown. His most characteristic expression was a frown, as if he were warning people not to get too close. He could have been anywhere from twenty-five to thirty-five years old, but Sarah guessed he was younger than the wrinkled sun lines around his eyes might suggest.

"I'm afraid there's no one racing for my time." Sarah bit back her words, wishing she could have said something cute or funny instead of the plain truth.

"Then the men in this part of the world must all be blind." Bart tried to keep his voice light, but the truth of his words showed in his eyes. He lowered her to the ground, allowing his hands to remain at her waist just a moment longer than necessary. "You look like an angel dropped from heaven to break a man's heart." He gently pushed the scarf from her hair. "A lovely little woman-child."

Sarah studied him as he looked down at her, and she saw the first sign of happiness in his eyes. The sorrow seemed to be pushed away for a moment as he pulled one of her long curls free.

"Lord, woman, stop looking at me like that. I'm afraid I'll start telling you my life story."

"And why, Bartholomew Rome, are you afraid to do that? You fly up in one of those planes every day, and yet you seem afraid of me."

"A plane might break my bones, but those blue eyes of yours could break my heart."

"A heart you keep well protected?"

"Locked safe away from tiny angels who might shatter it with a touch. You see, little lady, I'm as married to the sky as any man will ever be to a woman."

"And is the sky so jealous she won't share you for even a few hours?"

Bart chuckled and nodded his head. "When I fly, every

time I fly, it's like being part of a miracle. Here I am a huge toad, but with the help of a little canvas, wood, and wire I turn into an eagle. From the first time I saw a plane take off, I knew I was born to fly. Being a pilot is in my blood worse'n gold ever fevered a prospector. An editor once called us 'prophets of dreams, men who erase the word *impossible* from mankind's vocabulary.'"

Sarah loved the way his face lit up when he talked about flying. Flight was his mistress and would probably be his death.

He took her small hand in his huge fist, and they walked among the airplanes now sleeping quietly beneath tarpaulins. The fragile machines looked harmless in hibernation. Bart let go of her hand and patted a wing gently. "The danger is part of the fascination, you know." He talked more to himself than her, organizing his thoughts into words as he spoke. "Before planes, I raced motorcycles, then cars, like several other pilots. But with flying, the flirtation with death becomes intoxicating. I'm up there all by myself as near heaven as I'll probably ever get, and it all becomes a game. Each time I want to push myself just as far as I can go, to laugh in danger's face. Until one day I'll flirt too close and . . . well, I won't have long for regrets."

A shudder ran through Sarah that had nothing to do with the evening breeze. "I guess I always thought men flew for the money."

"Some folks might say that's the reason. But I don't see how that can be. The exhibition fee is five thousand dollars per plane, but the pilot draws only fifty dollars a day. Once you're up there, it's not the money you think of, or even the competition to see who can outdo the others; it's just you outdoing yourself." He looked down at her, and Sarah saw the hint of a smile brush his lips.

"Some guys want to fly the mail or run errands for someone with enough money to pay a pilot, but not me. There was a rich man just this afternoon looking for a sucker to make a trip from Washington to a farm a hundred miles down the coast. He'll find a daredevil like Cody to make the run if the money's good enough.''

Sarah leaned nearer, wishing he'd touch her again, but not knowing how to tell him to do so. ''Are the few of you I saw tonight the only pilots around?'' If she kept questioning him, maybe she'd find a way to get closer to this man who touched a plane so tenderly but didn't seem to know how to touch her.

''Hell, n-no,'' Bart stammered, as if the words had come out before he could stop them. ''Sorry, ma'am, about the language. I don't spend much time talking to ladies.'' He leaned against the plane and crossed his legs at the ankles. ''Curtiss has some men not more than thirty miles from here getting ready for a race coming up. He and the Wrights have been competing for quite a spell. They're fighting in courts over patents, but when they meet to fly, everyone seems friendly enough. Some think Curtiss has the better plane. Guess the truth will be in the testing.''

''What do you think?'' Sarah asked, wishing they could talk like this forever.

''Oh, I like Curtiss well enough. To be honest, a friend of mine taught me to fly using one of his planes two years ago. Back in those days there was room for only one man in the plane. So my buddy just told me how to operate everything and started the engine.'' Bart rubbed his right leg. ''It took me almost six months to recover from that first lesson.''

Sarah laughed at how lightly he talked of his injury. She wondered how many others he'd suffered without being able to laugh them off. ''Does your friend still fly for Curtiss?''

Bart looked away from her toward the open field. ''My friend was killed last year. He'd started flying when a pilot had to lie down and half break his neck in order to guide the plane. He was careful, too, always checking and rechecking the wind and the engine.''

"He died in a crash?" Sarah moved around the plane and looked at Bart through the parallel wings. The moonlight made dark and light angles on his face, and sadness glistened in his eyes.

"No." Bart laughed without any sign of humor. "His wife had talked him into giving up airplanes a few months before. He was killed in a car crash. He was racing a plane around a racetrack. The plane had engine trouble, and while the onlookers held their breath fearing the plane might crash, my friend missed a curve and rolled his car over."

Bart looked into Sarah's eyes. Slowly, almost timidly, he brushed a loose strand of ebony hair from her cheek. "I'm rattling on like a tent preacher on a hot night. Guess I'd better take you home." He backed away as if in a hurry to leave her.

"What is it?" Sarah hugged herself as a coldness passed between them. "Is something wrong?" She'd been brave enough to go riding with him, which Miss Willingham would have considered scandalous. It was after midnight, they were alone under the stars, and he was backing away from her as if he'd suddenly noticed she had smallpox. She hurried after him as he walked toward the hill.

"No, nothing's wrong. You're about the most nearly perfect person I've ever met." Bart didn't turn around to see the confusion in her face. Sarah opened her mouth, but he continued before she could speak. "I just don't want to get involved with any girl and leave her crying when I move on. It's better if we stop right now." Bart reached the rocks and stopped, as if debating what to do about helping her up.

Sarah stood just behind him. She didn't even come up to his shoulder in height, but she wasn't afraid. "It's not better," she whispered without anger. "Maybe I'm wrong, but I think we could both use a friend, someone to talk to."

Reaching out, she placed her hand on his shoulder, but he cringed away as if her fingers burned his flesh. "Don't touch me, Sarah. I don't think we could be just friends, no matter how much I'd like to. I've seen too many women left crying at crash sites. I can't afford the luxury of caring for someone or having anyone give a damn if I'm alive or dead.''

Sarah moved around him and stood on the higher ground ahead of him. She looked into his smoke-colored eyes, now divested of the hood that usually shielded his thoughts. "It's too late," she whispered, "I already care about you."

"No!" Bart balled his hands into fists as he shook his head. "I won't care for anyone. I want no face before me when I head nose-down to death. I want no woman aging ten years for every day I fly. No, Sarah, I don't care for you, so you might as well forget about caring for me." He pounded his strong fist against his leg.

"Then prove it, my brave pilot." Though she was not adventurous or outspoken, Sarah knew she could see through people. She could tell when someone was suffering and Bart was suffering now. Bartholomew Rome might lie to himself, but he could not lie to her. He might frighten most people off with his frowns and his tough act, but not Sarah.

She moved nearer. "Prove you don't feel anything for me."

"Name the task and let's go," Bart ordered.

Sarah knew if she told him to leave he would go, and she would have miles to walk home. If she told him to swear, he would do so without hesitation. Finally she named the only test she could think of: "If you care nothing for me, kiss me."

"Why?" He looked as if he'd been struck. "You make no sense."

"Because I've never been kissed, and a woman's first kiss is honest without any practiced affection. Yours must be the same."

"That's ridiculous!" he bellowed. "You're a child if you believe that."

"Prove me wrong," Sarah answered, determination echoing in her words.

Bart hesitated. He set his stance and his mind to the task. Deep lines burrowed across his forehead, as though kissing her were like moving into impenetrable darkness and having no idea how far below the ground lay. He pulled her brutally into his huge arms and pressed his lips to hers with calculated cruelty. When she made no attempt to pull away, he bruised her mouth with his force and split her bottom lip with his teeth.

Sarah pushed away in pain, and Bart let her go without hesitation. A cry escaped her as she backed away from him. Blood trickled from the corner of her lip.

Running into the shadows, she pulled a handkerchief from her pocket. Sarah wanted more than anything in the world to cry, but pride held back the tears. Her first kiss had been a brutal attack, not a loving touch as she'd always dreamed it might be. With a cry of loss, she watched Bart storm a few feet up the hill like a bull charging an impermeable gate. Slowly her tears began to fall—for him, not herself.

Halfway up the hill he slammed his fist into a rock and mumbled an oath. "What did you think would happen?" he asked himself. "That a fool like you could touch an angel and not feel anything?" He knew he should have ignored her at the dance hall, but those eyes, those wonderful sky-blue eyes, had drawn him. How could he have allowed her to disappear into the crowd without discovering why those beautiful eyes reached into his very soul and pulled out feelings he thought he'd buried long ago when he learned how unlovable he was?

When he turned around, he knew he'd have to try to talk to her. A man couldn't hurt an angel and then just walk away.

Sarah watched him storming back down the hill. He looked like a warrior ready to do battle with the devil. She sank deeper into the shadows of the trees and sat down on a log to watch him. He came toward her, his fists clenched in anger. Even in the shadowy light Sarah could see he had hurt himself with his cruelty far more than he'd injured her. When he was within twenty feet, he turned and retraced his path toward the top. His swearwords followed him as he ran up then turned to storm back down. Though tears streaked her face for his unhappiness, a tiny part of her suppressed a giggle at this huge man's boyish indecision.

Finally he came to her and sat down on the grass at her feet. She was afraid to say anything for fear of hurting him more than he'd been hurt already. He was silent for a long time, looking out over the open field. Slowly the cool wind calmed his breathing to normal and his iron-tight muscles relaxed against her leg. Sarah wanted to touch his hair and tell him it was all right, but she knew he would only pull away.

Why had he brought her out here to see the planes if he wanted no part of knowing her? He'd made sure several of his friends saw them leave. Could he have been playing some game that involved her? Could he truly care nothing for her? Or did he think he could bring her out here and enjoy the evening without allowing his feelings to surface? Sarah suddenly wished she were older and wiser . . . or Katherine. If she were Kat, she'd know what to do.

She pulled her midnight blue scarf from around her neck. "Let me see your hand," she said in her nursing voice.

Bart lifted his hand to her lap. Her fingers brushed his skin. Warm blood seeped from his knuckles where he'd slammed his fist into the rock. She wrapped his hand tightly with her scarf, knowing the pain of the wound was nothing compared to the hurt within him. Holding his hand firmly between hers, she tried to heal the wounds that were far too deep inside him to touch.

When he finally cleared his throat to speak, Bart sounded tired. "I had a bird once when I was a kid. A parakeet.

Prettiest thing you ever saw. I think I loved that bird more than I did my family.'' He wasn't looking at her as he talked. "One day the bird got out of his cage. I panicked. I just knew he would get outside and some hawk would eat him for breakfast. So I opened up my hand, and he flew right into my palm. I was so glad, I closed my fingers to keep him safe and ran toward the cage.'' Bart let out a long breath. "When I opened my hand inside the cage, the bird fell dead on the cage floor. I'd crushed his bones in my fingers by loving him so much.''

He was silent for a long while, and when he spoke, the sadness in his tone tore at Sarah's heart. "That's why I'm afraid with you. I can't help myself. When I saw you, I had to get nearer. I had to find out if you were as beautiful as those huge blue eyes promised. And you are, you are beautiful inside, like few people I've ever known. But you're tiny and fragile in body and spirit. If I get too close, I might just care too much. You need to fall for some banker who'll only worry you with gravy spots on his vest. A pilot's life would crush you as surely as if your bones were hollow.''

Sarah folded her hands in her lap and straightened her back. "Do you think so little of me? Quietness does not always cover fear, nor does meekness have to imply a weak spirit.''

"All I can add is I'm sorry I hurt you.'' He took a long breath that was almost a sigh. "I'll see you safely home. Maybe you're right. Maybe I am misjudging you, but I can't take the chance.''

"Wait.'' Sarah placed her hand on his shoulder. "I could argue with you, but I won't. I must say, however, that for a man who teases death daily, you're the greatest coward I've ever known.''

"Maybe.'' Bart's voice was so low Sarah felt she was reading his thoughts. "Maybe we're all a little bit cowardly in one way or another.''

He leaned his shoulder against her knees and rested his head on her lap, reminding Sarah of a lonely little boy. He was right about the cowardliness in us all, Sarah realized. She could bravely face hours of nursing one patient after another, but a crowd of people frightened her. Katherine could fight her way out of every fear, except the darkness. Sarah brushed Bart's hair lightly with her fingers. And this brave man, she thought with a smile, was afraid of her.

Four

BART DROVE BACK to the dorm trying to think of something to say to Sarah. He wanted to lay his hand over hers, but he wasn't sure what she'd do. She might tell him again how brave she was, but he knew a gentle soul when he met one. Never in his life had he been so fascinated with a woman.

He remembered once his mother had taken him to church when he was very small. While she prayed, he'd looked up at the face of a statue. Until tonight he would have sworn no woman could ever look as beautiful as that figure, but that was before he saw Sarah standing in the crowd like an angel among mortals.

"Stop the car down the road a little." She touched his arm to make sure he heard her above the engine. "I can walk from here."

Bart pulled the car over and silenced the engine. "I'll walk with you," he insisted as he opened her door.

Sarah took his arm without hesitation, and they crossed the wooded area beside the dormitory. When she reached the back door, Sarah tapped lightly three times and it opened.

Bart looked up the steps and met the angry eyes of the redhead he'd teased earlier. "Evenin', ma'am." He touched his forehead with a salute. "Nice night for a drive."

Green eyes stared down at him with enough sparks to set the Rockies on fire, but her voice was low and controlled. "I was worried about you, Sarah."

Sarah looked up at Bart. "You shouldn't have been, Kat. I was with Bart."

He could tell the redhead thought Sarah's reasoning somewhat daft, but he had to respect her for not yelling. He wasn't sure what he would have done if Katherine had yelled at Sarah. Trying to ease the tension, Bart asked, "I'm surprised you got away from young Cody. He's not a man to leave until the last waltz is played."

Katherine smiled, unable to hide her happiness any longer. "He's taking me flying in the morning."

"*What!*"

Sarah touched Bart's lips to quiet him. She didn't have to say anything. He knew he'd get them into trouble if they were caught coming in so late. The touch of her fingers on his mouth made him forget for a moment what he'd shouted about.

Katherine smiled victoriously. "I'll have to leave long before sunup to get to the field on time."

"You're not going without me." Sarah slowly lowered her fingers from Bart's face.

He could see there was no use standing in the cold arguing with these two. "Neither of you will walk in the dark to the test field. You'll fall and break your necks. 'Course, in your case, Red, you might hit your head and knock some sense into it."

"I don't remember asking for your approval."

Bart laughed. "No, you didn't, and you wouldn't have gotten it if you had, but I'm offering you a ride. I'll pick you up just before dawn."

Katherine opened her mouth to turn down his offer, but Sarah stepped between them. "That's very kind of you. We'll be ready." She shoved Katherine into the building and waved as she closed the door.

Bart stood for a while, staring at where they'd disappeared. She'd said he was kind. He could never remember in his life anyone ever telling him something he did was kind. Brave maybe, even daring, but never kind.

As he walked back to his car he remembered the way she'd touched his arm. He could still feel her light fingers against his lips when he'd yelled. Watching her move was like watching a miracle. Somehow on this earth perfection had come to life.

Katherine followed Sarah up the stairs in silence, feeling much older and wiser than her friend. When she closed the door to their tiny dorm room, Katherine could hold her tongue no longer. "I was so worried about you. The dance was over long ago."

Sarah fumbled in the darkness as she lit the lamp. "You sound like a mother," she said, trying not to giggle, "waiting at the door for me and scowling at Bart just as Miss Willingham would have done."

Kat's mood didn't lighten. She'd worn out the floor in the hall by pacing. "Well, maybe one of us needs a mother. I can't believe you left O'Grady's with that man. He's as hard as rock salt and as big as a mountain. I'd be surprised if he knows three civil words to string together."

Sarah turned up the light and faced her friend. "Bart's a wonderful man. I don't need a keeper, Kat. So stop acting as if I'm being committed to the state hospital next month and not just working there."

Katherine's frustration vanished as she noticed the tiny spot of dried blood at the corner of Sarah's lip. "Oh, my Lord, you've been hurt. He couldn't even see you home safely." Fear tightened her fists. "Did he hurt you? I'll kill him with my bare hands." Kat grabbed a wooden-handled button hook and swung it like a weapon. "When I'm finished with Bart Rome, he'll have to be sent to meet his maker in matchboxes. I'll make him think flying *was* dangerous."

Sarah laughed until tears bubbled in her blue eyes. She'd

almost forgotten the street-fighting child within Katherine. "He didn't hurt me, Kat. Settle down. Honest, if Custer had had you, he'd have won the Battle of Little Big Horn."

Katherine lowered her weapon and regained her poise, but her eyes still held the fire of battle. "Are you sure he didn't hurt you?"

"He kissed me."

Katherine returned her weapon to the dresser where she'd now only use it to attack the buttons on her shoes. "Cody kissed me too, but it was just part of my plan, nothing more."

"I don't think Bart planned to kiss me." Sarah blushed. "He makes me feel all grown-up inside, as if there's no little girl left."

Kat looked worried. She wasn't sure she wanted to think about Sarah caring for this man who might come between them. She knew such a thought was selfish, but Sarah was the only person she'd ever cared about. "Don't fall for the first guy who kisses you. Believe me, it's something men do without any thought. Don't trust him. He'll only disappear when you need him." She put her arm around Sarah, playing the part of big sister. "They take what you offer and then leave. Men weren't meant to stay around forever."

Sarah shook her head. "All men aren't like that. Just because your father left you . . ."

Katherine held up her hand as if she didn't want to hear any more. "He left me just as Bart will leave you if you start depending on him." Kat walked to the window and stared into the blackness. "I remember begging him not to let go of my hand. I was so afraid. But he pulled away.

"'I can't,' he said simply, 'I can't raise a child alone.' I remember crying and promising to be good, but he only mumbled something about being on the road."

Katherine continued looking deep into her own memory. "I begged him to promise to come back and get me, but he said, 'Never make a promise you can't keep.' He left me there at the cannery with a couple whose pledge to take care of me faded with the daylight. I cried so hard that first night that the Wards locked me in the cannery so they wouldn't have to hear me. I was so alone in the dark I thought my chest would crack open from the pain I felt inside. After that, I felt I'd never cry again.''

Sarah closed her fingers around Katherine's arm. ''You're not alone now. I'll always be with you, even when you yell at me worse than Miss Willingham would have.'' She knew Kat's anger with Bart arose from her fears for Sarah rather than with Bart himself.

''I remember the first time I saw you.'' Sarah's soft voice eased Kat's mind as always. ''A constable brought you from town, saying he had to put you at the farm because you wouldn't tell him where you were from. Most of us couldn't remember any life but the farm, so you were a real curiosity.''

Katherine turned away from the window. ''I'll never forget how all you lined up and stared at me.''

Sarah smiled. ''I'd never seen anyone kick a policeman before. He was just standing there holding you by the hair while you kicked his shins. I bet the poor man was blue from the knees down.''

Katherine's mood lightened. ''He'd told me I was going somewhere nice—a farm in the country. I took one look at that place and knew it was a work farm. I wanted to beat up the world.''

Sarah pulled Bart's wool scarf from around her neck. ''You about did. You beat up all the boys and started on the girls before you got to me. I decided being your friend was safer.''

''Without you, I'd never have run away from there.''

''Yes, you would have, just as you ran away from the cannery.'' Sarah laughed. ''You just wouldn't have known where you were going.''

Katherine looked around their neat little room. "We did all right, didn't we?"

"We did fine," Sarah agreed. "As long as we stick together, there's nothing we can't do."

"Forever and ever, no matter what," Kat whispered, knowing she'd never lose her friend.

"Forever and ever," Sarah echoed, remembering the day they'd bound their lives together in blood. "Now tell me how you snagged a birdman."

Bart tapped on Cody's door as he passed his room. Before he'd found the key to his own room across the hall, Cody poked his head out.

Cody's easy smile gave Bart no clue to what he'd planned for the morning. "Yeah?" Cody raised an eyebrow at Bart. "Need some advice about women, old man?"

Bart snorted like an ill-tempered bull. "Not from you, kid, but I do need to talk, if you've got a minute."

"Is it serious?"

Bart nodded.

Cody disappeared, then returned with a bottle of whiskey in one hand and a half-empty glass in the other. "I'm ready."

Bart opened his door and stepped aside to allow Cody to enter his room. He didn't miss the minor sidestep in Cody's walk, telling Bart his friend had already had more than enough to drink.

Cody turned and offered Bart the bottle. "Better drink up. I'm way ahead of you, partner."

Bart took the bottle and set it atop a cluttered dresser. "I don't think I've ever seen you this far into your cups. Is this some newly acquired vice, or are you celebrating having made a fool's promise to a redhead tonight?"

Cody sat down on Bart's newspaper-cluttered bed. "You still reading this hometown newspaper from upstate New York?"

"Every week." Bart knew Cody was stalling, but he had time. "It makes me feel like I've got a home field."

Lifting one of the papers, Cody tried to focus on the small print. "Did you ever live in this place?"

Bart retrieved a glass from the washstand and poured himself a splash of whiskey. "No, but my younger brothers went to live there after my folks died."

Cody rolled his glass between his open palms. "What about you?"

Bart drained his drink. "I was smack dab in the middle of eleven kids. All those older than me were able to take care of themselves when my father was killed in an accident. Within months, I watched my mother grow old and wither away. After her funeral, all the aunts and uncles got together and argued over who'd take the younger ones. My dad's sister in New York City wanted the three little girls, and an uncle with a farm upstate wanted the three boys, but no one bid for me. You would have thought I was damaged merchandise or something. Even then I was big for my age and uglier than a mud-covered toad."

Cody grinned. "Lucky for you, you never outgrew that look."

Bart laughed. He had no illusions about his looks, and somehow Cody's honest comments always made him feel better. He'd far rather fend off honesty than false flattery.

Cody interrupted his thoughts. "So what happened when they split up the brood? Where'd you go?"

"Nothing happened." Bart looked out his window into the darkness. "I overheard them talking about what a burden I'd be, a boy big enough to eat a man's portion but not old enough to pull his own weight. Folks think it's real charitable to take in orphans if they're little and cute, but nobody seemed to feel that way about a lumbering thirteen-year-old who could hardly walk without tripping over his own feet. So I told them both I was going with the other and lit out on my own."

Cody took another drink of his whiskey wishing he was either sober enough to say something to ease his friend's pain or drunk enough that it didn't matter.

"I learned a lot real fast that first year." Bart sat in the room's only chair. "It didn't take me long to figure out that not all people are what they seem. For a while I even gave up speaking to anyone and just roamed around stealing what I needed to eat. I learned to be satisfied with my own company. Eventually I figured out that if you're willing to flirt with death—be it in a boxing ring, on a racetrack, or in the air—people will pay to see you."

"So why the hometown newspapers?"

Bart shrugged. "It gives me a tie to somewhere. A man's got to feel like he's from someplace other than the streets. I've read it for so many years now, I feel like I know the people."

"Ever been there?" Cody had lost all interest in drinking.

"No, but someday I might drop in. I saw my uncle's obituary a few years ago and figure my brothers have scattered by now."

Cody crossed his arms behind his head and leaned against the headboard. "I would have liked to have brothers. Maybe my mother would have been distracted enough to ease up on me."

"Babied you, did she?"

"Not me." Cody laughed. "She babied the furniture. I was like a stray dog they had to keep and were afraid if they turned away for a moment I'd wet on something. I could almost hear her sighing with relief when I left home. I think she likes the idea that I fly. How much damage can I do to the sky?"

"Speaking of damage, what about your promise to take Red up tomorrow?"

Cody sat up and ran his fingers deep into his hair. "I must have been in a tailspin. Even if I'm lucky enough to fly without killing her, Wright will have my head if he finds out I took someone joyriding.''

Bart stared at him for a long time. He thought of yelling at him, but he knew Cody understood the danger as well as he did. Besides, he'd learned tonight that a woman could make a man do something he hadn't planned on doing. He figured women were born with some extra power. Hell, they could even make him think he was kind when he knew he didn't give a damn about anyone in the world but himself.

Suddenly Bart almost felt sorry for Cody, and in a strange way he felt lucky for having caught the same illness. ''Well, pardner, we'd better make sure you fly a clean flight and don't get caught in the morning.''

Cody met Bart's serious stare, and a bond of friendship formed between the two men. An eternal bond that said, No matter what happens, I'm with you.

Five

DAWN RIBBONED THE chilly November sky as Katherine and Sarah crept out the side door of their aging three-story dormitory and hurried toward the shadowy outline of a car waiting down the road. The bare oak branches swished near the darkened corners of the building as a breeze seemed to push both girls back into the protective shelter of the stone walls.

"This is crazy, Kat. We haven't had three hours' sleep." Sarah pulled her collar up around her ears. "I'm beginning to see why we're assigned to the state mental hospital for our first duty. If Miss Willingham catches us out this early—"

"We'll have time to sleep when we get back. We don't have to be on duty until midafternoon, so Miss Willingham will never know." Katherine laughed excitedly. "Besides this doesn't seem any crazier than you staying out half the night."

"I was with Bart," Sarah explained for what seemed like the hundredth time. "I wasn't going up in the clouds aboard an overgrown kite."

Katherine pulled her hip-length cotton coat closed around her. She'd wanted to wear her warm nurse's cape, but feared it might be too bulky. "Going out with Bart and going flying with Cody are in the same den of fright, if you ask me. I'm not finished with our discussion about your choice of men." They were almost to the car. Katherine lowered her voice. "Bart Rome is as wild as a March wind, Sarah. He's no good for you. I can feel it all the way to my bones."

"Yes, Mother." Sarah's reply bore no resentment, though she frowned at Katherine's uncharacteristic meddling. "Lucky for me he offered to give us a ride or you'd probably never let me see him again."

Katherine lightly slapped Sarah's arm. "All right, I may be interfering, but at least I have sense enough to bring you along as a chaperon when I go to meet Cody Masters." She couldn't help remembering his last words—that she should be willing to pay anything for a plane ride. With Sarah and Bart along, Katherine felt she would be safe enough. The only time they would be alone was in the plane, and then he'd have his hands on the controls. Katherine felt a warmth brush her cheeks even though the morning air was freezing. Cody Masters was like fire. Being around him made her feel warm and wonderful, but she knew if she stepped too close she might get burned.

"Morning, ladies." Bart's low voice met them through the shadows. He straightened his huge bulk and stood at attention as they neared. He held the car door open. The automobile had been freshly washed so that even the Firestone labels on the wheels shone as white as when the tires were new. Even Bart's long cream-colored duster looked as if it had just been laundered.

Katherine climbed into the back seat and watched the gentle way Bart helped Sarah. His face seemed full of kindness until he looked up and saw Katherine watching him. "So you talked Cody into taking you flying, Red."

"He was the only one of you birdmen who looked as if he might have sense enough to fly," Katherine snapped. "And don't call me Red!"

Bart started the engine and climbed in beside Sarah. He hadn't spoken to her, but Katherine didn't miss the touching way he reached over and patted Sarah's gloved hand before putting the car in gear.

"I can't say I think much of taking people joyriding," Bart yelled above the roar. "If you get up there and start screaming and jerking around, it will be the death of you both." He paused. "Cody is too good a friend to lose." His last words left little doubt about the lack of value he placed on Katherine.

Katherine hated his condescending tone. "I don't plan on getting us killed. I wonder if it's my being a passenger or the fact that I'm a woman that bothers you."

"Both," Bart answered honestly. "Women don't have any business flying. You should stay home and have little redheaded babies."

Katherine might have exploded in anger if Sarah hadn't started laughing, making her realize Bart was baiting her.

"Just remember when you're up there that the first person to die in an airplane was a passenger," Bart mumbled.

Katherine remembered the headlines when a Lieutenant Selfridge was killed while riding with Orville Wright. They were on a test flight to persuade the army to buy planes at Fort Myer, Virginia. "That was three years ago." She tried to sound confident. "Planes have come a long way since then."

"Yeah, a long way," Bart answered. "We're testing the final model of a plane called the Wright B. The army is planning to buy several. I'm not too crazy about it. The pilot has to sit on the wing to fly the thing, but it may be the best plane yet.

"I remember my first air show last year over in France," Bart continued as he drove. "Every pilot and every plane that could get off the ground was there. We flew for a solid week, and not a man got hurt. The people of Reims called it 'aviator's luck.' They all thought pilots lived charmed lives. But this year I've already counted thirty-two men who've been killed.''

Katherine huddled down in the seat for warmth, wishing she could close out all Bart was saying to her. "I just want to go up once before the fad is over," she said as she fought a shudder she knew was from his words and not from the cold air.

"It's not a fad." Bart sounded definite. "The army has a hundred uses planned for airplanes, and there's big money out there in showing off to crowds. I can even see, in a few years, planes carrying mail on a regular basis."

"And passengers?" Katherine added.

"I doubt it. There aren't that many people who want to risk life and limb just to get where they're going a few minutes faster. No, the money will be in performing. The Wright brothers have a team of air-show pilots touring the country now. Sometimes I wonder if crowds come out to watch us fly or to see us crash, 'cause we surely do both."

Katherine was silent for a moment. "You think I should reconsider?" she finally asked.

Bart shook his head. "I'm a firm believer in letting what's gonna happen happen. I guess if you've got your heart set on flying, there isn't anything I can say that will stop you."

"Thanks." Katherine was starting to like him just a little. "You're right. This is something I have to try, and I don't plan to stop until I've seen the thing through."

Bart nodded his understanding but added, "Well, take care of yourself. I'm kind of getting used to you, Red." Bart pulled the car to a stop beside a Model A Ford pickup at the top of the test sight. "'Course, if flying excites you, you're hanging around with the right folks."

Katherine looked up and saw Cody Masters getting out of the cab of the truck. His lean body was clad in tight brown pants and a leather coat with a chocolate-colored fur collar turned up against the morning chill. He looked dashing in his polished knee-high boots and creamy white scarf. Katherine watched his every movement as he walked toward them. His hands were shoved deep in his pockets, and his sandy hair caught the first touch of sunlight. She thought once more she could love this man, for he was her image of a hero, but when he drew nearer, she saw that his eyes looked cold and remote.

"Ready to fly under the rainbow and touch the stars, Katherine?" Cody opened her door.

"Ready," she answered, climbing out of the car. The old trousers she'd found in the charity bin at the hospital flapped around her legs in the cold breeze. If it hadn't been for the belt, they'd have fallen down. Her blouse was simple, without ruffles, and she'd braided her hair in a long plait. Her light jacket had been meant for summer evenings, not fall mornings.

"I didn't think you'd have a suitable jacket, so I borrowed this from young Taylor." Cody pitched a leather jacket to her.

"Thanks." Katherine pulled off her cotton coat and slipped into the jacket. The excitement of what she was about to do was drumming in her ears. In a few minutes she would be above the earth, one of the few people in the world ever to have left the ground. She wasn't going to allow Cody's mood to put a damper on her spirits. Not even the fear of what payment he might demand later could stop the adrenaline from rushing through her veins like a wildfire in a hay barn.

"Katherine," Sarah said, "are you sure?"

"I'm sure." Katherine winked as she looked into Sarah's worried eyes. "I'll be fine; I promise."

Without another moment's hesitation, Katherine accepted Cody's offered hand and they hurried down the hill. She knew that if she waited any longer she might back out, and Katherine would never allow herself to be a quitter.

Glancing back, she saw Sarah and Bart leaning against

the car talking. Sarah was smiling shyly at Bart, and
Katherine wondered if it wasn't already too late to change
her friend's mind about that man. There was something
between Sarah and Bart—maybe a shared secret, a common
dream, or an invisible bond that sometimes formed between
two people the first time they met. Katherine felt somehow
left out and a little envious.

Cody pulled her faster down the rocky hill. "We'll only
have an hour before the others start to get here, so we have
to hurry. We're lucky the Stardust Twins are in Denver."

"The who?" Katherine managed to say as she hurried
beside Cody.

"Hoxsey and Johnstone, the Stardust Twins." He slowed
a little but continued holding Katherine's hand as they
hurried down the uneven slope. "I know you thought I must
be the Wrights' star pilot after seeing me crash the other
morning, but in truth I'm only a beginner compared to
Hoxsey and Johnstone."

"They're the best?"

Cody laughed. "Thinking of changing your mind about
flying with me?" He stopped as they reached level ground.
"Well, you're out of luck, because both men are in Denver
at an air show, which puts them out of your grasp as well as
Wilbur Wright's control. He gets raving mad every time a
report comes in on how they almost splattered themselves
across half a mile. Wilbur hates the way they compete to
thrill the crowds. He's even threatened to fire them both, but
threats lose their vigor when you're half a country away."

"If you're trying to frighten me, it won't work. Bart's
already tried." Katherine lifted her chin.

"I'm not. I said if you were willing to pay any price, I'd
take you up this morning." Cody looked away, and his
voice took on a cold formality. "The wind is just right at
dawn. I'll fly a clean flight for you, Katherine. No tricks, but
I expect payment when the show's over."

Katherine looked toward the planes, not wanting to think

about what payment he'd ask. One biplane was uncovered and had been pulled out away from the others. A little man in dirty overalls hovered over the engine. He looked like a brown weasel slithering around a woodpile.

He glanced up as they neared and smiled a quick toothless grin. "About time you got here, Cody, no?"

Cody pulled Katherine in front of him. "Katherine, I'd like you to meet the best mechanic in Ohio, Wheeler DeJon."

The little man tipped his head back so he could study her through his glasses. He smelled of castor oil, and his words were flavored with a French accent. "So this is the passenger, no?" He looked her up and down as boldly as a rich old maid examines a suitor. "I've been pouring a little oil on the engine, and she's ready to fly."

Katherine was glad the smelly man didn't seem to want to shake hands with her. His hands were black with dirt and oil.

Wheeler rubbed his stubbly chin with a dirty rag. "Cody tells me you no more want to be a land hugger, mademoiselle. Once you go up in this machine, you are joining a new club and you will never be the same."

"I'm ready," Katherine answered. She fought the urge to back away from the mechanic. He frightened her. Something in his eyes. A touch of insanity? Or was it a touch of genius? Or both?

Wheeler dropped to his knees and scooped up a handful of dirt. Cody's firm grip on Katherine's fingers kept her from backing away as the mechanic stood and moved closer to her. "I never let anyone go up before I first brush some of mother earth on them for good luck." He spread his dirt-filled hand over her shoulder, then turned and did the same to Cody.

"Thanks, Wheeler," Cody said with a wink. He made no attempt to rub off the dirt. "You've been doing that for a year and I've always come back alive."

Katherine managed to say thank you to Wheeler, though she had to force herself not to brush the dirt off her shoulders. She wasn't superstitious, but she had the feeling she might need all the luck she could get today.

Cody's hands encircled Katherine's waist, and he swung her up into the plane's bench seat and settled her on the right side, squarely on top of the engine. "I'm going to tie you in with a rope." He didn't look at her as he continued, "Most aviators think it's safer to be thrown from a crash if the plane goes down, but I'll feel better knowing you can't fall out when I'm banking. I figure when we land you'll be safer inside the plane than rolling over the meadow. You're in what we call the center balance seat. All you have to do is sit still and let me do the balancing, just the way you did last night."

"What's this?" Katherine touched the lever beside her.

"That's the warping lever. I have to turn that in the right direction or we'll crash. Whatever happens, don't touch it."

Katherine was too excited to speak. She nodded and watched as Cody and Wheeler started the engine. The airplane looked so flimsy. Somehow she'd thought it would look sturdy up close, but it was made mostly of wire and cloth. The motor's rhythmic popping sounded much louder than it had the other morning when she'd been watching. Cody climbed in on her left side with the rudder-control and wing-warping levers between them. He yelled, "Hang on!" as Wheeler pushed the machine into motion.

They rolled down the field with the wind blowing against them and the noise of the plane blocking out every other sound.

Katherine nearly screamed with excitement as the plane moved faster and faster until suddenly it lifted off the earth and headed toward the horizon. She grabbed the rope around her waist and held on for her very life as they climbed above the treetops. Cody was busy moving levers while the plane rose toward a tiny cloud.

Intense fear and ecstatic joy surged through Katherine at the same time, making her feel as if she might explode. The engine roared with deafening force in her ears while cold wind turned her cheeks red and pushed her scarf away from her hair. She could taste the moisture in the wispy morning cloud around her and feel the early sun's warmth on her face. Though her hands were frozen with fear around the rope that held her in her seat, tears of excitement welled up in her eyes and were swept away by the wind.

Katherine turned toward Cody and knew he felt it also—that once-in-a-lifetime feeling of knowing this moment in time would be the one you'd always remember, always dream about. These few minutes would be the gauge against which, when she grew old, she would measure all the rest of her life.

Katherine looked down at the world below. The cluster of trees looked like a lake of dark brown surrounded by the rust-colored land. The hill at the back of the test field looked like little more than a slight rise in the landscape. She could see the blue of Sarah's dress beside Bart's mustard-yellow car. Sarah waved frantically, but Katherine didn't dare let go of the rope long enough to return the greeting.

She watched as the plane followed the road toward town. The narrow country road appeared smooth, without dips and holes. It was no longer bumpy and dusty, but had been transformed into a shiny ribbon sparkling in the early morning sun.

A few minutes later Katherine saw the two rectangular buildings where she lived and worked. The larger structure was the hospital with its manicured garden. The other building was the dormitory with a tiny walled garden for Miss Willingham.

Katherine leaned slightly to her right and looked down into Miss Willingham's enclosed garden where no student was ever invited. She felt as though she were spying, but curiosity wouldn't allow her to turn away. Winter-brown flowers surrounded an iron table and a solitary chair.

Cody circled the hospital and turned back toward the test site. Katherine craned her neck to look into the garden again. With this passing she saw a huge stone rock beside the table. She couldn't tell if it was natural or a monument. Or a huge tombstone amid brittle flower beds.

She turned away, not wanting to see more and wishing she hadn't looked so closely.

Everything looked so different from the air. The land seemed so well organized and peaceful beneath them—the woods, the rectangular fields, the square roofs. It was as though sure hands had taken a bag of earth-colored scraps and pieced them together. She thought of how grand it must be to be a bird and see this wonderful scene every day.

Glancing at Cody, she was disappointed to find him gazing straight ahead. She wanted to scream her delight above the deafening engine, but she was afraid of distracting him. She thought of reaching out her freezing hand to touch his fingers as they gripped the controls, but the memory of his angry eyes stopped her. For her, this was a miracle. If she looked at him and saw that flight for him was nothing special, it would pollute her happiness.

They circled the field once more and then headed down toward the earth. Katherine closed her eyes as the field rushed up at them. She quickly whispered every prayer she'd ever memorized.

As he maneuvered the plane into a landing, Cody made sure the tail touched the earth first. That first touch rattled every bone in Katherine's body. They rolled to an easy stop, and she took her first deep breath. Her mind was whirling, and her body felt as if she'd been treading water for hours.

Cody cut the engine and jumped down. ''Sorry we couldn't stay up longer, but the wind was whipping us a little more than I like. An air current can slap you as hard as an elm branch if you're not careful." He untied the rope around her waist. "I hope you enjoyed your short ride."

"Was it short?" Katherine couldn't move. Her limbs seemed to be made of lead. "It seemed like forever."

After pulling the rope free, Cody placed his hands around her waist. "I take it you like flying."

Katherine looked down at his face, still red from the wind. His eyes danced with the excitement of a child sharing the wonder of a treasured toy. For a moment she saw only gentleness in his brown gaze, a gentleness found in those who are forever young, forever learning. She moved into his arms willingly and allowed him to lift her down from the plane. There was no need to answer his question, for their eyes spoke the pleasure they'd shared.

The ground felt wonderful beneath her feet. So solid. Cody slid his arm around her shoulders and they walked in silence toward the others.

Just before they reached the end of the field, Cody murmured, "Was it worth any price?" His eyes darkened slightly. Gone was the gentleness she'd seen moments before. But she *had* seen it, and she knew the truth about this man no matter what game he chose to play with her now. She would see that look again, she vowed silently, just as she would meet his stubborn, mischievous streak with one of her own.

She hated his reminder of how dearly she might have to pay for this joy he had allowed her to experience, a joy that every bird, even the tiniest sparrow, knew.

Before she could question what the payment might be, Sarah and Bart came running toward her. Wild rounds of hugging and laughter passed between them. Sarah asked a stream of questions while Bart and Cody discussed the new part Orville had invented that simplified turns.

In all too short a time, they had pushed the plane back into place and returned to the cars. Katherine pulled off the jacket and handed it back to Cody. The sun now warmed the air, making her cotton coat sufficient for the ride back to the dorm.

Cody accepted the jacket in silence as he stared into her eyes with a mixture of emotions. She thought she saw a touch of passion, but it seemed laced with disapproval. Why, if he disliked her so much, had he taken her for a ride in the heavens?

"Come along, Red. I'll take you back to the dorm!" Bart shouted from his car.

When Katherine turned to move away, Cody caught her wrist and pulled her away from the car. "I'll see Katherine home, Bart!" he yelled as Bart started his engine.

Katherine glanced at Sarah, already sitting in Bart's car. "I have some things to ask Cody on the way back." She hoped her voice gave away none of the fear welling up inside her. Could she have been wrong about what she saw in Cody? Could he yet prove to have an evil core beneath his handsome face? This was her mess, and it wouldn't be fair to get Sarah mixed up in it now. Whatever the price, she would have to pay it alone.

"Fine." Bart nodded, even though Sarah frowned. "I'm going to take this little lady by the bakery and see if we can't find some coffee and a few rolls."

Sarah smiled at his suggestion, then turned to Katherine. "I'll meet you back at the dorm in an hour."

Katherine watched as they pulled away, leaving a whirl of dust in their wake. She knew Sarah had judged Cody an honorable man or she wouldn't have left Kat alone with him. But perhaps Sarah's usual keen assessment of people was beginning to fail her. After all, Sarah seemed to think Bart was wonderful. What if she was wrong about Cody as well?

Katherine suppressed the urge to call Sarah back. A riverboat gambler must have been one of her own ancestors, for she was risking a lot on one roll. But there were two things Katherine promised herself she would always do:

never betray Sarah and always finish what she started. She'd started this, not Cody. She was the one who had set a course toward what might be the destruction of her reputation, at the least. Now it appeared he was going to see that she followed it to the end. The chance to know the man behind those burning brown eyes just might be worth the risk.

"Let's go," Cody said sharply between clenched teeth.

He opened the pickup door and waited for her to climb in.

Stepping past him, Katherine crawled into the truck with a knot in the pit of her stomach. She looked into his face bravely and saw once more the tightly held anger and dislike in his eyes. An anger she didn't understand. A flash of disapproval she found both fascinating and frightening.

Six

KATHERINE WATCHED SILENTLY as Cody drove through the dusty streets. People moved about in their early morning rituals as the city came to life. She wanted to shout to all of them, "I flew across the sky today!" but she knew that even if some of them believed her, they wouldn't understand the way she felt.

Turning toward Cody, she studied his profile. His sandy curls were windblown and unruly. His clean-shaven jawline was set as he concentrated on driving, but there was a hint of kindness in the curve of his lips, in the fluid movement of his hands on the steering wheel. Katherine found honor in his face and a love of life and maybe part of the little boy he would always be, but cruelty did not rule this man.

She broke the silence. "Thank you for letting me go with you this morning." He didn't take his eyes away from the road. "I think I understand why you're angry. I know I'd be mad if I thought someone was trying to use me. But no matter what, I'll always be grateful that once in my life I was able to fly."

Cody slowed the truck in front of a two-story white frame house with a small sign in its tiny overgrown yard: Room for Rent. When he cut the engine, he looked at her for the first time since they had left the test field. His face was as hard as his words: "Don't say a word. Don't thank me. Don't be grateful. Don't talk at all."

Katherine watched him open the cab door. He seemed angry with himself as well as with her. She climbed out of the pickup without accepting his offer of assistance. Fear overtook her. Fear and excitement. Silent, formless fear that was impossible to see, impossible to battle, impossible to kill. Faceless excitement that rang in her ears as the wind had when she was flying.

Cody motioned her toward the steps at the side of the house. "My room's upstairs."

Katherine hesitated at the first step, turning her face to the morning sun.

He didn't attempt to make her follow, but walked alone halfway up the steps with his hands crammed deep in his jacket pockets. When he turned to look down at her, his voice was low. "Backing out of your bargain?"

Cold brown eyes watched her. Even in his anger he was giving her a chance to run. She could turn and walk away and he wouldn't try to stop her. He'd already branded her a manipulator. What difference did it make if he also thought she was a liar?

Katherine took the first step. It didn't matter what he thought of her, but it mattered what she thought of herself. "I'm not afraid of you, Cody Masters." She tried to make her mind believe her words. "So name your fee and be done with it." Her heart told her this man was honorable. If she was wrong? Well, there'd never been a scrape she couldn't get out of.

Cody climbed the rest of the steps and she followed. He opened the outside door, and they entered a long hallway. He tried not to look at her, but she'd seen the surprise in his face when she fell into step behind him. He fumbled with his keys beside the first door they neared. Within seconds Katherine found herself standing in a man's bedroom.

As Cody pulled off his jacket, she looked around. To her amazement the room was spotless. Even the bed had been neatly made. The furnishings were plain, and the rugs were worn from years of lodgers, but everything was in order. A large box-seat window looked out of place with its white lace curtains and dark blue pillowed seat. To the left, a row of books lined the desk top, and maps almost covered one wall.

Katherine watched Cody wash his hands and face in a basin. Whoever he was, whatever he was, this man was neat to a fault. Somehow this trait contrasted with her image of a birdman, and she suddenly found this new knowledge comforting. Any man who planned to ravish a woman would hardly take the time to make his bed before dawn. Fear cooled in her blood, and she relaxed slightly.

"I'm an honest person." She pulled the scarf from around her head and moved to the window. "No matter what you may think of me. I've waited long enough, Mr. Masters, to hear the terms of our bargain. I have to go on duty soon. Name your price, be it laundry or cleaning"— she slowed her words as she fought to hide her fear—"or whatever."

Cody folded the towel over the washstand and turned to face her. The hatred that had been in his eyes seemed to have lightened to a questioning hue. "Would you like a whiskey?"

Katherine shook her head. "It's a little early, don't you think?"

Cody poured a drink from a bottle on the dresser. He held it out toward her. "It's a little early for a lot of things, but that won't stop us . . . will it? My guess is you've never tried whiskey, so let me suggest you down it fast to fight off any chill you may have gotten this morning."

The glass felt cold in Katherine's fingers. His eyes dared her to drink. She lifted the glass and gulped down the whiskey.

Tears rolled from her eyes as the burning liquor traveled through her. She sucked in air, trying to breathe away the fire within her.

Cody took the glass from her hand and downed the rest of the drink, then turned to refill the tumbler with water from a pitcher before handing it back to her. "That was your first drink?" A smile touched his lips.

"And my last." Katherine's voice whistled slightly. She gulped the water and held the glass out. "More, please."

Cody's laughter cracked the hard shell he'd tried so resolutely to maintain. He refilled the glass and handed it back to her, his gaze never leaving her face. She could see the gentleness in his eyes once more and knew she'd been right to trust him.

Silently he brushed his thumb across her cheek to wipe away a tear. "I was angry when you tried to use me last night. I hate women who use their looks to twist men around their finger." His hand balled into a fist, circling a strand of her hair. "I'd like to make you pay dearly. I'd like to teach you a lesson."

He turned away from her and sat on the window bench, one leg tucked under him, the other stretched out in front of him. "But I can't." He sounded defeated. "I've never forced myself on a woman, and I won't start now—even if she does need to be taught to be careful about the bets she makes. I guess deep down I can't blame you for feeling the way you do. I remember a time when I would have promised anything for a chance to go up in a plane."

Unafraid of him, Katherine moved closer. She smiled to herself, knowing she'd guessed right when she'd picked her birdman. "What about the debt?"

Cody leaned his head against the curtains and closed his eyes. The sun was shining through the lace, brushing gold across his hair. "I'll call it up someday." He opened one eye. "But not in a physical way. Don't misunderstand, I'm still very attracted to you, but I don't believe in taking. Whatever may happen between us will have nothing to do with a debt. Agreed?"

"Agreed."

Katherine leaned against the other side of the window frame. There were still so many questions, and she had never been shy about asking. "Then, Mr. Masters, why did you bring me to your room?"

"I wanted to frighten you off." Cody's lopsided smile wrinkled half of his young face. "I didn't figure you'd ride back with me, and I never thought you'd climb the stairs." He laughed suddenly. "I should have known better. You proved your bravery in the plane. I guess I was testing your honesty."

"And did I pass?"

Cody nodded. "You looked pretty frightened in the car. I knew I was wrong about you when you thanked me for taking you up and didn't try to weasel out of the bargain."

"But you brought me here anyway?"

"I was still mad and didn't want to admit I was wrong about you." He reached out and touched a strand of her golden-red hair. "But when I saw you almost choke on the whiskey, the anger went out of me."

"You knew the whiskey would burn."

"Sure, but I wanted to teach you to slow down. You don't have to take every dare you're offered, Katherine."

"Thank you, professor." Katherine bowed low. "I'm glad to have found someone so much older and wiser to teach me how to live my life."

"Now, don't get cocky. I *am* older. I'll be twenty-one next spring. You may not know it yet, but there is a lifetime of knowledge between eighteen and twenty." Cody pointed his finger as if the two years between them were a great span. "It's lucky you're a girl or who knows what crazy things you would have tried by now?"

"Oh, yes, sir. Lucky I'm a girl."

Cody raised a questioning eyebrow. He couldn't tell if she was making fun of him. "I hope you see I had to frighten you for your own good." She looked so appealing in the sunlight that he was having trouble keeping his thoughts straight.

Katherine nodded, but Cody could tell she hadn't heard his last words. She looked around the room as though his speech had been addressed to someone behind her.

"This looks like a nice boardinghouse," she said. "I understand rooms are hard to find in town during the winter."

Cody nodded, not really following her train of thought.

"If I scream"—Katherine showed no hint of teasing—"several people will come running and you'll be evicted."

"You wouldn't!" Cody jumped toward her just as Katherine drew in the breath to scream. He closed his hand over her mouth and pulled her close to him.

Katherine giggled and pulled free. "Now who is afraid?" She moved out of his reach. "You bring a frightened girl to your room and then you don't know what to do with her." She laughed, enjoying Cody's discomfort. "My reputation will be ruined when I'm discovered, and everyone will blame you."

He advanced, but she darted out of his way. "Miss Willingham will probably have you ridden out of town on a rail for corrupting one of her young ladies. Tar and feathers might suit you, birdman."

Katherine neared the door. "The town fathers will ask me if you forced me to go to your room after drugging me with liquor, and I'll pause a long time before I answer."

She put the back of her hand to her forehead. "I'll have to say I don't remember." Katherine giggled as Cody darted toward her once more.

"You're not going to scream." Cody didn't sound very sure of his statement.

"I'll have to say that, whatever happened, you were merely teaching me a lesson. Everything you did was for my own good. I'm sure the sheriff will understand."

"Why you . . ." Cody grabbed her as she passed the

window and encircled her in his arms. The power of his lean body jolted through her as she struggled against him. The memory of the night when they'd been so close made Katherine long to feel his heart pounding next to her own once more.

"Scream," he whispered, "and you'll ruin us both."

"Don't order me around."

"Don't threaten me." His words were warm against her cheek. Though he wasn't smiling, his eyes were dancing with the challenge of their game.

Before Katherine could answer, his lips captured hers. His kiss was hard against her mouth and she made no coy pretense of resistance. When she didn't pull away, his kiss turned gentle. The excitement that shook her body was echoed in Cody's. Katherine knew she should stop. She wasn't even sure Cody liked her, but kissing him was like flying, a new adventure she couldn't turn away from. His mouth was firm against hers, and his body a wall of strength as she molded herself against him.

Slowly he parted her lips to taste her mouth. She cried softly at the new pleasures she was discovering with each moment, then wrapped her arms around his neck and pulled him closer to her. The excitement of flying returned to her as his kiss lifted her off the floor and onto a cloud of ecstasy. She could smell the slight hint of oil and leather. She could taste the traces of whiskey in his mouth, but the fire he now ignited burned far deeper in her than the whiskey had.

Katherine gave herself fully over to learning about this new wonder, this new height of feeling. His kiss was like dancing in an enchanted fire. She could feel the heat but wasn't burned by the flames.

When Cody pulled his lips away, he buried his face in her hair. His breathing was rapid; his heart thundered against her chest.

"I . . ." Cody pressed his cheek against her soft curls. "I didn't mean to do that. I hadn't planned . . ."

Katherine nestled against him and pulled his head down with her hands. As her fingers curled into his hair, her lips silenced his apology. She heard his low moan as he held her closer, pressing her tightly against the wall of his chest. The passion in his kiss exploded through her body, and every inch of her cried for more.

Cody lowered his hands to her waist and pushed her away. He leaned against the window frame, wanting her near, very near. Pulling her against him he let his lips travel down her neck.

Katherine leaned into him, loving the way his mouth trailed down to her throat, tasting her flesh lightly between kisses.

She knew little of lovemaking, but she was learning. Brushing her lips lightly over his hair, she returned his every caress, loving the way his skin felt against her cheek. Loving the taste of him on the tip of her tongue. Loving the smell of freedom that floated around her, encircling her with desire.

There was something so wonderful, so exciting about this man. She could see it in the warm depths of his eyes; she could feel it in his touch. Katherine remembered how once she'd touched an old flag a nurse had brought back from China. She'd felt the Orient between her fingers when she brushed the silk. She'd almost heard the foreign tongues and smelled the unknown foods. Now, touching Cody, she could feel the excitement of his life. She was suddenly a shareholder in all he'd tried, in all he would ever be. And she knew with shocking clarity that she would always be a part of him. A part of his past. A slice of his future.

"Katherine." Cody's voice was a low, warm whisper against her throat. "I've never met a woman like you. I keep fighting myself about whether to hold you or run as fast as I can away from you."

Cupping his chin in her hands, she raised his face until he

was looking into her eyes. She said the only thing her honesty would allow. "Don't run . . ."

Before she could finish, Cody pulled her down onto the window seat and gently lowered her to the velvet pillows. His lips found hers in a tender kiss while his fingers spread warmth wherever he touched. As he cradled her in his arms, he lay beside her allowing her to feel the length of his body without having the weight atop her.

When finally Cody lifted his mouth from hers, Katherine leaned her head into the pillows trying to stop the world from whirling around her. She'd dreamed of what it might be like to kiss a man fully, but this was so much more than she'd hoped.

Cody pulled at the top button of her blouse, and it gave way easily beneath his touch. "I'd better take you home before I ravish you right here and Miss Willingham does run me out of town." He laughed. "But first I want to give you something to think about in your dorm room tonight. I want to make sure you dream only of me."

He pulled her blouse open until he could see the rise of her breasts. Katherine watched his eyes darken as he looked down at her for a long moment. Her cheeks warmed, not with embarrassment but with joy at the pleasure she was bringing him.

Slowly moving his lips along her throat and down to the softness of her breasts above her camisole, he whispered against her flesh, "Sometimes, my sweet Katherine, loving is like liquor. It's better to enjoy just a little at a time and savor each drop." His lips were liquid fire on her skin. Her breasts swelled and strained against the cotton camisole as his mouth brushed the exposed softness.

"You're so beautiful." His words were warm between her breasts. "I'd like to show you all about the game of love, here in the morning sunshine. We could go flying again without ever leaving this window bench. We could play a game that would excite every part of you, just as flying did.''

Katherine shivered as his words chilled her soul. She pulled away, realizing Cody's words were no more than another game he played. ''I can't take love so lightly.'' Her hands were shaking, and she felt as cold as she had as they flew in the early light when the sun offered no warmth. ''I want your touch. I won't deny that. But this can't be just a game between us.''

''Life's too uncertain to be seen as anything except a game. And love—love is just an intimate sport between strangers.''

''Not with me,'' Katherine insisted, even though his warm body still fired her blood with need. ''It has to be all or nothing. I'd have to have promises and proof that you'd keep them forever before I cared about you.''

He planted a kiss on the bow of her camisole and pulled away from her with a moan of reluctant self-control. ''I've never loved except as a game. I make no promises to love forever. Only a fool would believe that. You ask a great deal from me. Maybe too much for any man.''

The sadness in his eyes tore her heart as he continued. ''I can't make a lifetime commitment to anyone. I never stay long enough in any town. I'm always on the road.''

Katherine raised her head stubbornly, blinking back tears she hadn't shed when she heard her father say the same words. ''I understand,'' she lied.

''I'll take you home now.'' He offered her his hand. He seemed to see her pain but had no idea how to ease it.

His fingers gripped her hand tightly as if daring the world to try to pull her away from him. For a long moment brown eyes met green, and they both knew it was he who stood in the path of their love. He wanted her—she could see that in his eyes—but was he willing to make the promises she had named as her price?

Katherine felt light-headed as she stood up. She forced

herself to smile. He was a good man, and one day, when he cared enough to give all of himself, she had to believe he'd come back.

She buttoned her blouse and followed Cody across the room. She'd had her first flight and her first taste of love in one morning and was filled with a need for more of each. The brooding in Cody Masters's eyes was all the assurance she would ever need to know there would one day be more of both.

Seven

THE MINUTE KATHERINE saw Sarah's face she knew something was wrong. Sarah always held her chin high in a valiant show of bravery when something dreadful had happened. Now her tiny friend stood beside Bart's car with chin lifted as her dark curls blew around her face.

Katherine jumped from the cab of Cody's truck even before the wheels completely stopped and ran toward Sarah. She swore to herself as she ran, "If that huge man has hurt Sarah, he'd better enjoy this breath, for it will be his last."

She slowed suddenly, noticing Sarah's tiny hands clutching Bart's massive arm.

"Are you all right, Sarah?" Katherine didn't miss the look Bart shot her at the question. It was as though he wanted to say Sarah would always be fine as long as she was with him.

Cody reached the waiting couple a moment behind Katherine. "What's the matter, Bart? You look as if we're about to be hanged for bringing the girls home late."

Bart swallowed hard, as if it took a great effort to speak. "I just came from town. Wilbur Wright was there and mighty upset. He wants to see you as soon as possible."

"He found out I took Katherine flying this morning, right?" Cody rubbed the back of his neck and looked skyward. "Well, I guess I'd better pack and see if Curtiss can use another pilot, though I'm not eager to fly a bamboo airplane."

Katherine felt sick inside at the trouble she'd caused, but before she could speak, Bart's booming voice filled the morning air.

"No, Cody. Wright knows nothing about this morning. He's upset because we got word that Johnstone was killed yesterday in Denver."

Cody jerked suddenly, as if Bart had knocked the wind out of him.

Bart shook his head. "Wilbur told Johnstone and Hoxsey to cut out the risky stuff. 'Straight flying,' I've heard him yell a hundred times. But the crowds loved the showy stunts, and Johnstone could never leave out the circus act. Hell!" Bart stormed as if mad at the world, then glanced at Sarah and some of the anger left him. "The Stardust Twins thought they could get away with it. Everyone thought they had pilot's luck."

"What went wrong?" Cody stared out at the low bank of winter clouds moving over the dorm.

"The air's thinner up in Denver. The telegram said Johnstone went into his famous spiral descent and just never broke out. He was dead even before the first rescuers could reach the crash. His back, neck, and both legs were broken. Said the bones were poking plumb through his leather flying clothes."

Kicking at a clump of dirt that had caked on the fender of Bart's car, Cody blinked away threatening tears. "I've seen Johnstone fly by and lift a handkerchief off the ground. How could he not have pulled out in time? He's been doing that trick ever since I've known him."

"Hoxsey was in the air when it happened. He said it looked as it Johnstone fell out of his seat and couldn't get control again. He was hanging on to the bench with one hand, trying to reach the levers with the other when the plane hit the ground."

Katherine had listened quietly for as long as she could.

Jodi Thomas

She grabbed Cody's sleeve. The reality that a man had died seeped into her brain. The knowledge that he was a pilot just like Cody hit her with full force as Cody turned his dark eyes toward her. She opened her mouth but could think of no words to say, realizing suddenly she was more frightened for Cody than she'd been for herself all morning.

He stared at her for a moment as if trying to understand the pain in her face. Then he folded her into his arms and held her tight. "Katherine, Johnstone knew the risk he was taking. We all know the risk each time we go up. It's part of the game. Even Orville Wright, who always thinks about safety, has had his body broken up more times than he'll admit."

Bart interrupted, his voice low but crystal clear. "Wright wants to see you, Cody. They want you on the afternoon train to Denver." His words came slowly. "You're Johnstone's replacement."

Katherine felt the excitement jolt through Cody's body. "I'm going?" he shouted.

Bart's smile was somehow sad. "You're on the team now, Cody. You get to finish the tour."

With a yell, Cody swung Katherine around. The dust of the road whirled around his feet. Trying to restrain his joy, he put her down and ran his fingers through his hair. He looked down at Katherine with a smile on his lips but a touch of sadness in his eyes. "I wouldn't have wished Johnstone harm, you know that. I'm only happy to have a chance to fly in the shows."

"I know." Katherine could understand Cody's joy. "This is your chance, your dream, isn't it?"

He nodded. "I'll be back in a few months."

Katherine fought back a tear. "Promise? I still owe you a debt I aim to pay, so don't go dying on me." She tried to smile and make light of his leaving. She knew he couldn't guarantee he'd be back, but she wanted to hear the words.

Just once in her life she wanted to believe a man would come back to her. "I was just starting to like you, Cody Masters."

He lifted an eyebrow slightly as a smile wrinkled the corner of his mouth. He glanced over his shoulder and noticed that Bart and Sarah were already halfway to the dorm. They had probably realized he needed a few minutes alone with Katherine, which was exactly what he planned to have.

Pulling her around between the cars he wished they were back in his room. "Say that again," he pleaded as he set her atop the wide car fender and didn't bother to remove his hands from her waist.

Katherine smiled at his daring. "I said I still—"

"No," Cody interrupted. "The last words."

"Oh." Katherine laughed. "I said I was just starting to like you—"

He stopped her again with his lips. She wrapped her arms around his neck and returned his kiss. She was too close to the dorm to be behaving so outlandishly in broad daylight, but she didn't care.

He pressed her against him. "I'll be back," he promised. "I swear I'll come back for another taste of these lips."

She could feel the warmth of his body through their clothing, his heart pounding madly against her own. A wild adventurous feeling blanketed her in the warmth of his nearness.

She needed his touch as desperately as she needed to believe his promise.

Cody leaned away, cupping her chin in his hands. "Take care of yourself until I get back. Because I think, Katherine McMiller, you just might be the one girl with whom love isn't a game for me. And that thought frightens me far more than anything will ever frighten you."

* * *

Bart walked Sarah slowly back toward the front door of the dormitory. Last night he had thought her the most beautiful creature he'd ever seen, but this morning, with the sun shining off her dark hair and her eyes bluer than any sky he'd ever crossed, she was even lovelier than he remembered.

"Were you good friends with the man who died?" she asked, looking up at him with tear-filled eyes.

Bart tried to swallow the lump in his throat, thinking it would almost be worth dying to have someone so perfect cry for him. "We knew each other, but men don't get too close in this business. It hurts too bad. I know he loved to put on a show. Johnstone had the blood of a carny. Sometimes he'd risk not only his job but his life to give the crowd a thrill."

"Did he have family?"

"Don't know." Bart couldn't believe all the times he'd talked to Johnstone, even had a few drinks with him, and never asked about his family. "Most of the pilots are light a full load of family. For some reason that makes it easier to go up."

Sarah shook her head. "I can just imagine how the crowd must have felt seeing a man die."

"From all the reports, people ran *to* the crash not away from it. They clawed through the wreckage for souvenirs, tore scraps of fabric from the wings. Someone even took the gloves from Johnstone's hands before Hoxsey could get to his partner and stop the madness."

Sarah didn't seem upset by his account. "Folks do strange things sometimes. They're like that when someone dies at the hospital. No matter how bad a dead person looks, there's always one family member who has to see the body and touch death before believing it."

"I'd be like that if someone I cared about died." He looked down at her and wondered if he'd ever cared about anyone as much as he cared about her right now, after knowing her for only a few hours.

"Not me. I want to do all I can for the living, but when they're gone, they're gone."

Bart wanted to change the subject as they neared the door. He didn't want death to be the last thing he talked about with Sarah. He also knew if he had any sense, he'd say good-bye to her. The last thing she needed in her life was him hanging around. But he couldn't bring himself to say the words that would end what had started between them. "So, in a few weeks you'll be graduating and moving on to a real job," he finally said, more just to keep the conversation going than out of any need to know.

Her mood lightened. "I can hardly wait. There's nothing greater than being able to help people. I think I was born wanting to be a nurse. Kat and I will move to Columbus at the end of the month to work at the state hospital. It's huge and pays better than most places."

"Need any help moving?" Bart could have slapped himself after he asked. Here was his chance to stop seeing her, and what did he do? Offer to help her move to Columbus.

Sarah cocked her head slightly, studying him. The action made his heart turn over inside a chest that seemed suddenly too small to hold it.

"Kat and I don't have much, but the trip would be easier if we could ride over in a car and not have to take the train." She looked guilty of being selfish. "But that'd be a lot of trouble for you."

"No trouble at all," Bart lied. He'd lose a day's work, but he would gladly have lost a week's pay to see her again. "What are friends for?"

Smiling, Sarah extended her hand. "Friends," she said.

Bart fought the urge to kiss her fingers as he covered her small hand with his. "Friends," he answered as if she had paid him great honor by speaking that word. He hoped she would just allow him to be close to her. Being near her and never touching her would be a small hell compared to the tragedy of not seeing her at all.

Suddenly Bart did something he rarely did. He smiled.

Eight

IN THE FIRST few weeks after Cody left for Denver, Sarah watched Katherine channel all her energy first into graduating and then into moving out of the dormitory. Katherine seemed unwilling to tell Sarah about her feelings, and she wanted no part of Sarah's close friendship with Bart.

She'd been moody and silent when Bart drove them and their belongings to Columbus. As early Christmas presents he'd given them both trunks, which made the move easier. Though he told them the gifts were also from Cody, Sarah knew that neither Bart nor Katherine had heard from Cody since the day he left to join the air show, even though he'd promised to write.

As Sarah dressed for her first day of work, she couldn't shake the feeling that trouble waited just out of sight. Katherine's refusal to talk about Cody worried her. It was almost as if Katherine believed any mention of his name might somehow endanger him. They both counted time in the number of days he'd been gone.

Sarah watched Katherine unpack her few belongings in their boardinghouse bedroom. Once again they were starting over, only now—unlike the time they ran away from the farm—they had direction and purpose. She broke the silence, wishing they had hours to talk and not minutes. "I wish we'd been given the same shifts at the hospital."

"Me, too." Katherine piled a handful of clothes in an old

pine dresser. The room they'd rented in Columbus was plain, but twice the size of their dorm room. It had lots of open space and floor-to-ceiling windows facing south. "We couldn't very well complain, though, since they at least gave us both a job. The state hospital may not be the best place to work, but where else could we make so much money? We'll be able to pay back our tuition in less than a year."

Sarah lifted her chin slightly. "I'm not sure I'll be able to work with the mentally ill. Remember some of the stories the girls in the dorm used to tell?"

Kat laughed. "It's my opinion there are a great many people running around outside who should be locked up. At least in the hospital we'll know who the crazies are."

Sarah shrugged. "Maybe. I don't mind treating pain, but how am I going to deal with wounds deep inside a patient's mind?"

Kat patted her friend's shoulder. "You can do it. I believe in you. Miss Willingham said you're a natural nurse, remember. Well, just do what comes naturally today. Then tonight when I go in, all I'll have to do is follow you."

Sarah pulled her ebony hair into a bun at the nape of her neck in what Kat always called the Miss Willingham style. "But we'll hardly see each other. I'll be here in our room at night, and you'll be here all day."

Katherine laughed. "Better that than the other way around. I'd hate being here at night. This way I can sleep all day and you can see Bart in the evening."

"Are you giving me permission?"

"I don't know. . . ."

"You don't see him as I do, Kat. Whenever he's near, the world's a little brighter for me. Even though our evenings are just friendly and quite formal, I can feel my heart beating faster just being close to him."

"But he's only a friend, nothing more?" Kat wondered if either of them believed that.

"We're just friends," Sarah agreed. "Only sometimes when we accidentally touch, it's all I can think about for hours. I daydream about him holding me in his arms."

"Sarah!" Kat tried to hold her laughter long enough to act shocked.

Sarah lifted her chin, refusing to be embarrassed. "We've spent hours talking, but someday I plan to do more. Far more."

"I don't think you'll get much of a chance, with him in Dayton and us in Columbus."

"He said he'd drive up to see me when he could." Sarah blushed. "Do you think I could make such a strong man fall in love with me?"

"I think he'd be a fool not to."

"You're starting to like him."

Kat shrugged, trying not to smile too easily and knowing Sarah would continue to see Bart no matter what she said. "I suppose he's not so bad. He did help us move and all. But I swear I'll thrash him if he ever calls me Red again."

Sarah laughed. "You *are* starting to like him!"

"He's growing on me. Maybe in twenty or thirty years, I'll be able to tolerate him."

"My guess is you'll like him by the time Cody returns in the spring."

The smile briefly faded from Katherine's face, then returned as she held Sarah's cape for her. "You'd better hurry or you'll be late on your first day."

Sarah could tell that Kat didn't want to talk about Cody, but they couldn't maintain this silence forever. "He's coming back, Kat. I feel it."

"All the way to your bones?" Kat's smile never touched her green eyes.

"All the way to my bones, and my predictions are far more reliable than yours." She crammed a biscuit in her mouth and ran out the door, waving and mumbling good-bye and praying her bones were more accurate about Cody than Kat had been about Bart. ''Cody will write,'' she said to herself as she left. ''He'll write and he'll come back.''

Quickly Sarah walked the several blocks to the hospital. Her new blue wool uniform and cape were enough to warm her in the early December air.

She felt very professional in her white starched apron and spotless round collar. This was it, what she had wanted to do all her life. She was a nurse at last. Sarah fought the urge to shout it out to every person on the street and push the tiny fear out of mind. Life had never been so wonderful for her, she realized. She was out of school, she was a real nurse, and she was falling love with Bartholomew Rome.

As she entered the grounds of the mental institution, excitement and apprehension built inside her. The dark brick had the look of a great wall devoid of any architectural design except the half-moon brickwork over each window. Large evergreens had been planted close to the walls as if the gardener had tried to hide what was inside.

Sarah studied the building in the morning light. She'd heard horrible stories of what happened in the hospital from nurses who'd tried to work there. Yet the building seemed solid and devoid of demons. She half expected to hear cries and screams as she neared. Bars striped all the windows, but other than that the hospital could have been any other in the state.

When Sarah reached the front door she was surprised to find it unlocked. She straightened her dress and shoved her fears aside as she entered the lobby in what she hoped was her most professional manner.

Walking to the desk, she wished Katherine were with her. A massive oak counter was strategically centered where several hallways converged. Doors of solid oak blocked each hallway. A clerk, dark circles under his eyes, stared at her with a bored expression.

Sarah cleared her throat. ''I was told to report here. I was just hired to—''

"I know." The clerk nodded as though he'd heard this speech a hundred times before. "You're one of the new nurses. Sit over there and I'll send for Mrs. Filmore." He waved a bony finger toward a long wooden bench against the opposite wall.

Sarah sat where she'd been ordered. She wanted to start work, not wait on a bench. She heard the low sound of someone crying. A door slammed somewhere deep inside the building and the crying stopped. Silence followed. Another door opened and Sarah heard a cry for help, an agonizing cry that tore at her heart.

She stood to ask the clerk if she could be of assistance. But before she could say anything, the front doors burst open with a thundering sound that echoed off the walls like a drumroll.

"Hold him down!" yelled an overweight policeman with sergeant's stripes on his sleeve. He barreled through the door with three men shuffling in his wake.

Sarah watched in horror as two other policemen dragged a screaming man into the corridor. The man twisted and thrashed as if Lucifer himself had a hold on him. Though his hands were bound to his sides, the officers held the prisoner tight between them. A cut on his head sprinkled blood over everything, but no one seemed to notice except Sarah. The man's clothes were filthy; there were urine stains on his pants, and caked mud hung from his cuffs. Sarah fought back the bile climbing up her throat.

The police sergeant slammed a fistful of papers under the clerk's nose. "Sign this guy in. We aren't keeping him any longer over at the jail. He's as crazy as any I've seen."

The clerk picked up the papers and smiled sarcastically. "You giving out diagnoses now, Sergeant? I thought that was the wing doctor's job."

The sergeant glared at the clerk with a long-nurtured hatred in his eyes. "Tell me, Ralph, did you get this job 'cause you're the lowest attendant in the place, or are you the top inmate? I never figured out which.''

Ralph twisted his head back and forth as if anger somehow made it loose at the neck.

The bound man screamed. ''No! I won't go! I won't be locked up in here!''

''Shut up!'' yelled the sergeant. ''Shut up or I'll slap you a good one with this nightstick.''

The clerk looked at the papers before him. ''Won't do no good to hit the man. Crazies don't have feelings like the rest of us.''

''Ya, but it would make me feel better.'' Before the sergeant could strike the man, two orderlies came from behind a locked door on the right. The policemen almost threw the bound man to his new captors. He fought as the two men in white jackets pulled him through the doors. One talked to him quietly as though he were a child who had a very limited vocabulary. The orderly's tone sent the bound man into even more convulsive attempts to free himself.

Grabbing his receipt, the sergeant glared at the clerk. ''I can't stand this place. Full of creeps.'' He hurried toward the door muttering, ''Hell on earth, that's what it is, hell on earth.''

The clerk dismissed the sergeant's words with only a slight lift of his shoulders. He pulled a towel from under the counter and wiped the blood off his desk. After a few minutes he looked up and noticed Sarah. ''I like to see them come in like that.'' He seemed to be talking more to himself than to her. ''When they come in fighting, there's more of a chance they'll get out of here. It's the ones who come in all quiet who never see the outside of these walls.''

Sarah jumped as a voice shouted from the end of a windowless hallway just as the stout frame of a nurse appeared. She was built like a tugboat, and her voice echoed like their low toneless whistle. ''So you're the new nurse? I'm Nurse Filmore. Fresh out of school, are you?''

Sarah nodded.

Mrs. Filmore came into the light. The head nurse looked as if she belonged behind locked doors rather than outside them. Her uniform was sloppy and in need of a washing with lye soap. She'd pushed her long sleeves up far enough to reveal hairy arms and dirty elbows. She smiled at Sarah like a hungry lioness who'd just found fresh meat. "You ever been in a nuthouse before?"

Sarah shook her head.

The nurse laughed with a snort. "Well, I'd like to start you out in the snake pit. That's where we keep the lowest of creatures. We have to feed them in a trough, and they mess all over the floor like animals."

She sighed unhappily. "But the doctor needs nurses on the infirmary wing. Crazy people get sick just like everyone else." She shook her head. "Start you with the worst of them is what I'd have done. That way no matter what you see after that, it ain't as bad as the pit."

Sarah let out a long-held breath. "Can you tell me where the infirmary is?" she asked the clerk before the nurse could give her any more information about the other parts of the hospital.

The clerk pointed without looking up from his papers. "Just knock on that door over there and someone will let you in. Check in with Dr. Farris."

Sarah said thank you and hurried away from Nurse Filmore. She hoped the remainder of the staff wasn't as lacking in compassion as these two. If so she would never be able to tell the patients from the employees. As she waited for the door to open, she could hear Nurse Filmore grumbling to the clerk about Dr. Farris. Sarah didn't hear all that she said, but it was plain the head nurse didn't think too much of working with him.

The lock on the other side clicked, and the massive door swung open. To Sarah's surprise, a kindly middle-aged man in a white coat appeared. Though he offered her a genuine smile, his eyes looked tired, and his was the kind of exhaustion from which it would take much longer than a night to recover.

"Welcome, nurse." His voice was low and slow, and a southern accent flavored his words. "I'm Dr. Farris."

Sarah introduced herself.

The doctor nodded formally, but again she noticed no life in his eyes. He looked like a man who had long ago given up on finding any meaning or joy in his life.

Dr. Farris pointed. "There's blood on your apron."

Sarah looked down in shock. Her first day and she hadn't even started work yet. "The man they brought in a few minutes—"

Dr. Farris smiled. "I know. I've already treated him. In the future bring an extra apron. In our infirmary we maintain high standards for our nurses."

As though they were on a stroll through a southern mansion, Dr. Farris offered her his arm and led her up a narrow hallway with closed doors on either side. "This is the infirmary. When patients are checked in, they're put in the infirmary for a few days of tests and observation. Then they're classified. The more violent and disruptive they are, the higher the floor they'll be assigned to." Dr. Farris could have been reading his speech like a bored tour guide.

"When patients fall ill or hurt themselves, they're moved here, and here they remain until they're well enough to return to the ward. The last two rooms are for patients with tuberculosis. When they become too ill to be violent, they'll be moved to the TB cottages out back. Many of our TB patients are not mentally ill, they simply have nowhere else to go."

He reached the center desk, where two men were playing cards. "These are our orderlies. You are never to enter a room without an orderly beside you, no matter how sick the patient." He turned to face Sarah. "Do you understand?"

Sarah nodded, but she thought she might be safer with

some of the patients than with these two men. One was muscular and tattooed, as though he'd spent most of his life at sea. He looked like a man who would kill someone for pocket change. The other orderly looked like his first cousin.

The doctor explained all the workings of the ward. Except for the locking and unlocking of doors and being shadowed by an orderly, Sarah found the procedures similar to those she would have expected in any other hospital.

"We try to treat all our patients with kindness, and most respond in time. Should any violent patients come down from the fourth floor, they'll be strapped into bed while recovering."

Sarah nodded.

Dr. Farris handed her a stack of folders. "Now if you will accompany me, I was just about to make my morning rounds."

Sarah followed him as he moved from room to room, unlocking door after door and examining each patient with unlimited kindness. To her surprise all the rooms were clean and the patients seemed well cared for. A few were talkative, but most were too sick to speak or chose to be silent. Even the man she'd seen enter an hour before was sleeping soundly on his bed, his arms still strapped to his sides. His clothes had been changed, but he hadn't been bathed. Several others had suffered broken bones, two had pneumonia, many were afflicted with fever or bowel trouble, and one had been severely burned.

As they left the burn victim's room, Sarah's curiosity overcame her discretion. His blackened, twisted body upset her far more than any illness or injury she'd ever seen. She still bore a small scar where she'd been burned once, and she couldn't imagine how painful it would be to have burns all over one's body.

"How was he burned?" she asked.

The doctor didn't even stop scribbling on the chart as he

answered. "A few years ago his family was killed in a fire caused by his carelessness. The police said he used to drink and never spent much time taking care of his wife and children. He thinks he should have died also. This is the third time he's tried to kill himself, but the first time while in the hospital. By now he's burning mostly scarred flesh when he sets himself on fire."

A chill passed through Sarah at the doctor's answer. "He wants to die?" she asked.

"Many in here do," he added. "And like all of us, he'll get his wish one of these days."

She looked up into his tired face, and for a moment she saw a kinship with the burned man flicker in Dr. Farris's eyes before he looked down at his work.

The doctor was one of the walking dead that Miss Willingham always talked about, Sarah realized. The dean believed that for many it wasn't the heart or the brain but the spirit that had to be active to keep them alive. Once it died they might still be walking around, but they were dead inside. These were the patients Miss Willingham had warned her students about, for if they became ill, she said, they would fight to die, not to live.

Dr. Farris closed the last file, and Sarah didn't meet his eyes when he looked up. "One other thing, Nurse Sarah. We have many orderlies and housekeepers in this hospital, but very few nurses. Make wise use of your time and your skills. Don't get too close to the patients or you'll burn out as fast as a candle in a fireplace."

As you did? Sarah wanted to ask as she accepted the files.

Just then an orderly interrupted them. "Dr. Farris, we looked everywhere but couldn't find them."

"Thanks," Dr. Farris shook his head and walked away from the desk. "Let's hope they burned."

"What burned?" Sarah asked the orderly when the doctor was out of hearing.

"The matches William got ahold of. If we didn't find

them it means he'll set himself afire again as soon as he heals.''

Sarah looked down the hall to the burned man's room. Suddenly fear blended with the compassion she felt for William. If he set fire to this hospital how would they ever get all the patients out from behind locked doors in time?

Nine

SARAH LOCKED HER hands in front of her and then stretched them toward the ceiling to relieve the ache in her back. She was finished with her first day of work, and the ten-hour shift hadn't been as bad as she'd feared. The only patient who'd been hard to work with was the burn victim, William.

Glancing toward William's locked door, Sarah pulled on her cape. He'd been sullen and much more uncooperative than any patient she'd ever had to deal with in school. The pain she'd seen in his eyes each time he moved tore at her like a blade across her flesh.

She'd sensed the emotional agony he felt in his heart as he begged for death while the physical pain made his reality a living hell.

Sarah frowned, remembering how the orderly had turned William on his side to change the bedding. A section of his skin had remained stuck to the sheets as his swollen red body rolled, staining the clean sheets even before they were on the bed. The smell of his rotting flesh stung her nostrils like ammonia, and the knowledge that he'd done the damage to himself angered her.

Sarah hurried past his room, pushing the man and his sorrow from her mind. She wanted to say good-bye to Katherine and be clear of the hospital. Both girls had been assigned to the infirmary, so the last two hours of Sarah's shift would overlap the first two hours of Katherine's every day. Katherine, in her usual outgoing way, had made friends with the other nurses living at their boardinghouse. They worked the same hours, but on different floors, and had promised to walk home with Kat after her shift ended at two in the morning.

Dr. Farris was finishing rounds with Katherine at his side as Sarah approached the infirmary desk. She wondered when the man slept.

"Good night, sir." Sarah smiled at the doctor. She'd learned to admire this thin, gentle man in the past hours. There was good in him that went all the way to the heart, as Miss Willingham would have said.

"Good evening, Nurse Sarah." Dr. Farris smiled his slow, sad smile. "I must say it's a pleasure having you on my ward."

Sarah thanked him and turned to leave. "See you before dawn, Kat."

"I'll walk you to the door and let you out." Katherine laid the files down and excused herself.

She waited until they were several feet down the hall. "The other nurses said this is the best place in the hospital to work. For one thing, it's the only place Nurse Filmore never comes, and for another, Dr. Farris is considered quite competent."

Sarah agreed as Katherine unlocked the door for her. It was surprising how, in only ten hours, she'd grown so used to the sound of locks clicking.

Shouting from the lobby made both girls jump. A man, fighting with all his energy, was being dragged through the door. Long evening shadows striped the front desk, making the struggling men look like dancers on a candlelit stage.

Sarah watched in horror as a fist whizzed through the air. One of the orderlies went flying across the floor almost slamming into her.

"I'm not crazy!" shouted a deep voice. "Touch me again and you'll be in the hospital as a patient."

"Hold him down, boys!" yelled the desk clerk.

"There's not enough of them to hold me down!" yelled the deep voice as the captive man sent another orderly flying across the lobby. "I'll see you all in hell before you take me anywhere I don't want to go!"

Panic flowed through Sarah. Every muscle tightened as she recognized the voice of the large man with his back to her. She hurried toward him with Katherine only a step behind.

The clerk leaned over the oak counter with his fist in the man's face. "They all say they're not crazy. I guess we got a whole hospital full of mistakes here." His voice rose with each word. "You hit another orderly and we'll throw you in a hole so deep you'll be ninety before you ever crawl out."

Two men in white grabbed the large man again, but before he could fight them off, Sarah raised her hand to stop him.

"Wait, nurse!" The desk clerk paled in horror as he watched the tiny nurse step between the huge man and the orderlies. Her hand gently stayed the powerful fighter's arm.

Sarah's voice was conversational as she looked up into the giant's flashing eyes. "What's the problem, Bart?"

The clerk didn't give Bart time to answer. "You know this man?" he yelled. His face burned beet red, and he shook his head as if he could not believe he'd just seen a feather stop an anvil.

"Yes." Sarah smiled. "Of course."

Bart's temper cooled at the sight of Sarah, but when he spoke, his words were still harsh. "I came here to escort Nurse Sarah home, and I was attacked on the grounds and dragged in here by a pack of white-coated idiots!"

One of the "white-coated idiots" behind Bart tried to explain what had happened. "He came up the north slope where there ain't no road or nothing! When I asked him how he got here, the crazy told me he flew in from Dayton."

The clerk snorted condescendingly. "So, you flew, sir? Many of our guests here fly from time to time. Some around the room and some to the moon."

Katherine's laughter shattered the tension in the lobby as she neared. She had watched as much of this comedy as she could endure. "Bart, you should feel right at home here. This place is full of birdmen." She patted Bart's shoulder as though he were a patient.

"Shut up, Red!" Failing to see the humor, Bart shrugged away from Katherine. "Of course, I fly!" He yelled as if the desk clerk were hard of hearing. "I've been a pilot with the Wright Brothers for over a year!"

Understanding dawned on the clerk, but he wasn't in any hurry to admit his mistake. "So you're one of those birdmen? Well, if you ask me, you belong in a place like this for going up in one of those flimsy machines." As he spoke, the orderlies backed away as if Bart's occupation made him not only crazy but dangerous as well.

Bart took Sarah's arm and headed toward the door. "Let's get out of here before they decide to keep me." He glanced back over his shoulder at Katherine. "Good night, Red."

Sarah could hear Katherine's laughter behind them as they walked through the door. Once they were outside, Bart's scowl turned to a boyish smile, and a low chuckle escaped him. "That was a close one," he said. "You may not want to be seen with me much."

Sarah moved closer, loving the protective warmth of his body beside her. "I love being seen with you, but why did you fly to Columbus instead of driving?"

Bart patted her hand as it rested on his arm. "A rich guy here in town thinks he wants to buy a plane, so I flew it over for him to look at. I'll get a room later and fly back to Dayton tomorrow, but right now I want to buy you dinner."

Sarah couldn't argue with that idea. Hunger pains pulled at her stomach, and the cold air brushed her face. The food in the hospital had been bland and starchy. After feeding several patients who drooled after every other bite, she'd lost her appetite.

They walked to a charming little restaurant with Irish lace curtains and red bandannas for napkins. Bart glanced at the menu on a blackboard against one wall and ordered two of the night's specials. A pleasant waitress brought their food, then disappeared, leaving them to enjoy their meal and each other.

"Well, little lady, tell me about your first day as a nurse." Bart smiled across the table at her. He'd longed all day to hear her voice. Suddenly he realized he needed her near him as much as he needed food to eat and air to breathe.

Sarah didn't hesitate. "I've been thinking about how I'd tell you everything. For the first time ever, I felt that I was doing what I was meant to do. The patients aren't that different from those at Miss Willingham's hospital. Only now everyone follows my orders and trusts my judgment."

"And well they should. I'll bet there isn't a finer nurse in the whole damn state."

Blushing, Sarah continued, his praise making her bold enough to admit her weakness. "Only one inmate upset me. He'd been burned so badly his flesh was almost gone. Every time I think I'm helping him I only hurt him more."

Bart patted her hand. "You can't be expected to take it all in and not feel upset. I wish I knew something more to say."

Sarah rubbed at the burn scar on her arm. "When Kat and I were running away from the farm, I accidentally turned over a lantern in the barn. I put out the fire, but my arm was burned slightly. I'll never forget how much I wanted to scream, but I couldn't give away where we were hiding. While we waited to make sure no one saw the lantern flame go out, I felt like the fire was still burning my skin."

She looked into Bart's caring eyes. "Today I could almost feel the pain of that fire again. I felt so helpless. The fire was out, but the man looked as if it still burned inside him.''

Clutching his hand, she held on tight for a moment, realizing he was her strength just as surely as the sun was the earth's warmth. Something in his gray eyes told her his friendship was unconditional. ''You say a lot by the way you look at me,'' she said. ''You make me feel that you believe I can do anything.''

''Can't you, darling?'' he teased.

Suddenly, like a child after her first day of school, Sarah couldn't stop talking. She told Bart everything, from how wonderful Dr. Farris was to how horrible the food was.

Bart listened silently, nodding his head now and then to let her know he understood. He tried to follow every word, but sometimes her beauty distracted him. He'd catch himself just watching her mouth and wondering how her lips would taste. What he found most amazing was that everyone in the restaurant didn't stop and stare at her. Couldn't they see he'd captured the most beautiful creature in the world and she was his, if only for a few hours? But folks passed her as if she were just another young woman. He alone saw her beauty.

Finally, after she'd eaten her pie, she murmured, ''Thank you for being so kind and for listening to me. I wish I could make Katherine understand how wonderful you are. Talking with you makes all the world fall into place.''

Her hand brushed his lightly, politely as always. ''I wish the evening wasn't over, but we seem to be the last people in the restaurant.''

Bart captured her hand for a moment, knowing he'd frighten her if he held her as close as he desired. ''If you're not too tired, I thought we might go for a walk and have a look at this town by moonlight.''

Sarah was tired, but she didn't want the evening to end. Every night they'd been together had been the same—peaceful, wonderful. ''A walk sounds nice.'' She smiled as pleasure brushed his rugged face. He pulled his hand away as though touching her a moment too long might offend her.

They left the restaurant and strolled in silence for a long while. The moon hung full in the midnight sky, and the winter air was crisp. Low, full clouds billowed like water-soaked cotton, while wind drifted around them, whispering promises of cold rain.

Sarah cuddled close to Bart's arm. "Dr. Farris says some doctors think the patients are more restless during a full moon. He believes a change in the weather can alter the mood of the entire ward."

"You like Dr. Farris, don't you?" Bart's words held a sadness that Sarah didn't understand.

"Yes, he's a nice man and a good doctor."

Lost in their own thoughts, they neared a neglected park. The hard and brittle ground gave their steps a lonely sound as they walked between the trees.

Sarah relaxed and just enjoyed Bart's nearness. They'd only known each other for a little over a month, but already the thought of life without him seemed unbearable. He was a rock she could lean on. She wasn't strong like Katherine; she needed him. He was the most wonderful man she'd ever known. She wasn't sure when she'd fallen in love with him—maybe that first night by the planes—but love him she did, and would until she died, even if he never returned her love. His feelings for her seemed to have crystallized at the friendship stage.

"Bart?" Sarah's voice broke the silence of the night. "Are we good friends? Honest friends?"

Bart turned his head away from the glare of the streetlight. His face was in shadows, but his words spoke his tenderness. "You are without a doubt the best friend I've ever had. I've never known anyone I could talk to so easily. I could spend a lifetime walking through parks with you."

Sarah gathered her courage. She'd been trying to ask him the same question every night for a week. She squeezed her eyes closed and blurted it out before she had time to change her mind. "And do you like me?"

Bart seemed surprised at the question. "Like you? I treasure you. You're a tiny angel from heaven, my lovely little woman-child. Before I met you I would go days without smiling or finding anything to make me enjoy life except the few minutes I spend flying." He patted her shoulder lightly. "I cherish our time together."

Sarah was losing her nerve, but she forced herself to continue. "Do you find me attractive?"

Bart's laughter made her jump. "Sarah darling, you are the prettiest little doll I've ever seen." He rubbed his chin with his thumb and forefinger and nodded as if suddenly understanding. "I know what you're thinking. You're figuring men notice Katherine before they do you and that you must suffer in comparison. Well, I'm assuring you that just about any man will turn his head when you walk by."

"I'm not interested in *any* man." Sarah looked down, avoiding his eyes. Even in the shadows, she was afraid he might read her thoughts.

Bart moved nearer and looked up as though talking to the streetlight. "Not any man, eh? Could there be one man? Maybe that Dr. Farris you talked about all during dinner?"

Sarah glanced up and saw his gray eyes grow darker in disappointment before he looked away. "No," she quickly said, not wanting him to think such a thing. "He's a wonderful man, but old enough to be my father."

Her next words were little more than a murmur. "The man I'm interested in stands beside me."

"I thought we agreed to be friends?"

"I agreed, Bart." Sarah placed her hands on his huge shoulders. "I don't want to tie you down in any way. I just want to be honest with you now." She had to tell him how she felt about him. She couldn't just go on pretending they were only friends, even if he wanted it that way.

Bart suddenly didn't seem to know where to put his

hands. He reached out to touch her, then jammed his huge fists into his pockets. "What do you want me to do, Sarah?"

"I want you to hold me," Sarah answered honestly as she moved into his embrace. His arms hesitantly surrounded her, and his breath brushed her cheek. Encircling his neck with her arms, she pulled his head lower. She felt enveloped in his warmth, in his protective hug.

Bart let out a long-held sigh and pulled her nearer. "Are you happy now, my angel?" he whispered into her ear as though he were enduring great pain to bring her pleasure.

"I don't want to be thought of as your angel or as a doll. I'm a woman, Bart. A woman who cares very deeply for you and asks nothing in return. See me for what I am—not some priceless treasure, not some child, but me." Sarah felt a tear cool her warm cheek. Would she go from a little girl to an old lady in his eyes without ever being seen as a woman?

Bart bent and kissed her lightly on the cheek, then pushed her gently away. "I think of you in many ways, Sarah." He patted her shoulder lightly as if humoring a confused child. "You're a fine little lady, and you're very young—"

"Stop!" Sarah stepped past him. "I don't want to hear any more." She suddenly broke into a run across the darkness of the park. She couldn't endure listening to any more. Did he think of her as his sister? Did he think she was being silly and needed to grow up? She wasn't brave enough to face the answer.

"Wait!" Bart yelled. He tried to follow her, but the shadows engulfed Sarah's navy cape and the wind whirled with sudden anger, muffling the sound of her footsteps.

Sarah ran from his voice. She didn't want to admit that she'd made a fool of herself. Why had she spoken so impulsively, when she usually thought about every word before she said it? She darted between the trees. The north wind whipped her skirts around her. The air was turning colder, but her face felt as if it were on fire.

Running until her legs ached, she ignored the overgrown shrubs pulling at her skirt as her arms ached from lifting up the woolen hem. She crossed the park back and forth until she could no longer find the walkway.

Finally, with the wind gusting around her, she stumbled into a long forgotten gazebo. Dried, twisted branches had overgrown the paint-chipped structure until the gazebo was little more than a pile of sticks losing its battle with nature. Sarah clawed her way through the vines into the blackened interior of the gazebo. She sank ankle deep in dried leaves.

Bart's low voice called her name through the trees outside her fortress. Tears streamed down her cheeks as she fought back each sob, fearing the noise would give her away. He saw her as a child, a toy, an angel, when she wanted him to see her as a woman. For the first time in her life she wanted someone other than Katherine to come closer. She wanted him to care about her as much as she cared about him. She wanted him to love her. Dear God, how she wanted Bart to love her.

Sarah roughly rubbed her palm against her cheek where he'd kissed her, wanting none of his brotherly kisses.

Her heart was breaking as rain began to pound on the roof of the gazebo. She began to care for Bart the moment she first saw the sadness in his gray eyes, a sadness that seemed to issue a challenge, daring her to ease his loneliness. Maybe she was only a foolish child, blind to the real world. Maybe she should have given their relationship more time. Why had she hurried as if there would be no tomorrow? Why couldn't she have left the friendship intact without ripping it apart looking for something that wasn't there?

Why couldn't he have kissed her with passion and not pity? She had dreamed of such a kiss, but now her dreams would only be a reminder of how she could feel the loss of something she'd never had to begin with.

Sobs rippled through Sarah and joined with the thunder. Outside the gazebo black velvet masses blocked the moon and darkened the earth to the gloomy shade of her mood. Sarah dropped to her knees and cried until her body shook with each sob.

An arm wrapped itself around her and tugged her to her feet. "Sarah!" Bart's voice resounded with worry and anger. He gripped her shoulders, shaking her roughly. "Why did you run away from me?"

She tried to wrench herself out of his hold. "Let me go!" she screamed in frustration.

Bart's hands closed over her shoulders like a trap snapping. He pulled her toward him with such force it almost knocked the wind from her lungs. "Why did you run?" he demanded.

Sarah slammed her fist into his chest. All her years of meekness seemed to explode in anger. If he couldn't love her, she shouldn't have to answer any of his questions.

"Stop it!" Bart yelled, grabbing her flailing fists and twisting them behind her back. He shook his rain-soaked hair out of his eyes as he lifted her off the ground. "What is it you want of me?"

Sarah could feel his hard chest flattening her breasts and his strong arms tightening around her like iron bands. His heart pounded violently against hers. Through her tears she realized she was angry, but she was not afraid of this giant who could have crushed her within his grip.

Bart's body warmed hers as he tried to bring his breathing to normal. "I . . . I thought you wanted me to kiss you. I didn't mean to frighten or hurt you." His deep voice rumbled with confusion. "God, I feel like such an ox when I'm around you."

Sarah stopped struggling and Bart released her. "You didn't frighten me and you didn't hurt me," she said. "But I want no pity in a kiss from you. I'd prefer our first kiss that split my lip to the brotherly peck you gave me tonight. And

I want no lectures about how young I am. I'm old enough to know my own mind." Thankful that the darkness hid her embarrassment, she pushed away from him. His nearness only made her longing worse. "In fact, I just want to be alone." She wanted to add that she was sorry, so sorry, but no more words would come.

She walked to the opening he'd made in the brush at the entrance to the gazebo. Leaning out into the rain, she no longer cared if her cape got soaked or if her shoes were covered with mud. She needed sleep, she needed dry clothes, and most of all she needed to be away from Bart so she could calm down. In the morning things would look better. Maybe she wouldn't feel like such a fool. Her need for him to hold her, to love her, was so great that she'd let it overshadow her reason.

Without warning, Bart grabbed her cape and pulled her back out of the rain. "If you want nothing but to be left alone, prove it!"

"What?" Sarah wiped water from her face.

"I said prove it." It was dark, but Sarah would have sworn Bart was smiling.

"How?" she yelled above the thunder.

"Kiss me. It's the only true test. You told me so yourself." He didn't wait for an answer. He lifted her into his arms and covered her lips with his.

Sarah tried to pull away, but he folded his huge body around her like a cocoon. Bart gently nibbled her bottom lip, pulling her mouth open. His tongue parted her lips, and the kiss became unlike anything she'd ever imagined. She pressed closer and felt his low moan against her mouth. He took possession of her, and the rain, the night, the world, faded away. There was nothing but his lips, his arms, his heart drumming against her own.

A wild beast had captured her and she was safe in his arms. She'd forced open the shackles that kept him at arm's length and now she would have to face whatever happened next.

Without breaking the kiss, Bart slid an arm under her legs and lifted her up, then carried her to a corner of the gazebo. After placing her on a damp cushion of pine needles, he blanketed her with his body. Sarah could feel the warmth of his flesh even through their soaked clothes. She loved the weight of him against her as he demanded her response to his kiss.

His body pressed hard against her, telling her boldly of the effect their kiss was having upon him.

Finally, when the world was spinning around her, Bart moved his lips to her throat, trailing a row of gentle kisses along her neck. The feel of his rough cheek against her skin made her sigh with pleasure. His large hands pushed back her damp hair as his lips moved along her neck, tasting her with a hunger that had lasted a lifetime.

When he returned to her ear his voice was already low with need. "Is this how you want to be kissed?" he whispered as he boldly slid his hand inside her cape and spread his palm across her abdomen. "Is this what you want, my beloved Sarah?"

"Yes," she whispered. "Yes!" This was everything, and it was a hundred times more thrilling than she'd dreamed it could be. She hadn't known exactly what she wanted until this moment, but she now knew this was what she'd dreamed of, longed for, ever since the first time Bart had carried her in his arms.

She ran her fingers through his hair, urging him to repeat the pleasure he'd given her, and this time her response surprised even her. She opened her lips to his exploration, loving the way his mustache brushed her skin, tickling the corners of her mouth. His damp black hair caressingly curled around her fingers.

Slowly he rolled over beside her. She tried to follow, but his arm held her on her back with gentle pressure. As his lips circled her mouth with kisses, his hand began to move across the damp wool of her bodice. He laid claim to her body with bold caresses. With methodical precision his hand moved to her breasts. She felt his palm spread over her fullness in gentle revolutions as his fingers tenderly tugged at the material. The buttons of her dress gave willingly to his demand.

Sarah gasped in surprise at the sensations boiling through her veins. The thunder and lightning around them dimmed in comparison to the volcano erupting within her body. A fiery need built inside her, a hunger that made her realize she'd been starving all her life. A longing in her heart and in her soul that only Bart could relieve.

He whispered against her ear. "I knew if I ever touched you I'd be unable to stop with a kiss." With one powerful tug he ripped her camisole from throat to waist. "I'm not sure I know how to be gentle, but I'll try, because you are heaven on this earth."

The pressure of his lips increased as did the pleasure he brought her with his hand. Sarah let her arms fall beside her head. Her damp lashes brushed her cheeks as she relaxed beneath the movements of his fingers over her body. He was bold and tender, teaching her of wondrous pleasure.

Reining in his wild passion for Sarah was the hardest thing he'd ever done. When she pressed her cheek against his arm and sighed softly he felt he would explode.

He shoved the damp wool of her dress aside in haste, not wanting to live a moment longer without the feel of her flesh beneath his open palm. Since the moment he'd seen her standing in the crowd at O'Grady's he'd thought of touching her. He'd convinced himself he could be content to brush her hand lightly or hold her under the protection of his arm. But his longing to touch her as a man touched a woman ate into his every waking hour and gnawed away at all his dreams.

As he explored her body from throat to waist, he

whispered, "You're very much a woman beneath that starched uniform." Pulling gently at her breast cradled in his large hand, he made her cry out softly with need for more. "You bring me great pleasure."

He flattened her full breast with his palm, loving her soft sounds of pleasure. "I plan to bring you much pleasure, my lovely angel."

All his life he'd been alone, fighting just to stay alive. Bart could never remember anyone really wanting him, but Sarah did. She wanted him as her friend and as her lover. He wasn't sure he had enough love inside him to give her all she needed.

He reluctantly released her breast and moved his fingers down her body. When he reached her waist, he roughly pushed her skirt off and covered her hips with his hands. As he pulled her against him, he whispered one plea: "Stop me, Sarah!"

"No," she answered. "Never."

"Stop me before the feel of you drives me mad."

Sarah closed her eyes once more and rocked her head gently from side to side amid the sweet smell of pine and the masculine scent of Bart. "No," she whispered over and over, lost in the pleasure he gave her. "I don't want you to stop."

She felt his damp lips at her ear as he asked, "Does passion bring you joy?"

Sarah didn't open her eyes. She was swimming in a sudden flood of sensations as his fingers played over her body. His mouth moved over her face teasingly, avoiding her lips as his hands brushed across the thin material of her undergarment.

"Does it?" There was an urgency in his words as he pushed her head back to expose her throat to his lips.

"Yes," Sarah said before pressing her hand over his fingers.

He pulled her against his muscular body. "You make me

drunk with happiness. I've dreamed of holding you in my arms, but the feel of you is a hundred times better than I thought possible.'' His tongue brushed her bottom lip. ''So much sweeter. If I died right now, I would have died at the happiest moment of my life.''

Sarah sighed and stretched beside him as he continued, ''Until I touched you, we could have remained only friends. But not anymore, because I'll never be able to look at you again without remembering the feel of you in my arms.'' Then suddenly he was kissing her again as though he'd been starving for her taste for far too long. Warm, frantic, loving kisses. He left her gulping for air as his lips moved across her face, then back to her mouth with more demands. Her breasts hardened in fullness. There was no world other than his touch, and he proved it to her again and again as he brought her to madness with his nearness.

Finally he pulled his hand away and fell back beside her. ''There is more.'' Bart sounded out of breath and almost out of control.

She knew there was more to lovemaking, but this was so wonderful she didn't think anything could be better.

''I want to bring you pleasure until you cry out. I could show you that passion now.'' Bart's voice blended with the whispering wind.

''I know,'' Sarah answered, again honestly. She had no intention of stopping him. ''Please hold me.'' She felt suddenly cold without his hands on her.

Bart hugged her to him, shoving all chill away with his warmth. ''Later. Just wait a little longer, my love. This is not the place.'' He stood and pulled her up beside him. ''Will you believe I want you, Sarah? I want you more than I've ever wanted anything in the world, but I must force myself to go slow. I want us both to enjoy each stage as I show you passion, not out here in the storm but in a warm bed.''

Sarah wanted to cry that it didn't matter where they were

as long as she was in his arms. She pulled his face down to her. "Promise me." She murmured her request against his mouth.

Bart groaned and lifted her to her feet. "I need to allow you time to make certain. If after a week you feel the same way, I promise, my darling, I'll show you all there is of paradise on this earth."

Sarah kissed his cheek, and somehow her love for him grew with his promise. "I love you, Bart."

He pulled her close under his arm. "I worship you, my angel, but the woman I just felt in my arms I will love until the day I die."

Ten

CODY PULLED HIS collar up against the brisk wind. As he and another pilot walked across Dominguez Field just outside Los Angeles, he wondered for the hundredth time how long it would be before he was back home. Flying in air shows had lost its thrill. He found himself longing again and again to be back in Ohio with Katherine.

Pretty women had been passing through Cody's life since he turned sixteen, but none had ever affected him the way Katherine did. Her spirit matched his, and he couldn't force her from his thoughts or his dreams.

"You think Hoxsey will go up today?" Walter Brookins, the pilot walking beside Cody, asked. "The wind's a bit too gusty for me."

Cody pulled himself back from his daydreams. It was the last day of the year. Surely they'd be heading home soon. "Hoxsey will go up if there are five people watching the show, no matter what the weather. Since Johnstone died, Hoxsey hasn't missed a day performing."

The men turned at the sound of an engine roaring to life at the far end of the field. Hoxsey's plane came into view and was airborne in seconds.

"He's going for a new world altitude record!" Brookins yelled above the noise. "I heard him say this morning that he was going to climb up to twelve thousand feet today."

Cody watched the Wright Model B climb into the clouds. "If he's going up in this weather, so am I."

Both men broke into a run for their planes and within
minutes were off the ground. But the winds played a
dangerous game with them, tossing the light planes like toys
in the air. In less than an hour Brookins and Cody were back
on the ground waiting for Hoxsey to join them.

Cody crossed his arms over his chest to fight back a
sudden chill as Hoxsey came out of the clouds in one of the
team's famous spiral glides. He was fine until he spun down
to only a few hundred feet above the ground. Then a gust of
wind caught the wing and flipped the plane over. Cody
watched in horror as Hoxsey and his craft somersaulted and
hit the ground.

Every man on the field ran toward the cloud of dust. As
the plane struck the earth, the sound of splintering wood
echoed in Cody's ears. A moment passed before he noticed
the air was now absolutely silent.

As Cody neared the crash he saw part of the propeller
lying across Hoxsey's twisted body. The pilot resembled a
half-empty scarecrow flung against the wreckage, his arms
and legs in unnatural positions. A jagged iron bar from the
transmission assembly had pierced Hoxsey's chest.

Cody froze, unable to accept what his eyes saw. Hoxsey
lay lifeless, his face covered with blood and dust. His eyes
stared up at the sky he no longer saw.

"Keep them back!" Hoxsey's mechanic yelled as he
grabbed a shattered strut from the wreck. "Don't let them
pick at his body like they did Johnstone's."

Cody turned and saw a crowd of spectators running
toward the plane. He nodded at the mechanic; he had heard
about people picking over Johnstone's crash site like
vultures, hungry for any souvenir.

"Stay back!" Cody yelled. "Stay clear of the crash!"

Cody wasn't sure if it was his order or the menacing way
the mechanic waved his stick above his head, but the crowd
kept its distance.

Walter Brookins stood at Cody's side ready to fight

anyone who came too close despite the tears streaming down his cheeks. A doctor, moving with what Cody thought must surely be an unnatural slowness, ordered a stretcher and covered Hoxsey's body. ''Both Stardust Twins are dead,'' he said as he walked beside the stretcher. ''The world will never know their like again. The Stardust Twins are gone.''

Cody wasn't sure how he got back to his room. He didn't bother turning on any lights, but knelt beside the small fireplace and brought the flames back to life.

Johnstone and Hoxsey were dead within two months of each other. Two of his heroes had vanished. Cody had watched them fly since the days when he'd only dreamed of being a pilot. They'd been the best, and they were gone.

Cody held his head tight as if to stop the pain throbbing through his brain. ''I can't fly again,'' he said aloud.

Slowly he looked up into the fireplace and pictured Katherine's hair in the firelight. She was smiling at him with her dancing green eyes, begging him to take her flying.

''Katherine,'' he whispered as though she'd come in answer to his call.

Suddenly a longing to see her stabbed through him. He'd never allowed anyone to slip beneath his skin the way she had. For as long as he lived, he would remember the joy he had seen in her eyes that morning he took her up. ''One hundred percent alive,'' he'd told her. ''You're totally alive when you fly.''

Then as surely as though he'd seen it written in the firelight, Cody knew he couldn't give up flying. The need to fly coursed through his blood the way a need to gamble or drink did in some men. The attraction might kill him, but at least it would be a clean way to die, one moment drifting through the clouds, the next lying broken on the ground.

Cody slowly stood and moved to his desk. He had to write Katherine before he slept. Even if he never mailed the letter, he would feel as if he had talked with her tonight.

* * *

Sarah finished the last of the paperwork for her shift and handed the charts and the job over to Katherine. "This week has been like a year. I can't wait to leave this place and be with Bart."

Katherine knew Sarah had been on edge for the past few hours, but she hadn't time to ask why. "Are you sure he's coming in tonight? The weather looks as if it might turn bad."

"He'll come." Sarah tried to sound sure. "He had as much trouble saying good night last week as I did." She remembered how much she'd wanted to run back into his arms one more time before he left, but several other boarders had been watching. She'd seen the need in his eyes also, that need to hold her and touch her as no other man ever had.

"I feel as if I've been on medication all week. I keep looking at the clock, not believing only minutes have passed when it should be hours."

"You sound like a woman in love. Next you'll be telling me he kissed you." Kat untied Sarah's apron for her and handed her a cape.

"He did—" Sarah laughed—"and it was wonderful. But that was last week. What if he's changed his mind about me? What if he never comes back? What if he's sorry?"

"Are *you*?" Kat asked honestly.

"No!" Sarah answered.

"Then I very much doubt he is." Kat walked her to the door of the infirmary. "It sounds as if you may have caught a terrible illness called 'falling in love.'"

"And if I have, will it be fatal?"

"For you, probably." Kat laughed. "Just let me know when you think it's happened."

"You'll be the second to know." Sarah hurried out the door.

''Be careful,'' Kat urged as she watched Sarah run down the hallway. ''Don't let him break your heart.''

Sarah waved and slipped outside. She hurried toward the boardinghouse, trying to hold her head high, but with each step she was more sure Bart wasn't coming. She tried to be sensible. He was older than she, and she wasn't sure she could handle being a pilot's wife. But then, he hadn't talked of marriage. He'd probably kissed a hundred girls the way he kissed her.

Bart Rome turned the sealed envelope over and over in his large hands as he walked out of the Wright Brothers' workshop and office. He'd already heard about Hoxsey's death, and Cody's letter was postmarked the next morning. He didn't have to steam it open to know what the letter contained.

He shoved the envelope into his vest pocket and climbed into his car. He knew he should give the letter to Katherine right away, but he wanted to see Sarah and talk with her before she learned another Wright pilot had died. Just as he'd promised, he had waited a week since their night in the park. The longest week of his life.

Driving toward Columbus, Bart reasoned through all his options. Cody had mailed the letter to the office in care of him instead of sending it directly to Katherine. That had to be his way of telling Bart to deliver it when he thought best. But the news was already headlines, so there was no way Bart could keep it from the girls. Katherine wasn't exactly pining over Cody anyway. The few times he'd seen her, she hadn't mentioned Cody's name. Maybe she was just too busy, or maybe she didn't want to think about what could happen.

By the time Bart reached Columbus and turned toward the hospital, he had decided that if it had been his letter to Sarah he'd have wanted Cody to deliver it right away. He parked in the shadows beside the hospital and gripped the steering wheel hard as Sarah walked out and turned toward home. He wanted to call out to her, but he had to see Katherine first. Then there would be time for Sarah and him.

After Sarah had turned the corner and disappeared, Bart got out of the car and walked through the front door. The strong, almost overpowering, smell of ammonia invaded his senses. Hospitals had always held a dread for him, and this one was no exception.

He asked the attendant at the desk if he could talk to Katherine, then tried to wait patiently. The bench looked too hard, so he paced back and forth, tapping the letter against his palm as he walked.

Katherine looked surprised when she stepped out of the infirmary. "Bart," She looked around. "You just missed Sarah. She couldn't have left more than a few minutes ago."

"I know." Bart handed her the letter. "I wanted to deliver this first."

He'd spent most of the drive thinking about how he'd say the words to Katherine. "Cody wanted you to know about another accident."

He saw her face tighten slightly before his words registered. "Cody wanted me to know?" she said. "He's all right?"

"He's fine." Bart almost smiled, satisfied that for once he'd used the right words. He hadn't frightened her unnecessarily by telling her about the accident first. "One of the team was killed, but Cody's fine. I'd like to tell Sarah about it in my own time. You know how worried she gets about the dangers of flying."

Katherine nodded and took the letter. She glanced at the doors to the infirmary, then at the attendant. Bart understood her dilemma. "Have a seat," he motioned toward the bench.

When she was seated, he stood in front of her facing the

desk. His huge body offered her a wall of privacy as she carefully opened the envelope and read.

Dear Katherine,

I'm sorry I've taken so long to write, but our schedule has been so hectic that the towns are starting to look alike. I find myself seeing crowds and not individual people anymore. Sometimes, I even catch myself acting the way they think I'll act and not the way I normally would.

It bothers me that people want to touch me just because I've flown. I don't mind the boys and their dreams or the old men with their questions, but the vicarious thrill seekers unnerve me. They are afraid to follow their own dreams, but they want to touch me, know me, because I follow mine. They pull at pilots as if they could snatch a piece of the dream.

Today I saw a man die. His wasn't the first or the last death I'll witness, I'm sure. Someday it may even be my turn, but I want you to know that I followed my dream to the end without regret and count my life fuller for having done that.

I had to write you in hopes you'd understand. I wish I'd held you once more before I left. Maybe then my arms wouldn't ache for you so much now.

I haven't forgotten my promise to you. I will *be back.*

Cody

Katherine blinked away the tears and stood up. She'd tried not to think about the dangers Cody faced, hoping somehow to push her fear aside by not dwelling on it.

Bart turned as she folded the letter. She looked up into his gray eyes and for the first time saw kindness there—a kindness Sarah must have seen from the first.

Looking unsure of himself, he awkwardly opened his

arms. "I don't know what to say." His low voice cracked.

Katherine stepped into his embrace. "Just hold me for a minute," she said, "and then I'll be all right."

Bart could count on one hand the women he'd hugged in his lifetime, and he'd never held one just to give her strength. He patted Katherine's shoulder lightly, wishing he had a few hours to think about the right words to say to her. But no words came, so he held her until he felt her inner strength straighten her backbone and she pulled away.

"Thanks." Katherine stood on tiptoe and kissed him on the cheek. "For bringing the letter and for being here."

Without another word she retraced her steps back to the infirmary. Bart stood staring after her long after she disappeared.

Slowly a smile spread across his rugged face. He wasn't sure what he'd just done, but damn if he didn't think he was probably being kind again. If he didn't watch himself it could become a habit.

Eleven

SNOW DRIFTED AROUND her, falling softly against Sarah's eyelashes, blurring her vision. She forced herself to follow the path home, fighting the urge to run to see if Bart was waiting at the boarding house, yet knowing that if he were in town, he'd have picked her up after work.

By the time she reached home, snow covered the ground. Though her hands and feet ached with cold, her cheeks burned warm and her eyes sparkled with unshed tears. She entered the foyer slowly. It only took one glance to know that Bart wasn't there. His bulk would have towered in the room. Dinnertime was long past, and most of the residents had gone up to bed. The few who remained only briefly nodded toward her as she climbed the stairs.

When she reached her room she closed the door and leaned against it, not bothering to turn on the light. Maybe without the light she wouldn't have to admit he hadn't come. If only she could hide in the dark forever. The very blackness that frightened Kat now gently cloaked Sarah from reality. Cold air from the open window chilled her skin, reminding her she had to face the truth.

As she reached for the light, a shadow moved across the moonlit windows. Sarah froze in fear. Someone was in her room!

The shadow moved again, closer this time.

Sarah wondered if anyone would hear her or bother to

check if she screamed. The intruder couldn't be a robber; surely a burglar would be wiser than to pick this room to rob. The only thing of value was the tin of cookies Cody had sent them for Christmas.

The shadow took another step forward. "Sarah," a voice said, "I'm sorry I'm late. I thought I'd catch you before you reached home." He moved a foot nearer. "When I realized I hadn't, I couldn't wait downstairs for someone to come up and get you. I had to see you and ask if you're sorry about what we did."

Sarah smiled as she watched the giant shift nervously before her.

"All I've thought about this week is that I might have hurt you," he said. "I almost didn't come, knowing I'd be doing you a favor if I stayed away."

Sarah moved without any thought but to be in his arms. "I'm not sorry—" she laughed as the warmth of him surrounded her—"and I would never have forgiven you if you hadn't returned."

Bart took his first deep breath in days. "I was so worried," he said as he kissed the top of her head. "I'll go slow, I promise, only I don't think I can live without holding you. I had to be alone with you or I'd probably have made a fool of myself in front of everyone in the boardinghouse." All week he'd dreamed of holding her again, and now she had come running into his arms. "Several nights I woke up and decided I must have dreamed of the way you felt."

Sarah brushed her hand along his cheek and felt the wetness of a tear. "You didn't dream it, my love."

"But I'm such a toad." He brushed his own hand over his eyes.

Sarah lightly pressed her lips to his jaw. "I think you're wonderful, Bart. The most wonderful man in the world."

He laughed. "You've seen little of this world, darling."

"I've seen enough," Sarah answered with no doubt in her voice.

Bart let out a breath and gave up without argument, though he knew he was right. "I heard my uncle say once that I was uglier than a fistful of swamp mud and about as useful."

Sarah spread her hands over his heart. "Here lies your beauty. Each time I feel your heart pound, you look more handsome to me."

She could say only what was in her heart. "Hold me," she murmured. "Please touch me again." He had come back to her. Her love was enough to draw him back. She pulled the tie and allowed her cape to fall to the floor, knowing she'd find in his arms all the warmth she would ever need.

Bart lifted her up and kissed her long and hard. His lips were warm and demanding as he drank in the wonder of her.

When finally he pulled an inch away, she whispered, "Hold me the way you did last week. Touch me as you did in the park."

Bart looked around the moonlit room. On one side stood a bed and a wardrobe, on the other a small sitting area with an overstuffed couch. Without a word he drew her to the couch. When she sat down, he knelt in front of her.

Sarah sat absolutely straight with her hands in her lap as he slowly unbuttoned her blouse. Gently, as if she were fragile, he moved, one button at a time, to her waist.

As he worked he said, "I didn't mean to tear your clothes last week."

"It doesn't matter. I don't think I could love you any less if all my clothes were in shreds."

Sarah relaxed against the sofa, loving the way he touched her. She watched him closely as he pulled her blouse free from her skirt and shoved it open. He seemed to study the ribbons of her camisole for several minutes before deciding what to do. His huge hands moved awkwardly as he untied each ribbon, revealing more of her breasts with each unlacing.

"You are so beautiful," he said as she leaned her head back.

She closed her eyes as his fingers gently uncovered her breasts. Then his callused hands covered her with a tenderness that made her catch her breath. She sighed as his hands began to circle over her flesh, pulling tenderly, brushing love's magic into her.

When she felt his mouth touch her skin, she almost screamed. His lips were warm and loving as they tasted her, lingering each time she sighed, repeating every action until she thought she might go mad with pleasure.

Finally he left her breasts and returned once more to claim her mouth. He kissed her until she felt there was no thought other than the pleasure he brought. She'd felt his hands moving over her body, touching, exploring, loving, but she wasn't even aware he'd unfastened the rest of her garments until her uniform slid to the floor.

"Lie down, my love," he whispered as he lowered her onto the soft cushions.

She expected him to cover her with his body as he had in the park, but he remained on his knees beside her. As she stretched out, he hesitated, whispering secrets only lovers knew. There was no part of her that he didn't touch gently, lovingly; he even rolled her onto her side facing him so that he could move his hands along her back and hips.

His fingers touched the scar on her arm where she'd been burned the night she and Kat ran away, and he paused to kiss it. When Sarah tried to pull her arm away, he whispered, "All of you is beautiful to me."

She relaxed as he continued to explore. His kisses roamed over her, building a fire inside her that blazed into a new and passionate paradise.

"Are you sure?" he finally said. "Are you sure you want me?"

"Yes," she answered and felt him pull away. She

reached for him in the darkness, voicing a soft cry at the coldness he'd left.

Bart's voice filled the darkness. "Patience, my lovely lady."

Her hand searched the darkness until she touched his bare shoulder. Her fingers traveled over the muscles of his arm and the soft hair of his chest.

Bart's laughter was loving. "Do you want to touch me?"

Sarah rose up on her knees on the couch. "Yes," she answered as her hands moved over him. He was a wall of strength. Hesitantly she slid her arms around his neck and pulled his bare chest against her. "I want to touch you with my whole body," she said and felt his arms go around her as he lowered her onto her back.

"You're so small and fragile," he whispered, almost mindless with the joy of feeling her body against his own.

"I'm woman enough to hold your love forever," she answered.

Bart laughed with pure joy. "That you are, Sarah. That you are."

Supporting most of his weight with his arms, he slowly let his body completely cover hers.

Sarah loved the feel of his flesh touching her from head to toe. She reached around him and pulled him lower, excited by the warm wall of his chest pressing against her.

Bart buried his face in her hair. "I don't want to cause you any pain, darling, but I understand it sometimes hurts the first time."

"I'm not afraid," she answered as she moved her hands up and down his bare back. "I want to be as close to you as I can be."

He kissed her long and gently, unable to say what his heart was exploding to tell the world. No one had ever loved him so completely. A part of him wanted to put her on a pedestal and worship her, but her exploring fingers reminded him of a need more forceful than any storm he'd ever flown through. He wanted to possess her and make her his, but he also wanted to give her equal joy in their passion.

He would have slowed down, postponing the moment when he knew she'd feel the pain, but Sarah would have none of his hesitancy. She moved her hips against him, silently pleading to feel him inside her. Bart's control shattered as she opened her legs in welcome.

When he entered her, he felt her cry against his lips, but he was beyond hearing anything except the pounding of his own heart. He pushed deep into the wonder of her and shattered the crust of loneliness that had built up around him over a lifetime.

He felt he might explode with happiness as he pulled her to him and they became one forever in a white lightning flash through his mind. He was loved. He was home.

For several breaths Bart didn't move above her. Her fingers drifted along his back, relaxing his muscles as his breathing returned to normal.

She wanted to push him away and ease the pain between her legs, but before she could move, she felt his warm tears against her cheek.

Her arms tightened around him as his need for her replaced all her discomfort.

"I love you," she whispered, brushing his hair back from his face.

"I never . . ." He couldn't find the words. "I never felt anything like this before."

Sarah kissed his eyelids. "Hush, darling. I know." She kissed the corners of his mouth.

Without a word or complaint, he watched her rise and move to the washstand. Slowly, in full view of him, she washed her body. He couldn't pull his gaze away from her, for she was all that was good and beautiful in his world.

He watched as she lifted the washcloth, now spotted with blood. "I hurt you," he said.

Sarah looked up as if only now aware he'd been watching. She wrapped herself in a towel and returned to the couch. "But you told me it would hurt the first time." She cuddled against him, unafraid, as always, of her giant.

Bart pulled her gently onto his lap. "If I could, I'd promise nothing would ever hurt you again, but no man can promise that."

Sarah leaned her head against his shoulder. "Promise me you'll never stop loving me."

"That I can do," he answered.

Sarah curled into his arms as Bart pulled a blanket over them.

As time passed in dreams for her, he held her to his heart, marveling at her strength and her uncomplicated love. In her way Sarah was far wiser than he would ever be. She trusted him and came into his arms even after he'd hurt her. She loved him without question or demand.

Sarah finally stretched.

Bart kissed her head. "Did you have a nice dream?"

"Yes." She moved against him, unaware of the effect her actions had on him. "Did you?"

"Yes," he answered, knowing he'd wouldn't have to close his eyes to have a dream in his arms tonight.

She raised her arms above her head as the towel slid low over her breasts. "You said in the park that we'd wait until we had the warmth of a bed."

Bart chuckled. "We almost made it."

She rose. "Do you think we could try it again?"

"But . . ."

"Is it possible?"

"Yes." Bart suddenly wondered if he shouldn't be afraid of her, when all this time he'd thought she might fear him. "But I don't want to hurt you again."

Sarah stood and pulled him toward the bed. "Don't worry, I'll go slow. After all, it's not my first time."

She sat him on the edge of the bed and slowly lowered

her towel. Without a word she lifted his hand and kissed his palm, then rubbed his fingers lightly over her breasts.

As he watched in wonder she moved slowly before him, lightly brushing her body against him. Her movements were a slow dance of love; she was driving him mad with her beauty. When he reached for her, she stepped away, but when he remained still, she moved nearer, teasing him with her body. After allowing her hair to tumble against his warm skin, she stepped away and turned around slowly to flood his eyes with beauty.

She placed his hand on her hip as she leaned forward until her full breasts brushed his shoulder. As she straightened, her breasts moved over his face and Bart, mindless with pleasure, closed his eyes.

Her slim legs brushed his knees as she drifted into his embrace. "Love me," she whispered as she moved against him. "Love me again."

Bart could not have stopped if his life were the wager. He pulled her back onto the bed and heard her laugh as though she were the victor in a challenge he'd never defend against.

Their loving was as deep and silent as a wide river, flowing over both their lives and changing their paths forever. Over and over, when he would have held back or slowed down, she encouraged him. She needed his loving as much as she needed his love, and for him she was the very breath of life.

Sarah knew she belonged in Bart's arms and there would never be another.

"Thank you," she whispered when they lay exhausted beside each other. "Thank you for making me feel that I belong. For making me a woman."

"Not *a* woman," Bart answered. "My woman. I'll never have another for as long as I live. I never knew beauty until tonight."

"And I"—Sarah placed her hand over his heart—"never belonged anywhere until this moment."

"Marry me." He stroked her hair lightly. "Marry me tomorrow."

"No."

Bart's entire body tightened.

Sarah giggled. "Not until we can tell Kat and Cody together."

Bart relaxed. "I'll love you no better in a few months."

"And I'll love you no less than I do tonight for as long as I live."

Twelve

SMOKE DRIFTED THROUGH the bar like a low cloud blurring everything into fuzzy shades of gray. Cody leaned back in a cane chair and watched the other patrons with about the same interest a six-year-old boy might watch ants. He'd been around strangers for so long he'd stopped looking at faces to see if he might recognize someone.

"Want anything else, birdman?" the waitress asked as she leaned toward Cody, her blouse unbuttoned just enough to tease the line of decency.

"No, thanks," he answered as he raised his beer mug and drained the last of the golden liquid.

The girl looked disappointed and moved on, swinging her hips.

DeJon smiled from across the table. "You could have had a soft pillow to sleep on tonight, boy, if you had answered that question correctly."

Cody frowned at his mechanic. The only reason he'd smiled at the woman in the first place was that her hair was almost the color of Katherine's. "I'm not interested."

The Frenchman laughed. "There was a time when every woman interested Cody Masters. Now you prefer to sit with me and practice your French. You must be suffering from a great illness, my son."

Cody tried not to let his irritation show. He *was* suffering. The longer he stayed away from Ohio, the more he wanted to see Katherine again. As the weeks had turned into months he'd decided his memory was playing tricks on him. He knew she couldn't have been all that wonderful and he could hardly wait to get home and prove it to himself. He'd take one good look at the flesh-and-blood Katherine and get her out of his mind.

"She wouldn't be a bad pillow," DeJon continued. "I like a woman whose breasts are more than a handful. They offer such a challenge."

"I'm not interested." Cody tried not to be rude to the man he admired more for his mechanical ability than for his taste in women. Sleeping with a memory of someone he cared about was better than sleeping with the reality of the barmaid.

DeJon finished his drink and motioned for another. "Drinking with you is getting to be as dull as drinking with Bart Rome."

"How is Bart?"

"Saw him just before I left." DeJon winked at the waitress as she delivered his beer. He was hoping to get lucky, but with his looks and smell the odds were piled against him. As the woman moved away without responding to his advance, the mechanic continued, "The huge guy is as silent as ever, but I did see him smiling the other day. I swear, he's so quiet he could disappear from the face of the earth and no one would notice unless you were standing in his shadow."

"Bart's a good pilot." Cody didn't know what else to say. That was about as fine a compliment as he could pay any man. He stood slowly, allowing his balance to steady his head. "I think I'll call it a night."

DeJon leaned back in his chair. "Not me. I learned a long time ago that if I stay until the bar closes, I sometimes find a nearsighted mademoiselle."

Cody wanted to suggest that DeJon start with a bath. He doubted there were many women who liked the smell of engine oil. But then, there was more to a man than looks and smell. In Wheeler DeJon's case Cody wasn't sure what that would be, but maybe the barmaid could find it.

"I think I'll go home and sleep with a memory." Cody tipped his hat.

DeJon smiled as the waitress glanced in his direction. "I think I might make a memory tonight."

Cody walked back to his hotel wondering how many more days it would be before he was on a train headed home. Suddenly he laughed to himself. He'd never in his life had a sense of someplace being home, but now he realized he did. Home wasn't a building or even a state. Home was a green-eyed wildcat who had written him last week that if he didn't make it back by the end of February she would never speak to him again. Home was a woman who wanted commitment with her kisses.

She'd speak to him, he was positive, even if it took him until March to get back. And eventually she'd figure out that no pilot could promise more than today.

Thirteen

April 1911

KATHERINE CLOSED THE door to William's room.

"Did you remember to lock the door?" Dr. Farris asked from the linen closet across the hall.

"Yes, sir," she answered. "He's getting better, Doctor. Yesterday he spoke to me, and tonight I think he was about to say something and then changed his mind."

Dr. Farris shook his head. "His wounds are healing into scars, but I'm not sure he's getting any better. If a man wants something, even death, bad enough, he'll find it."

Katherine looked at the doctor and wondered what he wanted. He was like a statue, always the same, never caring about anything around him, but never unkind. An emotionless void in only a shell of a body. She forced the thought from her mind and hurried to finish her duties.

"What a day," Katherine whispered, locking the last door. She'd traded with another nurse for the midnight-to-ten shift. Now every muscle ached with exhaustion, but there would be time to sleep when her shift had ended. In two hours she would be on the early train to Dayton to see her first real air show. And today . . . today Cody Masters was coming home.

Katherine had counted the days until she could go to Dayton. Cody's planned two-month tour had stretched into three, then five. But now he was coming home, and in a few hours Cody and Bart would fly together once more. The only cloud over their homecoming was Sarah's having to work. But Dr. Farris was a man of rules, and they knew better than to ask for a day off.

Besides, Katherine realized, Sarah had been half flying every day for months. Kat glanced over at Sarah unpacking medical supplies and smiled. There was no denying the obvious: Sarah was in love with Bart and nothing Katherine said about them slowing down would change that fact. When she wasn't talking about him, she had a look in her soft blue eyes that told Katherine her friend was daydreaming about the huge man who seemed to show up on their doorstep every time Katherine turned around.

Sarah woke up as Kat stumbled out of bed after her short nap. "I wish I could go with you," she said. "Today will be endless waiting."

Kat agreed with a nod as she handed the charts to Sarah.

"Say hello to Cody for me."

"I will." Kat forced herself to match pace with Sarah as they walked toward the infirmary door.

"And Bart," Sarah added.

"And Bart," Kat echoed. "You know the guy kind of grows on a girl."

Sarah silenced a laugh. "I've been meaning to tell you something you'll be the second to know."

Kat looked closely at Sarah. "You're in love?"

"Head over heels," Sarah answered. "I don't think I can keep it a secret any longer. He's the love I've always wanted."

"He does seem to cherish you," Kat admitted.

"I'm glad you're finally seeing his good side."

Kat shook her head. "I've looked all around that huge man and I'm not sure he has a good side, unless maybe it's inside. But before you go telling him I'm fond of him, I want you to know I don't think he's good enough for you."

"Feel it in your bones, do you?"

"Maybe," Kat answered. She didn't want to admit even

to herself that she was a little envious of the love between Bart and Sarah. Kat didn't want to take anything away from Sarah, she only wanted to feel that kind of happiness herself. Maybe with Cody coming home, her mood would lighten. Even if he didn't want a forever love, at least she wouldn't feel so alone on the outside of Bart and Sarah's circle of two.

Kat slipped out the door. "See you tonight."

"I'll be waiting." Sarah smiled. "And don't you and Cody get so busy with your reunion that you forget to bring Bart to take me out to dinner."

"Not much chance of that." Kat waved. The big man would probably walk to Columbus tonight if she and Cody forgot him. She'd known for weeks that Sarah and Bart loved each other. She could see it in their eyes, a passion that spoke of wanting to be alone together. Kat didn't have to ask if they were lovers; she'd known Sarah too long to have missed noticing changes in her.

Three hours later Katherine stood beside the airfield watching the newest Wright planes take to the air. A light layer of wool kept the chill from her, and a warm gray muff protected her hands. Katherine turned her head slightly, looking for a familiar face.

The crowd was small for the practice runs. The real show would be held in midafternoon. Most of the early watchers were farmers from neighboring fields and boys who'd ridden their bikes the mile from town to see their heroes. The boys talked excitedly as each plane went up. They knew the history of every plane and the life story of each individual pilot. The birdmen were their idols, and Katherine could see the hope of adventure in their young faces. The morning might be cold, but the lads in their knickers were warmly wrapped in their dreams of flight.

"Good morning, me lassie." A man's voice, thick with a Scottish burr, shouted from behind her.

Katherine turned as Cody crossed the field toward her. His full smile left no doubt of his delight in seeing her. Kat's heart pounded at the sight of him, and she felt suddenly very warm in her wools.

He looked taller, leaner than before, but just as handsome as ever.

"Cody!" she cried as he reached her.

With the enthusiasm of a child, he lifted Katherine and swung her around as if there were no one else in sight. "You're a beauty to behold." He laughed as she blushed. "I can never remember being so eager to see anyone in my life."

"Do I know you, sir?" Katherine teased. "I knew a pilot once, but he's been gone so long I'm not sure I'd remember him."

Cody slowly lowered her to face him. "When we have time, I'll try to refresh your memory." He studied her closely, as though to compare every detail of her face with that of his memory. "Everything about you has crystallized in my mind. Even after all these months, I'd know your voice, your smile, the smell of your hair, half a continent away."

Katherine didn't try to pull out of his embrace. She was so near she could feel the warmth of his breath against her cheek and see the tiny weather lines around his eyes. "Thank you for keeping your promise and coming back."

Cody couldn't seem to move his stare from her lips. "How could I not?" He leaned slowly toward her, drawn to her beauty.

When his mouth was only a breath away from hers, he paused, testing, exploring. "I've missed the sight of you, lovely one."

"And I, you," she answered honestly. His eyes were an even darker mahogany than she remembered and still full of mischief and fire.

"Do you remember that morning in my room?" he whispered into her ear.

"Yes," she answered, looking around to make sure no one else had heard.

"I've thought of the way the sun set fire to your hair that morning and the way I set fire to your eyes." Cody's hands at her waist moved ever so slightly, unnoticed by any onlooker. "I'd like to see that spark again."

Katherine's cheeks were afire with his last words, but she faced him boldly. He had the power to excite her and anger her as no man before.

Before she could answer him, she glanced over his shoulder and noticed the mechanic, Wheeler DeJon. With a quick and proper hug to Cody, she said loud enough for DeJon to hear, "It's good to see you again, Cody."

As she pulled away from a confused Cody, Kat turned to the Frenchman. "And it is nice to see you, Mr. DeJon."

Cody took the hint. "You look as lovely as I remember, Kat." His words were only conversational, the way he might have talked to anyone he hardly knew, but his eyes said so much more about the longing he felt. "How is Sarah?"

Katherine smiled, wishing she'd kissed him when they'd hugged, for now she saw the devil dancing in his brown gaze. "Sarah's fine. She and Bart are always together, and that makes her very happy."

Cody moved his tongue along his bottom lip, telling her he was also wishing they'd kissed.

"Bart doesn't seem to be in any too sad a shape either. I think the big guy may be falling in love. His good mood is driving everyone around here crazy."

Katherine didn't argue. She'd been around Sarah enough to see in her the mirror image of what Cody saw in Bart.

"Look!" Cody yelled. "There's Bart now. He drew the straw to make the first test run."

All three turned to the sound of an engine approaching. The roar of the plane grew louder.

Pointing skyward, Cody added as Bart's plane circled, "I can always spot him. He's worn that midnight-blue scarf of Sarah's every time he's flown since the day he met her."

A plane disappeared into the clouds. Wheeler rubbed his oily hands on an equally dirty rag as he looked at Katherine. "Good to see you again, mademoiselle."

"Nice to see you, Mr. DeJon," Katherine lied. She could still remember how the mechanic had rubbed dirt on her. "Are you still giving every pilot a fistful of luck before he goes up?"

Wheeler shook his head. "Didn't get here in time today. Had to fix one of the trucks."

Katherine wished she could think of something else to say. She glanced at Cody, hoping he would pick up the conversation, but he was just staring at the clouds. Katherine followed his gaze to the empty sky.

Cody thumbed up his cap, revealing worry lines across his forehead. "Bart's trying a new stunt this morning. When he does the loop, he's going to come out close to the ground and fly between those two barns."

"Is it very dangerous?" A brush of apprehension tickled its way up her spine.

"Not unless the wind gets up," Wheeler answered as they all turned toward a plane's roar.

They watched as Bart came out of the clouds and began his circle. The spectators on the field held their breath as he flew nearer. The roar of the engine grew louder, shattering the peace of the air. No one spoke, as though a whisper might distract the pilot. All eyes were on the delicate machine as the wind moved across the land like an invisible angel of death, a wind that crept up so slowly Katherine didn't notice the curl drifting across her cheek or the rustle of her skirts.

The plane's shadow passed directly over them, darkening their world for a moment.

"He's coming in too low!" Cody shouted and broke into a run toward the barns.

Katherine watched in horror as Bart's plane twisted in the air. "No!" she shouted as if her words could correct the error the wind had caused. "No!"

The plane gracefully spiraled once more like a dying swan and flew straight into the barn as if unafraid to face doom. The screams of the crowd and the sound of wood exploding burned into Katherine's brain as she lifted her skirt and ran toward the crash.

The thunder of feet replaced the noise of the engine. The smell of fire drifted across the cold air even before Katherine could see the flames.

When she reached the crash, the barn suddenly erupted into a blazing inferno. Smoke filled the air and blended with the cries and tears of the crowd. Katherine searched for Cody. She screamed his name over and over. He was nowhere in sight. Frantically she pushed her way deeper into the smoke, covering her mouth with her muff.

The fire burned white hot, but Katherine pressed a few inches closer. "Cody!" she cried. Her eyes watered as smoke filled her lungs. The sickening smell of burning flesh assaulted her. She could hear Wheeler, in his thick French accent, yelling for her to go no farther.

Katherine ignored his calls. She couldn't just wait among strangers. She had to do something. Cody was somewhere in that ocean of smoke, and Bart was beyond in the flames. Katherine moved a step farther and lowered her muff enough to yell their names, but only the crackling of flaming timber answered her call.

Out of the black floating death she saw them, Cody's lean form moving toward her with Bart's lifeless body beside him. Cody had Bart's arm around his shoulders and was dragging the bigger man forward. Cody's face was black with soot, and his jacket sleeve was smoking. He seemed to

weave toward her, struggling under the weight of Bart and
the lack of air around him.

Running toward them, Katherine lifted Bart's free arm.
His flesh was hot, crisp, and bloody at the same time. She
balanced beneath the extra weight and forced her legs to
move. Bart's foot scored the ground as he dragged it behind
him at an unnatural angle.

Cody staggered, but stubbornly kept moving one foot
blindly in front of the other as they dragged Bart's body
between them.

For what seemed an eternity without air, they moved
away from the barn. The first clean breath drained the last
ounce of Katherine's strength, and she collapsed to her
knees as others took Bart from her. The smell of burning
flesh was even more suffocating than the smoke had been.
Bart's jacket was burned completely away, as was his face
around the goggles and leather cap. Red exposed flesh was
patched with charred skin all across his chest and arms.
Katherine had to fight herself to keep from vomiting as she
looked for a place to touch Bart to comfort him. But his bare
chest no longer had skin to keep the blood from dripping
out.

Cody dropped beside her and rolled onto his back.
Suddenly other men were all around them, shouting, crying,
cursing, helping. Katherine couldn't bring herself to look at
Bart and hated herself for her weakness. She was a nurse.
She saw people in pain daily, but not people she knew, not
strong, hard Bart.

A man with a black bag stepped out of the crowd, and
someone ran for a stretcher. People were crying and
screaming and praying all at once until all she heard was a
rumble.

The man with the bag yelled, "Cover him quick!"

Several men pulled off coats and placed them over Bart's
body.

Katherine looked at Cody, unable to think of anything to

do to help Bart. "Are you all right?" she asked. His face looked sunburned beneath the black stains. His eyes watered from the smoke. Or was he crying?

Cody nodded and lifted his hands, burned and already blistering. "I had to pull part of the engine off him to get him out."

"I'll get you some medicine and bandages for your hands." She looked toward a supply truck parked by the road.

"No!" Cody shouted. "I have to stay with Bart."

They both watched as the doctor frantically worked on their friend. He had cut most of the charred clothing away and was trying to wrap the worst burns so that Bart could be moved.

"Bart!" Cody yelled. "Bart!"

The doctor shook his head sadly. "He's too far gone to hear you, son. We'll get him to the hospital and do what we can." The doctor looked at Cody's burned hands. "You'd best come along with us."

Cody climbed into the back of the truck that had been set up as an ambulance. He crossed his arms at the elbow and held his hands in the air. After settling in beside him, Katherine put her cape around them both to keep them warm in the open air. Bart lay stretched beside them, showing no sign of life. Katherine thought that at least that was a blessing, for if he'd been conscious, the pain would have been unbearable.

No one spoke during the ride to the hospital. As they pulled into the driveway, the entire hospital staff seemed to be waiting. Katherine remembered how excited everyone at Miss Willingham's hospital had been when they'd treated a pilot once. Now there was no thrill or curiosity in her.

As they unloaded Bart, Katherine turned to Cody. "I have to find a telephone and call Sarah."

"No!" Cody snapped at her, unaware of how sharp his voice sounded. "Wait until we can tell her he's fine. It would take her hours to get here, and there's nothing she can do but wait.''

Reluctantly Katherine nodded, knowing it would be better to tell Sarah in person that Bart was burned. Silently they moved past the nurse's station and into a small hallway leading to Bart's room.

Katherine explained to the doctor that she was a nurse, and the staff seemed happy to let her help them treat Cody. They brought cold water, and Katherine gently bathed his hands. She applied antiseptic and loosely wrapped them to keep infection from setting in. Cody didn't make a sound as she worked, but she could see deep pain in his dark eyes. When she finished, she saw he wasn't even watching her; he was staring at the room where they'd taken Bart.

''It'll be a while before they know,'' Katherine told him. ''Since your hands are bandaged, would you like me to wash your face?''

Cody looked at her for the first time. A slow smile touched his lips but never reached his eyes. ''Only if you'll wash your face as well.''

Katherine glanced at the wall mirror and saw hers was almost as black as Cody's.

''No matter what happens,'' Cody said, his voice sober, ''thanks for your help back there. You used your head and didn't pull back, as a lot of folks would have. I don't know if I could have made it out of the barn without your help. I couldn't have carried Bart much farther, and I wouldn't have left him.''

Katherine realized what he was saying. Slowly, uncontrollably, tears began to roll down her cheeks. Cody could have died in the fire.

He raised his bandaged hands, and Katherine moved toward him. She laid her cheek on his shoulder and cried. She cried because she'd almost lost Cody before they really got to know each other, because she'd been so frightened in the smoke, because in a few hours she'd have to tell Sarah that Bart was hurt or, worse, dead.

How long she wept, Katherine didn't know, but finally the tears stopped and she rested against Cody's arm. They sat on a long bench outside Bart's room and waited in silence, afraid to speak, afraid to hope.

The afternoon shadows were long when a nurse finally stepped out of Bart's room. "Cody?" she asked. "Are you Cody and Katherine?"

Cody stood up. "Yes."

"He's asking for both of you." When they hesitated, the nurse hurried to explain. "The man who was burned, he's asking for you. As soon as the doctor is finished, you may step in for a few minutes." Without another word she disappeared back into Bart's room.

Cody gently kissed Katherine's forehead, willing her to be strong. "I wish I could hold you." He lifted her hands so that she could feel his words against her fingers. "This may not be easy."

"I know." She nodded, wishing the hospital and the world would disappear. It seemed like years, not hours, since the crash, but still a million words needed to flow between them. In only a few hours they'd somehow aged, forever scarred by one morning's events.

His dark eyes drank in every detail of her. "God, how I want to hold you, Katherine." All the laughing youth was gone from his gaze, leaving only a raw need.

Katherine stood beside him unable to think of the right words to ease his pain as they waited for the nurse to open the door to Bart's room. She'd dreamed of his arms around her for four months. She needed him to hold her tight and make all the world step back a pace, but now was not the time. The nurse was waiting for them to walk into Bart's room. Cody's hands were burned so badly Katherine's slightest touch would have caused him even more pain. But she could see her need to be close to him mirrored in his eyes.

"I understand," she whispered.

Tenderly he laid his bandaged arm over her shoulders and pulled her to him. "I've dreamed of you in my arms." His words drifted in a whisper through her hair. "Sometimes I couldn't sleep for thinking of you, and at other times you invaded even my dreams."

She rested her fingers lightly on his chest. "I'm here now."

For a long minute he looked at her before he straightened and nodded slightly toward Bart's room.

Without another word they followed the nurse into his room.

Katherine had seen burn victims before, but never had the injuries so totally covered a patient's body. Even William at the state hospital had some flesh unburned. She'd seen men near death, but never someone she knew. She moved to one side of the bed while Cody stood at the other. Reaching out to touch Bart's hand, she realized how painful that would be for him and clasped her hands behind her.

"Cody?" Bart's voice sounded dry and raw.

"Yeah, pardner." The lightness in Cody's voice was obviously false.

"Thanks for pulling me out back there."

Cody smiled. "You would have done the same for me."

"Don't bet a week's pay on it. I've never been as crazy as you."

Cody nodded in agreement. "But you're always there when the chips are down. We'll fly side by side again soon."

Bart was silent for a long while. "The doc says my flying days are over. I just joined the land-huggers."

Cody opened his mouth to argue, but the doctor standing at the foot of Bart's bed nodded his agreement with his patient. Cody knew it would only be cruel to hold out false hope.

"Red?" Bart said from beneath the layers of gauze around his face. "Are you here?"

Katherine smiled. For once the dreaded nickname didn't sound so bad. "I'm here, Bart."

There was a long pause. "Kat, I want you to promise me something." His words were thick with pain.

"All right." He would probably tell her to look after Sarah if he didn't make it. "Anything."

"Swear?"

"I swear," Katherine answered.

Bart's voice calmed slightly as if in relief. When he spoke his words came slow and direct. "Katherine, tell Sarah I died."

"Oh, no!" Katherine couldn't believe what he was asking. "No, Bart, that would break her heart."

Bart sounded very tired. "Better to break her heart than to let her destroy her life by tying herself to me. If I live, the doctor says it'll be months before I can even sit up. My leg is so badly smashed up that I may never walk again." He tried to raise his arm, but straps kept him in place. All his pain came through in each word. "Tell Sarah I died. Don't let her see me like this!"

Tears spilled over Katherine's lashes as she shook her head, refusing to hear him say the words again. "No, I can't."

"You have to." Bart's voice faded, and the nurse hustled Katherine and Cody out of the room. Her hurried manner left no doubt she thought the burned man was about to make his statement fact.

Katherine tried to shove her way back in to argue with Bart. "I can't tell Sarah that, Bart." She fought to pull out of Cody's grip. "I can't crush her like that. I can't!"

Cody held her, blocking her way back to Bart. "We can't stay, Kat," he said as he almost carried her into the hallway.

She shouted at the closing door. "I can't tell Sarah such a lie. I can't!"

A long silence hung between them. Kat fought for air as if she'd run for miles.

Finally Cody's words came through to her as he pulled her into a hug despite the pain to his hands. "You have to do what Bart asked both for his sake and for Sarah's." His voice was hard, echoing down the long hall like the call of doom.

Kat's tears were blinding her. "I can't."

"If Sarah knew about Bart, she'd stay beside him. It would eat away at him worse than the fire did." Cody whispered words of reason into her hair as she cried on his shoulder. "Bart loves her too much to tie her to a cripple."

Katherine could see the distorted logic of Bart's request, but she would never lie to Sarah. "We swore when we were children always to be true to each other. I gave my oath in blood."

She tried to pull away, but Cody held her against him. "It's the only way, Kat."

"No, I can't. Sarah's my friend and far more. I've never, ever lied to her." She wished she could hit him hard and make him feel a fraction of the pain he was putting her through by even asking such a thing. "I won't do it."

Cody's anger surprised Katherine. "Bart's *my* friend." He held her shoulders lightly. "And I'm calling in my marker. You said once you would do anything I asked if I took you flying."

"But I meant doing your laundry or cleaning your quarters."

"Well, I'm asking you to tell Sarah that Bart's dead."

Katherine felt trapped. "So it's simple: I break my word either to Sarah or to you and Bart."

"That's about the size of it." Cody let his hands fall to his sides but he didn't move away.

"This will ruin Sarah's life."

"No." Cody's voice was now low with anger. "You'll ruin her life if you don't do as Bart asks. Don't you see? She'll never leave Bart if she knows he's alive, no matter how seriously crippled he is."

Kat fought the urge to run. "I wish I'd never met you and Bart. I wish I'd never gone flying."

"How can you say that?" Cody yelled, but Kat was too angry to hear.

"I wish I'd never talked Sarah into climbing that hill and watching you take off that first morning. I'd give anything if I didn't have to do this to Sarah." Her words broke her heart as she said them.

Turning away from him, she pressed her forehead against the cool wall of the hospital hallway. "I've always been an honest person." She spoke to herself now. "I swore to do what Bart asked before I knew the task. It'll rip me apart every time I look at Sarah."

Cody tried to turn her to face him, but she jerked away.

She knew she could never look at Cody again without reliving this day and all its horror. Without being reminded of her lie. How could she hold him and talk of the future when she was about to shatter Sarah's life forever?

All at once the weight of a lifetime of unfairness crashed down on Katherine. Sarah had never asked for much; she'd always only given to others. Now the first man who'd made her happy was being taken from her, not by force but by a lie.

"It's not fair," Kat murmured. "Sarah loves Bart. She never had a father or a brother. She deserves this one man. She deserves to be happy."

"It has to be, Kat, fair or not."

"But you don't understand. Sarah's never had anyone but me. Life should be kind to her this one time. I'll break her heart when I tell her."

"It's not your decision; it's Bart's," Cody answered. "He must love her a great deal to do this."

"But she'll never know that. I can't be part of this."

Cody placed his hand beneath her chin and forced her to face him. "Would you rather someone else told her?"

"No," Katherine answered.

"Someone has to. If you don't, I will."

Pride flickered in her eyes. "No! She's my friend. I'll tell her. She wouldn't want others to see her in pain."

"Then tell her."

Katherine lifted her head and faced Cody with cold green eyes. There was only one answer, no matter how unjust. "I'll tell Sarah that Bart died in the crash"—she braced herself for the final tie that had to be cut—"but I never want to see you again as long as I live."

"No!"

"It has to be. If I'm to sentence Sarah to a life without Bart, I can't see you again."

"You're not making sense." He reached for her, but she stepped away.

"Don't touch me!" Kat held her arms up as if to block him from her. "Nothing has made sense today."

"Let me hold you?"

"No!"

"We can talk about this later."

"There will be no later for us, Cody."

"But—"

"Never. I never want to see you again." She thought she saw a streak of pain in Cody's mahogany-brown eyes before he nodded soberly, sealing their pact of pain.

"All right, Kat. I won't argue with you now."

Kat turned and ran toward the door. "I won't talk to you again. If Bart is to die today, what is between us will die also."

"No!" Cody whispered, but she was too far down the hallway to hear him.

Fourteen

SARAH WALKED HOME from the hospital, thinking of how much fun Katherine must have had at the air show in Dayton. They had agreed to meet when Sarah got off work, unless Cody invited Katherine to dinner alone. Sarah smiled to herself as she thought Kat must now be with Cody. Her best friend's absence was all the fuel needed to flame Sarah's romantic imagination. She wanted to see them as happy together as she and Bart were.

Despite the chilly wind that whirled around her, thoughts of Bart warmed Sarah inside. He had become the center of her life in such a short time. He was always so kind, so loving, so strong. Since that night in the park when they had declared their love, they'd been like two starving orphans locked overnight in a market, unable to get enough of each other. Walking in the park. Talking. Sharing. And the passionate evenings when he'd surprised her with his need for her. The quiet times when they became one in body and spirit.

Hurrying up the steps of the boardinghouse, Sarah hoped she'd find Bart waiting for her. She wanted to feel his powerful arms lift her off the floor in a hug as she buried her face in his shoulder and breathed deeply of the leather-and-oil scent of his flight jacket. He'd probably be tired and hungry, but she knew he'd visit with the older boarders until she changed. Because Katherine had tonight off, she and

Cody might join them for dinner. Sarah could think of no better evening.

No one waited in the tiny front room Mrs. Parker called the parlor. Even the long sunny room referred to as the library because of its one shelf of books was deserted tonight. Sarah walked across the foyer, hearing only the soft brush of the housekeeper's table broom across the dining room tablecloth. Mrs. Parker was economical as well as proper. She set the table with linens, then brushed crumbs and rearranged plates until the cloth was so stained it had to be washed.

"Good evening, Miss Sarah." The chubby woman looked up from her work and smiled.

"Good evening, Mrs. Parker." Sarah didn't really want to stop and visit, but the empty room upstairs didn't appeal to her either. "How are you tonight?"

"I'm fine, just fine." Mrs. Parker turned to face Sarah, her tiny broom in one hand and the porcelain crumb tray in the other. "Which is more than I can say for Miss Katherine. She flew in here about an hour ago looking like she'd been in a train wreck. Her clothes were a mess, and that wild hair of hers was flying in every direction. Didn't even speak to me. Just ran up the stairs . . ."

Sarah didn't hear what else Mrs. Parker said. She lifted her skirt and bolted up the steps in what she was sure Mrs. Parker would tell the others was a most unladylike manner. Blood pounded in her head as a dozen reasons for Katherine's behavior sped through her brain.

The heavy door creaked on ancient hinges as Sarah entered their room. She knew something was horribly wrong the moment she opened the door; every light was on. Katherine sat in the middle of the bed in her petticoat. Her new dress lay crumpled and filthy on the floor. Her forehead rested on her knees, and her long fiery hair surrounded her shoulders like a protective blanket.

After throwing off her coat, Sarah crawled onto the bed

and faced the tearstained emerald eyes of her best friend. Fear choked Sarah's throat so tightly she could only whisper, "Kat, what is it?" Where was her brave friend, the champion who would try anything? What could have hurt her so badly?

Katherine buried her face against her crossed arms. Panic ripped through Sarah's soul.

"Kat, tell me!" Sarah tasted her own tears as she waited.

Katherine's voice came out as a whimper. "There was a crash before the air show."

Sarah bit into her fist and closed her eyes. "Oh, my God! Was Cody . . . hurt?" She couldn't bring herself to say the word "killed."

Katherine shook her head and Sarah let out a sigh of relief; but as Katherine looked up, Sarah saw pity in her green eyes and started to get up from the bed.

"No," she whispered as Katherine grabbed her arm and prevented her escape. Sarah didn't want to see pity in Kat's gaze. Not because of some crash. She tried to pull away, but Katherine held her shoulder, making her face reality's hell.

"It was Bart's plane," Kat said.

Sarah felt herself falling even though her body remained a frozen statue of denial.

"It hit a barn and went up in flames. . . ."

"No!" Sarah screamed as she closed her eyes and again felt herself spinning away from Katherine's voice and then falling, falling to where there was no pain, no reality, no loss.

"I'm sorry." Katherine held Sarah, but her words barely reached the abyss into which Sarah's hopes and dreams had plummeted. "He died before we could get to him."

"No!" Sarah said to herself. "He's always careful when he flies. He's not like the thrill seekers. He told me he'd take care of himself."

Katherine wiped away tears from Sarah's face. "He was trying a new stunt."

"No!" Sarah tried to close out all the world, including Kat's voice. "He told me he'd die of old age with me in his arms. He told me we'd have years together."

"Cody said it should have been an easy flight. But then the wind came up all at once."

"No!" Sarah's entire body began to shake as she tried to pull away from Kat.

"Listen, Sarah! Bart's gone! You have to face it." Even as she held her close, Kat felt that Sarah was slipping like sand through her fingers.

"I can't!"

"I know it isn't fair, but he's gone and you have to accept that fact. I'm here. I won't leave you. Together we can handle this."

"No!" Sarah's shouts sounded far away to her ears. "I want to die with him."

"No, Sarah. Stay with me," Kat pleaded. "I wish I hadn't had to tell you about the crash. I'll see that plane exploding into flames every day for the rest of my life. All I could think about was how much this would hurt you. I kept praying, 'Please, Lord, don't let Bart be dead.'"

Sarah raised her arms to Kat and held her friend tight. The need to comfort Kat sifted through her own grief, but her sorrow was a tidal wave washing away all other thoughts. "I'm not sure I can get through my life without him." She tried to hold her mind together even as her heart splintered.

Katherine's arms surrounded Sarah, pulling her back to the world. There was no need for words. Sarah wouldn't have heard them. They clung to each other, rocking slowly back and forth, sharing the heartbreak as they had shared everything since childhood, lost in their own private hell of grief.

For one had to live with her loss and the other, her lie.

Cody paced the floor of his room. The burns on his hands were nothing compared to the wound Katherine had opened across his heart. He couldn't accept Katherine's decision never to see him again. He could still remember every detail of the way she'd looked in the hospital hallway before they went into Bart's room. Her clothes had been stained with smoke, and her hair was wild and free around her shoulders. She'd looked at him with such need, as if she believed he could make everything in the world right and safe. As if with one hug he could take away all the years of not being loved.

But they hadn't had time to hug, and now they might never see each other again. He'd suffered enough death and said enough good-byes to last him a lifetime. Even if Bart lived, he would never fly with Cody again, so at best their friendship would be only a shadow of what it had been.

But Katherine belonged in his world. She was the one woman who'd made her way into his mind, and he wasn't about to just walk away from her because her twisted sense of justice told her she had to sacrifice her own happiness to atone for her lie to Sarah.

Cody grabbed his coat from the chair. He had to talk to Bart. There had to be an answer to this problem, and Cody was determined to find it. He wasn't going to let her walk out of his life without a fight.

On his way to the hospital Cody thought over everything he would say to his friend. If he could talk Bart into releasing Kat from her promise, maybe he could intercept her before she reached Sarah.

Cody parked his truck at the front door and ran into the hospital. He was inside the room where he'd last seen Bart before anyone could stop him.

Bart's bed was empty!

"I need to see Bart Rome!" Cody said to the nurse on duty. If Bart had died, Cody knew he'd have to see the body before he believed it.

"He's been moved to another room, Mr. Masters." The

nurse's voice was kind, showing no surprise at Cody's appearance.

"I have to talk to him." Cody hated the lack of control he always felt in hospitals.

"I'm afraid that's impossible. Perhaps in the morning."

"In the morning it will be too late." Cody noticed two orderlies step behind the nurse. "I have to talk to him tonight."

"He wouldn't hear you." Again the nurse's voice was kind but firm. "He slipped into a coma right after you left. God's granting him relief from his pain."

Cody wanted to scream, What about my pain? But he was facing a solid wall of professional detachment and had nowhere to turn. The day had been a thousand hours long, and now he felt his control slipping. He wasn't even sure he had the energy to walk back to his truck.

Gently, like a mother directing a child, the nurse rested her hand on his shoulder and led him to a small waiting room. "You're welcome to rest here. We'll call you as soon as he comes out of the coma."

Cody collapsed in a soft chair. His body and his mind closed down as completely as if someone had suddenly cut his engine. He floated silently into sleep.

Day after day passed, with Cody spending most of his time in the hospital waiting room. He knew it was too late to talk to Bart about the lie, but he had to see this thing through to the end. Finally, a week after the crash, Bart awoke from the coma. Cody was at his bedside within minutes after the doctors had checked Bart over.

"Hello, my man." Cody's Scottish burr was not as flawless as usual but his familiar greeting was still as warm.

Bart turned his bandaged head listening to the sound of a voice. "Cody?" His voice was raw and hoarse.

"In person," Cody answered, reaching for Bart's hand, then pausing a moment before withdrawing. "I had to hang

. around and see when you'd decide to come out of hibernation.''

Bart nodded slightly. ''You may not be able to tell, but the doc says I'm doing better. May get the bandages off my eyes in a week or so.''

''Great,'' Cody answered, wondering how long it would be before the miles of white gauze strips came off the rest of his body.

''I'm glad you're here.'' Bart turned his head toward Cody as though he could see through the layers of white. ''I wanted to ask you to keep an eye on Sarah and Katherine for me. Make sure they don't need anything.''

''I'll try.'' Cody wished he could say he'd take good care of them, but he doubted Katherine would ever speak to him again. ''They're strong women, used to taking care of themselves.''

Bart nodded slightly. ''The hardest part of dealing with the crash is knowing I'll never see Sarah again. But I know I'm doing what's right. She'll go on and marry some good man and have a houseful of kids to take care of. She doesn't need to be saddled with a cripple.''

''There's no changing your mind?''

''No,'' Bart answered stubbornly. ''I know I'm right about her. That will help me live with the loss. I may have messed up my life, but there's no need to mess up hers as well.''

''Sometimes the loss of what might have been is as great as the loss of what was,'' Cody said more to himself than to Bart. ''Katherine doesn't want to see me again.''

''She'll change her mind.'' Bart didn't sound so positive.

Cody leaned against the windowsill. ''Maybe men like us were never meant to love any way but hard and fast. Maybe the kind of love that lasts a lifetime was meant for men with both feet on the ground.''

''Maybe,'' Bart answered. ''They can give me stuff to ease the pain of my burns. Too bad there's not something to ease the memory of Sarah from my mind. When I woke up, I could feel the weight of her head resting on my shoulder. Her body warmed my side. I swear I could feel her low sleeping breath against my cheek.''

''You were dreaming,'' Cody interrupted, not wanting to hear about another man's loss.

''Maybe,'' Bart answered. ''It's hard to tell what's dream and what's real with my eyes all bandaged. I asked the nurse to tell me if it was morning or night. Not that it matters.''

Cody leaned closer. ''Do you need anything? Is there something I could bring you that might help?''

''I need to know that Katherine did as she promised.''

''She did,'' Cody answered. There was no doubt in his mind, for the look in Kat's eyes when he put her on the train a week ago was still burned into his brain.

''Then I'm dead to Sarah now?''

''Yes.''

Bart let out a long sigh as if all the happiness he'd ever known had passed from him. His words came slow, thick with drugged sleep. ''I'll go to my grave loving her.''

''You did,'' Cody said after a long minute of silence. He pulled the sheet up to Bart's chin and silently left the room.

Fifteen

SOMEHOW IN THE three weeks since the crash, Sarah had continued to function. She never missed work, but her nights were filled with a sorrow and loneliness Katherine couldn't share. She never asked Katherine for the details of the crash or where Bart's body had been shipped for burial. It was as though the mention of his name might rip her fragile composure to shreds.

Katherine's dishonesty ate at her while she walked to work, as it had every day and night since the crash. She doubled her pace as though she could outrun all the sadness she'd caused Sarah. Even though she'd sworn to Bart and promised Cody, the knowledge that she'd broken her vow to Sarah twisted away at her heart. She could tell herself a hundred times that Bart and Cody were right: Sarah would have sacrificed herself in caring for Bart if she'd known he was alive. But still the lie remained between them like a poison in Katherine's blood.

She jerked her glove off and stared down at the tiny scar that ran across her palm. They'd sworn always to be truthful with each other. They'd sworn in blood. Now that she'd broken that promise, Katherine hated herself for what she'd been forced to do.

Pulling her glove back on, she hurried through the hospital gate. She was an hour early for work, but that still might not be enough time to do all she planned.

The desk clerk frowned at the wind following Katherine through the open door and gave his usual bored wave as she passed. "You've got a message," he added after she'd already traveled several feet past him.

Katherine turned and waited as he rummaged through the papers on his desk.

"Here it is." The clerk held the message up, making no attempt to hand it to her. "It's a telephone number. The gentleman said to please call and ask for Cody." Finally the clerk handed her the paper.

Katherine stared at the numbers. The only reason Cody would call was if Bart had died. She'd made it plain enough she didn't want to hear from him socially.

Her fingers hurt as she gripped the single sheet of paper as though it were almost impossible to lift. A sob lodged in her throat, choking her. If Bart died, she hadn't lied?

She rang the operator on the desk phone, not caring that the clerk would overhear.

As the operator answered, Katherine silently prayed Bart was alive. She couldn't wish him dead to wash her lie clean.

Somehow she managed to give the number, then asked for Cody. The wait that followed seemed like hours as Katherine gripped the phone and glared at the desk clerk, who idly watched her with about much interest he'd have watched an insect climb a screen.

"Yes." Cody sounded out of breath. "Masters here."

Katherine waited, not knowing what to say.

"Kat, is that you?"

"Yes."

"Katherine . . ." Cody's voice relaxed. "I was afraid you wouldn't call after what you said at the hospital."

He sounded so wonderful, but she didn't want to hear his voice. It was only a reminder of what would never be. "I meant what I said." Then very slowly she added, "How is Bart?"

"About the same." Cody's voice hardened slightly, less

of the boy she remembered, more of the man. "There's still little hope that he'll ever leave the hospital. I visit him every day, but he's usually asleep. Even if he can walk again, his face and arms will always be covered with scars."

Katherine closed her eyes and forced the words out. "Then why did you call?"

Cody hesitated so long she wasn't sure he had an answer. When his words came, they were blended with pain. "I just wanted to say if you and Sarah ever need anything, let me know. . . . I'd like to keep in touch."

"That won't be necessary." Katherine bit her bottom lip to keep any hint of indecision from her voice.

"Katherine, listen. What happened was an accident. It doesn't mean we can't still see each other." Cody seemed to be searching for words. "We could wait awhile, give it time. I thought of you every day those four months I was gone. I can't just walk away without seeing you again."

"You have to." Tears formed in the corners of Katherine's eyes. "We both have to."

"But . . ."

"No," Katherine said and hung up the phone quietly, as though her last word were an epitaph.

Miles away in Dayton, Cody clutched the phone with his long fingers. "Come back to me, Katherine," he whispered to a dead line. "Come back to me!"

Silence.

"I need to talk to you, Katherine. We can't go through what we did that day and never talk of it again."

Silence.

"Come back and talk to me, damn it!"

Cody froze as a click sounded in his ear. "Do you wish to make a call?" the operator asked.

"No," Cody answered. "I only wanted to talk some sense into someone."

"Please replace the receiver."

Cody slammed the phone down and ran out the door. Within minutes he was on the road to Columbus. He drove without really being aware of what he was doing. All his thoughts were on changing Katherine's mind. She had no right to make such an insane request of him. If she didn't want to see him because she didn't like him, that would have been one thing, but to refuse to see him because Sarah no longer had Bart didn't make any sense.

Full darkness shadowed the city when Cody arrived. He knew it would be hours before she got off work, but he planned to be there when she walked out the door. After parking the truck directly in front of the hospital, Cody leaned back in the seat and waited.

The memory of Katherine played through his mind. He would never forget the way she looked when she appeared in the smoke and helped him pull Bart from the fire. Her eyes were burning from the heat, yet he'd seen a determination in them. She was the most alive woman he'd ever met. And also the most stubborn.

Cody drifted into a light sleep, waking every time the light crossed his face as the front door opened. Finally, after countless false alarms, Katherine stepped outside the hospital with several other nurses. He watched as she pulled the hood of her cape over her hair and turned her face toward the wind.

Suddenly Cody couldn't remember any of the speech he'd rehearsed. He seemed capable only of watching as the nurses walked toward him. Had it only been three weeks? It seemed as if he'd been starved of her beauty for years.

After the women passed him, blood started moving in his veins once more, and he stepped out of the truck. "Katherine?"

She paused and raised her head but didn't turn around.

"Katherine," he called, louder.

One of the other nurses looked back toward Cody but didn't wait for Katherine.

"I had to talk to you."

Kat turned to face him. Dear Lord, he thought. She was more beautiful than he remembered. The night was cold, and though her face was pale, her cheeks were red. Reflections of the lights of the hospital floated in her emerald eyes.

"I can't see you," she said, but didn't move to join the others. "We can never be together again." Her words sliced like a double-edged blade between them.

"I know." Cody tried to understand her reasoning. "I don't mean to bother you." He took a step toward her.

She turned as if to join the others but froze before she moved away. "You must go away. It wouldn't be fair to Sarah if you didn't."

Cody stepped up behind her until their bodies almost touched. He didn't dare reach for her, for he knew she'd bolt, but he waited, feeling the warmth of her in the slight space between them. "I had to try one more time."

Katherine didn't trust her voice to answer.

"I wanted you to know that if you or Sarah should ever need anything . . ."

"You said that on the phone."

"I know." Cody was having trouble thinking with her so close. "Katherine, I have to hold you once more. I have to know that you're real before my mind becomes completely lost in fantasy."

He could feel her trembling as he slowly closed the space between them. His hands brushed her arms so hesitantly she wasn't sure his touch was real.

His words brushed her ear. "You drift so lightly into my everyday reality, sometimes I wonder that someone doesn't see you there beside me."

"Don't make it harder for me, Cody. I have to live with the fact that I lied to Sarah. I have to make life easier for her. You don't understand what she and I have been through together. She can't be alone, not now. Don't make this any harder.''

"I understand," Cody lied. He didn't understand why he could never see Katherine again. "Only let me hold you one last time and I promise I'll never bother you again."

"Just once?"

"You owe me that. I saw your need to touch me in your eyes that day at the hospital before we went into Bart's room."

A cry whispered from her lips as she turned into his arms. As her fingers slid around his neck and into his hair his arms crushed her against him. Even through the layers of clothing he could feel her warmth pressing against him with a longing as great as his own.

All his life Cody had felt he was walking through someone else's house, listening to someone else's feelings, living someone else's dream. But now, standing in the predawn air with her in his arms, he felt whole. She was his reality and always would be, even if it took him years to convince her of it.

"Hold me tight," she whispered, "before you leave. I want to remember the way it felt to be in your arms."

"I can't leave you." Cody buried his face in her hair. "I can't just let you walk out of my life."

"You have to!" Katherine cried. "It's the only way I can live with the lie I told Sarah. When she was a child she always dreamed that the father she'd never seen would appear and care about her. Finally she trusted Bart, and he deserted her also."

"But—"

"There's nothing else to say."

Cody lifted Katherine off the ground with his hug. She felt so wonderful in his arms, so right. "No!" he whispered into her hair as he lowered her back to earth and watched her leave.

* * *

In the weeks that followed, Katherine's routine never varied. She arrived at work early, hurried to complete all her chores, then did as much of Sarah's work as she could before the shift was over. Knowing how much it upset Sarah to work with the burn victim, William, Katherine took extra time with the man for Sarah's sake. Somehow the unspoken kindness to her friend helped ease Katherine's guilt. But Sarah's blinding grief kept her from even noticing, for she moved like a sleepwalker through each day.

Late May brought the first changes. Sarah's spirit returned to the hollow shell of her body. Katherine had just waved good night to the nurses she'd walked home with when Sarah stepped out of the porch shadows. She greeted Katherine with such a whirling hug, Katherine was sure Sarah had lost her mind.

"I waited up for you." Sarah's voice was almost a laugh. "Maybe we could go over to the all-night bakery the way we used to do."

"What is this?" Katherine asked as Sarah locked arms with her and twirled her around. "You haven't had a doughnut attack since—"

"I know," Sarah interrupted, "but I have to talk to you, and the walls of this house have ears." Pulling Kat off the porch, Sarah continued, "We could walk toward the park. Bart and I always liked the park."

Katherine fell into step. They hadn't said Bart's name aloud more than a few times since the accident. She'd almost given up hope of Sarah pulling out of her grief. "Doughnuts and the park. What's the occasion?"

"I have great news." Sarah was almost dancing.

"What?" Katherine couldn't help but smile. Sarah's mood was contagious, and it had been so long since Kat had seen her happy. The quiet beauty had returned once again to her friend's blue eyes.

Sarah leaned close. ''Bart's not gone,'' she whispered. ''He's with me.''

''What?'' Katherine's breath caught in her throat, choking off all thought of another word. Somehow Sarah had found out the truth about Bart. Sarah knew of her lie.

''Katherine, don't look so worried.'' Sarah laughed. ''I'm not insane. Bart is with me because I'm going to have his baby.''

''No!'' Katherine was unable to say more than one word.

''A baby! *Bart's* baby.'' Sarah touched her abdomen with a soft caress. ''I went to the doctor this afternoon. He says I'm about ten weeks along.''

''But . . .'' Katherine couldn't believe it. She wanted to cry and laugh at the same time. Sarah would recover from Bart's death by having his child. Little Sarah, whom Katherine had always sheltered, was going to be a mother.

Sarah was rattling on so fast Katherine could barely understand her. ''I may have to quit work a few months before our year is up, but I'll find some way to pay back the rest of my tuition. I called Miss Willingham and told her. Funny about what you expect from people. All she said was she understood and not to worry about the money. She almost begged me to come back to the dorm to deliver, as if it would be some great honor for her to have me there.''

Katherine raised an eyebrow. ''Miss Willingham?''

Still glowing, Sarah added, ''I thought she'd give me a lecture about not being married, but all she talked about was how nice it was that Bart had left me with someone to love.''

Katherine remembered the view from the plane of Miss Willingham's garden. Maybe the stone statue was a gravestone and she'd been left with only memories of the man she loved. Kat shook her head. Not Miss Willingham.

Pulling at Katherine's coat, Sarah said, ''Kat, I know you're worried, but don't you see, I'll make it. When you told me Bart was dead, a part of me died inside too. But now

I'll always have a part of him with me." Tears threatened the corners of Sarah's huge blue eyes. "I've suspected for a few weeks. Each day I kept praying I'd be pregnant."

The full reality of what Sarah had said struck Katherine like an icy blast of wind. "But you're not married. How will we take care of a baby?"

"This is the twentieth century, not the Dark Ages. People will accept me and the baby. Anyway, we don't know that many people here." The first touch of doubt crossed Sarah's face. "I was planning on you helping me out. We could still work different shifts after the baby comes. I know it's a lot to ask."

Katherine thought of all their dreams of traveling after this year. She remembered their plan to join the Red Cross and see the world. She thought of the little house they'd always talked of buying. But now their plans were vanishing rapidly. She felt that somehow this was all her fault. She had the urge to tell Sarah the truth about Bart, but that would only add to her troubles. The coming of the baby would seal her lie forever. The lie had started building walls around her freedom, and the baby would complete the prison of her future. "Of course I'll be there to help."

Sarah was chattering again. "I don't see how we can come up with the money for a doctor, so I thought we'd go to Miss Willingham's, or, if you like, you and I could deliver the baby together."

"Oh, no."

"But, Kat, we're both nurses."

Katherine had to laugh at the thought. "We've been nurses for only a few months. Nurses who've never seen a baby born."

"But we saw pictures."

Somehow Katherine doubted the pictures would be anything like the real thing. "I'll get the money for the doctor and when the time comes we'll make it to Miss Willingham's or the nearest hospital."

"How can we afford a doctor?"

"You need rest, but I can work extra shifts or something." Katherine turned Sarah around. "Right now we've got to get you in out of the night's chill. Don't worry about the money. I'll find it. We've always made it together. Everything is going to be fine."

Sarah hugged her. "I'm so happy," she said. "A little part of Bart will always be with me."

Looking up at Kat, Sarah raised another topic they had both been avoiding. "Should we call and tell Cody? He might like to know about the baby, and maybe you could see him again."

Katherine closed her eyes, fighting back the tears. "No," she whispered. "It just didn't work between us." As Kat lied she could almost feel Cody's lips pressing into hers as he'd asked her not to leave him.

Sarah placed a comforting hand on Katherine's arm. "I'm sorry. Since I lost Bart I've been selfish and thoughtless not to ask about Cody."

"It doesn't matter. Cody wasn't the type of man to settle down, and I didn't want to wait around until he changed." Kat knew he was just the type of man she wanted, but she forced the words out, as if saying them aloud would make them true.

"But you'll see him again."

Katherine shook her head. "He's only a memory now." She knew it had to be so. If the tables had been turned, Sarah would have stood by her. As Kat followed her friend she almost wished she was in Sarah's place. With Cody's child inside of her, she'd have had more than a dream of what might have been.

"Hello!" a low male voice yelled over the static.

"Cody?" Katherine hated using the hospital phone, but it was the only way she could get in touch with Cody without Sarah knowing.

"Katherine?" Cody sounded shocked. "I can't believe it. How long has it been? Four months?"

"Almost five," Katherine answered. She had measured time in the weeks of Sarah's pregnancy.

"How are you?" There was a low, caring tone in his voice. For a moment she remembered the way the sun had shone on his hair the morning he took her flying. She thought of the boyish wink he'd given her when they met and wondered if he'd aged as much as she had over the months.

"I'm fine." Katherine swallowed the need to cry . . . the kind of deep crying that racked a body until there was no energy left. She'd been working seventy hours a week and still hadn't earned enough to cover all of Sarah's expenses. Now the doctor was asking for the rest of his money, and Katherine didn't even have this month's rent covered. "Cody, I called because I need to talk to you." She didn't want to say too much because one of the orderlies was listening.

"Are you in some kind of trouble?"

"No, it's Sarah. I wouldn't have called, but you said if we ever needed—"

He didn't wait for details. "Are you still working nights?"

"Yes."

"I'll be there tomorrow afternoon." Cody was silent for a moment. "Wait for me at your boardinghouse and I'll walk you to work."

"I think I can get permission to go in at eight."

"I'll be there before six." He paused a minute, and Katherine didn't know what to say. "And, Kat," he said finally, "whatever it is, I'll take care of it."

Katherine replaced the receiver and glanced at the clock. She still had a long night ahead of her, but she didn't feel tired. Cody's voice had lifted the weight from her shoulders. She knew she had to ask him for a loan—a loan it would probably take her years to pay back. But she had no one else to turn to.

The shift passed in a steady round of work. Katherine stayed long past her shift to work with William. He was almost fully recovered from the wounds, but his mind had never healed from the loss of his family. When he talked, he spoke only about wanting to join them. Katherine found herself wanting to scream to heaven that God should have taken William and left Bart alone.

As a gray dawn crept through the barred windows, Katherine unlocked the infirmary door for Sarah. She was two hours early because Dr. Farris insisted she rest during the middle of her shift. He hovered over her like a nervous midwife, always making her eat and rest. She and Kat shared many a laugh talking about the way he treated Sarah more like a patient than a nurse. But the doctor had had little to look forward to for many years. The patients also watched Sarah's pregnancy like little children watching a first garden. Most hospitals would have fired her, but Dr. Farris was too short-handed and too kind.

As they worked together, Sarah and Katherine exchanged small talk, mixing the news from the boardinghouse with the latest about the patients until an outsider wouldn't have known which was which.

"Nurse Sarah?" Dr. Farris interrupted.

"Yes, sir."

"I have to leave for a few hours, but I want to make sure you follow my orders."

"Orders." Sarah glanced at Katherine.

"Orders?" Katherine repeated.

"Yes." The doctor smiled. "I had a housekeeper clean the last room for you. Right after lunch I want you to sleep for two hours."

"Yes, sir." Sarah smiled at Katherine. They both tried to hide their giggles at what a mother hen Dr. Farris had become. He was interested in every detail of Sarah's pregnancy.

"I've left orders with the orderlies that if you don't sleep for two hours they are to lock you in the room next time."

"Two hours," Sarah answered. As the doctor turned to walk away both Katherine and she saluted.

"I saw that," he snapped with only a hint of mirth in his voice and without turning around. Both girls lost the ability to conceal their giggles any longer.

Katherine pulled off her stained apron and headed home. By the time she reached her room she was too tired to think about what she would say to Cody; she merely pulled off her uniform and crawled into bed.

Cody's dark eyes floated in her dreams. The memory of his kiss warmed her with bittersweet longing for what could never be.

As Katherine closed her eyes in her room in Columbus, Cody opened his eyes in the long bunkhouse-style room where most of the Wright Brothers' pilots now stayed, in Dayton. He hadn't slept more than an hour all night, but he jumped out of bed ready to go.

He didn't need a fortune-teller to inform him that Katherine needed money. That had to be the reason she'd called. Sarah was in some kind of trouble. He'd hang around the office until it was time to leave to meet Kat. Maybe he could pick up some ideas about earning some quick money. Someone was always willing to pay a pilot to risk his neck.

Sixteen

KATHERINE STOOD AT the top of the stairs and watched Cody pace the foyer of the boardinghouse. In his polished boots and worn leather jacket, he looked out of place in the ornate little room. His hair was, as always, windblown and unruly, but the autumn rain had darkened the sandy strands.

Although he was thinner than he'd been five months ago, his body seemed tighter, more powerful. Very little of the boy was left inside the man.

As she studied him, he glanced up at her and his dark eyes held her frozen in place. Those eyes said all was right with the world, and his easy smile almost made Kat believe it was true.

"Katherine," he whispered, watching her descend the stairs. His gaze drew her to him as he memorized every inch, every movement, every hesitation.

He took the first two steps in one bound and took her hand. The flicker of a dimple on his cheek told Kat he'd have hugged her had not the entire occupancy of the boardinghouse been watching.

Mrs. Parker stepped forward as the gathering's undesignated spokeswoman. "I see you're going out, Miss Katherine. And with a pilot, if what he tells us is true."

"Yes." Katherine resented the meddling but couldn't afford to offend the landlady. She had been nice enough to allow Sarah to stay on at the boardinghouse until the baby came . . . but only after Katherine had promised her more money. "Mr. Masters is an old friend. He's offered to drive me to work."

"Oh." Mrs. Parker crossed her arms over her ample chest. "Well, you be careful, now. You know all too well what can happen."

Cody smiled at the old woman, misunderstanding her warning to Katherine. "I'll drive carefully."

Mrs. Parker's frown indicated a car accident was not the kind of misfortune she was referring to.

"We'd better be going." Cody didn't miss the disapproving look the woman shot Kat, and suddenly he couldn't wait to get out of the landlady's sight. Her manner toward Katherine doubled his curiosity and his desire to help.

They ran out of the house and were in his car before either took the time to breathe. Cody paused before starting the engine. He wanted to let his eyes take in their fill of her. Could it be possible that she'd gotten even more beautiful?

"I borrowed this car from another pilot," he said as a part of him wanted to pull Katherine against him and hold her tight for as many countless hours as he'd spent dreaming about her. "I thought you'd be more comfortable." He fought the urge to yell at her for haunting every day of his life since they'd said good-bye months ago.

Slowly he set the car into motion and drove a block before daring another glance. "Lord, Kat, you look even better than I remember." A solemnity etched her features, making her seem older than the girl who less than a year ago had begged to fly. "Have you any idea how many nights I've thought of you? How many days I've almost driven down to see you?"

Katherine stared at the rain splattering against the window. The heavy clouds brought an early darkness to the evening. "I only called to ask a favor, nothing more. There can be nothing between us."

For several minutes Cody didn't answer. When he did,

his words came slowly as if he were testing the ground before stepping on it. "I know a café on the west side where we can talk without people like Mrs. Parker breathing down our necks." His smile silently called her last words a lie. Her cheeks wouldn't glow so red or her hands clench so tightly if there was nothing between them. "Have you got time for a cup of coffee before work?"

Katherine nodded and relaxed against the soft leather seat. She didn't want to tell him all her problems here in the cold rainy darkness. She wanted to enjoy being with him for a few moments before it ended. Somehow in the gray light her problems didn't seem so real. It was like the twilight after a dream, when the world wasn't clearly in focus.

Cody seemed to feel reality pause also for he cautiously dropped his hand from the gearshift and lifted her hand. When she didn't pull away, he slowly spread her hand atop his leg and covered it with the warmth of his own. "I've missed you." He murmured his thoughts. "I think I've missed the hope, the anticipation of what might have been more than I've ever missed anything in my life."

He watched the rain slide down the windshield. "Some days I feel that I have to force you into a corner of my mind so I'll have room to think of something, anything, else. I worry that if I'm not careful your memory will consume all of my thoughts."

Katherine didn't answer. She could say nothing that would change anything between them. Any comfort she gave would only widen the scar in her heart. She had to think of Sarah and the baby. There could be no life for her and Cody, but she let her hand remain and felt his warm fingers caress hers. It was a small thing to allow, a small action she would treasure during all the lonely years to come.

After several minutes Cody parked the car next to a tiny café. As he helped her out, he pulled her against him, shielding her from the drizzle with his open jacket while they ran for shelter.

After they passed through the entrance, he held her close, reluctant to let go. For a heart-wrenching moment they stood just inside the doorway seeing only each other. She felt so right at his side. Dear God, how could he turn away from her once more? The day of the crash had been hard enough; then as he waited in the shadows outside the hospital he'd felt himself being pulled apart. Now that she was facing some kind of trouble, he wasn't sure he could ever leave her again.

Someone inside cleared his throat, and Cody glared at the waiter. Hesitantly he lowered his arm from Katherine's shoulders and motioned for coffee.

Since no one else in Columbus seemed crazy enough to brave the rain on a night like this, the waiter expressed his displeasure at being bothered. With a loud grunt, he delivered the coffee and left.

Cody paid him no mind. Like a man starved for the sight of her, he lost himself in watching Katherine. Raindrops sparkled on her hair and face. He fought the urge to touch her as he forced his mind to think logically. "Would you like something to eat?"

"No." She looked down, knowing the time had come. She wasn't afraid to ask for money, only disappointed in herself for being unable to stand alone. "How is Bart?" she began.

Cody let out a long breath as if he'd been expecting the question. "He's going to live, but not much else. They transferred him to a big hospital in Dayton three months ago. Last week when I called, I learned that he checked himself out without leaving any forwarding address. I've searched everywhere, but he seems to have disappeared. You wouldn't think a man in a wheelchair with scars all over his face could just vanish, but Bart must have wanted it that way."

"How could he do that to you? You're his best friend."

"Was." Cody looked out the window and watched the rain pound the glass. "It got to where he couldn't stand to see me or any of us. We were still walking, still flying, still living, and all he was doing was cursing life. Bart wanted to be out of our lives as much as he wanted us out of his."

"Do you know where he's from?"

"There's a small town in upstate New York. I plan to look there next. I don't think he ever lived there, but some of his family did." Cody shook his head. "With the mood he's in, I doubt he'll contact any of his family even if he can find them. He's been on his own too long."

"I'm sorry he's vanished."

"Why? We both know you or Sarah could never go see him anyway. What difference does it make where Bart is?"

"None, I guess. Sarah believed me completely."

Cody leaned close. "How is Sarah? Something must be wrong or you wouldn't have called after all these months; and that damned woman back at the boardinghouse wouldn't have treated you as if you and Sarah had been robbing the collection plate on Sundays."

"Sarah's going to have Bart's child," Katherine said with rehearsed calmness as she looked past Cody at the empty café. She lifted her head slightly as if daring him to say anything against Sarah, but the room was silent except for the sound of someone cleaning the kitchen.

When she finally looked back at Cody, she saw only concern in his gaze. A sigh of relief escaped her as she realized he wasn't going to judge Sarah. Suddenly the months of being alone, of keeping the worry to herself, exploded within her and she told Cody all about the problems and about every failed plan she'd tried to make. He listened silently as she ended with the bills they would face in less than two months.

Cody ran his fingers through his hair. "How much do you need, Kat?"

"Three hundred dollars should pay the doctor and set us up in another place," she answered. "But it's just a loan, nothing more. I'll pay you back somehow."

Cody opened his wallet. "I've got a hundred and fifty with me, and I can get my hands on the rest by Friday." He handed her the money without hesitation. "One thing, though, I think Bart has a right to know he has a child."

"No!"

"But, Kat, it's only fair. Sarah wouldn't have to know about Bart, but Bart should know about the baby. Hell, it just might give him something to think about besides how miserable he is."

"You just said he'd disappeared."

"I know, but if our paths ever cross I'm going to tell him."

Katherine weighed her options. There was always the chance Cody would tell Bart anyway no matter what she said. She'd have to just pray he didn't find Bart and, if he did, that Bart would still insist on remaining "dead." Now with the baby he had double the reasons he'd had before. "Agreed," she said before she downed the last of her coffee.

Cody watched her closely. "Is there anything else I can do for Sarah?"

"No. I can handle everything."

He didn't miss the determination in her tone. "With the loan comes one favor."

Katherine looked up, stiffening as if preparing for battle.

"Would you consider keeping me informed about the pregnancy? I'd really like to know if the baby's a boy or a girl, in case I find Bart."

Katherine agreed.

Cody shoved his untouched coffee to the center of the table and folded his napkin neatly. As he stood, he pulled Katherine close beside him. "Kat, what about you and me?"

Katherine closed her eyes. "There is no you and me. There will never be. It wouldn't be fair."

Cody slid his arm around her waist and held her against his side. "How can hurting us help Sarah?"

"You'll have other girls to flirt with. There must be quite a number who are willing to do anything to fly."

For the first time Katherine saw anger in his eyes. "Do you think so little of me? Would you believe me if I told you that you were the first and only girl I've ever taken to my room? Would you believe that lately I dream I'm no longer flying, but standing with both feet on the ground and you in my arms?"

Katherine forced herself to pull away, not wanting to hear more. What if he was telling her the truth? What if he found it hard to look at another woman without thinking of her, just as she found it impossible to look at another man without seeing Cody?

"There can be an us, Kat." Cody slowly turned her toward him. "You can't sacrifice your entire life for Sarah."

"I . . ." Katherine's mind no longer formed words as feelings washed over her senses so completely. She raised her fingers timidly and touched his mouth, longing for the feel of his lips against hers.

"I want to kiss you," Cody whispered against her fingertips. "I need to kiss you."

Katherine couldn't take her eyes off his lips. "I wish . . ." She longed to put one dream into action. "I wish the world would stop for one moment."

Cody glanced over her head. "Let's get out of here. I need to be alone with you."

He turned Kat toward the door. Before she'd taken three steps, she almost collided with the cook. "Might be able to see it better from here!" he yelled as he ran out onto the sidewalk.

"See what?" Katherine followed.

"The fire," the waiter answered without looking back. "I think one wing of the state hospital is burning."

"What!" Katherine and Cody said in unison as they pushed past him.

"Yep, we're going to have some roasted nuts tonight," the waiter jeered.

Cody grabbed Katherine's arm as she swung at the crude man. He pulled her fist against his chest and almost lifted her off the ground to keep her from fighting. "There's no time. We have to get there fast." He pulled her with him to the car. "Sarah's still on duty, isn't she?"

Katherine nodded, her eyes large with fear.

Neither spoke as Cody raced toward the black cloud that billowed up from the earth. The evening grew darker, and blackness closed in, suffocating her. All Katherine could think about was Sarah and how it had upset her to treat William. Now many patients might be burned, and Sarah would have to work with them. She thought of Sarah's round little body trying to run from the fire, and suddenly a fear froze Katherine from deep inside, making her shake even as her hands began to sweat.

Cody saw her start to tremble. He pulled her against him. "Easy, honey. Sarah's probably fine." Holding her tight, his chin brushing her forehead, he couldn't help pressing his lips against her hair and wishing she'd allow him to hold her out of love.

But Katherine's energy and thoughts were directed toward Sarah. All Cody could do was get her to the hospital as fast as he could.

Sarah leaned back and stretched. The child inside her was growing heavy, but she would never complain.

"How do you feel?" Dr. Farris asked without looking up from the chart on which he was writing.

"Fine," Sarah answered, wondering how he always seemed to sense her discomfort.

"I've heard women say that babies are never less trouble than they are right now." Dr. Farris looked up and winked at her with a fatherly smile.

Sarah opened her mouth to ask a question, but a scream from the other end of the hallway cut off her reply.

"Fire!" an orderly shouted as he ran toward the smoke. "Fire!"

Sarah stared at the linen closet door in the center of the wing. Smoke billowed out from beneath the closed door in thin gray sheets. Another scream came from behind the door.

Dr. Farris grabbed Sarah's arm. "Leave! Now!" he yelled. "Tell the desk clerk to call for help."

Panic filled his face. "Be careful, Sarah, but get out as fast as you can."

Before she could answer, Dr. Farris turned away, yelling orders like a seasoned general. "Unlock all the doors on the back of the hall first! Let's get everyone out fast!"

The orderly nearest the linen closet reached for the knob as another scream came from behind the smoking door. He grabbed the handle and pulled the door open just as Dr. Farris yelled, "No!"

Smoke, flames, and a running mass of human fire exploded from the closet. The blackened man rolled on the tile as the orderly crumpled to his knees, holding his own face.

"My eyes!" the orderly screamed as fire spread out the open doorway.

Dr. Farris grabbed a towel from one of the hall trays and wrapped it about the orderly's head. Then he hurried past the burning man, now curled into a fetal position, and pulled the orderly to his feet.

"Come on, Jake."

"I'm blind!" the orderly cried.

Dr. Farris glanced up. "I told you to get out, Nurse

Sarah!'' he yelled, all of the kindness gone from his voice.
''Take Jake with you.''

Sarah pulled Jake down the hall, now gray with smoke.

''Fire!'' she yelled as she unlocked the hallway door.
''Fire in the infirmary!''

She'd expected men to come running to help, but
everyone seemed interested only in getting the patients out
of their own wards. No one ran to help Dr. Farris and the
one orderly left in the infirmary wing.

Sarah deposited Jake on the front steps, grabbed his keys,
and ran back to help. Two men would never get all the
patients out. At least she could unlock the doors for those
who could walk. She would stay on this side of the linen
closet. She'd be safe.

When she returned, a thick gray cloud filled the hallway.
Patients screamed from behind every door. Sarah unlocked
the first door as the remaining orderly almost knocked her
down carrying a woman out.

''Put a wet towel over your head!'' he shouted. ''And
push those who can walk in the right direction.''

Sarah did as ordered and moved from room to room. She
tried not to breathe the thick, hot air.

''Go!'' she shouted again and again. ''I'll be right behind
you.''

The patients were like children, not wanting to leave her,
fearing the unknown more than the smoke and fire.

She pulled her apron off and soaked it in a tub, then
wrapped the wet cotton around her head.

Wanting to open one more room, she forced herself to
move deeper into the smoke. She could see the flames from
the closet now eating away at the desk where the orderlies
sometimes played cards. In another minute the flames
would close off the other end of the hallway. One more
room and then she would have to leave. She turned the key
and felt the doorknob burn her hand as she twisted it.

The black billows choked away all air now and heat

burned into her throat and lungs. "Run!" she yelled as the man in the room almost knocked her down to obey.

Sarah stumbled backward in the hallway, tumbling out of control as something tripped her.

She curled up in pain and felt blindly for whatever had made her fall. A root seemed to extend from a pile of clothing bundled on the floor.

Sarah pulled herself closer, biting into her bottom lip to keep from screaming at the stabbing pain in her abdomen.

The root materialized into an arm, and Sarah cried out for help. The bundle of cloth became a body wrapped in a blanket.

"Help!" Sarah pulled a frail old woman toward her. "Someone help us!"

Eyes liquid with fright stared up at Sarah from beneath the folds of the blanket. "I can't get out like they told me," the old woman said as she clung to Sarah. "Don't leave me here. Make the smoke go away."

"Over here!" Sarah yelled, knowing she hadn't the strength to help the woman stand and walk.

She fought back a cry of pain as another stabbing sensation ripped across her abdomen. "Please God, don't let my baby die in this fire."

She didn't care about herself but the thought of her baby dying before breathing its first breath angered her.

"Come on!" she yelled at the old woman. "We've got to get out."

"No!" The patient tried to pull back against the wall, wrapping her blanket around her as though it could protect her from the fire. "I don't know which way to go."

Smoke was thick even at floor level, and the air was hotter than the blast from any oven.

"Well, I know the way." Sarah grabbed the woman's blanket. "Hold on to this and crawl behind me."

The woman whimpered in protest, but followed.

Sarah ignored the whining patient. She ignored the pain

in her lungs and abdomen. All she thought of was the baby. Bart's baby.

"Come on!" Sarah yelled, pulling the old woman along with the blanket. "We're almost at the door."

"Sarah!" Dr. Farris's voice drifted through the blackness. "Sarah!"

"We have to go, Doctor," the orderly's voice answered. "Everyone's out."

"Sarah isn't outside." Dr. Farris moved closer through the blackness. "Sarah!"

"I'm here!" she yelled and a moment later felt his hands pulling her to her knees.

When she cried in sudden pain, he lifted her into his arms. He was not a big man, nor was he strongly built, but he carried her easily, as if unaware of the burden.

"The woman . . ." Sarah tried to pull away from him.

"Get her, Sam!" Farris yelled at another shadow moving through the smoke.

"Got her, Doc," Sam answered.

They stepped from the infirmary into the main hallway where air was still smoke-filled but lighter.

"I'll get you to safety," Farris said as he passed firemen charging through the wing. "I thought everyone else was out, but I couldn't find you."

"Thank you." Sarah cried against his shoulder. He'd done what she'd always prayed her father might do when she was a child. He'd appeared out of nowhere and pulled her to safety.

"I should be angry with you for not following orders." Dr. Farris walked into the cool drizzle outside the hospital. "But I'm so relieved you're alive."

"You saved my life," Sarah said. "And my child's."

Farris slowed as he walked along the path toward the cottages behind the hospital. "Once, when I was just starting my practice"—words seemed to choke him more than the fire had—''a mother and child died because I didn't get to them in time.''

"You got there in time tonight." Sarah now understood the sadness always lingering in his eyes.

Farris nodded, then stood a little straighter. ''I'll put you in one of the huts. You'll be out of the rain and safe. I'll be back as soon as I can. Are you burned?''

"No, only slightly, but I felt a pain." She touched her swollen stomach and there was no need for more explanation. ''But it's gone now.''

"Someone should stay with you till I get back."

"I'll be fine." Sarah wanted to hug him, but could hear the authority returning to his voice.

He lowered her gently to her feet at the door of the hut. ''And you stay put.''

"Yes, Doctor." Sarah held her abdomen, gently calming the child within. ''Please help the others, then hurry back.''

"I will," he promised, placing his hand over hers.

When Cody and Katherine arrived, people and trucks surrounded the hospital. No visible flames rose from the building, but smoke still boiled out of the infirmary. Katherine jumped from the car and ran toward the smoke.

A constable grabbed her before she could get within thirty feet of the building. ''Can't go any farther, miss!''

"I have to!" Katherine fought at his arm. ''I work here. My friend may be inside!''

"Everyone's already out of the building."

Cody halted beside the policeman. ''Was anyone killed?''

The constable released Katherine's arm. ''We were lucky. Only several hurt as far as I've seen. One of the inmates set a fire in the linen room. It's a wonder half the place didn't go up in two minutes. They took all those who were hurt out back to the lunger huts.''

Katherine lifted her skirts and ran toward the tuberculosis

cottages behind the hospital where TB patients were allowed to spend their last days. She heard the cries of pain and orders being shouted even before she saw the huts between the trees.

"Sarah?" she cried. "Sarah?"

Mass confusion and suffering confronted her as she stepped into the first hut. Patients lay everywhere. Those already ill had been moved from the infirmary. Others were burned and screaming in pain. Their blackened skin bubbled with blood as they waved injured limbs, trying to avoid even caring touches. Mixed through all the suffering walked unharmed patients who were disoriented at having been moved from their rooms. They cried and pouted like frightened children in a strange environment, begging for help from everyone they passed.

Katherine moved among them, comforting them when she could but pausing only long enough to ask if they'd seen Sarah.

As she stepped into a tiny bedroom, she saw Dr. Farris bending over the blackened body of a man. The smell of burned flesh almost suffocated her, but Katherine moved to the doctor's side.

She looked down, unable to recognize the body. "What happened?"

Dr. Farris raised his red-rimmed eyes. "William finally succeeded in joining his family. He was doing so well; he talked one of the orderlies into leaving his door unlocked." Farris pulled the smoke-blackened sheet over the charred body. "At least he no longer suffers."

Katherine stared at the bed, horror pulsing through her brain. William had started the fire. He had caused all this pain because he wanted to die. The memory of the plane crash filled her mind as the stench of flesh filled her lungs. A fire had started Bart's suffering, and now a fire had ended William's. She turned and ran from the room, not wanting to see more.

"Sarah?" Katherine's cry sounded almost like that of a child who'd been separated from the only person who loved her.

Cody caught Kat just outside the doorway. "We'll find her," he promised.

"Wait!" Dr. Farris yelled just behind Kat. "Sarah's safe. I know where she is. We almost lost her."

Katherine looked up at him. The sadness in his eyes chilled her. "Where?" she managed to ask.

"I'll take you." He was moving before she could ask more.

The cold, damp air pushed against her, slowing her progress as she ran behind Farris down a path that connected the cottages.

"Was she hurt?"

"Not by the fire," Farris answered without slowing his progress.

Tears filled Katherine's eyes so completely she had to rely on Cody's arm as guide. His fingers held her close as they moved along the path.

The entrance to the other cottage was surrounded with men and women in their nightgowns holding on to one another for comfort. Dr. Farris disappeared among them without a backward glance at Katherine.

Cody held the door open for Katherine as though he couldn't enter without her. She could feel his need to protect her, but he seemed unsure where danger hid.

Katherine let her eyes adjust to the light of the room. Sarah lay on a worn couch with an old quilt thrown over her. Streaks of blackened smudge crossed over her ghostly white face, now contorted with fear. Dr. Farris stood beside her looking at his watch.

"Sarah!" Katherine knelt at her side. "I was so worried when I couldn't find you. Are you all right?"

Sarah tried to smile. "We got everyone out, thanks to Dr.

Farris," she said, "but I fell. Oh, Kat, I think the baby is coming."

"But it's not time."

Sarah's face twisted in pain. She grabbed Katherine's hand and held on as though to life.

Kat could feel the blistered burns covering Sarah's palm. "I'll get salve for your hands."

After a minute Sarah took a deep breath. "Don't worry about my hands. Get me out of here. I don't want my baby to be born in this place."

Katherine looked up at Farris.

"I agree. Let's get her out of this mess," he echoed Sarah's plea. "I think she may be right; the baby is coming. The contractions are still quite far apart; there's still plenty of time to move her."

Kat glanced at her environment for the first time. The room was a shambles. All the TB patients were huddled together watching her. Their coughing rattled in a low undertone like constant thunder. Most of these people were too ill to take care of themselves and these cottages were the purgatory before death.

Katherine glanced at Cody. He nodded as though he'd been awaiting an order and stepped forward.

"Sarah?" he asked as his hand brushed damp ebony hair from her face. "Would you grant me the honor of escorting you?"

Sarah looked up and smiled as politely as if Cody were asking for a dance. She raised her arm to his shoulder and he lifted her.

"You've gained a little weight, darling," he chided. "But on you it looks quite grand."

Sarah didn't answer, but held on to him. Cody pulled her close, trying to shield her from the drizzling rain as he followed Katherine out of the cottage and through the mud to the car.

Dr. Farris was never more than a step behind, giving

constant orders on how to treat her labor and the burns on her hand. When they reached the car, he added, "I'll make sure everyone is all right, and I'll meet you at the hospital as soon as I can."

Sarah's voice was weak, but she made an effort to act unafraid. "I'm fine, Dr. Farris. You worry about the people who are burned."

Farris glanced toward the cabin, then back at Cody. "You'll make sure she gets out of here? I must stay to help. We'll be in chaos for hours."

Cody nodded. "I'll get her somewhere safe."

Farris glanced once more at Sarah. "Take care, young lady."

"Thank you for saving my life." Sarah smiled up at the doctor.

He seemed uncomfortable with such a compliment, for he nodded quickly and disappeared into the night.

"If it wasn't for the fire, he'd never have let you out of his sight with you in labor," Katherine told her. "I think he'd been planning all along to help with the birth."

"I know," Sarah answered. "But maybe these are only false contractions." Her tone left no doubt she knew they were real.

When Cody lowered Sarah into the back seat, he kissed her on the forehead. "I'll have you safe in a hospital in only a few minutes, little mother, and we can check you and the baby in."

"No," Sarah whispered. "I have to go to Miss Willingham's hospital. Please take me. It's the only home I've ever had and I promised her I'd come when the pains started."

Cody shook his head. "It would take over an hour. Sarah, there are hospitals here in Columbus. We can't risk having you deliver between towns."

Her face was white and weak, but her hand clutched his sleeve with a steel grip. "I read in a book that first labor takes hours. I want to be at Miss Willingham's when the time comes. Please, for my baby. Bart's baby. I don't think I could bear to have my baby where people are looking on with disapproval. Miss Willingham will understand and help.''

Her words stopped abruptly as she hugged herself in pain for a minute. Finally she took a deep breath and looked up at Katherine and Cody.

"We better go to the nearest hospital just to be safe," Katherine whispered.

Sarah shook her head. "You don't understand." Tears blended with the rain on her face. "I need to be with Miss Willingham. She lost a baby years ago. She buried him on the hospital grounds in her private garden. If she could help me have mine, it might allow some of the grief that's settled in to pass. I have to go for everyone's sake." Her huge blue eyes held a world of pain in their depths.

"I understand, but . . ." Cody began. He looked to Katherine for help.

But Katherine stood like a granite statue, her eyes fixed on the blood on Cody's jacket and sleeve. Sarah's blood!

Seventeen

CODY DROVE AS fast as the car would allow. With the beginning of each contraction Sarah cried Bart's name softly, and Cody's knuckles whitened around the steering wheel. He would rather have flown through miles of thunderstorms than driven now, but Sarah was depending on him, maybe more than anyone in his life had ever depended on him.

"How much farther?" Katherine asked from the back seat.

"Five, maybe ten miles." Cody almost said, two, maybe three more pains. "When we get there, where do I take her? To the hospital or the dorm?"

"The dorm," Sarah answered. "Miss Willingham promised to help us deliver the baby." Another pain stopped all talking.

Minutes later Cody carried Sarah through the front door of the dorm and into Miss Willingham's private suite. Student nurses, drawn by the shouting, lined the halls in their robes, and were quickly enlisted as handmaidens to Sarah's ordeal.

Mamie Willingham showed no shock or anger at the interruption as she gave orders to all who came within hearing. She was the queen and this was her realm. Within minutes she had Sarah cleaned up and settled in an empty room across the hall from her suite. Cody was sent to fetch the young doctor, Daniel Lockhart, who might still be at the small hospital across the grounds. Katherine was told to scrub; she would be assisting.

It took Cody several minutes to persuade the young doctor to leave his other patients and come to the dorm. However, when they returned, Dr. Lockhart took one look at Katherine and started acting as if he considered it an honor, not a bother, to help out.

Cody watched them disappear into Sarah's room and leaned against the hall wall wishing he hadn't persuaded Dr. Lockhart to come. What good would one young doctor be? Cody mumbled to himself. Lockhart had seemed more interested in staring at Katherine than in delivering a baby.

Cody got shoved aside as supplies were moved down the hall. "He said he'd never even seen a baby delivered," Cody grumbled. "Hell, I'd probably be just as much help, but you'd think I was invisible around here."

Yet any young nursing student whose curiosity brought her within Miss Willingham's sight was put to work. She even had the floor scrubbed in what was now Sarah's room while everyone counted time by contractions.

"Strap her arms!" Miss Willingham ordered as she stepped from the room and began backing Cody down the hall with one bony hand on his chest. "Thank you, young man, for all you've done, but this is not something you need to see or even hear." They reached the front door, so she raised her voice slightly. "You should be on your way now."

Cody resented being dismissed like a first grader. He dug his heels in and faced the woman. "I'm not going anywhere, Miss Willingham, until I'm sure Sarah's all right."

Miss Willingham pressed her lips together so tight that blue veins formed around her mouth. She might be forceful, but never unkind. "No men except doctors are allowed in this dorm. You can wait on the steps in the rain or across the way in the hospital waiting room. Someone will let you know when it's over.'' She studied his worried face and added, ''Everything will be fine. Babies come every day and night on this earth, and most do so without very much help from anyone.''

Cody stepped out onto the porch and leaned against the building, hardly noticing the drizzle. He knew he'd be more comfortable in the hospital waiting room, but he couldn't force himself to move any farther away. Bart should have been here, he thought, but there was no way of finding him. Cody had even written to an address in New York State— the one Bart had put on his application when he first signed on to fly with the Wrights—but Cody was told the house had been vacant since Bart's parents' death years ago. His huge friend had managed to vanish.

As the hours passed, Cody found himself growing angry. ''If I ever find him,'' Cody mumbled, ''I'll tell Bart what I think about what he did to that young lady in there, and then I swear I'll punch him, burns and busted leg or not.''

It was almost dawn when Cody watched a car slide into the mud beside his own vehicle. A lean man carrying a black bag jumped from the Ford and ran toward him.

''Dr. Farris,'' Cody said more to himself than as a greeting.

Farris looked up as he reached the porch. ''I had the devil of a time finding you. If one of the other nurses hadn't remembered Sarah saying she wanted to deliver here, I'd still be looking.''

Cody slowed the doctor as he tried to open the door. ''I'm not sure they'll let you in there.''

Dr. Farris looked puzzled. ''Let them try and stop me.''

He opened the door. Cody couldn't resist following the doctor.

The dean of nursing stepped out of Sarah's room, her face set with determination.

Dr. Farris removed his hat as only polite southern gentlemen could do. His body seemed to relax, but his eyes were steel with determination. "Evening. You must be the wonderful Miss Willingham. I've heard such fine things about you."

The head nurse raised her chin slightly. "Yes."

"I'm Dr. Farris, and I'm here to offer my assistance. There was a time in my career when I specialized in helping babies come into this world. Nurse Sarah is a fine woman, and I'd like to do what I can to help."

Miss Willingham looked at him closely as though she could gauge his skill on sight. "We welcome your help," she said after a moment of hesitation. "Our Dr. Lockhart almost passed out a few minutes ago. I'd like to have a doctor who can be of some use." As she spoke, two student nurses helped the young doctor through the door.

Lockhart looked as if he'd been bled one too many times. His already pale face was ghostly white.

Miss Willingham patted him on the back. "Go back to the hospital, Daniel, and get some rest."

"I think I'll do that." Lockhart tried to look professional, but in truth, he looked as if he might turn green any moment.

Miss Willingham turned her attention back to Dr. Farris. "There have been some problems. . . ."

Dr. Farris hurried past her into Sarah's room without waiting for her to finish. The nurse looked at Cody as if he were a stray dog that had somehow gotten into the house.

"I know." He raised his hands in surrender. "I know. I'm leaving."

He walked back out onto the porch. He could never remember having felt so useless in his life. For all the good he was doing, he might as well have gone home, but somehow he couldn't bring himself to leave. He leaned back against the cold brick and tried to sleep on his feet while the early sun warmed his face.

"Cody?" a voice called from the doorway.

"Kat?" Cody straightened, realizing he must have dozed

off, for the sun was well over the treetops. "How's Sarah?"

Katherine hesitated in the archway. Her face was white with worry, and her apron was splattered with blood. She turned huge green eyes to him, then bolted toward him as though he were the only refuge in the world. "Oh, Cody," Katherine whispered against his neck. "She's bad, really bad. The baby's out, but Dr. Farris says Sarah's had a great deal of damage." Katherine clung to him. "She's very weak. If she makes it, she'll have to stay in bed for a month, maybe longer."

"I thought Dr. Farris knew how to help?"

"He did. If he hadn't been there, I don't think she would be alive now. Dr. Lockhart tried, but he didn't know what to do."

Cody pulled her against him and buried his face in her hair. "The baby?" he whispered. "Did it live?"

"Yes, but he's so small. Half the size he should be. The doctor says he's seen them live when they're born that small, but it'll be a gamble."

Rain sparkled in Katherine's hair, and he brushed it away gently with his hand, wishing he could brush away the worry in her eyes as easily.

"It's going to be all right," Cody said against her cheek, trying to believe it himself. "I wish I could do something to help."

Katherine smiled up at him. "You've helped a great deal. You got us here and you're holding me now."

"I'll hold you whenever you need me, Kat." Cody wanted her to believe he would always be there for her, but he wasn't sure he believed that himself, either.

"Katherine," a student nurse said as she joined them on the porch. "Sarah is asking for you and someone named Cody."

"We'll be right there," Cody answered as he pulled his handkerchief from his pocket. "Dry those eyes, beautiful. We don't want Sarah to see that her heroine has been crying.

She doesn't have anyone but us, and we've got to convince
her that everything is fine.''

Without answering, Katherine moved into his arms holding on as tightly as she could. He could feel her shake with
grief and fear and realized all Katherine's strength would
vanish if she lost Sarah. Cody wrapped his arms around her
and hugged her just as tight, praying he'd be strong enough
for her whenever she needed him.

After a long moment Katherine slowly pulled away and
followed the student nurse back into the building. The room
had already been cleaned, and Sarah was resting quietly.
She smiled as Cody knelt beside the bed.

''How's the finest little lady in the world tonight?'' he
asked as he kissed her hand. ''Ready to go dancing?''

''I'm a little tired right now, but I'm happy. Did you see
Bart's son? He doesn't look much like his father now, but
he'll grow.''

''We wanted to see you first,'' Cody answered. ''Miss
Willingham is taking care of the baby.''

Sarah looked at Katherine. ''We did it, Kat. We delivered
a baby.''

''With Dr. Farris's help and Miss Willingham's,'' Kat
agreed. ''You get some sleep. I'll pull a chair up and stay
right beside you in case you need anything.''

Sarah nodded. ''I'm going to name him Matthew. It
means 'gift from God.' Matthew Rome.'' Sarah's eyes
closed and she drifted into sleep. She looked so small in the
large bed with pillows and covers all around her.

Cody stood watching her for a long while. Sarah's
happiness made all their troubles seem so small. Her inner
strength probably made her the strongest one of them all, he
thought.

The student nurse interrupted them again by pointing
toward Miss Willingham's private rooms. ''You can see the
baby now,'' she whispered.

Cody crossed the hall and tapped lightly on the door.

When he got no answer he turned the knob and entered a darkened office. He walked into the sitting room and pushed a door open to a small kitchen. The night was warm, but the stove made the room hot.

"Come on in and close the door before you let the heat out," Miss Willingham ordered.

Like everyone who ever came in contact with the woman, Cody did as he was told. Miss Willingham sat at the table with Matthew in her arms. Her hair was disheveled and her apron bloody, but she didn't seem to care. Dr. Farris relaxed beside her, blowing on his hot coffee without taking his eyes off the baby.

Cody pulled up a chair and watched as she rocked little Matthew Rome. "He's small," she said, "but he's a fighter. This little fellow is going to make it fine. I know a few tricks." She glanced at Dr. Farris and for once her smile was genuine. "First, we're going to keep this room warm twenty-four hours a day. Except for the times he's with Sarah, he'll sleep in here. I'll have a cot moved in and we'll take shifts. We'll hire one of the student nurses to sit with Sarah when Katherine or I can't be there."

"I'll cover all the expenses for that." Cody looked up as Katherine entered. "I'll also pay for anything you need until Sarah and little Matt are on their feet."

"Matthew," Miss Willingham corrected. "I'll not have him called by any nickname. Christ didn't call his disciple Matt for short, and we will have the same respect for the name."

"Matthew, then." Cody laughed as he leaned forward. "And Miss Willingham, I think I'm in love with you." He kissed the cheek of this woman who tried to be so tough.

"Nonsense, young man. I'm only doing my job as a nurse." Her back was as straight as ever, but a blush stained her cheeks. "And hadn't you better go do whatever it is you do."

"Yes, ma'am." Cody stood, his hand brushing the baby's cheek one last time in farewell.

"Young man," Miss Willingham added when he'd reached the door. "You may come back to visit Matthew." She glanced down at the baby and smiled. "If we're going to have one male living in the dorm, we might as well have one visiting."

"Or two," Dr. Farris added.

Exhaustion lapped over Katherine in slow waves of numbness. She poured herself a cup of coffee and smiled, first at Cody, then at Dr. Farris. The life was back in the doctor's eyes. Whatever had made him so sad had vanished with the birth of this tiny infant. Even without sleep Dr. Farris seemed ten years younger.

Farris took the cup from her hands. With a wink he told her he guessed she'd hold it until the coffee was cold without having the energy to drink. "Nurse Katherine, why don't you walk this young man to the door while Miss Willingham and I talk? By the way, I think it best if you don't report to work for a week. You look as if you could sleep that long without waking."

Katherine followed Cody into the hallway. "Thanks for being there last night."

Cody fought the urge to hold her. Instead, he took her hand and pulled her outside with him, unwilling to say good-bye in front of the others.

"Does this mean you've finally seen the light and we can start being together again even when there's no disaster?"

Kat slowed her steps. "I've been thinking about that." She spoke clearly even though her heart screamed that her words were a lie. "There can be no us." Only hours ago she'd almost given in to her feelings for Cody, but that was before she'd seen how desperately Sarah needed her. She wouldn't turn away from Sarah and the baby. Not now. Not even for Cody. Not even for her own happiness. Yet she delayed this last parting, knowing she should go back inside but wanting to feel him beside her one last time.

They walked almost to the car before he gave conversation another try. "I know where I can make five hundred dollars this week. I want you to have it for the baby."

Katherine shook her head. "We can manage."

"I know you can, but I want to help."

Katherine leaned against the door of his car. "What do you have to do to make that kind of money?"

"Fly and land."

"There's more to it than that." Katherine took a deep breath of the fresh-washed air. "I know an ordinary flight, even at an air show, doesn't pay that much money."

Cody lightly looped his arms around her. "Some railroad men made a bet that a plane couldn't land on a moving train car. I heard them talking yesterday. I bet I could do it if they lined up enough flatcars."

Katherine opened her eyes, all sleepiness forgotten. "You can't!"

"For five hundred dollars I can."

"What if you crash?"

Cody shrugged. "That solves your problem of never running into me again." He tried to laugh, but the joke fell flat between them.

Katherine swung and hit his shoulder with her fist. "I want none of the money. I'll never speak to you again, Cody Masters, if you do such a foolish thing."

Cody caught her fist in his hand. He loved seeing the sparks in her eyes, even though he was the source of her anger. "I wasn't aware you were speaking to me all that much in the first place. In the second place, landing the plane will be no problem as long as they keep the train going in a straight line at the same speed."

She pushed him away and turned back toward the dorm. Staying away from him was right, not only for Sarah's sake and Matthew's but also because he would break her heart by gambling with death as surely as Bart had broken Sarah's.

"You'll speak to me, Katherine!" Cody yelled after her. "You won't get rid of me so easily this time."

Katherine increased her pace. She would think of the baby and Sarah and forget about this crazy pilot who threatened to crush her heart. They needed her; Cody only wanted her. She had lied to Sarah once, and now she planned to make that up to her if it took a lifetime.

Cody tried to sleep the next day, but by nightfall he was wide awake and ready to fly. He walked toward the airplane thinking more of Katherine than of what he intended to do.

Wheeler DeJon, as always, had oiled the engine and prepared everything. The Frenchman pointed one long finger at Cody as he neared. "I think you're insane to try this, Cody. If you miss by a foot you'll not only be dead from the crash but the damn train will probably run right over your bones."

Cody laughed. "Sounds like one hell of a mess to clean up, old friend. Guess I better not miss."

DeJon snorted. "I checked the train cars. The surface is flat. I also tied the boards between the cars so they can move slightly with the rattle of the train and still make a platform."

"Good." Cody knew DeJon would take care of all the details. "All I have to do is fly a straight flight going the same speed as the train, then drop down onto the cars. A piece of cake."

DeJon spit a long brown stream of tobacco juice. "I'm going to be riding on the train. When I hear your engine, I'll light a torch at the end of your landing space."

"Thanks." Cody slapped DeJon on the back. "But stay clear. If I should slip off, I don't want you grabbing the plane and being pulled off the train."

DeJon laughed. "Unlike your mother, my mother had a smart child who lived and plans to go on living."

Cody dropped his smile. "One more thing. If something happens, tell—"

DeJon interrupted, not wanting to hear any last request from a pilot. "I know. Tell each mademoiselle that you loved only her."

"Something like that." Cody only had Katherine on his mind, and she'd threatened never to speak to him if he flew tonight.

DeJon dropped to the ground and scraped up a handful of dirt. He rolled it in an oily rag he'd used to clean the engine. "I don't have any train dirt, but this should work, no?" He dusted the oily mixture on Cody's shoulder. "Don't forget to come back in one piece."

Cody winked but couldn't bring himself to say anything. This would be the riskiest flight he'd ever made. The fact that it was being flown at night made it even worse.

An hour later he climbed into his plane, suddenly impatient to meet his fate. Within seconds he was airborne and flying across the cloudless sky. The stars hung huge and sparkling, dusting the earth with a glow almost as bright as shadowy daylight. The rain from the night before had dampened the land, making it seem new in the moonlight.

Cody followed the tracks until he heard the sound of the train. He circled high and flew parallel with the locomotive. Even as he lined his plane up with the flatcars he couldn't get Katherine's angry face out of his mind. He wished he'd told her that he would have flown this trick for half the money. Oh, he needed money fast, but he could have gotten it some other way for her. He was flying tonight for the thrill and probably always would. Still, if something happened, he knew she'd blame herself.

As he began to descend, he laughed. "Better a fast death than dying by inches." But the words seemed hollow. For the first time in his life there was something he wanted to do beyond this moment. Someone he wanted to talk to. Someone he wanted to love. Katherine.

DeJon's torch blazed in front of him and smoke from the train blackened Cody's face as he slowly lowered his plane onto the flat surface of the railway cars. Suddenly Cody felt the sensation that he had been waiting, even yearning, for. It had always come to him when he flew. The feeling that time was falling away, that he and the airplane were one. Cody was in his element. The canvas and wire that covered the machine also extended to his being. At that moment he knew he would succeed.

As the wheels touched down, the plane rocked, tipping first one direction then another. Cody forced the brake with all his strength as the plane rolled to a stop on the flatbed railroad car. He closed his eyes as the sounds and images of the night came flooding back to him. Safely down, Cody and machine could once again separate . . . until the next time.

He heard the clink of metal as bands were thrown over the wings to secure the plane on the car.

"You've done it!" DeJon shouted. "You've done it!"

Cody took a deep breath and relaxed the death grip he had on the controls. "Want to try it again?" he shouted to DeJon. Cody tried to swallow the heartbeat pounding in his throat as he climbed from the plane.

DeJon's smile acknowledged the joke. "Sure, boy. Some other night."

They both laughed as they sat down in front of the plane to wait for the train to stop so they could collect their money and go have enough to drink to turn this night's fool's play into heroics.

"Morning, Mr. Masters." Miss Willingham looked very much as if she had come from a long line of palace guards. "Won't you come in? We were about to take tea."

Cody pulled off his hat and tried to comb his hair with his fingers. What was it about this woman that always made him feel as if he still wore short pants? "I hoped it would be all right for me to check on the baby today."

"Of course." Miss Willingham ushered him into her sitting room, which now looked far more like a nursery. "We've seen you twice a week for over a month. Why would our hospitality change now? I'll go get Matthew." She moved through the doorway just before Sarah entered.

"Cody!" Sarah cried.

As he had every time he'd seen her, Cody hugged her warmly. She looked so frail that a snowflake might crush her, but her smile left no doubt of her happiness. "I wanted to see how Matthew has grown." Cody helped her to a rocker. "Plus I hoped to catch Katherine."

Sarah patted his arm. "She took the train back to Columbus over an hour ago."

Cody tried not to allow the disappointment to show in his face. He'd seen Katherine only once—the day after his night landing on the train. She'd argued, then finally taken the money from him, promising to pay it back as soon as she could. He'd left so angry he wasn't sure he could see her again without strangling her. Yet, as each visit passed, anger turned to longing.

"Kat's been working double shifts, hoping to finish up my year there as well as her own." Sarah's smile faded. "On weekends she insists on coming to Dayton to care for Matthew, and then it's back to work. She's looking so pale, I'm starting to worry about her."

"Is there anything I can do?" Cody fought the urge to add, Besides beat some sense into her stubborn head.

"No." Sarah lifted her shoulders. "Matthew's stronger every day. Soon we'll all be able to sleep at night. If Kat can just keep working for three more months, Miss Willingham has offered us both teaching jobs here."

"Is that what you want?" Cody tried to read her face closely for the truth.

"It's what I want." Sarah nodded. "But not Kat. She

tells me it is, but I know her. She needs more.'' Sarah's blue eyes were an ocean of concern. ''She'll die here. I can't allow her to give up all her dreams just because mine have changed. She's always wanted to travel, see the world, work at some big hospital. Teaching here would wither her, but she won't accept that. One person can't live another's dreams. This is mine now, not hers.''

''What can I do?'' Cody felt as helpless as Sarah.

''Talk to her,'' Sarah pleaded. ''Make her start living again before the Kat who flew with you disappears forever.''

''I'll try,'' Cody said as he heard the door open.

Miss Willingham ended the conversation as she entered with the baby. ''Here he is, awake and dry, Mr. Masters.'' She looked at Cody and raised a questioning eyebrow. ''Did you wash your hands?''

''Yes, ma'am,'' Cody answered as he held his arms out for Bart's son.

Eighteen

THE CALENDAR TURNED from 1911 to 1912, but Cody Masters did not celebrate. Instead he counted the last minutes before midnight with the names of his friends who'd died over the past months. Though he hoped Bart Rome was still alive, Cody had included his name among the casualties. What started for Cody as a bright adventure had become an addiction. At first the excitement of flight thrilled him, then it drove him to push faster and higher, and now it seemed to be the only thing that made him feel alive.

The memory of Katherine haunted his dreams, though she wanted none of his attention. Sometimes he felt like a kite flying high in the wind, untouched by anything or anyone. She was his only connection to the earth. She remained the only person, male or female, he'd ever met who could understand him, who could hold him without his wanting to fly away as he had from every other relationship that might bind him.

He'd made a point of dropping by the hospital every time he had a chance, but Katherine was rarely there. When she was, she seemed too tired to spend more than a few minutes with him. Somehow she made him feel guilty for taking up any of her time. But he felt bound to her by something far stronger than the secret they shared.

He'd watched Sarah's world center around little Matthew, but Katherine's world had no center. Katherine plodded through life like one of the patients pacing a ward at the state hospital. She had no hope of escape, but her survival instinct wouldn't allow her to stop walking the boundaries.

Cody pulled his Model A pickup onto the state hospital grounds and cut the engine. Miss Willingham had told him Katherine slept at the state hospital in Columbus during the week so she could work both Sarah's shift and her own until their contracts were completed. On weekends she caught the train to Dayton and helped with the baby.

Now, almost fourteen months after she'd started work, tonight Katherine would complete both her year and Sarah's at the state hospital.

He watched the door for almost an hour before Katherine walked out and headed toward the train station. For a moment he didn't recognize her, bundled up in her long dark cape. She looked thinner than he remembered. She'd pinned back her hair harshly from her face, and her bearing remained, as always, tall and straight. She might not be the natural nurse Sarah seemed to be, but she was a fighter; he could see it in her stride.

"Kat!" Cody shouted as he started the engine.

Turning toward him without a smile, she spoke his name so softly her voice caught in the frosty air and hung between them like a thought. In the months since Matthew's birth, Cody couldn't remember seeing her smile. The day of Bart's crash she'd locked all emotions away except her loyalty to Sarah. No matter how hard he tried to break the lock, it stood between them and any happiness they might find together.

"I thought I'd offer you a ride back to Dayton." He held the door open for her, wondering if she'd make this small concession.

"Sorry I couldn't borrow a car, but this truck drives better in bad weather." He waited for her to accept his offer. So far all she'd taken from him was the money she needed for Sarah. She seemed to have removed him from her life with a clean cut and bandaged the wound with her pride.

Katherine hesitated, allowing the icy wind to pull at her cape with freezing fingers before she nodded and climbed into the warm cab.

"Miss Willingham said this was your last night at the state hospital." He noticed Katherine didn't even look back at the building. "Not much of a farewell party."

Leaning her head against the seat she said, "These last few months seemed endless. I start Monday at the Willingham Clinic and Hospital."

"That's great." Cody was thinking more of the weekend than of the new job.

"I guess." No excitement colored her words. "I'll be an instructor, and so will Sarah when she's able. I think Miss Willingham offered us the job more to keep Matthew close than anything else. She even offered us a private suite right across from hers."

"Is that what you want?" Cody knew it wasn't, but he had to know if she lied to herself as well as to him.

"Yes, though I had another offer." Katherine let out a long breath. "Dr. Farris left the state hospital two months ago to open a practice in gynecology and pediatrics. He told me I could have a job with him if I ever needed one, but it would be here in Columbus and that's too far from Sarah and the baby."

Cody pulled the truck onto the main road as snow began to fall. He couldn't tell by her words which job would have been her choice if the baby hadn't been a factor to consider. "I thought you'd be more comfortable driving than riding the train tonight. I also figured this was the only way I'd get a chance to talk to you."

Katherine closed her eyes. "Thanks, but you shouldn't have gone to the trouble. I would have been fine taking the train."

Fighting back a reply, Cody concentrated on his driving.

Why was it that whenever he tried to do anything for her, she fought him so? When he was with her, he felt like he was flying high and always about to destroy their fragile relationship with any sudden move.

After driving in silence for several minutes he realized she'd fallen asleep. Carefully he pulled her near and adjusted her head against his shoulder. He untied her cape and blanketed it over her. She cuddled into his warmth, and Cody's heart tightened with longing. She felt so right by his side, like a puzzle piece in his life that had always been missing. He'd always been alone, an only child born of parents who worried more about how tidy his room was than about whether he was happy. Cody couldn't remember ever minding the loneliness until he met Kat, but now her slightest touch made him long for more.

He tightened his arm around her, loving the way she molded herself against him. They drove for half an hour before a light up ahead waved them to the side of the road.

Cody rolled down the window, trying to move as little as possible. "What's the problem?" he shouted at a man waving a lantern.

"Car wrecked on the bridge. It'll be a few minutes before they get it cleared."

After closing the window, he pulled Katherine closer and looked down into sleepy green eyes. "How long has it been since you've had any sleep?"

"Two days, almost three." She moved away slightly.

"Don't pull away from me, Kat." Cody fought the urge to hold her to him even if it was against her will. "I'm not poison."

"We shouldn't be here like this." Her words were thick with sleep. "We shouldn't be alone."

"Why? Because you dislike my nearness so much, or because you allow yourself no happiness?" Cody knew he was shouting at her, but he'd bottled all his emotions up since Bart's crash. "Do you have to punish us both for the rest of our lives because you told one lie to Sarah? At least she and Bart had each other for a few months before they were separated.''

Katherine turned away, and something inside Cody snapped like a tight kite string. He grabbed her by the shoulders and twisted her in the seat until they faced each other. ''Tell me you don't care for me and I'll disappear forever.'' Seeing no resistance, he pulled her close so he could memorize her face in the shadows. ''Tell me, Kat, just how much you hate the sight of me.''

She tried to pull away, but he held her fast and shouted, ''I'm through playing this game by your rules! Now we play by mine and the only thing that's going to stop me is if you say you don't dream of being in my arms as much as I dream of holding you in mine.''

He saw it first in the depths of her tear-brightened eyes. A need as deep as his own. A longing for what they'd never had but both desired.

She slowly raised her hand to his cheek, but no words came.

Her fingers brushed his face lightly as if trying to decide if he was reality or dream.

''Kat, let's declare a truce. Right here, right now, we're in no-man's-land and all hostilities are suspended. Let me hold you for these few moments. Let's pretend there is no place else just now. No one, not even God, will miss a few minutes.''

''Right here, right now,'' she whispered in a sob. Her fingertips brushed his lips as softly as one might try to touch a dream. ''For only a little while, then never again?''

Cody wasn't sure which of them moved first, but all at once he was kissing her. Wildly, passionately, as he had in his dreams. Her arms encircled his neck, pulling him to her.

He twisted his fingers into her hair and heard the pins fall like tiny nails against the metal floor of the truck cab. When her hair tumbled around her, he grabbed a fistful and held on as if holding on to life.

Snow silently fell against the windshield, curtaining them from the world while his heart pounded violently. This was the Katherine he knew, wild and free. Her kisses grew more demanding as she came alive in his arms. Gulping for life once more, she no longer sat back allowing it to happen.

Her kiss told him what her words would not. That she had dreamed and relived the other times he'd held her. He'd felt that oneness with her when he first touched her during the game at O'Grady's when they balanced so perfectly together atop the board. Being with her balanced his life.

Cody wasn't sure what he'd said that had broken her shell, and right now he didn't care. He had to feel the Katherine he remembered beside him once more. He was holding the girl who'd flown with him that morning so long ago and the woman who'd first come to life in his bedroom an hour later.

He pulled her onto his lap and rested her back against the steering wheel. He wondered if he'd have the energy or time to breathe if they continued. He wasn't sure he cared as long as he could die holding her. Nothing mattered but Katherine in his arms.

Finally he broke the kiss and threw his head back with sheer joy. "Lord, Kat!"

She raked her fingers into his hair and pulled his head to her. "Again," she whispered in a voice blended with demand and need.

Cody kissed her once more, loving the way her mouth opened to his probing. Her fingers snaked through his hair, sending lightning across his brain, and her breasts pushed into his chest begging to be touched. With her, there was no art of loving, but only raw need. He wondered if he could handle her in bed, then smiled, knowing he'd love to die trying.

Slowly he stroked her back and arms, attempting to tame

her. His mouth softened to a loving caress, and she responded willingly, melting against him. Long and deep, his kisses pulled all the loneliness from her. He wanted her, had wanted her from the moment their eyes met. Katherine wasn't a flower to be picked, but a wild, wonderful garden to be nurtured and cherished for a lifetime.

His hands circled her waist and pulled her close. Tenderly he brushed the sides of her body, slowly climbing upward to the swell of her breasts. As his fingers brushed lightly across the wool, he closed his eyes and pictured what rested just beneath the material of her uniform.

When his fingers climbed higher, he felt her moan against his lips. Their kiss grew into liquid fire, sparked into flames again and again by the brush of his fingers across her breast.

When finally he broke the kiss to breathe, Cody buried his face in her wonderful hair. "I want to taste you," he whispered, "here." He bit lightly into her throat. "And here." He ran his tongue lightly along her lip. "And here." He molded his hand over the swell of her breast.

Kat leaned her head back and closed her eyes.

For a long while Cody watched her face as he touched her, loving the pleasure he brought her and wishing there was no material between his hand and her flesh. When he could stay his hunger no longer he pulled her closer and kissed her open mouth. She tasted of a passion he'd never have enough of to be satisfied.

She welcomed his kiss as she had his touch, as though she'd been starved of it for too long. Her fingers slid through his hair again and again, demanding he continue the pleasure he was bringing her, demanding he give totally during the moment they had together.

Someone tapped on the window, bringing Cody back to earth. "You folks can move on now. Wouldn't want to freeze out here." The man wandered off toward the next car.

Katherine looked up, her eyes fiery green, her cheeks red

with passion. She laughed suddenly. "I'm not in the least danger of freezing."

Cody trapped her face in his hands. "I was growing rather warm myself." He kissed her nose.

"Once more," she pleaded as she lifted her fingers to his mouth. Lightly she tasted the skin at his knuckles. "Can time stay stopped for one more kiss?"

He couldn't have found the words to answer if he'd tried. All he could do was obey her request. He pulled her against him and kissed her with a heart full of need and a lifetime of longing.

When she finally lifted her head, she smiled down at him. "Thank you," she whispered. "We have to start the clock again."

Without another word she cuddled next to him, and Cody pulled the truck back onto the road. They moved slowly through the snow, both lost in their own thoughts.

Hours later Katherine snuggled against him like a child in her father's arms when he carried her into the dorm. He nodded to Sarah as she rocked Matthew, then headed for Katherine's bedroom. She didn't awaken when he slipped her shoes off and covered her with a blanket. The lines of exhaustion had relaxed around her face. He couldn't resist one last taste of her lips before moving away.

Even with the taste of her still in his mouth he already hungered for more.

When he walked back into the sitting room, Sarah laid the baby lovingly in his crib.

"Want a cup of coffee?" She smiled at the baby as she asked.

"Sure." Cody tried to think of something besides the redhead in her bed only a few feet away. He knew if Sarah hadn't been up, he would have been very tempted to lock Katherine's door and crawl in beside her. There'd have been hell to pay the next morning, but he would have had a night of heaven first.

"Milk and sugar?"

"What?" Cody ran his fingers through his hair, trying to clear his brain. He looked down to accept the cup and noticed blood on his hand.

Sarah saw it, along with the crimson stain along his hairline. "You're bleeding." She hurried to examine the scratch.

"It's nothing." Cody gingerly felt his scalp. "Just a little scratch. I must have bumped into something."

As Sarah examined the cut, he fought to keep from laughing. He had run into something all right. A redheaded wildcat. He doubted even Sarah's gentle caring hands could cure the fever Katherine had started within him.

"I'm glad you brought Kat home." Sarah opened a small medicine cabinet.

"So am I," Cody answered with total honesty.

"She cares for you"—Sarah pulled a bottle out—"even if she won't admit it."

Cody touched his scalp. "I'm beginning to see a few signs of that myself."

Sarah pushed him toward the rocker. "Don't give up on her. Give her time."

"I'll try." He wanted to add that Katherine wasn't exactly making it easy for him. When she wasn't giving him frostbite with her coldness, she was burning him with passion.

Cody folded himself into the chair beside the crib and watched Matthew sleep while Sarah mothered him as if the scratch were a war wound. His easy smile slowly faded to a frown as he realized Bart was somewhere alone tonight not even knowing of the baby's existence. Bart had a right to know, even if he decided never to tell Sarah the truth. A man should know he was a father.

He set his jaw and looked up at Sarah. "I've been offered a lot of money to go on tour. I'll be gone for more than a year. I wonder if that will give Kat enough time." He had a gut feeling Bart was out there somewhere still hanging around planes. If he made enough stops in enough towns he might run into him. And if he could find Bart, maybe he could rid Katherine of her guilt.

"We'll be here when you return, as far as I know."

Cody looked up into her soft blue eyes. "Are you happy?" he asked without thinking how very personal the question was.

Sarah smiled. "Yes." She glanced at the baby. "I miss Bart every hour of every day, but I am greatly blessed."

Sarah lifted her coffee cup, but didn't take a sip. "What about Katherine? If you go away on tour you won't see her for a long time."

Cody wanted to tell her he'd wait for a hundred years if he thought Katherine would love him, but he wasn't sure how Kat felt about him. He had a feeling if she came through the door right now, she'd probably tell him to get out for good and deny everything that had happened in the truck. But then, he had the scars to prove it.

She needed time to think and so did he. "I'll be around for another three days. All she has to say is one word and I'll stay." He spoke more to himself than to Sarah as he stood. He had finally found someone who made him long to end his wandering. "If I don't hear from her by the end of the weekend, I'll see you both in a year."

Sarah stood on tiptoe and kissed his cheek. "Take care of yourself, Cody."

"Take care of little Matthew," Cody answered as he almost ran from the room, sealing his fate.

Nineteen

THE NEXT MORNING Katherine stood staring out the dormitory window in the direction of the test site. She wanted to run to Cody and never look back. She knew she should probably be ashamed of the way she'd acted when they were alone, but she wasn't. She'd taken the moment he offered and tried to cram into it all of her passion for him and for life. Those few minutes would have to last her a long time, and she had wanted to feel all there was to feel, including the pain that followed.

Sarah walked up behind her. "Go to him, Kat."

Katherine shook her head. No matter how much she wanted Cody she would never leave Sarah. Not now, when Sarah needed her so desperately. "No. I promised to meet Dr. Lockhart at the hospital this morning. We need to go over my duties."

"You need to see Cody," Sarah answered.

"I don't know. . . ."

"Don't let Matthew and me stop you." Determination echoed in Sarah's voice. "I feel he's right for you, Kat. You have to give it a chance."

"Do you feel it all the way to your bones?" Kat tried to make light of Sarah's suggestion.

"All the way to my heart," Sarah answered. "If you're hesitating because of me, I won't have it."

Katherine suddenly saw a resoluteness in Sarah that had

never existed before. Somehow Bart's death, the baby, the hardship, had forged a strength within her.

"It's not because of you and the baby." Kat tried to sound convincing. For one instant she saw the reflection of herself in Sarah's gentle blue eyes and wondered who needed whom the most. Perhaps she wasn't the crutch but the crippled. Cody's gift of a year would give her the answer. "It wouldn't be right to go to him," Kat added. "He's not ready for ties."

"Sometimes you have to do the wrong thing for the right reason." Sarah was looking at Kat, but her mind seemed far away. "At least let him know you'll be here when he gets back."

Or the right thing for the wrong reason, Kat wanted to add, but she said for Sarah's benefit, "It wasn't right between us. We're both too young to know what we want. Men like him don't settle down. All he thinks about is flying, and I want roots." She almost added, "To make a home for you and Matthew," but she stopped herself. None of this was Sarah's fault. Somehow their problems had started with her lie. "I need time to think. I feel as if I've been on a merry-go-round moving too fast for months."

"Cody won't wait forever."

"I know," Katherine whispered.

Sarah's expression showed her sympathy for Katherine. "Someday you'll find the kind of love I found with Bart." She looked out the window into the morning sun. "Sometimes I can still feel him, as if he's not dead, as if he's out there somewhere thinking of me just as I am of him. Maybe he's in heaven waiting for me and watching Matthew grow each day."

Katherine fought back a sob as Sarah continued, "I'll never love another. It would cheapen what we had those few months."

Katherine patted her friend's shoulder and quietly left Sarah to her own thoughts.

A few minutes later she forced herself to smile as she walked into Dr. Lockhart's office. He was searching through papers and didn't notice her. His white-blond hair brushed his glasses as he worked. He was still in his early twenties, but because of his poor eyesight, he bent over like an old man to look at everything.

"Morning, Dr. Lockhart," Katherine said.

Daniel jumped at the sudden interruption. He looked up frustrated, then smiled when he noticed her. "Oh, Katherine. Welcome." He stood, spilling his papers and knocking some of them to the floor.

Kat knelt to help him pick up his things. "I'm sorry. I didn't meant to startle you, Dr. Lockhart."

Daniel accepted the papers. "It's not your fault, Nurse McMiller." He looked nervous. "I just get so busy reading I push everything else away, even sounds." He tried to organize the files, but couldn't seem to get his long, thin fingers to cooperate with one another.

Katherine felt she should help him before the poor man had a heart attack. They would never be able to work together if he couldn't even talk to her without blushing and dropping things.

"Do you think we could start over?" Before he had time to answer, Kat stepped back out of the office and knocked on the open door. "May I come in, Doctor?"

Daniel laughed. "Of course." He straightened to his full height and offered his hand. "I'm Daniel. If we're going to work together I'd like to start off as friends."

Kat accepted his hand. "My friends call me Kat."

His light blue eyes danced with pleasure. "I'd like very much to be the friend of the great Katherine. The student nurses talk about you as if you can work miracles. But if you don't mind, I'll call you Katherine. It fits you somehow, and my father said never allow folks to shorten your name; it lessens your value."

Katherine nodded. "Is your dad any relation to Miss Willingham?"

"What?"

Daniel didn't understand her comment and Katherine didn't want to explain. She could tell he was still nervous, for he was still shaking her hand, but at least they were talking. "Forget it." She changed the subject. "I'm afraid my reputation may have been exaggerated."

Daniel shook his head. "You delivered Sarah's baby and then went back to work double shifts in a place where most nurses couldn't handle a single day's work."

"I had a little help with the baby." Katherine pulled her hand back. "And sometimes folks just do what they have to do."

The look in Daniel's eyes told her he was determined to see her as a heroine. "Well, Katherine, shall I show you the hospital?"

"Please." Katherine wasn't willing to tell him that she'd grown up in these wings and already knew every room better than he ever would.

Daniel slowly relaxed as they moved from station to station. His intelligence surprised Katherine. By the end of the morning she wondered if he was one of those doctors who knew every theory but had no healing power in his hands.

As he walked her back to the dorm, he grew silent for several steps before he finally said, "Katherine, I enjoyed this morning. I think we'll work well together."

Kat smiled up at the thin man whose almost white hair was blowing in his face. "I'm sure we will," she answered. She'd almost forgotten how young he was after hearing him talk all morning of medical advances. Something about his light eyes made him seem like an old man inside a young body. "Good day, Daniel."

"Good day, Katherine."

* * *

The weeks passed into months. Katherine found it pleasant to work beside Miss Willingham, Sarah, and even Daniel, but sometimes she'd catch herself looking up to watch the clouds. Cody's letters came regularly from different parts of the country, each one carefully addressed to both her and Sarah, with no personal note to Katherine. As the year ended, Katherine's longing for Cody remained an unhealed wound in her heart that bled only in the darkness when she was alone, making her hate the absence of light even more than she had as a child.

Winter passed slowly, draped in dreary rainy days. Katherine walked down the icy pathway toward the hospital one morning thinking of the last time she'd held Cody. He glided so easily through her dreams that sometimes it took her hours after waking to push his memory into the corners of her mind.

"Morning." Sarah hurried up from behind her. "You're out early."

Katherine tried to pull herself back to the real world. "I thought I'd have breakfast with Daniel before class."

Sarah nodded, glad Kat showed some interest in a man, even if it was Dr. Lockhart. Not that he was so bad, Sarah reminded herself. He was a kind man, but his love for life was folded inside the covers of his books. He seldom talked to anyone except Kat.

"I had breakfast with Matthew. In fact I'm wearing some of it." She pointed to an oatmeal stain on her apron.

"How is our darling little Matthew this morning?" Kat tried to allow Sarah her private time with Matthew in the mornings.

"When I left, Miss Willingham was talking to him about which college he planned to attend."

"Has he decided?" Kat tried to sound serious.

"Not yet." Sarah held the back door of the hospital open

for Kat. "I think he's more interested in trying to cut his first tooth on the arm of her rocker."

"I'm sure he'll decide as soon as he has time." Kat laughed. "Between Miss Willingham and Dr. Farris, he'll be enrolled in a good school by the time he learns to walk." In the past year Matthew Rome had been more work than Kat had ever dreamed one little baby could be. He'd also been more joy. Sarah's love for him was limitless, but she hadn't abandoned her calling as a nurse. Most days she put in as many hours teaching and nursing at the hospital as Kat did, then spent the rest of her time with her son.

"See you at lunch." Sarah waved as she hurried down the hallway.

Kat stepped into Daniel's office. Her life had begun to flow into an endless river of sameness. She even knew what Daniel would say when he saw her. Lately she'd sometimes found herself having fun by disrupting his predictable life.

"Morning." She waited until she was in front of his desk to speak, knowing it would startle him.

Daniel jerked slightly, but didn't drop anything this time as he looked up at her. "Katherine. I'm glad you're early. Wait till I tell you about this article I'm reading."

Katherine tried to act interested. "Can we read over breakfast?"

Daniel stood up and gathered his papers. "Of course."

Katherine didn't step back as he moved passed her. She knew she made him nervous when he had to be so close. She could almost see his hair thinning. But she couldn't help herself; mischief just grew inside her sometimes like weeds in a garden, without purpose or intent.

"Katherine?" Daniel stopped before he opened the door.

"Yes," she answered, looking directly into his ice-blue eyes.

As always he lost his nerve when she looked directly at him. "Nothing," he finally said as he pulled the door open.

Kat wanted to scream. He'd been playing this game for

weeks now. Ask me, Daniel! Whatever it is, ask me. How are you ever going to find a wife if you can't even talk to a friend?

But aloud she said, "Want to come to dinner with Sarah and me tonight?"

Daniel nodded so fast she knew she'd guessed what his unasked question had been.

As they began their day, an idea formed inside Kat's mind. Maybe Daniel wasn't dashing or even all that good-looking, but he was stable. What better man to step in as a father for Matthew than a doctor right here in town?

Kat's daydream of Daniel as Sarah's future husband was short-lived. For though he talked with Sarah all evening, his gaze never left Katherine.

As the days passed, Kat tried everything to get the two together, but they were like two rain-soaked sticks. No matter how hard she rubbed them together, no sparks flew. Friday dinners became a habit with the three of them. Daniel talked of medicine, Sarah played with Matthew, and Katherine tried not to yawn.

Finally one Friday afternoon Daniel spoke first. "Would you like to go for a drive before dinner?"

Katherine stared at him for a moment, not believing that after all this time he'd asked a question of her. She smiled at him, loving his sudden bravery.

"Then it's a yes?" Daniel said when he saw her expression.

"Sounds nice," she said as she grabbed her coat. "As long as we're back by six so I can help Sarah with dinner."

As they drove outside the city, Daniel's words began to sound rehearsed. "Katherine, we work well together, don't you think?"

"Yes," Kat answered, watching the sky and wishing it would snow.

"In all the months we've been together I can't remember

one time when you were unpleasant or harsh, and you share my interests."

Katherine wasn't fully listening. She'd learned months ago that most of what Daniel said required only a small amount of attention. He liked to reason out loud, and as long as Kat nodded her head now and then, he seemed happy.

Daniel pulled the car to the side of the road and faced her. "Katherine, I want to ask you something, and I hope you won't take offense."

Kat couldn't imagine him saying anything less than proper.

"You can stop me at any time and we'll forget I even brought the subject up."

"Ask," Kat almost shouted. For once he'd captured her full attention.

"I want you to know first that you don't have to answer right now. I'm willing to wait."

"Ask."

Daniel straightened. "Katherine, would you consider becoming engaged?"

Kat knew her mouth was open, but she couldn't seem to remember how to close it. "Are you asking me to marry you, Daniel?"

"Well, not exactly." His hands gripped and released the steering wheel several times. "Actually, I'm asking you to get engaged. I thought we'd talk about marriage in a year or two."

Katherine turned to stare out the window without saying a word. She knew she could do a lot worse than marry Daniel Lockhart. He'd been offered a job teaching in a local medical school. She'd have a nice life and always be close to Sarah and Matthew. Even if Cody came back, he might not be ready to settle down. He'd promised to return in a year and the date had passed. Katherine couldn't decide whether to laugh or cry. She'd just been offered everything she thought she wanted—by the wrong man. Or was he? Had she really given him a chance?

Slowly she turned to Daniel. "No one has ever asked me to get engaged. Shouldn't you kiss me first?"

"Of course," Daniel said. Then he leaned over and pressed his lips against hers as if he were performing a duty.

Again Katherine wanted to scream. Where was the passion? Where was the love? She closed her eyes. Maybe that was her problem. She'd had only the passion and never the day-to-day reality. Cody's kind of love was wild and free. If she tried to tie him down, his love might die.

When she looked at Daniel, Kat saw the kindness in his eyes. He would never leave her. He'd never promise her rainbows and stars. His feet were planted solidly on the ground. He didn't even like traveling to out-of-town medical conferences.

"You said I could have some time to think about it. Did you mean it?"

Daniel smiled with satisfaction. "Of course. I think that would be practical." He pulled the car back onto the highway. "We'll talk of it again when you're ready."

Katherine didn't say another word all the way home. When he walked her to the dorm, she raised her face to him expecting a kiss, but he wasn't so daring in front of the dorm.

"I think I'd best call it a night, Katherine," he said. "I've several things to read before tomorrow."

"But what about dinner?"

"Please give my apologies to Sarah."

Katherine didn't try to argue. After their drive she needed time away from Daniel to think. Without a word she nodded her acceptance of his cancellation.

"Good night, Katherine," he said. "See you at breakfast."

"Good night," she answered, still confused by his tentative proposal.

* * *

As spring drifted into summer, the headlines spoke of the danger of war in Europe, but Katherine's life had become a treadmill of predictability. Daniel had kept his promise: He never again mentioned his suggestion of that winter night, and Katherine thought that he had forgotten all about it. She taught classes in the mornings, kept Matthew in the afternoons, and worked the late shift at the hospital most nights. She fought the urge to run as fast and as far away from her life as she could, but she knew she'd designed and built her own prison. Expenses for the baby were high, but she saved all she could. By midsummer she had enough to make the first payment to Cody and found her opportunity in the paper.

Occasionally Katherine read Daniel the news of Cody's triumphs, knowing he cared little.

No longer a junior member of the flying team, Cody had become a star in his own right. His stunts across the country had made him a dashing hero in many a young boy's eyes. While flying he'd raced around a track against some of France's top drivers. And finally he was coming to Dayton to fly a sunset race with pilots from around the world at the end of a week-long air show and fair.

Each time she read about Cody, she had but one plan: to see him again. Katherine wouldn't allow herself to think of anything beyond giving him the money she owed him. Yet she couldn't help remembering the smell of excitement that always surrounded him. She could almost taste the danger and fear clinging to his skin. He was more like her than anyone she'd ever met. She might be a nurse at a small hospital, but in her heart she flew every time Cody took to the air.

"I suppose you plan to attend the air show," Daniel said, breaking into her thoughts at breakfast.

"Yes." Katherine tried to hide her excitement about

going. Daniel had never said a word against Cody, but she knew he thought that flying was a suicidal occupation.

"If we were officially engaged it wouldn't be proper."

Kat straightened. "But we're not."

"I've tried to be patient, but in two weeks I'll start teaching at the medical school. I would like an answer." He tried to keep his voice from shaking.

"I'll give you my answer on Sunday," Kat answered. She wanted to go to the air show and see Cody one last time. She wanted to see if the embers she carried for Cody still burned in her heart or, after all this time, her love for him had grown cold.

Several student nurses walked along with Katherine toward the air show the following evening, but she was not quite part of their group. Her thoughts were still filled with what to do about Daniel. She felt comfortable and safe with him, but she never felt the need to touch him as she hungered to touch Cody. Daniel would give her everything she'd dreamed of since she was a child. Everything but adventure and passion.

A sob caught in her throat when she realized how much like Miss Willingham she'd become over the past year. Her carriage was straight and tall, her hair carefully molded to her head. Even though only a few years separated her from students, she was no longer part of them. Somehow, while she'd been too busy to notice, the young girl had disappeared, leaving a woman in her place.

Unsmiling, Katherine entered the fairgrounds where the airshow was being held. Banners of all colors gave the spectators direction. A steam calliope had been placed beside a ticket booth adding to the carnival atmosphere. Several vendors hawked their wares, everything from popcorn to fresh cider as the last warmth of summer died in the air. Adults congregated in small groups while children ran among them.

Katherine and the students found a place by the border of banners roping off the runway, close to a stage that had been built to announce the winner of the race. The nurses squealed in unison as pilots strode out of a row of low buildings that had been set up as living quarters during the week's stay. As varied in size and appearance as their planes, all of the men were dashing, each in his own way. Katherine stood apart from the others watching for only one man to step into the arena he seemed to love so dearly.

The sun hung low against mountain-high clouds when she first saw him coming toward her. His long, lean body looked more powerful than she remembered, and sunlight danced in his hair. He walked with a sure stride of a veteran warrior, his scarf snow white against the dark tan of his face, his boots polished as always.

With only a quick wave at the crowd, Cody jumped into his plane and raised his thumb to signal to the ground crew that he was ready whenever the field was clear. Katherine's heart pounded. She could almost hear Cody saying, "Come on, Katherine. Join me. Let's fly under the rainbow and touch the stars."

Suddenly the deafening sound of the engines roared in her ears, and the taste of excitement rose in her throat. As Cody aimed for the clouds she could feel the wind in her face and the frost of the air above the earth.

The crowd watched the planes dance in the air like flying square dancers listening to the words of an unheard caller. But Katherine didn't see the others; her gaze never left Cody's plane. As he flew, all the months of feeling alone crumbled around her. The problems of her day-to-day life melted like a wax shell, and she felt suddenly light and free.

Each time he dived and soared, she was with him in spirit. Somehow their souls were bound together, and no separation could cut the feelings free. She closed her eyes and tried to imagine what he saw as he circled the field. Did he still thrill to the beauty or had another year callused his vision until the sight was only ordinary?

Darkness settled around the crowd. Ground crewmen lit barrel torches to help the pilots land. People held their breath as plane after plane appeared out of the night sky. Each man drew a cheer as he leaped from his flying machine and walked to the platform to receive his award.

Moments later she watched as Cody jumped to the ground. He walked toward the crowd waving, as if he saw no individuals, but only a mob he'd seen many times before in many cities.

When he stepped into the light, she noticed the windburn on his face and saw in his eyes the same wild excitement she'd seen that first morning so long ago. He still felt the magic when he flew; she knew it.

But Cody wasn't thinking of the magic of flight or of the noise of the crowd. Ever since he landed in Dayton only Katherine had been on his mind. He'd stormed across the country trying to forget what a fool he'd made of himself with her by almost begging her to love him.

At first he'd spent most of his time drinking and romancing any woman who offered her charms, but finally he'd realized he was only digging deeper the hole she'd left in his heart. So he had come back to Dayton determined not to fall at her feet. He knew she wanted a commitment from the man she fell in love with. He also knew that even if he could offer her a promise of forever, she probably wanted no such gift from him after all this time.

"Cody." She whispered his name as he passed through the mob he'd long ago given up seeing as individuals.

Like a man awakening from a dream, he turned toward her.

Over the dancing flames of the torches, she saw him. He took a step toward her and she couldn't break his stare, even with the squeals of the student nurses at her side.

Cody walked to the ropes that separated the spectators

from the field. Without a word he reached for her hand and pulled her closer. His eyes were filled with longing, yet no smile of welcome touched his lips.

"Katherine," he said as the students giggled, "I can't believe you're here."

She smiled up into his handsome face. "How have you been, Cody?" There were a million things she wanted to say to him, but this was not the time or the place.

"Fine." His stare made his words a lie. "How are Sarah and Matthew?"

"They're both fine." Katherine felt as if they were speaking some nonsense language instead of saying what was on their minds. "He's walking now."

"I hope to stop by and see him." Cody pulled her gently against the ropes so that their bodies were almost touching. The crowd seemed like a wave threatening to wash her away from him.

He lightly brushed her cheek with a kiss and whispered, "Meet me behind the stands." She could not mistake the promise in his eyes.

"I-I . . ." she stammered, afraid to allow him to know how much she needed him. People suddenly surrounded them, shoving them apart.

In the flickering light of the torches she watched pain shoot through his eyes, as though he'd broken a promise to himself by asking.

Then he was gone, leaving her with the young nurses and their questions. Katherine tried to explain to the students that Cody was only an old friend as they wandered toward the carnival, but none of the girls believed her explanation and all of them looked at her in a new and even more admiring light. She had mystery about her because she knew a pilot.

As soon as she could slip away from the student nurses Katherine hurried to the living quarters to the left of the field. She'd endured enough of crowds for one day. With sudden determination, she made a plan. She would find Cody's quarters and leave the letter she'd written him, then she'd rejoin the student nurses. The money had to be paid back before anything could grow between them.

The buildings were laid out in rows with one light at the end of each row. Katherine walked from one little house to the other, wondering how she would know which one was Cody's. They all looked the same except for the numbers over the doors.

All of the doors were ajar like those of the rooms in a home; there was no need for privacy. As she walked down the row, she glanced inside a few houses. Most were untidy, with piles of clothes lying everywhere and muddy boots standing outside the door. Each had a bed and a small table with only one chair. Several smelled of stale cigar smoke or whiskey. Others were so plain it was apparent they were rarely used.

Her gaze caught one pair of dress boots outside a door that were not muddy and suddenly, she knew which room was Cody's. Katherine hurried up the steps and opened the unlocked door. Just like his boardinghouse room, this place was spotless. His bed was made with tight military corners; and, though the table was covered with maps, they looked as if they'd been organized. His clothes were lined up in the closet as if in formation.

As she stepped into the room, she wondered at Cody's unusual tidiness. His neat, orderly habits seemed inconsistent with his wild, free way of life.

Hesitantly she lifted the pillow and placed the letter beneath it. She wished she could have held him, but there had been no time to explain when they'd touched earlier in public.

Somehow the picture of her life, which had once been so clear, now seemed smeared with the moisture of her own tears.

She'd thought she sacrificed for Sarah, but Sarah was strong enough to stand alone and take care of Matthew. By the time Kat realized that fact, Cody had been gone a month. And now, now it was too late to pick up the pieces again. Her mind told her she'd be better off with Daniel. They worked well together. But in her heart she could see only Cody's mahogany-brown eyes looking at her with life and fire.

Lightly brushing the pillow with her fingers, she wondered if he even cared. She must be just one of many young women he'd known in towns all across the country.

The door creaked slightly and Katherine whirled around, knowing she was trapped. For the first time since she'd thought of this plan, she realized how far from the others she'd gone. If a drifter had followed her into the camp, she'd be easy prey for a robbery, or worse.

Cody's tall frame blocked the doorway. He took a step forward and struck a match to light a lantern. He studied her as though trying to decide if she was real or a dream.

"I only . . ." Katherine turned and reached for the letter. She had to explain quickly why she'd come to his room before he got the wrong idea. Her fingers absently brushed the pillow as if to remove all traces of her presence.

But Cody stepped behind her before she could turn around. He pulled her back against his chest and encircled her with strong arms. She felt his long intake of breath as he drank in the smell of her hair.

"I wanted to give . . ." She couldn't remember the words as his mouth brushed the side of her throat, planting kisses along her neck. "I . . ."

His lips warmed her blood as light kisses brushed her skin. She was afraid to move, afraid he might continue, terrified he might stop.

"Hold me." She voiced her one thought, her one need. "Hold me, Cody," she cried as she turned in his embrace.

He jerked her cape off in haste as his mouth reached her

lips. A sigh escaped her as she parted her lips to welcome him home. One arm held her to him while his free hand dug the pins from her hair, which seemed to be bound as tightly as her heart. A long-unsatisfied hunger drove his actions, as though he, too, had to make a memory come to life.

He held her close against him, needing to feel her in his arms.

"Don't let go," she pleaded. "Please don't let go."

Cody crushed her against his heart as her words melted the restraint he'd built up to prepare himself for her rejection.

"I won't let go," he whispered as he kissed her tears. "I've never wanted to let you go. I'd like to hold you all night."

He tilted her head with his hands and lowered his mouth over hers, drinking deep of the taste of her.

Katherine felt herself flying again, and she didn't want to touch the ground. Her mind kept telling her to stop, but her body begged for his touch. Her cheeks grew warm and her mouth felt dry from excitement, but she couldn't pull away from the reality of her dream.

She returned his kiss with a passion that made him moan with pleasure.

His hands touched her waist and slowly drove her mad because they didn't complete the journey to her breasts. His mouth pulled all the longing and loneliness from her with a passion of need that left her light-headed.

Finally, she pulled an inch away. "I didn't plan . . ." She didn't want him to think she'd planned to meet him here like this. And kissing him had only been a part of her dreams.

"Hush," he whispered against her mouth. His kiss was not the young kiss of an excited boy, but the demanding kiss of a man. The taste and smell of him were the same as always, but the power within him was now intoxicating.

"Let me hold you for a while first before we let words get in our way."

The time apart had changed them, hardened them to life and its shortcomings. But now neither could deny the longings exploding within them.

The memory of the night they'd kissed in the snowstorm drifted through Katherine's mind. She'd relived it so many times she was unsure which parts were real and which were dreams. Had his mouth really tasted so wonderful? Had she really been so wild?

Now she knew the answers to her questions. His mouth tasted of adventure, and the air around him was charged with a frenzy of freedom.

"Kiss me back," he murmured against her ear. "Kiss me the way you did that winter night when the world stood still and we stole time."

Katherine wanted to cry out in pleasure. *He remembered.* It had been special to him as well. Suddenly she could no longer control her need to feel him against her. She pushed her fingers through his windblown hair and pulled his lips to her, demanding as much as she gave.

His fingers pulled at the material hiding her flesh from his touch. "I've missed you so much," he whispered against her lips. "Dear God, Kat, I think I started missing you the day I met you."

Suddenly they laughed at the pure joy of being alive and together. He lifted her off the floor and held her against him, planting hungry kisses along her neck, and chuckled when she pulled his mouth back to her waiting lips.

His actions fed energy to her dying spirit, and she felt herself come alive once more. She shoved his shirt open so she could feel his smooth, hard chest beneath her fingers. A light dusting of sandy hair covered the center of his chest and trailed downward. Katherine boldly ran her fingers over his skin, loving the tight strength just beneath her touch. She placed her palm over his heart and closed her eyes, trying to forever match its pounding in her own heart.

A hundred things needed to be said between them, but all that seemed important was their nearness.

When finally he took the time to breathe, he said, "I love you. I think I've always loved you."

She moved closer, pressing her body against his. She'd been numb for so long she welcomed all the feelings back into her heart. His fingers were strong around her waist, his breath warm against her cheek, his mouth hungry along her neck.

"Let me love you?" Cody slid his hands beneath her jacket and over the silk of her blouse, and he brushed passion against her as his hand covered her breast. "I've dreamed of you so many times, I think I must be dreaming now."

He boldly pulled the blouse away so that he could touch her.

"No, we can't do this," she said, no longer able to think clearly. She hadn't even talked with him, just fallen into his arms.

He lowered his hands to her hips and tried once more. "I have to catch a train to the East Coast before dawn and from there a boat overseas for a short tour. Come away with me." He began to unbutton her skirt. "I'll show you Europe." His words warmed her like liquid fire as he moved to the next button. "Come away with me, Kat, before I go mad wanting you."

"I can't," she whispered as she touched his hair. "I'm needed at the hospital. Stay with me. Don't leave again so soon."

"I've signed a contract, and the news releases have gone out. With all of the trouble in Europe, this may be the last tour. Come with me. We'll be back in three months."

Kat's mind was whirling. "I can't, but I'll wait for you."

"Three months?" Cody whispered into her hair. His

fingers twisted into a fist and he pulled her head back, exposing her neck. His free hand moved up from her waist and captured her breast. As his grip tightened, his mouth covered hers in a kiss that demanded all.

"Three months or three years," Kat answered when he released her lips. There could be no man in her life without passion, and there was no passion without Cody. She tried to breathe as his mouth touched her throat and his hands shoved her clothes to the floor, telling her forever how clearly she belonged to him.

"You'll wait." He whispered against her skin as his fingers lightly circled her flesh. "While you're waiting, remember tonight."

Kat could feel fire all the way to her toes. She barely had the strength to stand as he moved his hands over her.

"Tell me again to hold you," he demanded in a voice low with passion. Her skin was softer then he'd remembered even in his dreams. He slid his fingers low over her hips and pulled her against him.

Suddenly Kat thought of Daniel's cold kiss and winter-blue eyes. "Hold me, Cody. Please hold me."

Her plea melted his heart. He lifted her in his arms. "Remember once I told you loving was something you took slow, like liquor. Well, tonight I'm going to give you something to remember for the next few months." He kicked the door closed with his foot. "But we're not going all the way on the journey. I won't leave you with a child. I'll only leave you with memories."

He pushed her gently until the back of her legs touched his bed. "I'm going to make you want me so desperately that you'll never pull away from me again."

He sat on the bed and encircled her with his arms. His eyes were full of desire as he admired her body. Slowly, tenderly, he kissed the flesh between her breasts, gently brushing his cheeks against the swell of each mound.

"Cody, I . . ." Kat began.

He silenced her by leaning backward and pulling her atop him. "No more talk," he whispered against her lips. He rolled over her, warming the length of her body with his own.

Kat stretched beneath him, loving the weight of his body over hers. "I love you," she answered as she pulled him closer.

His hands were magic along her body. Making love to her with his touch. He brought her pleasure with each kiss and promised her more with each caress. Tonight he would take her on a flight of passion, molding her feelings into dreams and shaping her need into love. With his touch the world suddenly had color and her life had reason.

Twenty

KATHERINE SAT DOWN at the foot of Sarah's bed. "Cody's gone. Another three-month tour. I couldn't hold him even when I wanted him to stay."

"Kat, you talked to him! That was a start." Sarah pulled her robe on and looked out at the gray predawn light. "Come on, I'll make coffee."

"I feel as if I'm fighting myself half the time and him the other half." Kat followed Sarah into the little kitchen. "He wanted me to pack and leave with him tonight."

"Why didn't you?" Sarah asked. "If you stayed because of me, I'll borrow one of the doctors' cars and drive you to the train station myself."

Kat laughed, but her tears sparkled in her eyes. "You can't drive."

Sarah looked as though she'd been insulted. "I'd learn by the time I hit the station."

"*Hit* the station would probably be the right word," Kat added. "But no, I'm not staying just because of you. Though I do have responsibilities here I just can't walk out on." She helped with the coffee as she continued, "I'm needed here. I'm not sure Cody will ever need me. Oh, he wants me, but I need him to need me."

Sarah understood that. She had always let Kat be the strong one because Kat needed to be. "He'll be back in three months. Wait until you see how much he misses you.

And you might be surprised at how much he may need you with him.''

"Anyway," Kat added, "I couldn't just run off with Cody without telling Daniel good-bye. I owe him that.''

"He's a good man." Sarah nodded her agreement. "We'll miss him around the hospital when he leaves in a couple of weeks. Once he got over being sick at the sight of blood, he became a promising doctor.''

Kat smiled through her tears. "You wouldn't consider marrying him?''

"No!" Sarah said quickly. "I may want a quiet life, but not a dead-boring one. To be honest, I've been waiting for months for you to part ways with the man so I wouldn't have to have dinner with him every Friday night.''

Suddenly Kat's tears turned to laughter as she learned Sarah's real feelings about Daniel.

"We'll wait for Cody," Sarah announced, leaving no room for argument.

"And I'll tell Daniel good-bye at breakfast." Kat raised her hand in promise. "Then I'll start counting off the days until Cody will be back.''

But three months stretched into four and four into eight. Katherine spent another winter alone without Cody. As spring came to Dayton his letters were few, but those few were filled with news of the storm building in Europe. He never spoke of the night they held each other, but Katherine knew he remembered. Sometimes she'd lie in her bed at night and try to cross half a world and send him her thoughts . . . her love.

As his three-month tour stretched to more than a year, Cody's prediction came true. By late summer war spread like a huge prairie fire across Europe, with Cody in the center. He wrote about how it began, with parades and promises that the soldiers would be home before the leaves began to fall. As the months passed, everyone in the world realized this was not to be a short war but a bloody conflict in which men would die facing machines.

Katherine and Sarah watched the mail each day for word from Cody. His letters were now filled with sorrow. He'd remained in France, teaching Frenchmen to fly since, as an American, he couldn't fight beside them. He told of how the French marched proudly into battle with their bright blue and red uniforms, only to be splendid targets for the German machine gunners. He reported seeing rivers flowing red with the blood of German troops who had been cut down while trying to cross.

Cody described the planes the French had called into service. They were of every shape and size, piloted by young men who'd learned to fly in an afternoon. Through each letter he kept reminding Kat not to worry. Planes were used only for observation and he would rather be in the air than near the fighting on the ground.

Katherine read his letters over and over, always fearing each one would be his last. Finally a short note came just after Christmas almost eighteen months after he'd left.

He wrote: "They've started shooting at us in the air. One of the pilots reported a German Taube flew over him and dropped a brick. Another was fired on with a rifle. The men are going up armed now. I don't know how long I can stay out of the fight."

Each night Katherine lay awake staring at the light burning in her room and waiting for the next letter. She and Sarah, along with Miss Willingham, searched the papers for news of the war and of the pilots' role. The young men who took to the air were rapidly becoming the Knights of the Sky in a war that was short on heroes. Foot soldiers who marched by the thousands to their death received only short reports in the paper, but pilots' escapades were written up in detail, drawing Americans into the spirit of war despite President Wilson's determination to keep America neutral.

By the time Cody's next letter arrived, the war in the

trenches was in full swing. Two parallel scars had been cut across Europe with bodies piled up in the barren land between. The machine gun had made it impossible to fight with charges and advancements, so mighty warriors became nothing more than targets within their opponents' sights. With each day of battle on the ground there were no heroes, only survivors.

As she opened the next envelope, Katherine couldn't keep her hands from shaking. "They've begun to kill one another in the skies," the letter began. "France figured out how to mount a machine gun synchronized to fire bullets between the whirling blades of the propeller. The boys I'm training are dying faster than I can get them ready for the air. I've decided to join the Foreign Legion and fly for France. Something's got to stop the slaughter before every young man in Europe is dead. I only wish I knew what."

All three women began to cry as Katherine continued, "I know my chances of living through this as a pilot aren't good, but I've got to help."

Katherine passed the single page to Miss Willingham, who finished it despite tears running in a steady stream down her face.

Cody told of men who were cut down by guns with no one left in their squadron to pull them back to the trenches. Often they bled to death waiting for help or cried out only a few feet away from safety. Sometimes the blood made the mud in the trenches red for hours. With the rain and the filth, the mud never dried in the walkways along the trenches. Those who weren't being shot were ill from poor food and wet clothes.

When Miss Willingham finished the letter, she looked up at Sarah who watched little Matthew playing on a blanket at their feet. "I want to go," she said with the determination of an old warrior. "I've spent my life trying to stop suffering. The need for nurses in that awful place pulls at me, and I'm not too old to help."

Sarah was too kind to comment on Miss Willingham's age. She simply said, "You're needed so desperately here. I also feel the need to go. If Matthew were old enough to be in school, I'd be tempted to answer the Red Cross's call for nurses."

Both women looked toward Katherine.

Katherine tried to shake the thought from her head. She could feel her direction being changed as surely as if Miss Willingham and Sarah had put both their oars on the same side to alter her course. "I can't leave you and Matthew. I have to help you take care of him." Her words were hollow, for her thoughts were only of Cody. If she went to Europe somehow she'd find him. If he wouldn't come back to her, she'd go to him.

The thought of seeing all that dying frightened her at the same time the lure of the adventure called her. Nursing had never really seemed exciting enough for her spirit, but working in a field hospital sounded like a challenge. But she would never leave Sarah.

"Nonsense." Miss Willingham stood up and laced her hands together at her waist as she always did before starting a lecture. "Sarah and I are perfectly able to take care of one little boy. Nurses are desperately needed in Europe, and you must answer that need. I'd go myself if they'd have me. Our calling is to relieve suffering."

Once more Katherine tried to remember ever having answered a calling. She'd become a nurse because it was Sarah's dream. Now it looked as if they planned to put her on the next boat to France because it was Miss Willingham's dream. She was afraid to admit, even to herself, that it was also her dream.

As Katherine listened to Sarah's arguments she wondered briefly why the strong were so often manipulated by the meek. She wouldn't have dreamed of trying to talk Sarah into such a thing, but Sarah would stand fast next to Miss Willingham, a firing squad of two against all her objections.

"I . . ." Katherine could think of no words that didn't make her sound like a coward. How could she fight both her *calling* and her heart?

In less time than she thought possible, she found herself on the train to New York for training with the Red Cross. The blood was pounding in her head with uncertainty, and her white gloves were already dirty from being twisted and pulled on in her lap.

As she sat quietly among the other travelers, Katherine closed her eyes and thought of Cody. What if he were dying in the rain-soaked trenches? What if his eyes closed forever, all because she didn't come to help? She had to go. She had to do the best she could. He would probably be far too busy flying to even know she was in the country, but somehow knowing he'd be near made her warm inside.

Hours later a woman in a Red Cross uniform met her at the station. New York should have fascinated Katherine, but the hours on the train had shaken out all response. All she could think about was stretching out in a bed.

The training school reminded her of the state hospital. Day and night it was drab and cold. The outside doors were kept locked most of the time, and by the third day Katherine began to wonder if the locks were meant to keep the public out or the trainees in.

The Red Cross philosophy was pounded into them eighteen hours a day. Though they operated under military-style discipline, the workers saw themselves as neutral, ready to aid the injured from all warring nations. The Red Cross provided temporary shelter, medical and nursing care, and even sanitary engineering if it was needed.

Katherine handled all the nursing procedures with practiced efficiency, but she had difficulty making herself believe she could dig privy lines. Strangely, the memory of Miss Willingham's face kept her going when the training seemed endless. Katherine would simply picture the dean working beside her, doing chore for chore while she inspected everyone's hands for cleanliness.

Every night, no matter how exhausted she felt, Katherine wrote a short note to Sarah and Miss Willingham. Sometimes she'd include something she'd learned about field nursing, knowing the information would be incorporated into next year's curriculum at the Willingham School.

The time passed quickly, and Katherine was walking up the gangplank almost before she realized she was about to leave her homeland. All the other nurses danced with excitement. A few hugged their loved ones as they said good-bye or talked with friends they'd made in school. But Katherine walked alone to the ship's railing and watched all the people move like ants on the pier below. Because of her training and experience, she'd been appointed the leader of the troop of women. As in the nursing school, the position held her apart from the others.

Watching the land recede as the ship left the harbor, she felt suddenly very alone. "Sarah," she whispered as she looked down at the scar along her palm, "stay with me in spirit." She closed her empty fist, almost feeling Sarah's hand inside hers. "Forever and ever," Katherine whispered her oath. "Forever and ever, no matter what."

Summer of 1915 was half gone when Kathcrinc crossed the English Channel and landed near Abbeville. Trucks met the nurses and hauled them southeast to Amiens on the Somme River.

The land was beautiful, with wonderful little high-pitched houses scattered over the countryside, but the rainy day made the cold seep all the way to Katherine's bones. She was told as she bounced along the rutted road that the armies on the western front had dug in along a four-hundred-mile line from the North Sea to the Swiss border.

Closing her eyes, Katherine tried to picture how all those miles of trenches must look. Within an hour she no longer had to imagine. She stood in horror with the others and took her first view of the conflict people were already starting to call "the great war."

A network of trenches with narrow passages just taller than a man stretched miles into the distance. Huts of sorts were carved out of the dirt walls with boards placed across the top to serve as roofs. Barbed wire marked the other border of the trenches, destroying any beauty that might have existed before them. Fog settled just behind the wire, hiding the other side and the enemy. Every now and then Katherine heard the rapid fire of a machine gun somewhere beyond the wire. It seemed unreal, like a ghost firing on unseen targets as if hoping to hit something by luck through the fog.

The constant shooting made Katherine's nerves tighten. She took a deep breath and forced herself to relax, only to have another burst of fire shatter any calm she'd mustered. Don't think about the firing, she told herself. Think about the job you've got to do. Think about finding Cody.

As the days passed, the firing became almost as routine as the endless rain. The Red Cross had set up a field station far enough from the front to be safe but still within hearing distance of the war. Two days passed before she had time to unpack her bags. The work was endless. The small tent hospital was organized and ran like a well-oiled machine. Only the human element sometimes faltered.

Katherine took pride in excellence. By the end of her first week she'd proven herself to the head doctor, who could have been a twin of Dr. Farris back at the state hospital. He regarded the world with the same lifeless stare.

On the morning that marked the end of her first week he called her into his office. "Nurse McMiller," he began as he lifted a stack of letters on his desk, "are you aware that almost half the women have already asked to return home?"

Katherine nodded. Sometimes she thought the only reason she didn't request a transfer was because she'd been too tired to write the necessary letter. She'd come all this way and hadn't even had time to look for Cody.

The doctor slapped the letters down. "How can we win against death without an army?"

She'd been there long enough to understand his desperation, but he needed more than understanding. "Those of us who are left will have to fight harder." Suddenly Miss Willingham and Sarah were at her side. "It's our duty to help where we can."

Dr. Wells smiled at her with an ounce of respect blended into his pound of doubt. "Will you take over as the head nurse, Katherine? I need a fighter at the top because this threatens to be a long war."

She fought the urge to cry out she couldn't, she'd never heard the calling, but his sad eyes penetrated into her sense of duty. "I came to France to find someone I love, Doctor." She had to be honest. "But I'll stay to help."

"Do you know where this young man is?" The doctor didn't have to ask if it was a man.

"I don't even know." Katherine realized how foolishly she'd been to think she could find Cody so easily. Even if he'd told her his location, his letters always took months to arrive, and he would have moved on by the time she could get to him.

"You'll wait until he finds you?"

"Yes." Katherine had written him several letters. Surely it wouldn't take much longer.

"And you'll be head nurse in the meantime?"

"I will," Katherine answered and returned to her duties before she had time to change her mind.

That night when she wrote a note to Sarah and Miss Willingham, she described every detail of her nursing assignment, told of the long line of men trooping through the mud bearing heavy-laden stretchers. They looked like death's porters bringing body after body to the hospital door. As she put down each detail, she knew the two women would write back with suggestions.

"Thank you—both of you—for urging me to come to Europe," Katherine wrote. "I see now that waiting wasn't the answer. I'm glad I'm here near Cody even if he doesn't know it or can't get to me. Someday I'll find him."

During Katherine's third week the fighting increased, and casualties tripled. The wounded were carried to the tent door in an almost endless procession. Dr. Wells finally gave up trying to run back and forth and waited just inside out of the rain. He'd look at the body for a few minutes, then raise his finger. If he pointed left, the man was assigned a bed. If he pointed right, the body would be taken farther down the road and covered until a truck could take the soldier home.

Katherine watched him at the entrance for so many hours that she finally saw him as Saint Peter at the gate of heaven, only in this place of endless damp, she was unsure if hell was to the right or to the left.

So many had became faceless bodies covered with mud and blood. Once, after three days without sleep, she thought she saw Cody on a stretcher Dr. Wells had assigned to the right. A sob ripped through her before she could stop it. Through tears of fear and exhaustion she ran outside and grabbed the arm of one of the soldiers who carried the stretcher. She stared at the dead soldier for several moments before she realized it wasn't Cody.

Dr. Wells noticed her behavior and ordered her to bed for a few hours in a voice that was both fatherly and professional.

Walking back to her little half-tent, half-office Katherine resolved to become as ruthless in her fight to save the men as the machine guns were at shooting them. She would become a machine, emotionless, tireless. Miss Willingham's voice lectured inside her mind, telling her what she must do. Calling or no calling, there was a job to be done and no one except Katherine to do it.

When she reached her tent, she took the time to do paperwork until her eyes would no longer focus, then she collapsed in her bed without even undressing. As slumber began to relax her, she looked out into the darkness. In her mind she saw Sarah's hand reaching across the ocean and gripping her hand as she had done when they were children.

"It's all right," Sarah whispered in Katherine's mind. "Someday we'll live in a house with lots of windows, and we'll leave the lights on all night long."

Katherine smiled and allowed sleep to possess her, blocking out the sounds of war rumbling in the background.

Katherine's only peace in a world gone mad was her dreams. They were filled with Cody. Even if he never returned out of the clouds to her, he would always have a place in her heart. His arms would protect her in sleep even if they were not there to do so any other time. Somehow she felt closer to him here at the front. They were fighting against the same enemy. He was close: she knew it.

Twenty-one

1915

For almost a month Cody Masters had been grounded west of Verdun, France. He'd paced the camp's perimeter until he knew every inch of the place. He'd complained to everyone who would listen and still couldn't get his men airborne.

Several of the pilots fighting for France were American, though the French didn't like to take anyone without military experience into the Foreign Legion. Cody had already met one man who'd listed five years with the Salvation Army as his armed service background. There was talk of a new all-American flying squadron by April.

The only snag in the plan lay in the waiting. And waiting seemed to be what they'd done all year. Pilots were never long on patience. Asking them to all sit around together was like throwing ammo into a fire. They were a mixture of dreamers and drifters, each of whom had joined for a unique reason. For hours they played cards and told stories of flights they'd made. Finally the conversation turned to women.

As his men argued over who was the most beautiful woman they'd ever seen, Cody leaned back in his chair half asleep. He had his own memories, and the fact that his mail hadn't caught up to him in six months only made Katherine's last letter more valuable. She'd been careful to write nothing personal in her note, but Cody knew what was left unsaid, for he'd always left it out in his letters also.

One American named Hall, who'd been driving a cab in Paris when the war broke out, insisted that the most gorgeous woman in France was an American nurse he'd seen in a small Red Cross station near the Somme River. "She's got hair that teeters between red and auburn, and her green eyes make you want to lay down your pension at her feet. But she's fiery. Got a tongue that'll cut a man in half if he steps out of line."

Cody pulled out of his daydream to listen as Hall continued, "I was just trying to get acquainted, and she about took my head off for interfering with her work."

Cody opened one eye and stared at Hall. "Did you get her name?" He knew it couldn't be Katherine and almost resented Hall for interfering with his dream.

"Nope," the man answered. "Not even when I told her I was a pilot. If that won't soften a lassie's heart, nothing will." He laughed as everyone nodded. "The beauty just looked at me and told me she'd been up in a plane once herself back in Dayton."

Cody was out of his chair and to the door before anyone noticed he'd moved. "Katherine," he whispered as he grabbed his jacket and headed for the field. It couldn't be possible. She couldn't be only a few hundred miles away without him feeling her nearness. She'd been so much a part of every dream he'd had for so long, he'd begun to think of her as someone he'd made up to help him pass the lonely hours. He'd never been homesick in his life, but his arms ached to hold her.

It took him over an hour to talk someone into letting him use a plane. He had to lie his way through three officers and several clerks, but finally he was on his way, with a drudge of a plane and a twenty-four-hour pass. Even if this turned out to be a wild-goose chase, at least he was doing something.

He flew northwest, staying well behind the lines. Troops were everywhere. The Allies had built a road toward

Bar-le-Duc they called the Sacred Way. Thousands of men and tons of supplies were rolling toward Verdun. Cody couldn't help but watch the sky, daring a German plane to cross the line. Katherine might be in his mind, but he was always ready for a fight. The young German pilots weren't much of a challenge for him with their few hours of flight time and unsteady hand on the controls. Someday he hoped to meet the one named Baron von Richthofen, who'd painted his plane bright red as though he thought this was a game.

War hadn't been a game for Cody. He'd felt every loss until sometimes he thought there was no more feeling left. Even at meals, he'd find himself looking around and wondering who would be next to die. Finally he avoided meeting the new pilots because he didn't want to think about them not returning. He didn't even like shaking hands, for he felt he'd just touched the doomed. In the end, though, a part of him died whether they'd been his friends or men he'd refused to know.

The sun was almost out of sight by the time Cody spotted the Somme River. He landed on a small airstrip well behind the lines. The tents of the Red Cross hospital were on his left when he jumped down from his plane. He gave the canvas a heavy pat, thinking the horse was old, but she'd run the race. He would have flown the same plane the Wright Brothers used at Kitty Hawk to get here.

A tall man with one crippled leg hurried toward Cody and offered him a hand in pushing the plane off the runway. Cody hid his surprise at the powerful strength of the frail-looking man whose clothes hung on him as though he were no wider than a clothespole.

Cody tried to talk to the man, who was covered with oil and dirt, but the Frenchman didn't seem to understand his accent. He simply nodded when Cody asked if the plane could be ready to fly again tomorrow afternoon.

Hurrying toward the hospital tents, Cody felt a sudden

need to dust a bad feeling off his shoulders. Something about the mechanic made him uneasy. Never one to put a great deal of faith in luck, Cody still had a feeling bad luck would follow him if he ever let the man touch him. Mechanics were an even stranger lot than pilots, but this one bordered on frightening. He was missing the easy smile Wheeler DeJon always offered pilots when they landed.

Cody broke into a run toward the hospital. Suddenly all he could think about was the hope of seeing Katherine. He had to hold her. It didn't matter how many times he left her, she always seemed to go with him in his thoughts.

"Don't say something stupid," he reminded himself. This time all the words he said to her would come from his heart, not his past.

"You've got to make her realize how important she is to you," he continued talking to himself, not caring that soldiers he passed were staring at him. "You've got to let her know that you couldn't help breaking your promise to be back in three months. She's got to understand you had no choice but to stay and help. This time, you have to get it right!" he whispered as he opened the tent hospital flap. "You may not get another chance." He smiled, knowing if his men could hear him talking to himself they'd have him grounded.

The lights were low inside the tent, giving those moving among the cots long ghostly shadows on the canvas walls. Several beds were empty, but stacks of supplies along each wall helped to keep the warmth in as well as to prepare for the next onslaught of wounded.

An older man in white walked slowly toward Cody. He paused every few cots to check the patient there as though he considered Cody's problem of little importance since no blood was leaking from him.

"Evening, sir," Cody said when the man finally raised his gaze to look at him.

"Evening, son. What can I do for you?" The older man's

eyes looked as if he'd stared a moment too long in death's face.

"I am looking for a friend."

The doctor started shaking his head. "Sorry, son. I don't know most of these boys' names." He glanced at the flight helmet hanging out of Cody's pocket. "'Course if he's a pilot, you might ask the mechanic who works out on the airfield. He knows everyone who flies into here. Don't let his looks scare you. Last week he crawled under the wire and hauled out a pilot who'd crashed in the middle of no-man's-land. Both sides were firing over him, but he somehow made it to safety with the man on his back."

Cody felt suddenly a little guilty for misjudging the crippled mechanic. In wartime people weren't always what they seemed. He'd known men who talked brave on the ground, then froze at the controls in the air. Cody made a mental note to take a few minutes to talk to the Frenchman as he directed the doctor's attention to his reason for coming. "I'm not looking for a pilot, or for any soldier. I'm looking for a nurse who might be here. Her name's Katherine McMiller."

The doctor shook his head and Cody's hopes fell. "Wouldn't do you any good to talk to her," he said, with a look of feeling sorry for Cody in his eyes. "She's been here four months and hasn't given a healthy man the time of day."

"She's here!" Cody fought the urge to grab the doctor and shake all the information out of him at once.

"Sure." The doctor shrugged. "But she won't have anything to do with any man who isn't bleeding."

Cody wanted to scream that his heart had been bleeding for her since the day he looked into those emerald eyes, but he simply asked, "Could you tell me where she is?"

The doctor nodded. "Over there with the worst of them, I'd guess. She always ends her shift by sitting with those who are dying, just to hold their hands one last time before they pass on.''

Cody barely heard the last words, as he moved in the direction the doctor indicated. The far section of the tent had been draped off from the others. He pulled one of the thin curtains aside and froze at the sight before him. Katherine knelt beside a cot, slowly pulling the sheet up over a soldier's head. When she looked up at the slight sound of Cody's movement, he saw tears in her eyes, and all his resistance against falling totally in love seemed to collapse.

Silently she stood and straightened her uniform. He could see the tired lines around her eyes and the blood on her apron, but she'd never looked more wonderful to him. He opened his arms to her, and she walked toward him, moving faster and faster until she was running.

He lifted her into his hug and twirled her around, loving the way she buried her head against his throat and held on to him as if to life itself.

He couldn't stop holding her. There were probably a million things he needed to say, but all he could think of was that she was here with him. Katherine, the foundation of his every dream and desire, was in his arms and hugging him just as tightly as he held her.

''You folks know each other?'' the doctor interrupted with almost a laugh.

Katherine turned her head slightly, but didn't let go of Cody. ''Dr. Wells, I'd like you to meet Cody Masters, a very dear friend.''

The doctor stretched out his hand. ''Pleased to meet you, young man. Katherine's the finest nurse in this outfit. If she says you're a friend, then a friend you must be.'' He had seen and understood the way they clung to each other. ''And if you're her friend, you'll take this lady out of here and get her some food before they close up the mess tent for the night. Go on.''

Cody didn't need to be told twice. He pulled Katherine with him through the flap doors and out into the night.

When they stepped outside, he looked around. "Which way to the mess tent?"

In the moonlight her eyes were the color of evergreen. She stared at him without moving or showing any indication she'd heard a word he'd said. He knew food was something neither of them needed.

A smile slowly spread across her lips as she stepped into the shadows of the tent hospital. "Cody," she whispered before he joined her in the darkness.

All the months of doing without her touch exploded within him. He pulled her against him and found her mouth as a dying man might find the last breath of air. He wanted to tell her all the things he'd never told anyone in his life. He wanted to hold her silently for hours, just hearing her heartbeat next to his, but first he had to taste her.

His demand parted her lips with the violence of a love too long held at bay. Without slowing, he swallowed her cry of delight and felt her arms tighten around his neck. He could taste blood on her lip, but he couldn't slow the pace. His need for her was too great to allow anything to stop him, and he wasn't sure she'd allow him to pull away even if he tried.

As the kiss deepened, she melted against him and moaned her pleasure softly against his lips. She tasted of peace to his troubled mind, and she felt like love and home. A home Cody had never known. A home where he was loved for what he was and not for what he did.

He wanted to carry her away from the war and the world and hold her to him all the days of their lives. "I was wrong," he whispered as he planted little kisses across her face. "I told you we should go slow. I was wrong. The only way to make it through this life is to take big gulps and never look back."

"No," Katherine answered. "I'm the one who was

wrong. I thought I had to have forever. In the last few months I've learned there is no forever.''

Katherine dug her fingers into his hair and pulled his lips back to hers, silencing him with her demands. When she'd driven him mad with her mouth, she moved her hands underneath his jacket and shirt and clawed his chest.

"I need to feel you next to me," she pleaded as she leaned her head back to allow him to brush kisses along her neck. "Cody, don't leave me until you've loved me."

Her words were a cry that answered all the longing within him.

Cody's words brushed her ear. "Where?"

He didn't need to say more. She knew what he was asking, and she had no thought of denying his request.

She laughed softly and buried her face in his chest. "I can't believe you're here. I knew you were in France, but I'd almost given up hope of finding you. I thought you'd only be a part of my dreams forever."

"I'm real, Kat," he whispered as he hugged her. "Here and now is as real as life will probably ever be again."

"Here and now," she whispered as a promise.

A shadow moved between the tents in front of them, and Cody pulled Katherine suddenly to his side. He'd thought they were on safe ground, but they were too close to the front line to drop their guard. Silently Cody slipped the safety strap off his revolver.

"Pardon." The shadow advanced with a limp. Then in slow, broken English a man said, "Thought you and the lady . . . would like dinner."

The mechanic handed Cody a basket and retreated into the shadows before Cody could even thank him.

"Who is that man?" He looked down at Katherine.

She shrugged. "Folks around here call him Hoot because he's like an owl, moving only at night. He takes care of the planes, I think. He looks scary, but he's harmless. I've found him a lot of nights sleeping out behind the hospital tent. Guess he doesn't want to bunk in with the others any more than they probably want him. He smells worse than your mechanic, DeJon, and I hadn't thought that possible.''

Cody pulled Katherine toward the tents. ''Do you sleep in one of those tents?'' He nibbled at her ear, already wishing her hair was loose and free.

Katherine put her arm around his waist and guided his path. ''No, I'm the head nurse. My room is behind my office tent in a little place all by itself.''

Cody let everything fade from his mind as Katherine drew him toward the fulfillment of all his dreams.

Twenty-two

KATHERINE WATCHED CODY in the tiny mirror mounted on a pole in the center of her office. Removing her cap, she allowed her hair to tumble, wishing suddenly it were brushed and shiny as it had been the day they met. That girl who'd promised anything in return for a ride in a plane seemed like a stranger to her now.

Cody looked out of place in her little office. The top of the tent almost touched his sun-bleached hair. He seemed too wild and free to ever be closed into the small canvas shelter. His leather jacket battered but clean, his tall boots were polished and his white scarf spotless. With his handsome looks, he looked more like a poster pilot than a real man. Only his eyes reflected imperfections in his life. They told of a loneliness that went all the way to his soul.

"What's in the basket?" she asked, not really caring but not knowing what else to say. A part of her wanted to admit that she'd never entertained a man in her quarters and had no idea what to do. But somehow she managed to talk of ordinary things while in her mind she dreamed of possibilities. "The mess kitchen is quite good at making up late snacks," she said as she remembered the way his chest felt pressed against her own.

He gave her a glance that said he had no idea what she was talking about, then he opened the basket. "Sandwiches and cookies. You hungry?" As he watched her every move, his warm brown eyes told her of his hunger, a starvation that no amount of food could satisfy.

Katherine removed her apron and washed her hands in the small portable sink. "Not really." She doubted she could eat anything. All she could think about was wanting to be in Cody's arms again, but somehow, now that they were alone and in the light, it was hard to know where to start. She smiled, wondering if he'd follow her if she suggested they step outside into the darkness.

"How are Sarah and the baby?" Cody moved around the office restlessly. His hand traced first one thing then another as if only something with warmth would satisfy his touch. "Matthew must be four by now."

"They're both fine. She writes that Matthew grows every day and looks more and more like Bart," Katherine answered, trying not to stare at his hands as they brushed along the familiar belongings in her world. "I mailed a letter yesterday asking Sarah to consider coming for six months. We need trained nurses badly, and she has an entire dorm full of girls to take care of Matthew."

As if suddenly aware of what he was doing, Cody locked his hands behind him and widened his stance. "I've looked for Bart but never found him. The few clues I have only hint that he's still alive, nothing more. It's not easy to find a man who wants to disappear."

Katherine didn't want to talk of Bart or Sarah. For once in her life she wanted to be selfish with the precious little time she and Cody had together.

Cody seemed to sense her feelings, for he resumed his pacing. He lifted the flap that separated her sleeping area from the rest of the office and Katherine cringed. She remembered how neat his room had looked. Hers was a disaster, with clothes, boxes, and books strung everywhere. There never seemed to be enough time to pick up. Besides, until tonight no one had ever been beyond her neat office to discover the mess.

Cody glanced at her and raised one eyebrow. "Lucky you can afford a maid. I'd hate to think of what this place would look like without one."

She was almost to him when she realized he was joking, but it was too late to stop her playful attack. Her fist struck his chest more in a release of tension than in insult. He lost his balance and tumbled backward onto her bed. When she felt him pull on her hand, Katherine realized he was taking her down with him in the fall.

Carelessly he shoved the covers aside and pulled her on top of him. "I surrender." He couldn't stop smiling as she wiggled above him. "Just don't hit me again or smother me with all these clothes."

Katherine planted her arms on either side of his head and laughed for no reason, experiencing joy for the first time in more months than she could remember. "Be quiet, Cody Masters. Every time you open your mouth, I end up mad at you."

His hands moved slowly up and down her back as his eyes darkened. "What would you have me do?" His fingers were bold in their movement over her hips and feather light along her spine. He'd waited too long to touch her to hesitate now.

Katherine answered him with her lips brushing his. "Kiss me. Hold me." Her mouth moved lightly over his face. "Make me feel alive."

Cody whispered a breath away from her mouth, "Only one request at a time." He rolled her beneath him. The promise in his eyes contradicted his words, for he had every intention of granting all her requests and more. "I've lived a great deal since I kissed you last, but I've never felt alive."

"I know," Katherine replied, kissing his eyelids.

"I don't want to play any games or follow any rule but loving you right now."

"Agreed." Katherine loved the way his day's growth of beard felt against her lips.

He kissed her, spreading fire through every part of her body. She loved the feel of him against her, pressing into every curve with his need for her.

"There's never been any woman for me but you." His thoughts seemed to tumble from his lips.

"I thought I told you to stop talking." Katherine bit at his bottom lip, wanting to taste him, wanting to memorize every smell and touch so he'd never be fully gone from her mind.

Cody laughed as he nuzzled her neck, loving the way she moved her head to offer him more soft skin to touch. "Are you ordering me, Head Nurse? You've gotten mighty bossy in your old age." He mumbled as he kissed her. "Fortunately, I'm a man accustomed to following orders."

"You missed a spot below my ear," she answered as she closed her eyes and cherished the feel of his lips sliding along her throat.

"You're the most manipulative female I've ever met." He unbuttoned her uniform. "If you're not trying to hit me, you're ordering me around. Now you think you can tell me how to make love to you."

He reached the button between her breasts. Unbuttoning it slowly, he enjoyed her pleasure when his hand brushed her breasts as he completed his task. Her skin was velvet beneath his touch. He slowly pushed her clothes aside, loving the way she moved slightly as his fingers reached beneath the material to touch her.

"I'm not leaving until I make love to you." He spread his hand over her flat stomach. A storm of pleasure was already whirling in his mind, blinding him to all but her. He twisted her hair into one fist and kissed her hard as his fingers spread wide and moved slowly from her throat to below her breasts and back again.

Gripping the material of her uniform, he jerked the blouse completely open and allowed himself the luxury of staring at her. "Dear God, but you're beautiful." He shoved the camisole below her breasts with a haste born of urgent need.

Katherine watched his eyes darken with pleasure as she arched toward him, loving the fire of his gaze. She wiggled slightly so her white cotton underclothes could slide down to her waist. When his hands touched her once more, they were gentle, worshiping, loving. His fingers felt warm and strong moving over her, branding her with a passion that was only his.

As he molded her breasts in his hands, he kissed her throat, feeling the pounding of her pulse against his lips. When his hands tightened slightly over their tender treasures, her pulse increased sending passion's heartbeat all the way to his soul.

Without another word, he lowered his mouth to her breast and loved the cry of pleasure that escaped her lips before she bit it back with her fist. He laughed against the sweet smell of her skin. His tongue slid over each peak, testing her efforts to stifle her cries of passion. Without his mouth leaving her breasts, he pulled off the rest of her clothes and moved his fingers over perfection. Her body was all he'd dreamed of and more. No other woman would ever feel right in his arms now that he'd touched Katherine. Every curve, every swell, was like a work of art. His mind kept telling him to go slowly, but he had no speed other than full ahead. He'd waited too long for heaven to stand at the gate now.

When he finally returned to her mouth, she moved freely and mindlessly beneath him. She returned each kiss with as much pleasure as he'd tried to give her. With each touch she learned about passion and gave it back to him with great delight.

Then, with a sudden impatience he'd grown to love, she shoved at his shirt, ripping the buttons in her haste. Cody straightened away from her and laughed as he removed his own clothes. For the first time in his life, he tossed them aside without a care. Before the last garment hit the floor she was pulling him against her once more, demanding he return her kisses as their bodies curved together. Only now flesh touched flesh, making them both forget to breathe as newly discovered joy whirled them into passion's raging storm.

When her soft breasts pressed into the hard wall of his chest, he thought it possible to die from pleasure. He wondered briefly how he'd ever lived without her beside him.

Though unsure he could stop, he had to force himself to pull back. He looked into her face with desire, her eyes fiery with need. He'd planned to ask if she was sure, but when he looked at her lying against the pillow with her hair wild and her mouth already bruised with passion, he knew there were no questions to ask, only dreams to fulfill.

She reached up to him, then moved her hands over his body slowly, loving the difference between his skin and hers. "Take me flying, birdman," she murmured as she pulled him to her.

Cody's restraint shattered. Loving her became not a pleasure but a need. Strong and fierce with desire, he tried to think of ways to make her happy, but all he could do was that which was basic to life.

He kissed her until she moved beneath him like a dancer to a rhythm played only in her mind. When he could stand the movement no longer, he slowly nudged her legs apart and joined in the dance.

As before when he'd kissed her, he swallowed her first cry and continued until she rose once more with passion and met his rhythm with one of her own. He gave himself fully to her, holding nothing back.

A bomb could have struck the tent and Cody wouldn't have noticed. He felt all the love he had within him pour into her, and all the love he'd longed for radiated from her to him. The passing was far more than physical, for they became one in a white lightning flash that would forever bind their spirits.

He collapsed, wanting to whisper words of love and beauty, but all he could do was hold her against his heart and marvel at how the reality of her could be so much more wonderful than his dreams.

Tears rolled down her face as she cuddled beneath his arm. Ever since she could remember, Katherine had dreamed of being held close to someone who loved her. His passion and need had driven her to the point of madness and back with pleasure. But now, as time passed and his arm never lessened its grip, he satisfied the longings of the child within her. Even when he reached out and switched off the light, she didn't feel afraid, for his long, powerful body was solid against her, and there was nothing in the darkness that could reach her.

At some time during the night they both fell asleep with only their love between them.

When Katherine awoke hours later, dawn had turned the room to smoky gray. Cody sat beside her gently wiping the few drops of blood off her legs. "It won't hurt next time," he whispered with so much love that his voice shook slightly.

"Next time?" Katherine rose up on one elbow. "When is next time?"

"Whenever you're ready." Cody laughed at the way her emerald eyes turned to fire.

"Now," she answered.

Cody leaned slowly down and kissed her shoulder, smiling as she groaned with impatience. "All right," he whispered against her skin. "Only this time, we'll take it slow and easy." He wanted to leave her with wonderful memories of loving, not just the memory of fire.

But Katherine had no such desire. She wanted all the passion they'd had the night before and more. Within a few minutes she was driven wild by his slow touch and once more pushed him into the passionate rhythm of their dance.

She wanted to touch him and bring him the pleasure he brought her. As her hands moved along the long, lean muscles of his body, she burned his insides with the need in her kiss. She opened herself to him, welcoming him with her body and her heart.

An hour later, when Cody rested beside her, he decided this redhead would kill him if he stayed another night in her bed. He pulled her to him and tasted her salty skin, damp with perspiration, and decided he didn't care. He'd lived a lifetime in one night in her arms. What she didn't know, she tried, and what she tried, she quickly mastered.

Smiling, he closed his eyes and forced out the sounds of artillery that had started up sometime after dawn. "Go away, world," he whispered into her hair. "Go away and let me love Katherine forever."

Twenty-three

CODY HELD KATHERINE until he was sure she was asleep again; then he pulled his arm slowly away. He knew they had only a few hours left together, but he couldn't bring himself to awaken her. Silently he dressed and slipped from her room into the tiny office. A part of him realized it might be better to leave her sleeping. She'd have all the hopes and dreams he'd whispered during their loving to keep her until he returned . . . if he returned. But Cody decided to get a pot of coffee and some breakfast from the mess tent, then talk to her of the future before he left. He had to be Katherine's friend now, not just her lover.

Closely checking his appearance in the tiny mirror, he tried to hide the night of pleasure from his face. He wouldn't dishonor her by walking out of her tent with satisfaction showing. Their happiness was too private a thing to share with strangers.

At the door he almost tripped over a tray of food that someone had placed just inside Katherine's office. As he knelt down, he smelled coffee.

Cody lifted the tray, a question raising one eyebrow. He knew of only two people who might have guessed they'd need breakfast delivered. One was the doctor who'd smiled like a father about to marry off his last daughter, and the other was the mechanic who'd brought them the basket of food.

When Cody turned, the sight of Katherine in the doorway to her room took his breath away. She'd pulled on the wrinkled white blouse of her uniform, but she had buttoned only the last button. The blouse hung just below her hips, revealing her long legs to his view. Her hair was a cloud of curls that tumbled below her shoulders in fiery softness. And her eyes, her wonderful emerald eyes, were huge and liquid with tears.

"I thought you'd gone without saying good-bye," she said in a voice that would have broken the heart of a statue.

Cody set the tray on her desk, not caring that coffee sloshed everywhere. Then Katherine was in his arms. He held her so tight the world could have stopped turning and they wouldn't have noticed.

"I only went for breakfast." He couldn't stop kissing away her tears. "I thought you'd sleep until I got back."

Katherine placed her arms around his neck and swallowed her pain. "I know you have to leave soon, but promise me you'll always say good-bye. I couldn't take it if I woke up and found you gone."

There were so many things he wanted to promise her. A future. A lifetime of loving. A world of happiness. But all he could promise was that he would say good-bye before he left.

He kissed her long and hard. A kiss that had little to do with passion. "We have to talk," he finally told her as he held her head close against his heart. "I'll come back whenever I can, but if I don't—"

"No!" Katherine pulled away. "I won't listen!"

Cody pulled her hands away from her ears. "Please listen, Kat. You have to." He knew his words would upset her, but he could not allow her to refuse to face the future.

"If I don't come back, I want you to promise you'll forget about me and go on with your life." He couldn't bear the thought of her spending her life as Sarah did, living on memories.

She tried to break his hold, but she couldn't.

"Promise me, Kat!" he ordered.

She fought his words as her body physically fought his hold on her wrists.

"Promise me!" he pleaded.

Fire danced in her eyes, but she stopped fighting and faced him. "If you don't come back, Cody Masters, I'll hate you for the rest of my life."

Cody laughed with relief. "And if I *do* come back, will you promise to love me for the rest of your life?" He loved the strength in this woman almost as much as he loved the passion.

"I'll let you know when you come back."

Cody rattled the tent with his laughter as he lifted her in his arms and carried her back to bed, forgetting all about breakfast.

The day passed in a lovers' dream as they talked and slept and touched with hearts and hands. Finally, when the shadows were long, Cody knew he had to go.

They dressed without looking at each other and moved silently out of the tent toward the airfield. Her hand rested on his arm lightly as they walked. She wanted to pull him back and hold him forever, but they both knew that was impossible. Words were unnecessary. They'd said all that needed to be said when they were next to each other in bed. Now was a time to cloak their feelings along with their bodies.

As they reached the end of the tents, Cody turned to hold her one last time. "I want to leave you here, not at the field," he said. "Promise me you'll never watch me take off when I'm flying away from you."

Katherine grabbed his scarf, which hung loose around his neck. She wanted to make him promise he'd come back, but she knew that would be foolish. He would come back if he was alive, and if he was not, she didn't want a false promise to be the last thing said between them. "Take care, my love," she said as she lightly kissed his cheek.

As Cody moved away, a stirring between the shadows of the tents caught his eye. He quickly stepped in front of Katherine and reached for his gun.

"Masters," a voice, thick with a French accent, whispered. "Masters."

"Who's there?" Cody challenged. His one day of love was over; he had to come back to the real world. A world at war. Cody's mind cleared of all thought except survival.

The mechanic moved only far enough out of the shadows for his outline to be recognized. He carried a standard black medical bag of Red Cross supplies. "I need your help, Masters. I found a pilot hurt." The man's words, half French and half English, were almost lost in the sound of gunfire from the front. He moved closer, but turned his face so it was hidden in the shadows. "He's hanging in the trees." The Frenchman pointed toward a clump of trees well behind the hospital tents.

"Well, call the ambulance drivers and tell them to get to him as fast as possible." Cody didn't try to hide his anger. Why had the man come to him with the problem when a pilot could be dying? "He'll need a doctor fast. Hurry, there's no time to waste."

The Frenchman hesitated, his tall frame almost shuddering with indecision. "But he's German," the man finally said.

Katherine felt a scream begin at the base of her throat before she stopped its escape from her mouth. She could imagine a wounded German pilot hanging from a tree while French soldiers shot him down. "Dear God, what will they do to him?"

Cody did not hesitate. "Take us to him," he said. "We've got to get him down before anyone else finds him." He grabbed Katherine's hand, and suddenly they were running into the blackness of the trees beyond the camp.

As they searched, panic mounted within Katherine. What would they do if he was still alive? Turn him over to the army? Kill him? Let him go so he might someday shoot Cody down?

The woods were dark and confusing, with paths running between the trees in all directions. The brush and low branches were tangled together in places, making thorny walls across the maze of paths and natural tunnels. Katherine tried to keep up with Cody and at the same time prevent the bushes from ripping her skirts.

''I've found him!'' Cody yelled at the Frenchman several feet ahead of him.

Katherine looked up into the branches that spiderwebbed across the moon. Slowly the outline of a body took shape among the dried branches. It looked as if his plane had crashed almost a quarter mile away, but he'd fallen into the tree.

''I thought he was dead at first,'' the mechanic said in broken English, ''but then he moved.'' He slapped at his leg with his fist. ''I can't climb with this leg or I'd have gotten him down alone. I had to ask for your help, Captain Masters.''

Cody nodded his understanding. He removed his jacket and gun belt and began to climb toward the twisted body above him. ''You were right to ask me.''

Katherine held her breath and watched. Once she heard a ripping sound as though a branch had torn Cody's shirt. Several branches broke under his weight, but he continued to move toward the body hanging like a rag doll in a thorn bush.

Finally Cody reached the pilot and pulled off his helmet. It was too dark to see where he was wounded, but the moon cast enough light on his face to tell Cody that he was more boy than man.

The soldier raised his head slightly. Blood from a head wound covered most of his face, but his eyes narrowed in fear. He twisted violently, but there was nowhere for him to go except downward, and the fall would mean death.

Cody slowly extended his hand to the wounded man.

The German hesitated. If he reached for Cody's hand, he would give up the safety of his branch. If he didn't, he'd die in the fall when he could no longer hold on, or he would be shot at daybreak when the French troops would see him. He raised his hand, and the two pilots locked forearms.

Slowly the soldier let go with his other hand, and the branches twisted around him, setting their captive free. He swung like an acrobat with Cody's arm his only support.

The branches snapped in protest as Cody lowered the man inch by inch. Finally the French mechanic was almost able to touch the wounded boy.

"Drop him," the mechanic said.

Cody let go. The enemy pilot fell into waiting arms far stronger than Katherine would have guessed. He carried the boy several feet to a clearing and gently placed him on the ground. Moonlight offered all the light she needed to see that he had both a head injury and a shoulder wound.

Katherine stood frozen above him. The blood dripping from his head and arm didn't bother her, but the thought that this very man might someday kill Cody turned her muscles to stone.

"Help him, Kat," Cody said from behind her as he set the bag of supplies at her feet.

"I . . ." She wasn't sure she could touch this man. He was the enemy. He and his people had caused all the pain and hurt she had worked to relieve every day since she'd been in France.

The scarred, dirty face of the mechanic looked up at her. "You must help him. He'll bleed to death if you don't," the man said. "He's a pilot."

"But he could live to kill Cody," she answered the

Frenchman without looking at him any longer than necessary. Even in the moonlight Katherine now understood why
the man called Hoot lived in the shadows. His face was a
mass of scar tissue.

Cody's hand gripped her shoulders. "I'll take my chances
with him fair and square in the air, but on the ground he's
one of my kind. I can't just hand him over to the French to
be shot as soon as he's well enough to stand."

"But it's treason to aid the enemy."

"For me, yes, but not for you. You're sworn to help the
suffering no matter what side they're on. Isn't that the Red
Cross philosophy?"

Katherine closed her eyes and remembered the oath she'd
sworn before she left New York. Suddenly Miss Willingham's words seemed to flow through her, warming her
hands so they could relax: "We have to help those who
need us." The dean of nursing had never once mentioned
nationality.

Looking down at the black bag, Katherine knew what she
had to do. She knelt beside the boy, her fingers automati-
cally working at the job she'd been trained for.

As she cleaned the wounds and wrapped each, the young
German watched her. At first she felt him tense with fear
each time her hand brushed his wounds. When she tied the
bandage tight to stop the bleeding, he flinched with pain, but
he never said a word. He might have little idea what she had
planned for him, but he faced his fate bravely.

Cody and Hoot talked in the shadows, keeping watch
over her as she worked. When she completed her task, she
patted the boy's arm and started to stand.

He reached out suddenly with his good arm and grasped
her hand. Slowly, awkwardly, he raised it to his lips and
brushed a feather-light kiss over her fingers. For the first
time, Katherine saw his eyes clearly in the moonlight. They
were the clear blue of an Ohio sky, and a tear made its way
across his unwrinkled face. He might not understand a word

she said, but he knew she'd saved his life. She realized how few differences separated the two armies. Both were mostly boys with fears and dreams, boys who would die in the battles they never even knew the names of.

Cody pulled her to her feet and planted a quick kiss on her cheek. "We have to hurry. Go back to the hospital tent and be at work by the time I take off. If something happens, I don't want you involved. You've done enough already. And please, Katherine, never speak of this to anyone."

Katherine nodded. He didn't have to tell her about the danger she'd place both men in if she told anyone what they'd done. "What about him?" She had to know what the plan was even if she could take no more part in it.

"Hoot will carry the man through the shadows to my plane. I think I know a few places where I can cross the line in the darkness." Cody didn't sound very confident. "All I have to do is land and let him out. Come morning someone will find him, and by that time I'll be back at my base."

He pulled her against him. "I know you may not understand this, but somehow, even though he and I are on different sides, he's a part of me. I have to do what I can and hope he'd do the same."

The French mechanic lifted the German onto his shoulder and limped away as silently as fog might steal toward the horizon.

Katherine rested her head against Cody's jacket breathing deep of the leather smell before she asked, "Can we trust the Frenchman? If he tells anyone what we're doing, I'll be sent back to the States and you'll probably be charged with treason."

"We can trust him," Cody answered. "He took a big chance telling us about the pilot. We could have turned on him, too."

Cody slowly pulled her arms away. "I'll get word back to you as soon as I can and let you know I made it safely to my base. Stay here a few minutes so no one will see us leaving together.''

She wanted to say, ''Don't go!'' but she couldn't. He had to do what needed to be done. His honor would allow nothing else. He'd told her his unit would take to the air any day, and she knew he had to be with them. All the things she wanted to say, like ''please come back'' and ''I love you,'' were lost somewhere in the flood around her breaking heart.

Cody looked down at her one last time and said, ''I know.''

Then he was gone, vanishing into the shadows as easily as a dream vanished at dawn. Katherine closed her eyes and fought back her tears until he was out of hearing.

While she waited, the night grew cold. When she opened her eyes, she felt suddenly very alone. The blackness closed in around her as it always did. She could feel more than hear movement at her feet and knew the creatures of the night were surrounding her before they attacked and bit at her flesh.

Fighting back her screams, Katherine ran from the woods. She didn't have to see the creatures to know they were there. They were always there. She'd felt them in the blackness since she was a child, and they were no less frightening to her now.

The moonlight guided her until she reached the rows of tents. Katherine slowed to a walk and tried to stop the pounding of her heart. She made herself walk in measured strides without looking up when she heard a plane overhead. Closing her eyes, she said a silent prayer as Cody flew into the night and away from her.

When she could no longer hear the sound of his engine, she made herself a promise. She would work as hard as she could until he returned. Nursing would keep her hands busy, and if she was tired enough she wouldn't wonder where he was or if this day would be his last.

A cold, damp wind chilled her face as she walked toward

the hospital. When she looked up, she saw a long line of men standing outside the main Red Cross tent. Katherine quickened her pace. As she passed among their ranks, she discovered many of these men were not shot, but ill with fever.

Entering the hospital, she was shocked to find every bed filled. Dr. Wells hurried toward her. "Thank God you're here, Katherine. We need to separate these men from the wounded as fast as possible."

"Start setting up more beds," the doctor said, "before we lose more men from fever than from bullets."

Katherine hurried to do what was needed. By the time she'd divided the hospital into two parts and organized the nurses so that those working with the wounded did not come in contact with the men with fever, she was exhausted. She looked down at her watch and realized she'd worked almost twenty-four hours without a break and with only coffee to keep her going.

As she stepped out of the tent, Katherine was amazed at how cold the weather had turned. The wind had grown bitter, and now the sky was dark and brooding. The sudden change from the hot damp hospital tent into the crisp night air made Katherine's head swirl.

In exhaustion she lost her way and she wandered off into the blackness.

She ran without direction or plan, for what seemed like an endless time, toward the only light she saw in a sea of blackness, a light that wasn't constant but flashed in the dark like fireflies blinking. The muddy earth pulled at her shoes, but she forced herself to keep running toward the flashes of light. She wished Cody's arms were around her again. She needed Sarah to calm her fears. She had to reach the light before the night creatures came out.

Someone in the darkness shouted for her to stop, but Katherine didn't react. In one moment the earth slipped away and she was falling, falling, falling.

Twenty-four

SEVERAL PAIRS OF strong hands reached out of the blackness and pulled Katherine up from what seemed to be a long grave. She saw explosions of gunfire above her head. The sound was like rapid thunder and much closer than she'd ever heard it before.

"Crazy lady!" a voice above her yelled in a British accent. "If this foxhole hadn't stopped you, you'd be at the front line by now." The soldier turned to his men. "Lift her up easy, boys. No telling what she broke in that fall."

"I'm all right," Katherine lied. Her body felt numb, as if she'd landed flat, bruising everything equally. "I just got turned around and thought I was running toward the hospital." She wanted to tell all the men yelling at her that it wasn't her fault. She was tired, and she hated the night, but she doubted they'd understand.

"Well, pardon me for saying so, miss, but you don't seem in such good shape to me. How'd you get this far into the lines without someone stopping you?" The soldier yelled again as though he had only one volume level. "If you don't mind, I'll have my men carry you back to the hospital."

The thought of being placed on a stretcher and carried into the tent horrified Katherine. "No!" She pushed at the hands that held her. "I can walk."

The officer hesitated, then told his men to lower her slowly to the ground. "All right, if you say so. But I'm sending a few men along with you to make sure you get there. We've got a war to fight here and we can't have nurses dropping in on us.''

The last thing Katherine wanted was to be alone. She wasn't sure she could cross the black space between the trenches and the hospital without screaming. She accepted the offered escort.

A firm hand rested beneath her arm as she moved toward the tent lights. The man touching her didn't speak but only walked formally at her side as though if he got too close he'd catch her insanity. Another soldier followed a step behind, silent as a shadow. When they reached her quarters, both saluted and disappeared without a word.

Katherine took a long breath, realizing she'd just done a very foolish thing, running into the night. There were men who needed her. She couldn't afford to allow her fears to rule her again, no matter how tired she became.

Hurrying inside, she quickly lit the little stove and washed. Several places looked like they would be black-and-blue tomorrow, but at least tonight she was safe.

Her thoughts were filled with Cody's love as she huddled between the stove and her desk. She didn't notice a letter from Sarah on her desk. She moved the thin envelope around twice while she finished her paperwork before it fell unnoticed to the floor.

Katherine finally stood and stretched. Every muscle ached from either the fall or from exhaustion. It seemed like a lifetime since she'd been held. Her lips were still puffy from Cody's kisses and the very private parts of her were sore from his loving, but her entire body longed to touch him and be touched.

His memory was almost tangible in her little room. She brushed the top of the tent where she'd seen his sunny-colored hair touch. With a smile, she wandered around, caressing all the things he'd touched only hours before. The smell of leather, wool, and Cody lingered in the tent as if refusing to leave.

A sudden draft of cold air whispered across her cheek and she whirled toward the opening of her tent. No one was there. She'd almost expected to see Cody walk in and open his arms in silent greeting.

Forcing back the tears, Katherine looked down. There, just inside her tent, lay a small package wrapped in newspaper. She walked slowly toward it, hoping it was good news, fearing it might be bad. As she knelt to pick up the package, she looked through the opening in the flap, but couldn't see anyone outside.

Written on the package were these words: "When you fly into a little field near the Somme River, deliver this to a mechanic named Hoot. He'll know where to take this package. Thanks, Cody."

Katherine tore into the wrapping like a child with only one present at Christmas. She shoved all the paper away and opened the box. Folded neatly inside was the long silk scarf Cody had been wearing when he left her.

Carefully she lifted the scarf and held it to her cheek. She could smell the wind and adventure just as plainly as she could smell Cody's strong masculine fragrance woven into the cloth.

A note lay in the bottom of the box. For a moment Katherine couldn't bring herself to pick it up. Part of her would rather have faced no news than the possibility of bad news.

Carefully she unfolded the single piece of paper and read the bold handwriting:

Kat,

I made it back after delivering my cargo. All hell's about to break out near Verdun. The battles will be costly and fruitless. The ground they'll pour blood into looks worthless from the air.

Don't know when I can get back, but I'll carry you in my heart until then.

Love,
Cody

Katherine crumpled to the floor. She cried until no more tears would fall. She wanted to sleep in Cody's arms. Like a child she was tired and hungry and in need of rest, yet she couldn't stop crying or make even herself stand up.

Finally, exhausted, she curled into a ball on the cold floor and closed her eyes to the world.

Some time later, in the space between dreams and reality, someone lifted her in his arms and carried her to bed. He laid her down gently, like a father; then Katherine felt warm covers being tucked around her. She smiled and stretched beneath the warm blankets, too sleepy to open her eyes.

Several hours later when she finally rolled over, Katherine felt as though every bone in her body had been rearranged. Without opening her eyes, she remembered all that had happened the night before, even the part where she'd dreamed she'd been tucked into bed by someone who cared about her. Somehow the dream of being cared for gave her comfort, reminding her that there was kindness in this world filled with fever and dying.

The months that followed were cold and damp. Work and gray skies seemed endless. Katherine sometimes had trouble remembering what day it was. Occasionally, when planes landed from the south, they brought short notes from Cody, never more than a few lines quickly written.

He reported that his men, now called the Escadrille Américaine, had been moved to a quiet sector at an airbase called Luxeuil. The men were restless and ready for action, but the French seemed reluctant to allow the Americans to fly near the front.

The Escadrille had made its first kill. One of the men was

returning from his first patrol when he spotted a German two-seater observation plane. The American had never before fired his machine gun, but he made a hit and the German plane nose-dived to earth. The hit created an overnight hero and made headlines across the ocean.

Cody's next letter came from Verdun where the Escadrille had been transferred once more. Miss Willingham sent all the news clippings of the battles near Verdun, telling Katherine that Cody was also still in touch with those back home. The clippings told of troops ordered "over the top" by the thousands and cut down just as quickly by enemy machine guns. The news reported that so many artillery shells were fired, the ground between the trenches was potted and devoid of all life.

Within weeks the Escadrille became famous. They were the American heroes of the skies, fighting the very best German planes and men. And like all heroes, many were dying.

As the year progressed, Katherine used all her energy working so that at night she was exhausted. Finally, on a rare afternoon off, she decided to clean her quarters. With her usual determination she set to work, resolving she wouldn't spend the day worrying. The office was half cleaned when she found Sarah's letter.

Katherine opened it excitedly and almost screamed aloud when she read the first line: "I can neglect my duty no longer. I'm coming over in the spring."

The next few days were lost in a happy whirlwind of activity. Katherine should have had months to prepare for Sarah's coming, but the lost letter had cut the time short.

Arranging for a two-day pass, Katherine rode to the coast in a supply truck to await Sarah's ship. The weather was warm, and France was beautiful away from the front. At times as they bumped along the road, she found it hard to believe this country was at war, for peace rested so easily over the landscape.

Knowing she'd arrived early, Katherine booked a room in a little inn that allowed her to see the ocean. She could have stayed at the Red Cross headquarters, but she didn't want to spend her one day away from the front talking to the other nurses about the war.

She spent over an hour soaking in a real bathtub, then put on the only dress she'd brought to Europe other than her uniforms and ventured downstairs to the restaurant.

The place was smaller than the dining room at the boardinghouse in Columbus. Little tables for two and four were arranged around the sides of the room with one large round oak dining table in the center. All the tables were covered with linen and place settings, but except for a tired waiter leaning against the wall in the far corner, no one was in the room.

When she took a seat, the waiter brought her a menu and a glass of wine. Katherine felt terribly wicked as she sipped her first glass of spirits since she'd downed a glass of whiskey the morning she flew with Cody. What would Miss Willingham say if she saw her prize student all alone in a foreign country, drinking?

Katherine laughed to herself and tried to figure out at least one word on the menu. She might be very hungry by tomorrow afternoon if she didn't come up with something to order.

"May I help the mademoiselle make a selection this evening?" a low French-accented voice said from behind her. "Would you like more wine?"

Katherine nodded as he set another glass in front of her. She stared at the red wine and his leather sleeve a moment before she realized the pieces didn't fit together. The waiter hadn't been wearing a jacket.

Katherine turned slowly, afraid to hope. She'd waited months, looking for Cody in every stranger's face. She'd stopped counting the times she thought she saw him.

"Cody!" she whispered as she looked into his dancing eyes.

He tried to hide his smile. "Do I know the mademoiselle?" he asked in an imitation of a French accent that was almost flawless.

If she hadn't been so glad to see him, she might have been angry. But there was only mischief in her look when she answered, "Oh, I'm so sorry. I thought you were a dear friend of mine. I hope you'll excuse me."

He lifted her hand to his lips. "This dear friend," he asked, still using the French accent, "does he love you dearly?" Cody kissed her palm and closed her fingers.

Kat fought down a giggle. "Yes," she answered. "He loves me wildly."

Cody lifted her other hand and moved his lips over her knuckles. "And do you love him?"

Kat could feel the warmth of his breath against her fingers. "Yes." She pulled her hand from his grasp. "So you see, sir, I cannot allow a stranger to join me at dinner and taste my fingers."

Cody's laughter reminded her how dearly he loved the fire in her. He straddled the seat across from her and stared at her for a while before speaking. "Would you allow this stranger to share your bed?"

"I might, if the night is cold," Kat answered.

"I promise the night will be very hot," Cody said.

The waiter moved to set a place in front of Cody, forcing him to alter his speech.

"I had one hell of a time finding you. No one in that hospital of yours knows what day it is, much less where anyone is. If it hadn't been for my old buddy, Hoot, I'd have given up and headed back to my base."

"Hoot knew where I was?" Katherine wasn't really surprised. The mechanic seemed to know about everything going on around the camp.

"He pointed me in the right direction. Told me some new

nurses were coming tomorrow. He said you seemed more excited than usual.'' Cody sipped her wine. ''So I put two and two together and came up with Sarah.''

Katherine raised an eyebrow. ''So you're here to see Sarah?''

Cody winked and nodded. ''You guessed it, baby.'' He lowered his voice as the waiter moved away. ''After I spend the night with you, of course.''

''And what makes you believe you're invited?''

Cody's eyes darkened slightly, and his full mouth lost its smile. ''There are few things in this crazy world I am sure of, Kat. I don't know how much time we'll have together, a few nights or a lifetime, but I plan to live all I can in whatever time I have. And I plan to live as much of it as possible with you beside me.''

The waiter stopped at their table once more, and Cody ordered in French without even looking at the menu.

When the waiter left, Cody turned to Kat. ''Want to go upstairs, lovely lady? I don't think I can sit here looking at you for many more minutes without going nuts.''

''Take me up, birdman.''

Cody rose and offered her his hand.

Katherine looked confused. ''But what about the dinner you just ordered?''

Cody laughed as he led her out of the restaurant. ''I asked him to deliver it to your room.''

Katherine tried her best to look shocked, but she took his hand and hurried up the stairs.

Beyond the landing the stairs were shadowed and hidden from view of the lobby.

''Kiss me,'' she whispered.

Cody backed her up against the paneled corner and kissed her gently. ''I've missed you.''

Katherine moved her hands beneath his jacket and spread her fingers out on his chest. ''Sometimes I wanted to fold up, because my longing for you felt like a huge hole in my heart.''

"I know," he answered as he lightly brushed her face with kisses. "I don't know how many times I've awakened from a dream so real that I could feel you by my side.''

"How long do we have?" Kat hated to ask, but she had to know.

"Until tomorrow night," Cody answered as his hands moved lightly over her clothing. "Long enough for me to let you know how completely I love you.''

"You think you're up to taking all my love, birdman?"

"I'll do my best." He laughed.

Suddenly Katherine could wait no longer to be alone with him. She bolted from his arms and ran toward her room. "You have to catch me." She laughed, feeling very young and alive.

Cody caught her just inside her bedroom door and pulled her to him. His grip was sure and powerful now. "I want you so desperately." His fingers boldly roamed her body. "I thought I'd have to sit on my hands to keep from touching you downstairs.''

"Stop talking and take off your clothes," Katherine ordered. "Maybe I'll be the one who frightens you." She unbuckled his belt as she talked.

Cody laughed. "There you go again, bossing me around." He held his hands up in surrender. "I thought you'd want to talk first."

Katherine shoved his jacket to the floor. "We'll talk later."

Their clothes tumbled together onto the floor as they laughed and raced each other to bed. Katherine had dreamed of holding him every night since he left, and she could no more hide her desire than she could deny the fact that she loved him.

They rolled among the covers, kissing with a passion that had waited too long to be quenched. When he would have slowed the pace to a more loving stroll, she pushed him faster, driving him mad with the way she moved.

Finally he rolled on top of her and pinned her arms beside her head. "Kat, we have all night. We don't have to try and kill each other in the first hour."

She twisted beneath him, more to tease than to escape. "Can't keep up with me, can you, old man?"

Cody bit at her neck. "I'm not that much older than you, kid."

"If I live to be a hundred, I'll never slow down with you," Kat answered as she struggled in earnest, freeing one hand to rake her nails across his back.

Cody closed his eyes in pleasure. "If you don't slow down, I'll never live to be a hundred."

She answered by clawing his chest as she moved her hips beneath him.

He wasn't sure if his words had been thoughts before they came out of his mouth. "Marry me, Kat," he whispered as passion consumed him. "Marry me tonight."

Kat bit into the skin at his throat. "Maybe," she answered, "if there's time."

All thought left Cody's mind except loving Katherine as they danced to their own rhythm and soared into a world that would always be theirs alone.

Early dawn light drifted through the stained-glass windows and sparkled in the dusty morning air of the old church. A French priest stood before them speaking words Katherine couldn't understand. She and Cody hadn't slept, but she didn't feel tired. Not today. Not on her wedding day.

As the priest finished and blessed them both, Cody turned to her. "I think we're married now."

Kat smiled up at her handsome husband. "I don't feel married."

Cody seemed to understand. He gently held her shoulders and turned her to face him. "I, Cody Masters, take you,

Katherine McMiller, to be my wife. I promise to love and cherish you every day of my life whether the flying be smooth or stormy. Even if we can't be together every day, you'll be with me always in my heart."

"And I take you," Katherine replied. "Always."

Cody kissed her lightly, almost reverently. "I always felt I didn't belong until I found your arms. You alone make me believe in forever. No matter what happens in this war, never doubt that I love you."

Katherine felt the same. Somehow in this little church in the middle of a war, she'd sealed her fate with Cody's. Not just for today but for every day.

The priest handed them a piece of paper. "God's love," he said in English.

They both watched him leave, but they didn't move. They wanted time to stop for them once more.

"When we're old, we'll come back here and be married again." Cody held her hand.

"And stay at the little inn again?" Kat asked.

Cody laughed. "If I'm still able, we'll stay there again."

An hour later they stood arm in arm waiting for Sarah's boat to dock. Katherine looked up at her husband. "I know why you married me."

Cody glanced down at her. He could think of a hundred reasons, but he wondered which one she would choose. Maybe she'd say it was the wine or the craziness of war when nothing made any sense. Or maybe she'd mention the numerous bruises she'd left on his body. He'd teased her that if he was shot down the Germans would think there was some kind of code hidden in the scratches and bruises on his chest. Or maybe she really understood that he wanted to spend the rest of his life, however long that was, with her.

"You were afraid of what Sarah might say if she knew we'd slept together."

Cody laughed. "I don't remember sleeping, darling."

Katherine poked his ribs. "You know what I mean. You think of Sarah as an angel who would never understand such a thing."

Cody played along. "Right. We could hardly make love all night with Sarah around. What would she think? She'd probably have me tarred and feathered and run out of the war for even thinking such a thing."

"She'd understand," Katherine reasoned. "After all she has a child. It's Miss Willingham who would have you shot on sight."

Cody couldn't resist nibbling at Katherine's ear. "Matthew was the result of an immaculate conception, I'm sure. Sarah's too much of a sweet little angel for it to have been anything else." He pulled her an inch closer, wishing they were back at the inn. "My marrying you had nothing to do with Sarah. I only felt it was my duty to save the life of some other poor soul who might have accidentally fallen into your arms."

"That was kind of you."

"It was the least I could do, offering myself." Cody whispered future plans into her ear, but Katherine wasn't listening as she searched the row of nurses coming down the gangplank.

Suddenly she broke away from Cody and ran toward a short nurse with a blue scarf tied around her dark curls.

Cody stood back and watched as the two friends hugged each other wildly, dancing and screaming at the same time. He realized that to love one was to love both. They might be as different as night and day, but they were a part of each other. Katherine might be his wife and love him dearly, but she would die for Sarah and he had to accept that as part of the package. He knew only a fool would ever try to come between them.

If a war couldn't keep them apart, one man wouldn't have a chance.

Twenty-five

SARAH HUGGED KATHERINE tightly against her. "I've missed you so desperately, Kat," she said. "A part of me didn't seem alive when you were away."

"I know," Kat agreed. The months they'd been apart had seemed like years, but hadn't weakened their friendship. "If you only knew how many times I've sat down and tried to figure out what advice you'd give me."

"I came to France to answer the call for nurses, but seeing you was a part of what swayed me." Sarah couldn't let go of Kat's arm. "I asked for a six-month leave from teaching. Miss Willingham agreed we needed to do more to stop the suffering."

"I only wish I had time to prepare you for what you're going to see."

"You've been preparing me for months with your letters. No matter how bad it is, Kat, I'm here to help."

"And Matthew?" Kat hadn't realized how much she missed seeing the baby until she saw Sarah. Suddenly memories of home flooded her mind. "He's growing up without me."

"Miss Willingham has him on a schedule already. You wouldn't believe how fast he learns. He'll probably be bored with school by the time he's old enough to start. We'll be back before he misses us."

"Sarah!" Cody called from several feet away.

Without letting go of Katherine, Sarah reached for him. Sarah took one look at their faces and knew Kat and Cody had finally realized they were in love. They could have lit up a dark room with their brilliance, and Sarah couldn't have been happier for them. A part of her remembered that glow, but her son now warmed the darkness she would live in for the rest of her life.

"So tell me"—Sarah crossed her arms and tried not to laugh—"what's been happening half a world away while I wasn't looking?"

Kat laughed. She knew Sarah would know. "We're married."

Another round of hugs followed. Sarah kissed Cody on the cheek and said, "Welcome to the family, Uncle Cody."

Sarah had always thought of Cody as a part of her family, partly because he'd been Bart's friend and partly because he'd been there when Matthew made his entrance into the world. All at once they all tried to talk. Katherine asked questions about Matthew and home, while Cody wanted to know every detail about the voyage over. There didn't seem to be a second when someone wasn't talking until it was time to board the trucks that would take the nurses to the hospitals at the front.

Cody lifted Sarah into the truck. "I have to fly back before dark. I'll see you when I can." He couldn't seem to take his eyes off Katherine even though he was talking to Sarah. "Take good care of my wife."

"I will," Sarah answered and moved away to allow them a moment alone.

Cody looked down into Katherine's face and thought he'd die if he had to say good-bye to her one more time. The gentle wind played with a free strand of her auburn hair while the late afternoon sun sparkled in her eyes.

Katherine sensed his feelings, for all of his emotions were in her heart also. "I'll love you forever," she promised, then leaned close to add with mischief, "Take off your clothes."

Cody laughed suddenly. "Right here, right now?"

"You said anytime, any place, birdman."

Cody knew she was teasing, but the fire in her emerald eyes held a promise. "Thank you, pretty lady. You've added love and wonder to my life."

Katherine raised her arms and hugged him as close as she could. "I'll love you every day I breathe."

Cody lifted her slowly into the truck as the driver started the engine and waved for them to hurry. "Good-bye, my love, my wife, my life."

There was no need to say more. As before, all the words had been said. He watched the truck pull away and wondered how long it would be until he'd be with her again. He felt as though his heart had stopped beating and would only resume with her touch.

Cody smiled to himself as he watched the truck disappear. He'd been right; there was a great deal of pain in caring for someone. But he was wrong about one thing; even the pain was a reminder of what they'd had, and as such, it was welcome. He'd live a thousand days without her if God would just grant him one more night with her in his arms.

"I'm coming back to you, Kat," Cody vowed. "You can stop worrying about me crashing. If I have to walk through the hell of this war on foot, I'm coming back to you."

Sarah sat close to Katherine and held out her hand. They watched the lights of the town grow smaller as they both prayed for an end to this war that had overturned their lives, even though America was still officially neutral.

Finally, when the port town had disappeared, Sarah said, "I'm afraid, Kat. All these months I've thought of how brave you were to come here. I wanted to be like you, but now that I'm here, I'm afraid I won't be able to handle the job."

Kat put her arm around Sarah. "Of course you will. I'll be near to help."

"But I wasn't there for you."

Kat laughed. "Yes, you were. I can't tell you how many times I felt you beside me."

"I wanted to come sooner, but I had to wait until Matthew was old enough for me to leave."

"You'll be back with him before you know it." Kat tried to sound confident.

"Oh, he'll be fine. He's braver than I'll ever be."

"What do you mean? Have you forgotten the night we ran away from the farm? Or when you ran into the fire to help save lives at the infirmary?"

"I had to help those people. Just as I have to help now."

Kat tried to keep her voice calm. "In many ways you'll be running into the fire again."

"But you'll be with me."

Kat nodded. "I've asked for an extension of three months so we'll be going home together."

All at once the other nurses could stay quiet no longer. They had to ask questions about what they were headed into.

Kat remembered her first days near the front, and she knew no words of warning or encouragement would be enough. Each woman would have to find her own strength. All she could do was try to help.

When they pulled into the camp, Sarah jumped down like a child who'd just found her home. Thanks to Katherine's letters she felt she knew the place already. This was her one chance to prove herself as a nurse, and she planned to make good use of the time.

"That's the main tent," Sarah told the others. "Our tents are behind it."

Light blinked across the sky like a huge lightning bolt.

All the women turned and caught their first glimpse of artillery fire from the front lines.

Katherine held Sarah's hand. "I'm glad you're here."

Sarah's blue eyes were full of excitement and fear. "One little war shouldn't be too much for the two of us to handle."

Katherine laughed. "Together forever."

"Forever and ever," Sarah added. "Now show me the hospital!"

"Don't you want to sleep first?"

Determination sparkled Sarah's gentle eyes. "I spent days sleeping on the ship. Now I want to begin what I came here to do."

Katherine directed the other nurses to their tents, then took Sarah into the hospital. As they walked among the beds she saw the field hospital through Sarah's eyes. For the first time in months, she felt the old anticipation and somehow believed that together they could make a difference. She realized that, to some, the wounded had become numbers in a faceless war, but to Sarah each man was an individual.

Within an hour Sarah had met Dr. Wells and the other veteran nurses.

"So you're the Sarah we've all heard so much about." Dr. Wells pumped her arm. "Not much bigger than a minute."

Sarah showed no fear when she smiled at the doctor. His eyes might be the same cold gray as Dr. Farris's, but she knew he could change. After all, Dr. Farris had joined Miss Willingham as a full-time grandparent to Matthew. "I can hold my own as a nurse."

Wells pushed up his bottom lip and looked at her more closely. "That I bet you can, Nurse Sarah. When would you like to start?"

"As soon as I find my apron," Sarah answered. "I'd like to work the rest of this shift before I unpack."

"Heavens be blessed!" Wells shouted. "I think you must be molded from the same clay as our Katherine."

Katherine winked at Sarah. "One mold," she said, "named Miss Willingham."

Both girls washed and set to work. As the hours passed they talked when there was time and smiled at each other across the room when work was heavy. The hours flew by so fast that Katherine was surprised when a new wave of nurses arrived for the shift change.

She and Sarah ate dinner together before finally giving in to aching muscles and heading toward the sleeping quarters. Sarah insisted on rooming with the staff because, after all, Katherine was not only the head nurse but a married lady now. Katherine wanted them to stay together, but didn't protest too much when she learned Sarah's quarters were just next door.

As in the state hospital, Sarah and Katherine balanced each other's strengths and covered each other's weaknesses. Before her first shift was over, Dr. Wells commented twice that Sarah was the most natural nurse he'd ever seen. She seemed to feel the patient's pain even before he'd been examined.

Sarah missed Matthew desperately but the work kept her so busy she had little time to think about home. He was being well cared for by Miss Willingham, and all these mothers' sons needed her. As the days warmed into summer the battle at the Somme built. There were reports of thousands dying to the southwest at Verdun. Newspapermen predicted 1916 would be the year of Europe's great bloodletting.

Sarah and Katherine read everything they could find about the pilots. The Americans flying in the Escadrille were the favorites of the reporters. They wrote about the pilots as though they were great knights fighting battles in the sky. When one made five kills, he became an ace and was elevated to godlike status.

Sarah watched Katherine closely, sharing her happiness and understanding her fear. They never talked about the chances of Cody dying, just as they never talked of the future except in terms of Matthew.

As before, as soon as Sarah learned the rules, Katherine took the night shift and Sarah the day, only Sarah noticed that Kat never left the hospital until well after dark.

After a few weeks Sarah learned to take a break just as the sun set. She'd slip out behind the hospital tent where no one else ever ventured and watched the night approach. The ground became rocky and uneven only a few feet from the tent, providing her with a natural bench to sit on. This became her favorite time of day. If she closed her ears to the constant rumbling from the front, she could almost believe the world was at peace.

One evening, just after sunset when the light still lingered, Sarah realized she wasn't alone. Someone had stumbled upon her secret place.

"Who's there?" she said as she backed up against the tent. She'd never told anyone about this place. If a German had crossed the front line, he could kill her without anyone knowing.

"Who's there?" she said again, trying to sound brave. With her height and weight he'd have to be a pretty puny soldier not to be able to kill her with his bare hands. Sarah clenched her fists; she'd fight as hard as she could anyway.

"Pardon my intrusion," a French voice said, and relief flooded her senses. "I did not mean to frighten the mademoiselle."

Sarah relaxed as the shadowy form of a man she'd heard called Hoot materialized between the rocks. He limped toward her but stopped before emerging from the darkness.

Sarah took a long breath. "It's all right. I didn't think anyone knew about this place except me."

The man moved slowly to a rock several feet away and

sat down as if to reassure her he meant no harm. "I come here when the others go to dinner."

Compassion filled Sarah's heart. "Don't you want to eat?"

He shook his head, and black hair almost covered his face. She knew he was lying. His hunger had nothing to do with the reason he never came to the mess tent. When she thought about it, she realized she'd never seen him inside the tent, not once. Sometimes she'd noticed him at the back door picking up a sack of food, but he was always alone.

In a world filled with people who seemed to come in pairs, Sarah had stumbled upon someone who must be even lonelier than she was herself. At least she had Katherine and Matthew. This poor soul looked as if no one had ever cared for him in his life. He wore his solitude like a badge of honor.

Her need to ease his pain was as great as any calling she'd ever had to help, but she forced herself not to look at him as she said, "I like to come here and watch the sunset, but I also miss dinner." She hesitated, unsure if her request would cause him an inconvenience. "Would you mind picking up something tomorrow night and bringing it to me along with your own dinner?"

"If you wish, mademoiselle."

She tried to see his face. "I think it would be nice to enjoy a meal with a friend as I watch the sunset."

The tall man stood up and disappeared into the night without saying a word. Sarah leaned back and wondered if she'd helped ease his loneliness or merely added to his problems. She'd heard Katherine say the man was like a shadow around the camp. Katherine and the Frenchman had a kind of unspoken trust between them as though they shared a secret. The shadow man always delivered the notes Cody sent, and Katherine had said more than once that she felt him following her when she walked from her tent to the hospital, as if to ensure her safety.

Sarah stood and stared into the night sky. She would not call him Hoot, she decided. She would call him Shadow.

The next day passed quickly, and Sarah was almost late in coming to watch the sunset. As she rushed around the corner she was surprised at what lay before her. On a rock beside where she'd sat was a little white tablecloth and a tray laden with food and coffee.

"Hello?" She looked around, but her shadow man was nowhere.

The smell of coffee lured her to her seat. She leaned back and watched the day's passing as she sipped her coffee and ate most of the food he'd brought.

When darkness once again blanketed the earth and none of the sun's glow remained, she heard a movement in the rocks beside her and knew her shadow man was once more at her side.

"Hello?" She relaxed, unafraid.

"Did you enjoy your meal alone?" With his voice so low and the French accent, she could barely understand him.

"Yes, I did. Thank you for bringing it." She tried to see him clearly, but the light was too poor. "Only I thought you were going to join me."

"I was nearby."

Sarah could hear the loneliness and pain in his words, but she wasn't sure how to reach him. If she went too close, he would disappear into the blackness. She decided that being honest with the man might be the only way to become friends. "I like it back here, away from the war, but it makes me a little homesick."

The shadow man moved a foot closer. "Tell me about your home." He sounded like a man who'd never had a home and wasn't sure what the word meant.

Sarah smiled, knowing she'd just found a way to ease his pain. Like most people, he desperately needed someone to talk to, and her need was no less.

"I live in Ohio." She began a long description of the

country and how far it was from where they sat. As she talked, she could almost feel him relax beside her even though he didn't say a word. She guessed he probably didn't understand many of the things she said, but it felt good to just talk to someone. She told him all about the hospital and Miss Willingham and even how she'd worked at the state hospital to pay off the cost of nursing school.

Finally Sarah stood, not wanting to say good-bye but knowing she'd stayed long enough to give both their tired minds a rest. "I have to go. It's getting late. I'm sorry I rattled on so."

The shadow man rose beside her. "Thank you." He sounded as if he meant it all the way to his core. "I enjoyed hearing about Ohio."

"Thank you," she answered and was surprised at just how deeply she meant it. "If you'd like, we could have dinner tomorrow night. I'll try not to talk so much."

He stepped away to allow her to pass. "I enjoyed it greatly."

Sarah was almost to the corner of the tent. "Well, don't get me started on my son or I'll never stop." She moved away, speaking more to herself than to the shadow man. "That Matthew Rome is one bundle of joy. He keeps me and Miss Willingham as well as most of the nurses busy."

She didn't see him slip into the trees or hear his cry of loneliness in the night.

As summer faded, the work increased daily. Many nights Sarah missed the sunset and her talk with the shadow man, but she always felt him close, like a guardian angel watching over her. When they were together, Sarah found herself doing all the talking while he only listened. Slowly, as friendship grew, he became a part of her life. She told him all the news from Miss Willingham as though he knew her and cared. She even found herself talking over the problems of the hospital with him, as if he might somehow have an answer.

One evening, well after sunset, Sarah walked around the back of the tent, hoping to find him waiting.

"Hello?" She walked to the rocks where they always sat. "Please be here tonight."

A movement reassured her of his presence. "I'm here," he replied in a voice that had come to mean stability in her world.

"Thank goodness." Sarah relaxed against the stone wall. "I need to talk to you."

All day she'd been trying to figure out in her mind what she would do, and again and again the answer seemed to be to talk with her shadow man. "I don't know what to do." She knew he would probably be of no help, but she had to talk to someone. "Katherine is urging me to go with her to Paris to meet Cody this weekend. They want to introduce me to a friend of his."

The shadow was silent.

"I don't want to go. I know it would just be all in fun. I don't want to meet anyone, but telling Katherine no is impossible. She has this idea that I should meet someone and get married someday. Then Matthew would have a father, and I'd have someone to take care of me. She's been telling me that Cody wouldn't introduce me to someone unless he's an honorable man."

There was a long silence before the shadow spoke, and then he said just one word: "Go."

Sarah stepped forward and tried to make out his face in the shadows. "So you're on her side?"

"She's right."

Anger bubbled in Sarah's tiny body. "I thought you were my friend."

She stormed toward the corner of the tent, but a strong hand reached out of darkness and gripped her arm. "I am your friend," he whispered. "I only want what's best for you."

Sarah shoved his hand away. "Well, I don't want a

husband. I don't think I could ever love another man after my Bart.''

He released her arm without comment and slipped back into the shadows.

Sarah ran all the way to Kat's tent. "Kat!" Sarah cried, needing her friend.

Katherine jumped up from her desk and ran to meet Sarah. "What's wrong!"

Sarah pulled herself together, realizing suddenly how small her problem was compared to those around them. "I can't go with you to Paris.''

"But of course you can." Kat started to go on, then stopped when Sarah raised her hand.

"I'm sorry. I worded that wrong. I don't want to go to Paris. My six-month hitch will be over soon and I want to work every minute I can.''

"But . . .''

"The answer is no," Sarah said simply.

Katherine realized for the first time that she couldn't talk Sarah into something.

Sarah continued, "I'll be here, so you won't have to worry about the hospital.''

Kat wanted to argue, but she knew it would be wasted effort. She slowly walked back to her desk and pulled a chair up for Sarah.

"Would you like some hot tea?''

Sarah smiled suddenly. "You sound just like Miss Willingham.''

Kat poured the tea. "I guess we're all changing." As she handed Sarah a cup, she added, "I always thought I'd welcome change and love adventure. But when you change it's somehow frightening. I'm looking forward to a time when the days will pass without change.''

Sarah, as always, understood Kat. "Don't worry, we'll always be blood sisters.''

"I know, but we seem to be constantly readjusting.''

"Maybe that's how we've stayed friends for a lifetime."

Kat looked over her teacup. "Maybe Miss Willingham was right about the tea also."

"Maybe feeling it scald all the way down makes you forget what you were worried about." Sarah laughed. "I have to apologize to someone. Then I'll come back and help you pack."

"I'd like that," Kat agreed. "It may take an hour to find my suitcase."

Sarah walked out of the tent and almost collided with her shadow man.

"I'm sorry," he said as he backed away into the blackness between the tents.

"No," Sarah answered. "I need to thank you for caring. I shouldn't have gotten angry. You do so much for me. You bring me dinner. You listen to all my problems. You even give me advice that I don't want, which must be the mark of a true friend. I wish I could give you something in return."

The shadow moved into complete darkness and murmured to himself, "You do. You give me a reason to live."

Sarah didn't quite hear his last words, but the warmth of his caring remained.

Twenty-six

"SARAH?" KATHERINE WHISPERED as she entered the shadowy darkness of the nurses' tent. "Where are you?"

Sarah rose up on one elbow. "Over here."

She could hear Katherine stumbling over trunks and corners of cots. "I have to talk to you!" Kat's voice sounded almost panicky.

Sarah shoved her covers aside and stood. "Stay where you are. I'll lead you out. This place is a maze at night."

One scarred hand reached out of the darkness to touch another. "Follow me."

Within moments they were in the yellow glow of the outside lantern. Sarah closed her robe in front of her and tied the belt.

"I've got to ask you a favor," Katherine said softly. "And you have to swear no one will find out. What I'm about to do could get me in big trouble."

Sarah raised an eyebrow but nodded, knowing she'd go along with whatever Katherine wanted, short of killing someone.

"A pilot landed about an hour ago with a message. He said Cody's plane was shot down."

Sarah pressed her fist to her mouth to fight back the cry shaking her body. "When?"

"Come dawn it's been three days." Katherine didn't miss the terror in her friend's eyes, so she continued rapidly.

"He's all right. Or at least he will be. Just bruises, no broken bones. He managed to crash-land on this side of the front."

"Thank the Lord." Tears were already flooding the corners of Sarah's eyes. "Is there anything we can do to help? Could they fly him here to the hospital?"

Katherine shook her head, then looked around before lowering her voice. "The pilot and I decided it would be easier to fly me to him."

"What!"

"I could fly out at dawn before the Germans even get up for breakfast and be back before my shift starts tomorrow night."

Sarah backed up as if she could push away from the problem. "No!" She looked at Katherine in disbelief. "You can't. The fighting's bad all around; everyone says so. What if you accidentally crossed the line and were shot down? No, Kat, you can't go."

"I have to," Katherine answered. "If he's hurt, I have to go to him."

"No!" Sarah felt as though death had walked between them. "It's too risky."

"The risk is small. I flew once before, back when planes were not nearly as sturdy. I need your help, please, not arguments. I'm going—that's a fact—but I have less than an hour to find a pilot's uniform that will fit me so I can get into Cody's barracks."

"Isn't there anything I can say to stop you?" Sarah didn't try to stop the tears rolling down her face. "The thought of you flying over the battlefields frightens me."

"If it were Bart, could I stop you?" Katherine turned away suddenly as the pain of her long-ago lie slammed against her heart. She had stopped Sarah from going to him; and until this moment when she compared Bart and Cody, she'd never known the magnitude of her lie. What if someone told her Cody had died? She'd hate the liar forever. And the liar would deserve her hatred.

Katherine shook with a pain so deep it clawed into her heart and ate away at her soul. She had to remain silent about Bart, but she hated herself for her reprehensible lie. At first she'd thought she was being merciful, but now she saw that Sarah should have been given the right to go to Bart and know the truth. For even if Cody had been scarred and burned in a crash, she would still want to be at his side. She'd had no right to alter the future for Sarah, no matter how much Bart begged her.

Sarah touched Kat's shoulder. "You're right, Kat. If Bart had been injured instead of killed, I'd have wanted to be there. I'll help you. Go to your room and get ready. I know one person I can trust to find us a uniform, if there's one in camp."

Katherine nodded and turned to hug Sarah. "I love you more than I could ever love a sister."

Sarah smiled at Kat's sudden emotion. "I know. Now go to your husband."

Before Kat was inside her tent, Sarah ran between the barracks and supply tents lining the small airstrip. She'd heard someone say that the mechanic slept in one of the tents where airplane supplies were stored. Several officers had ordered him out because if a shell hit the place, he'd go up in one big explosion of gas and oil. But Sarah suspected he'd still be sleeping among the spare parts and fuel tanks.

She followed her nose until there was no mistaking which tent was his. The smell of oil that always drifted around when he was near filled the air now.

"Hello?" she called as she entered.

No answer returned.

"Hello, my friend. I need your help." She felt a little silly talking to the crates and barrels.

"Please answer me. It's Sarah."

"I know who you are," the shadow man answered. "Even in total darkness I can feel your presence."

Sarah moved toward the voice. "Will you help me?"

"Yes," came the answer. No explanation was necessary for he clearly had no desire to deny her anything.

"My friend Kat has a chance to fly down to visit her husband, who's been injured, but she needs a pilot's uniform within an hour." Sarah moved closer to the shadow. "Is there such a thing around here?"

The toe of her shoe caught on the corner of a box, and she would have tumbled forward if a strong hand had not appeared out of the blackness to steady her.

He held her arm only a breath's passing longer than necessary, but Sarah felt in his hand the power of his need to touch her. Then his support was gone and she was alone in the darkness once more.

The shadow's voice came from a few steps away. "I'll find one and deliver it to her in half an hour, but I can't guarantee it'll fit. If you do any alterations, you have to return it to its original size."

"I can manage that. Anything else?"

The Frenchman was silent for so long she wasn't sure he planned to answer her.

"Don't dust the dirt off the shoulders," he said at last.

"But why—"

"It is the custom."

Sarah couldn't imagine such a custom, but she half remembered a Frenchman dusting Kat and Cody with dirt the first day they flew. "I promise," she answered as though she believed the dirt could have some importance.

"That is all," he added formally as though he'd given his first order.

Sarah took a deep breath of the air now thick with emotions as well as the smells of flying. "Thank you, my friend."

The man held open the flap of the tent for her to pass.

"Ask anything of me that you need. I'd move the earth for you, *ma chèrie*."

Sarah tried to see his face as she passed, but she couldn't make out his features. She walked into the open air with the memory of his touch still tangible against her skin and his words whispering through her mind. The only thing she could ever want was to have her Bart back in her arms, and not even her shadow man could grant such a request.

An hour later Katherine climbed into a plane for the second time in her life.

"We should be there a little past dawn, Mrs. Masters!" the young pilot yelled above the engine. "Wrap yourself up in that blanket and you'll stay warm enough."

Katherine wanted to tell him she was fine, except for the way her heart was pounding in her throat. She could imagine what Dr. Wells would do if he caught his head nurse flying off into the night. Briefly she wondered if he'd have her tied to a cot and shot at shift change.

As the plane rolled down the field, Kat looked toward the hospital and saw Sarah waving. Several steps behind her, Kat could just make out the thin shadow of the crippled mechanic. She had no idea where he'd found a pilot's uniform and there hadn't been time to ask, but when she returned she planned to hug the man, scars or no scars.

The flight was smooth. Except for the flashes of light along the horizon, she could almost have believed the world was as peaceful as the early sky. The young pilot seemed to take no chances of encountering the enemy. He flew straight and low as he neared the airfield. When they touched the ground Katherine laughed, thinking they hadn't made much progress with landings; it still shook every bone in her body.

"When the plane stops," the pilot yelled, "hop down and run toward the buildings. Captain Masters's quarters are in the third building you'll come to."

Katherine nodded and unwrapped herself from the blanket. "Thanks!" she yelled back.

The pilot shook his head. "You may not be so thankful when you see him. He's been in a devil of a mood since the crash. Even told the doctor where he could put all his pills. That's why I volunteered to bring you here. None of us were sure how much longer we could stand him if you didn't come."

The plane rolled to a stop and Katherine jumped free. She waved to the pilot, then ran toward Cody's quarters. The long line of buildings, half wood and half canvas, seemed to offer neither the warmth of real houses nor the mobility of canvas.

As she stepped inside the third structure Katherine froze and considered backing out before she was discovered. The place was a mess. Clothes and food trays were scattered everywhere. Dried mud and cigarette butts littered the floor. Empty whiskey bottles lined one wall, and one wine bottle was balanced atop another on the room's only table.

"Go away!" someone shouted from behind a curtain made from a blanket. "I don't want anything, least of all company."

Katherine carefully stepped around the filth. She couldn't believe this was Cody's room, yet the angry bear behind the curtain did sound like him.

She kicked a half-empty rations box out of her path and kept going.

"Get out, I said!" the bear yelled. "I've had about all the good cheer I can stomach."

Before Katherine could move, the curtain was shoved aside.

"I . . ." Cody froze as his gaze met hers.

"Morning." Katherine smiled innocently, as if it were her everyday greeting at this time.

Cody glared at her, exhaustion blurring his vision. His sandy hair, looking as if it hadn't been combed in days, hung over a bandaged forehead, and a light brown brush of beard covered his chin. He'd never looked better to her than he did at this moment. His eyes turned liquid with pleasure as he studied her like a man watching a dream take form.

Then suddenly she was in his arms, holding him tight while he buried his face in her hair. It had been almost a month since their night in Paris. One long month of lonely nights, worrying and waiting, melted into the reality of their warm embrace.

"Kat," he whispered into her fiery hair. "How did you get here?"

"I flew." She laughed at his expression. "Honest. Your men couldn't stand you any longer, so they sent for a real nurse to look after you. I only have a few hours to give you the very best of care."

"I'm fine. It was just a little crash," Cody answered, resisting when she tried to pull away for a look at his wounds. "You shouldn't have taken such a risk."

"A *little* crash?" Katherine looked at him closely. His ribs were strapped. His left forearm was bandaged, and a dark purple bruise marred his left shoulder.

"It was nothing. I was lucky. I got thrown out of the plane, and I must have landed on my head. When I came to, I didn't even remember hitting the ground."

"How long were you out?" Kat ran her fingers lightly into his hair, feeling a swelling just past his hairline.

Cody looked around the room. "Long enough for my squadron to do this much damage to my living quarters. They were worse than a bunch of wet nurses with a collicky baby. Sometimes I can't tell the pilots from the mascots around here. They all act like animals. None of them would leave until they knew I still had at least part of my brains remaining."

Kat followed his gaze. "I hadn't noticed the mess," she lied.

Cody winked at her. "You wouldn't. Or if you did, you'd

think I had decorated my quarters this way to make you feel at home.''

Kat raised her hand to strike him, but thought better of it when she had trouble finding an unbruised target. She planted her fist on her hip and cocked her head. "Now that we're married, I've noticed a few things about you that need to be changed. Like this neatness problem of yours.''

"Already trying to remake me?''

She slowly looked up and down the length of him. "No, I like the basic design. When it's in a little better condition.''

Cody's eyes darkened, and he leaned closer to kiss her.

"No!'' Katherine stepped back. "Before you touch me, I need to examine you completely.''

Cody hesitated, but she turned him toward his private quarters. "March, soldier, and strip off those trousers.''

"Anything you say.'' He chuckled while lowering the curtain to insure privacy. "You're always trying to get me to undress.''

"Now, don't get sassy with me, birdman, or I'll wrap that bandage around your neck instead of your head.'' She pulled a box of almost untouched medical supplies off his dresser.

She hadn't verbally fenced with a patient in some time, and it felt good. Somehow her sharp tongue made it easier for her to hide all the emotions welling up inside her. She could fight her fear that Cody had come close to dying by teasing him, even though they both knew this war wasn't a game.

"Yes, ma'am.'' Cody broke into her thoughts as his clothes hit the floor. "Damned if I didn't marry the bossiest woman in France.''

"I'm not listening.'' Katherine knelt in front of him and slowly ran her hands up his legs. She enjoyed the feel of hard, tight muscles beneath the soft dusting of hair. With or without clothes, he was a man to delight the senses. When she reached the first bandage, she didn't hesitate. "These wounds will have to all be redressed."

"They're fine!" Cody snapped, as if he hated being mothered, but the determined lines of his face were already softening to her touch.

Kat worked at what she'd done every day for years. She cleaned each wound, spread medicine where needed, and expertly bandaged the injuries. Only now the task took on a different mood. She was no longer only nursing; she was caressing, loving. And her touch healed his lonely spirit better than any drug could stop the physical pain.

When she reached the bandage on his forehead, Cody could feel his blood running through every vein in his body. The need to hold her made his muscles hurt as if he'd strained them. He watched her closely as she worked, loving the nearness of her.

When she finished treating the head wound and applying a fresh bandage, she said, "Now I think you're going to live."

"I'm not so sure." Cody's smile was filled with secrets only she'd shared. "I think now it's my turn."

"But I'm not injured."

Cody pulled the jacket from her shoulders and let it hit the floor. "I have to make sure."

"So you want me to take off my clothes?"

"No." Cody pushed two of his fingers inside her belt and pulled her toward him. "I'm going to take them off."

Slowly he unbuttoned her blouse. "Tell me," he whispered. "How come you get more beautiful each time I see you?"

Katherine closed her eyes and enjoyed the feel of his fingertips traveling over the flesh he uncovered. "You've been hit in the head. Maybe you don't remember."

Cody unbuckled her belt. "I remember every detail about you. And there is nothing I don't love." He slid his hands along her hips and lowered her slacks.

Closing her eyes, she leaned closer. "You mean you love my body?"

"Not just your body, but you. Katherine, I love you. The you that was brave enough to fly, the you who works far too many hours a day at that damned hospital, the you who holds me close at night because she's still a little afraid of the dark."

Cody cupped her face in his hands. "If I loved just your body it would be like living near a great lake and only swimming in the shallow part. There's far more depth to explore and enjoy within the woman I married."

Katherine brushed her fingers up and down the walls of his rib cage. "Do you think we could play in the shallows for a while and save the deep water for later?"

Cody laughed and pulled her gently to his bed. "Do you think you're the cure the doctor ordered?"

"I'm just the medicine you need. Don't worry; I'll try not to bruise you any more."

He kissed her soundly. "Before I met you I always felt I was flying toward the wrong end of the rainbow. If we ever get out of this mess . . ."

"Shhhh." Katherine pulled the covers over their bodies. "We'll talk about it later."

Twenty-seven

As EVENING DARKENED into midnight Sarah continued to work long after her shift was over. She knew it would be useless to try to sleep, with Katherine up there somewhere in the skies over France.

Dr. Wells asked about Katherine twice, but the duties were slower than usual. He convinced himself she must be catching up on paperwork. When he made his rounds for the third time, he ordered Sarah to leave and get some rest.

Sarah walked between the tents. The night air cooled her body, and Katherine's absence chilled her heart. Kat had said she'd be back before her shift started. That was hours ago.

Absently Sarah walked toward the tent where her shadow man slept. She couldn't endure the thought of being alone, and he was the only other person who knew Kat wasn't in camp.

"Hello?" she called as she stepped into the tent.

"Ma chèrie," a sleepy voice answered.

"I know it's late." Sarah moved toward him. "But I couldn't sleep with Kat not back yet."

"I understand." His English sounded almost perfect in his sleepy state. "How can I help you?"

"Can I stay here with you for a while?"

The shadow stood, his dark outline tall and lean. He hesitated for a long while before finally saying, "Of course, *ma chèrie.*'' He held his blanket out to her. ''You'd better wrap up in this to keep warm.''

''Thank you.'' Sarah allowed him to drape the blanket over her, wondering if his hands had held her shoulders for a moment in almost a caress or if she'd just imagined it.

''You don't smell so much of oil,'' she said, unaware that her comment might have offended him.

A low laugh rumbled from him. ''It's dark in here or you'd have noticed I'm only wearing my long johns. My clothes get soaked with oil . . . and never come clean. . . . I do try to bathe and smell like a human most nights.''

Sarah couldn't think of what to say. He'd just said more words than he'd ever put together in her presence.

''I'll get dressed if it would make you feel more comfortable.''

''Oh, no. Please. I've invaded your privacy, and the dark makes us both sightless.'' Sarah moved near the crates looking for one low enough for her to sit on. ''I'm so tired I wouldn't be able to keep my eyes open much longer even if it were daylight.''

''Would you like me to walk you back to your tent?''

''No, please allow me to stay. I have to wait for Katherine.''

''We'll hear the plane and have time to light the runway.'' He hesitated. ''Please sit down.''

Sarah gingerly lowered herself to the cot where he'd been sleeping. ''I'm so worried about her. If I lost Kat, I'm not sure I could handle life.''

Suddenly the tears couldn't be stopped. Sarah let go of all her banked fears and allowed the tears to fall freely. She'd grown so weary of always trying to be brave. Bravery was for Katherine, not her.

In the darkness she felt an arm encircle her and push her back on the cot. Silently the Frenchman pulled the covers over her and stood aside. In the night the action seemed more like a dream than reality. An action that might have been considered wrong in daylight now seemed natural among the shadows.

Sarah relaxed beneath the covers. She knew he stood only a few feet away protecting her.

"Rest, *ma chèrie*," he whispered an inch from her ear. "I'll wake you when the plane arrives."

She rested her head on the pillow and closed her eyes. As she drifted into sleep she felt his hand brush away a curl from her forehead.

Some time later the low rumble of a plane startled her out of a sound sleep.

"Careful," he whispered. "You'll fall off the cot." A hand crossed the blackness to steady her.

"Katherine?"

"Sounds like her plane coming in. I'll go light the strip. You stay in here where it's warm until they've landed."

Suddenly the shadow man was gone and Sarah felt cold and alone once more. She could hear him dressing only a few feet from her. "Thank you," she said.

"Any time, *ma chèrie*."

The noise of the plane grew as he left the tent. Sarah knew she should take his advice and wait inside, but she had to see Kat, had to know she was safe.

Sarah kicked off the covers and ran from the tent onto the field. The shadow man was lighting torches along the runway to guide the pilot in. Hugging herself, Sarah watched as the tiny plane circled, then landed and bounced along the grassy runway like a wooden rocking horse.

Sarah broke into a run to meet her friend halfway, but Kat's long legs covered most of the distance. They hugged wildly, though it had only been hours since they'd last seen each other.

"Kat!" Sarah yelled above the engine. "How is Cody?"

"Meaner than an old bear." Kat laughed, knowing Cody

would never show sweet Sarah his temper. "But he's healing. Did Dr. Wells miss me?"

"Not really. I think he called it a night not long after dark."

Katherine placed her arm around Sarah as they hurried toward the tents. "I need to talk with you as soon as we have some time."

"You're not planning to go flying off again?"

"No." Kat rubbed her backside. "I love the flying, but the landings are murder. I made a decision while I was flying."

Sarah linked her arm in Kat's as they hurried to Kat's quarters. "As long as you and Cody are safe, nothing else really matters."

"That's how I feel." Kat took a deep breath. "I won't be going back with you in two months. I've decided to stay longer with the Red Cross."

Sarah looked up at her friend. "Thank God," she said. "Because I signed my reenlistment papers yesterday and hadn't had time to tell you. I miss Matthew terribly, but I'm needed here. Maybe he'll understand."

Kat filled the teapot with water. "I hope you're not staying because of me."

"No," Sarah answered. "I'm staying because I'm needed. We have a massive job to do."

Kat lit the tiny stove. "Maybe between the two of us we can make a difference."

"Maybe." Sarah laughed as she reached for the two cups. "Shall we have tea?"

Twenty-eight

DEATH MOVED ACROSS France with endless artillery in one hand and the sword of typhoid fever in the other, killing equally with both weapons. Sarah worked each day until her hands bled, but the lines of wounded soldiers seemed endless.

Her only refuge hid in the quiet hour she spent each night with her shadow man. Gradually he began to talk more, asking her questions, telling her news of the pilots who flew into the small airstrip. Though he came to her only in the darkness, she knew there were subtle changes in him. She no longer smelled dirt and oil when he was near, and once when she touched his hair accidentally, it felt clean and soft.

She walked behind the main tent at sunset toward the one place where she could hide from the horror around her. During the months she'd been here, the French mechanic had become an island in a stormy sea. Katherine was close, but she had enough to worry about, with Cody and running the hospital. Sarah saved her problems each day until sunset, when she could talk with a man whose face she'd never seen clearly.

"Hello?" she called as she moved near the rocks, already guessing he was near.

"Sarah," came his answer. He said her name as though it were the beginning of a prayer. "I was afraid you were not coming tonight, *ma chèrie*."

"I'm sorry I'm late."

"It doesn't matter," he said. "Sit down. I brought you some cream for your hands."

Sarah did as he'd instructed and he knelt in front of her. "I bought this in the village. The farmer said it's made from goat's milk and aloe oil from Africa."

Sarah pulled her hands away, not wanting him to see the swollen red cuts along each crease. "My hands don't hurt so badly," she lied. "You shouldn't have gone to so much trouble."

Her shadow man didn't answer but simply took her hands firmly in his. His fingers were long and strong. With a gentle pressure, he rubbed the cream into her palms.

"That feels wonderful." Sarah leaned back against the rocks and relaxed.

He continued to slowly circle her chapped hands until he'd rubbed all the cream into them. Then he wrapped each with a bandage.

Sarah watched his dark outline before her. He'd grown to mean so much to her. His kindness seemed endless and without demand.

"Thank you." She leaned forward, but as always, he backed away, pulling a few feet out of her reach.

He was still, as though he thought she might advance and he would have to run. Sarah smiled. As thin as he was, he was far more powerful than she. Did he really think she might grab him and force him to stay? She knew his face was jagged with scars, but because the scars were a part of this kind man, she didn't find them repulsive.

"You're a nice man." She brushed his jawline with her fingertip.

He stumbled away from her as though he'd been shot at point-blank range.

"Wait." Sarah grabbed his cotton shirt. "I'm sorry." Her fingers closed around the material. The only way he was going to disappear into the darkness this time was if he dragged her with him. "I didn't mean to startle you . . . or hurt you." She hesitated, trying to find words he'd understand. "I'm sorry I was so forward. Please don't take offense."

He stopped pulling away, but he turned his face as far away from her as her hold on his shirt would allow. "You wouldn't touch my face if you saw me in the light."

His pain was as thick as oil, and Sarah felt her heart twist with compassion. "The man I touched is my friend, and I would have done so in daylight or darkness. You mean so much to me. More than you'll ever know." She released his shirt and turned her back to him. "Please don't disappear. Don't leave me alone tonight."

Sarah fought back her sobs. She knew she'd gone too far by touching him, but it was too late to go back now. "Some nights I need someone to talk to so desperately. I won't touch your face if you promise not to leave me alone."

He moved behind her and lightly rested one hand on her shoulder. "I'll be here if you need me."

He leaned an inch closer, and she did the same until her back pressed against his chest.

Sarah drew strength from his nearness. "Everything in the world is dying. I'm so afraid."

"I know how you feel," he whispered. "Until you came, I felt the same way."

Sarah couldn't stop herself. She had to tell him how she felt. "When I came here, I thought I could save lives, but all I seem to do is wipe up blood. I thought I was called to help the suffering, but the dying goes on and on. No matter how many times I wash my hands, I can't get the bloodstains off."

She wished she could curl up in his arms. "Since the day we entered nursing school people have been telling me I'm a natural nurse. But I'm not; Katherine is. She can pull far enough away from the suffering to get the job done. If I feel any more of their pain, I'll explode.

"I should go back home. I'm a good mother. I'm a good nurse to women having babies and old people with rheumatism, but this job is too great for me. I don't belong here."

"Yes, you do, *ma chérie*. You belong here."

"No." She stared up into the stormy night sky. "I don't belong anywhere. You see, I'm dead inside. I died the day the father of my child was killed. My heart is cold and dried up. Only the living should try to save the living."

"You're not dead inside." His voice was so low that the comment could have been a thought that passed between them.

Sarah brushed away her tears with her bandaged palm. "Yes, I am. All I'm able to feel is pain. I've pushed all other feelings aside for so long that they wouldn't return even if I summoned them."

"You're a beautiful woman."

"No," she answered. "I'm a mother and a nurse and nothing more. The woman part of me is dead."

The shadow moved slowly away from her. "Sometimes," he murmured, "it's unwise to declare even a part of yourself dead permanently."

She turned to question him, but he was gone.

As Sarah worked through the shadows, she missed her son desperately, but the sons of thousands of other mothers were dying, and she had to help. Her six months stretched into nine, but she still didn't feel her work was done. She and Katherine were awarded the Florence Nightingale Medal, the highest honor a nurse could receive. Both mailed their medals home to Miss Willingham.

Twenty-nine

KATHERINE WATCHED SARAH all day, knowing something was wrong, but remained unable to corner her long enough to find out what it was. The weather had been cold and rainy for days. Everyone in the hospital felt the dreariness outside. Even the war seemed to have taken cover for a rest until the weather cleared.

Finally, as Sarah's shift ended, Katherine watched her friend slowly remove her apron and walk toward the entrance. She looked so tiny among the rows of beds, almost like a lost child. She didn't stop every few bunks as was her habit, but held her chin high and moved slowly down the aisle.

As she reached the entrance, Sarah crumpled like a wet paper doll. She fell so quickly, she was on the floor before anyone in the tent could react.

Katherine dropped the tray she'd been carrying and ran toward her, as did several others. By the time Katherine could get close, Dr. Wells was already kneeling over Sarah, checking her pulse.

Katherine dropped beside him, holding her breath as she waited for his diagnosis. She forced herself not to reach out and touch Sarah. If she had simply fainted from exhaustion, Kat didn't want to embarrass herself by overreacting. If it was more serious, she had to be prepared to do what was necessary. After all, she was the head nurse; the others took their lead from her.

It took Dr. Wells only a moment; then he nodded as he always did when he'd made a diagnosis. "She's got the fever," he whispered to Katherine. "We have nowhere to put a woman patient. We'll have to ship her to the French hospital closer to the coast."

"No!" Katherine wasn't about to have Sarah sent so far away.

"Be reasonable, Katherine. We can't keep her here with the men."

Kat motioned for the medics to lift Sarah onto a stretcher. "I'll make up a bed in my tent."

The doctor nodded and turned to continue his work. Sarah was one of his troops, and he didn't have a replacement for her. "I won't have you tying up other nurses."

"I understand," Kat agreed.

The doctor's hard features softened. "I'll check in on her as soon as I'm finished here. Keep her warm."

"Yes, sir." Katherine knew he was as worried as she was, but he hid it behind his professional manner.

By nightfall Katherine had her tiny office organized like a private hospital. She'd had a cot delivered and all the supplies she might need. Sarah was dressed in a nightgown and resting quietly. Her fever was high enough to worry Katherine, but not dangerous. Katherine sat beside her, holding her hand, trying to force her strength into Sarah's body.

"This is all my fault," Katherine murmured. "If I hadn't come to France, you wouldn't have followed." She smiled, a sad smile that never reached her eyes. As she remembered, she hadn't had a great deal of choice about coming.

Sarah opened heavy eyelids. "It's not your fault," she said. "Stop blaming yourself for everything bad in my life." Her voice was weak, but her will was strong. "Ever since that day when we were eight and I asked you to cut my hand you've taken responsibility for every injury I've suffered."

Kat smiled, realizing Sarah was probably right.

"I only have a little fever. I'll be fine after I get some rest." Sarah closed her eyes.

Katherine knew this wasn't just a little fever. "Just get well." She traced the scar on her friend's palm. "Blood sisters forever," she added. "Please get well."

Someone rattled the tent flap. Katherine didn't want to talk to anyone. She just wanted to be alone with Sarah. If she could have figured out a way, she'd have loaded Sarah up and gone home. Miss Willingham would know cures for fever that even Dr. Wells wouldn't know. Miss Willingham would make them both feel better.

The tent flap rattled again.

"Yes?" Katherine snapped as someone stepped just inside her office but still in shadow.

"I come to check on the little nurse." The French accent was thick with worry.

Katherine looked up at the mechanic she'd grown to trust. "It isn't good. She's got the fever."

"I want to help." The shadow moved nervously as if preparing to fight an opponent. She knew it had taken a great deal of courage for him to move out of the darkness and come to her tent.

"There's not much to do except wait. I've told the other nurses that I'll take care of her. They promised to check on her at night while I'm at the hospital."

A long silence stopped even the air in the tent from moving before the man spoke again. "I could bring you food and supplies. I could sleep just outside in case you need something." He seemed desperate for a chance to help. "I could sit with her at night."

"It's too dangerous. You might get the fever."

"I don't care. I want to help." His words were both a plea and a demand.

Katherine's fear and worry over Sarah's illness made her impatient with this poor man. She was a breath away from asking him what he knew of nursing and how on God's earth he thought he could care for someone when the only thing he ever worked on was engines. But she stopped herself. She'd known him for a long time, and he'd just said more words to her than he'd ever uttered. She realized he must care a great deal about Sarah.

"You could be a great help if you'd fetch her meals so I don't have to leave her to do that. And at night, if you wish, you can make a bed just inside the door. That way if Sarah cries out, you can come and get me." Katherine wasn't sure she wanted this man touching Sarah with his dirty hands. She didn't bother to tell him he'd have to be very quiet; the man was always as silent as a light breeze. She had decided she might as well put him to work because she had a feeling he was going to be a step away watching, whether she accepted his help or not.

"I'll go get my things," he said without hesitation and disappeared.

After he'd gone, Katherine wondered if she'd made the right decision. No one in the camp knew anything about Hoot. He seemed to have no past and no future, and no friends or enemies for that matter. But if he'd been a bad man, she reasoned, she would have heard something by now. He had helped her once when she needed the uniform. She owed him for that. Cody trusted him with their mail, so maybe she should trust him just a little.

An hour later Katherine had to return to her shift. She left Sarah sleeping while Hoot sat in the dark corner by the door. She reminded him to come and get her if Sarah called out, but she wasn't sure how much the Frenchman understood. Finally she left the tent, vowing that if he so much as touched Sarah's hair she'd kill him ten times.

The lights were low, like circles of fireflies drifting around her, when Sarah opened her eyes. Her mouth felt sandy and dry, and her arms were too heavy to move. Her head felt as if she'd slept with her face against the oven door, but her body shook with a chill.

She turned her head slowly and saw the outline of a man standing over her, but she couldn't seem to focus her eyes. He was only a dark form hovering nearby.

"Water," she whispered.

The outline moved away and returned with a cup. He sat on the edge of the cot and lifted her carefully into his arms. When she was secure against his shoulder, he raised the cup of water to her lips. She swallowed a few drops, then rested her head against his heart. He felt so good to be close to. The nightmare she'd been having disappeared as he rocked her gently in his arms.

"Thank you," Sarah whispered.

"You're welcome, darling."

Sarah cuddled closer, rubbing her hand lightly over his chest. "Don't leave me," she said. "Don't ever leave me."

He kissed the top of her head. "I'm right here if you need me, *ma chèrie*."

Sarah drifted in and out of her dream. Sometimes she awakened burning hot and felt someone place a cool cloth on her forehead. Sometimes she'd begin to shiver, and even before she asked, blankets would be tucked in around her.

When the tent was bright with daylight, Sarah knew Katherine was always near; but when the room was in shadows, it was the man who saw to her every need. He slept in a chair only an arm's length away. Once, when she moved her head slightly, she felt his head resting on her bed. She didn't have to open her eyes to know he slept. Gently, so as not to awaken him, she brushed her fingers over his soft hair. He wore it longer than most men did, and it felt wonderful in her fingers, reminding her of Bart's thick, coarse mane.

When she finally grew too tired to continue, she pulled her hand an inch away and rested it beside his face. She could feel his warm, slow breath brushing across her fingers. After several minutes he moved slightly and kissed her hand with a feather-light kiss that could have been more in her dreams than in the real world.

After an endless time during which the days and nights seemed to be strung together like smoke rings, Sarah awoke and her vision was clear. She felt weak, but fog no longer fuzzed her mind until no thought could catch hold.

Looking around, Sarah was surprised to find herself in Katherine's office. Everything was neatly arranged as if Sarah had been sleeping there for a long time.

The door flap rattled and Katherine rushed in followed by a brisk wind and a watery morning sun. She paused for a moment and stared at Sarah.

Sarah rose up on one elbow and gave her redheaded friend a weak smile. "Morning. How long have I been asleep?"

All at once Sarah found herself in Katherine's arms. She was being hugged so wildly that she feared the room might start spinning again.

When Katherine pulled away, tears shimmered in her eyes. "You've been ill for over six weeks now. I've been so worried about you."

Sarah tried to comprehend Katherine's statement. How could it be possible? She felt as if she'd awakened after too long a night's sleep. The faint memory of sleeping in Bart's arms warmed her for a moment. It would almost be worth being ill if she could dream again of him. But he could only live in her fantasies, for there was no place for fantasy in reality.

"What's happened?" A feeling that life had passed her by filtered through Sarah's sleepy mind. "The war—is it over?"

"Not by a long shot," Katherine answered. "I'm beginning to think the war will never be over."

"Cody?" Sarah's eyes widened at the despair in Katherine's eyes.

"He's fine." She didn't seem very sure. "He's been up to see us twice since you've been ill, but he could only stay a few hours each time. The fighting in the air grows more deadly each day." Katherine didn't want to talk about Cody, and Sarah recognized the worry lines along her brow. He was alive today; that was all they could hope for.

Katherine picked up a stack of papers. "You've got tons of mail to read. Miss Willingham sent you some of Matthew's drawings. They look like scribbles to me, but she insists they are designs for airplanes. Can you believe that? I'd bet my pay that Miss Willingham didn't encourage him in the least, but he's got flying in his blood just like his father."

Sarah rested back against her pillow. "He'll never fly. I'll see to that with my last breath."

"Maybe that sense of adventure is born into a man and he can't help it." Kat wondered if any mother could keep her son from following his dream.

Sarah shook her head. "No! He's going to be a doctor. Miss Willingham and I agreed."

Katherine wanted to laugh, but she feared Sarah might be serious. "People can't be talked into being what you want them to be."

"I talked you into being a nurse. Are you sorry?"

"No," Kat said. "But Matthew Rome may have his own dreams. He may want to fly."

"I couldn't bear it if he died like Bart."

Katherine turned her back and Sarah realized she'd been thoughtless. Katherine was also in love with a pilot. That would explain why Kat never mentioned Bart even though it had been years since his death. She must fear every day that what happened to Bart might happen to Cody.

As if their thoughts had caused the sound, both women looked up at the tent ceiling as a plane flew low overhead. "Cody!" Katherine cried and ran to the entrance of the tent. She looked back, debating leaving Sarah alone.

"Go." Sarah fought back the tears in her eyes. "Thank God he's safe." Sarah leaned back on her pillow and fell asleep as though she'd been up all night instead of a few minutes.

It was dark when she woke again. The shadows in the tent overlapped one another making gray and black triangles inside the small space.

Something moved in the shadows.

"Who's there?" Sarah asked, hoping it was Katherine.

"Don't be afraid, mademoiselle." The shadow moved closer until she could almost see his face. "Katherine said you were better, but I thought I'd come by and check on you just in case you needed anything."

"No. Thank you. I don't think I need a thing except sleep." Sarah had a feeling her shadow man had been by every day to check on her. He'd probably driven Katherine crazy. "Unless you'd like to keep me company for a while. You could sit in the chair there by the lamp and tell me all that I've missed."

The shadow man backed away slightly. "I have to go," he said. "I have to have Cody's plane ready to fly at dawn."

Sarah didn't want to be alone again so soon. She wanted to talk to her friend if only for a few minutes. "Where is Cody?"

The shadow man seemed in no hurry to leave her. "Dr. Wells gave Katherine the night off. He told them to take one of the extra tents for the night. Cody has a new assignment, and he needs to talk to Katherine in private before he leaves. They have to have time to say good-bye."

"It's nice that they can be alone."

The shadow looked nervous. "They only have until dawn."

Sarah could sense he knew more than he was telling her. "What is it?"

The shadow man debated leaving without telling her, then hesitated a long moment. "Katherine may need you

when Cody leaves at daylight. It's no secret: Cody drew a
mission no other pilot would volunteer for. He's going to fly
straight over no-man's-land. Our generals believe there's a
new big buildup several miles behind enemy lines. If Cody
can find it and drop one flare, we'll know where the next
assault is coming from.''

Sarah relaxed. The assignment didn't sound that difficult.
''He should be back in a few hours.''

The shadow's low groan told of his disbelief. ''They have
to know the location by tomorrow or it may be too late for
thousands of troops on the ground to move. His orders are
to fly until he finds out where the buildup is or until he runs
out of gas.''

Moving from the bed, Sarah was almost to the door
before he caught her. ''Let me go!'' she cried, too weak to
fight to free herself. ''I have to stop him from going up.''

Iron fingers held her tiny frame. ''There's nothing you
can do. Get back into bed. You're still very weak.''

Her eyes brimmed with tears when she looked up into the
shadow man's dark face. ''You don't understand. I have to
do something. I can't let Cody die. I can't let Katherine feel
the pain I felt when Bart died. You don't understand.''

His words were tight with emotion. ''There's nothing
we can do. Cody drew the assignment. What would you
have him do, refuse the assignment and have another pilot
take the death flight?''

Sarah wanted to say yes. Men were dying every day in
this war. The average pilot only lasted three or four weeks.
But Cody couldn't die. She and Kat couldn't both lose the
men in their lives. ''I don't care. We have to stop Cody from
making that flight. Let someone else be a hero; Katherine
deserves to have someone love her.''

The shadow never slackened his grip. After several
minutes, Sarah saw his logic. She didn't have the right to
send another man to his death just because Katherine loved
Cody so much.

Suddenly Sarah felt very old, as if all the emotion within her had been used up and there was no way to replenish it. She leaned into her shadow man and allowed his strong arms to support her weight.

"I'll do something," he whispered as he rocked her to sleep in his arms.

"Please," she whispered. "Please help him."

"I promise." His words were an oath.

After a long while the shadow lifted a sleeping Sarah into his arms and carried her back to bed. He tucked her beneath the covers and straightened her beautiful ebony hair.

"Good night, my darling," he whispered as he pressed his lips to her cheek. "Good-bye, my lovely woman-child."

Thirty

KATHERINE COULD HARDLY wait to get out of the dining hall and have Cody all to herself. Every officer within five miles wanted to talk to a real flying ace from the newly named Lafayette Escadrille.

"Come on," she said as she pulled Cody out of the mess tent.

He laughed at her eagerness. "I thought I'd just have a few more words with—"

She punched him playfully in the ribs. "I've been waiting all day to get you alone for a few hours. How dare you think of talking war when you have to leave in the morning?"

One rakish eyebrow lifted on Cody's handsome face. "Are your intentions honorable, Mrs. Masters?"

Katherine fought to keep from hitting him again. "Of course not. I've been trying to get you in bed since the moment I laid eyes on you."

Cody hugged her wildly. "That's what I've always suspected." He laughed as they ran to their tent.

He closed the flap and tied it securely while Katherine caught her breath. She stared at him through the shadows, wondering how such a perfect man could be real. She could hardly wait to mess up his hair and turn his eyes wild with passion.

Neither one thought of lighting a lamp as they faced each other. Cody straightened and reached for her, but she stepped away from his grip.

In the twilight Kat raised her hand, palm forward. He did the same, lightly touching her fingers with his own. As his hand brushed hers, Kat closed her eyes with pleasure, telling him that his slightest touch moved her deeply. As their fingers locked, she moved toward him, coming into his embrace gracefully.

He held her against him, wishing he could pull her right into his body until their flesh and blood blended into one. "I love you, Kat," he whispered.

She pulled his mouth to hers and bit at his bottom lip, loving the way he always held her as if he felt afraid that something might pull them apart at any moment.

He crushed her against him and kissed her with a passion that surely had taken more than one lifetime to build. His mouth pressed hard and demandingly against hers as his hands moved up and down her sides, pulling at her uniform.

As the kiss softened, his hands slowed to loving magic. Each stroke was a fraction closer to her breast, an inch lower on her hips.

When he released her, he smiled, satisfied at his effect on her breathing. Love darkened her gaze. Cody stood his ground as she dug her nails into his back as though she were trying to claw the cotton from his flesh. "Tell me you love me, Kat," he said without moving. "I need to hear the words."

She stopped teasing as quickly as she'd started. She'd never really thought of Cody needing anything from her, but now she saw a longing deep in his eyes. "I love you," she said as she planted little kisses across his face. "I love you more than I've ever loved anything or anyone in my life. I'll love you a moment longer than I breathe." She ran her fingers into his hair and pulled slightly. "I love you for a hundred reasons and for no reason at all."

He felt his muscles relaxing. This was all the heaven he had ever asked for. All he'd ever wanted. To have one woman love him. He'd never heard his parents say loving

words to each other or to him, and he needed right now to
know that Kat cared deeply for him.

Katherine's body pressed against him, begging him for
attention as he stood so controlled before her. She moved
her hands over his hips and pulled him close telling him of
her need without words.

Cody lifted her into his arms and moved to the small bed
that stood in one corner of the vacant tent. "We have to
talk." He sat down and tried to pull her with him.

"Later," she answered as she knelt beside him. She
smiled as she slowly unbuttoned his shirt. Her fingers
slipped inside, and she smiled as his chest hair tickled her
palm. When he reached for her, she leaned away but smiled
up at him with a look that asked only a small amount of
time.

Cody gripped his legs to keep from touching her as he
watched her remove the pins from her hair. Suddenly her
mass of curls tumbled over her shoulders as she shook her
head. When he would have touched her, she leaned back
again and smiled as she began opening her uniform button
by button. He watched her undress as his hold on his legs
whitened his knuckles.

She stood and let her uniform fall to the floor, then knelt
once more in front of him to push his shirt from his
shoulders. A moment later when her warm lips touched his
chest, he was consumed by the passion that he felt only for
Katherine. He pulled her against him and kissed her wildly,
proving that she'd driven him to the point of madness with
her teasing. He rolled onto the bed, taking her with him.

Her body moved beside him setting fire to a need for her
that never died. His tongue parted her lips as his hands
roamed over the silk of her body, loving each part of her
flesh. His fingers moved over her, warming her skin with
his gentle touch.

Katherine loved his caress, light with love at first, then
strong and demanding with desire. His touch reminded her

of a warm rain. Light and soft at first, then building into a great storm that made her mind whirl until there were no thoughts left but of Cody and his love. When his hands cupped her breasts, she whispered her pleasure in his ear.

As he pressed her into the mattress his body replaced his hands. His lips moved lightly against her mouth as his chest pressed against her own, making her heart explode with passion.

Kat raked her fingernails across his back as he lowered his head between her breasts. He leaned into her soft flesh and heard her heart beating. The pounding was a music he would never tire of hearing. He pressed his body against her, needing to feel all there was to know of his Katherine.

They made love wildly and without bounds until they were both so tired they could only hold each other close and marvel at what they'd done. Cody wouldn't allow himself to sleep because he didn't want to miss one moment of time he had left with Katherine.

They lay awake listening to the sounds of the camp coming alive an hour before dawn. Cody pulled her close and knew he could delay no longer. "We have to talk now."

"No." Katherine kissed his cheek. "I don't want to hear it." She knew it would be bad news. She'd known it when she saw Cody climb from his plane. Something about the way he walked toward her had told her he'd come to say good-bye once more.

"Not putting it into words won't make it go away, Kat."

"I know." She buried her face in the hollow of his neck.

"I have to fly a mission at first light." He wanted to lie to her and tell her he'd be back in a few hours, but he knew the words would ring false. "Two planes will go up. One will fly on this side of the line; the other will fly parallel but on the other side of the enemy line. As soon as the pilot on the enemy side sees any sign of a troop buildup, he will fire a flare, then try to make it back across the line."

"Sounds like a simple plan." She played with the light patch of hair in the center of his chest as though what they were saying wasn't already pounding against her heart.

He stopped her hand, spreading her fingers flat.

"You'll be back in a few hours." She could hear the ring of her lie even in her own ears. How good she'd become at believing lies. This one should be just as easy . . . shouldn't it?

Cody was silent for a minute before continuing, "Our orders are to stay in the air until we spot the buildup or run out of gas." He tried to ignore Katherine's gasp. "Once the pilot who flies over enemy lines spots the buildup, his signal will tell his partner where the troops are, but it will also tell every German for miles where he is."

Katherine rose up to look him directly in the face. "So you're saying the one on the other side doesn't have a very good chance of making it back."

"That's about the size of it."

She didn't want to ask, but the words slipped out. "Which plane will you fly?"

Cody stared into her face, trying to remember every line so that when he went down he could put her face before him. "I'll fly the plane that crosses the enemy line."

Katherine wished she could have cried, but her sorrow was too deep for tears. A hundred thoughts came to mind. They could run for the coast. Cody could desert from this war his country wasn't even fighting. He could refuse to fly.

Among all the thoughts, she could find no reason. They both knew he had to go no matter how much he loved her and life. It was his duty, his honor. Somewhere he'd made the choices of this day a long time ago, and now he had to complete the ride. She had to be ten times braver to let him go.

She rose and picked up her clothes, knowing he had to fly this mission. "We'd better get dressed. I'll walk you to the field." There was nothing more she could say.

Cody could almost see her pain, yet she didn't cry or beg him to stay. In one shattering flash he realized how much stronger she was than he'd thought. Maybe stronger than he.

They dressed in silence, afraid to look at each other for fear they might shatter the thin sliver of control they were managing to maintain.

"Ready, Mrs. Masters?" Cody finally turned.

Katherine lifted the hood of her cape over her hair. "Ready, Captain Masters," she answered.

As they walked toward the field, he knew he was holding her hand too tight, but he couldn't seem to loosen his grip. He'd never loved her as much as he did right now. If he had a thousand years, he couldn't tell her how much she meant to him.

When they neared the other tents, Sarah joined them.

Katherine frowned. "Sarah, you shouldn't be out of bed."

Sarah looked as if a sudden wind might blow her across the trench line. "I had to come to say good-bye to Cody." She moved to the other side of Cody and locked her hands around his arm.

When they reached the field, light was just blending with darkness on the horizon. The world looked almost peaceful with gentle breezes and low rain clouds to the south. Two planes were lined up, ready to take to the air. The other pilot already waited next to his plane. He had no great good-byes to say, for with any luck at all, he'd be back in a few hours.

Cody turned to Sarah and opened his arms. "Take care of that nephew of mine."

Sarah stood on her toes and hugged him. "Come back safe," she said as if she believed that was a possibility. "Go with God."

Cody held her in a brotherly hug, then opened his other arm to Katherine. "Take care of each other," he ordered, wanting to add, *because the men in your lives haven't done such a great job,* but he only said, "because I love you both."

An engine sputtered several yards away. Cody spun around, knowing the whine of his own plane the way a mother knew her child's cry.

A tall, powerful man dressed in a pilot's uniform limped out of the shadows toward the craft. At first Cody watched him without reacting, thinking he was only the mechanic who worked on the planes. The overalls had been replaced by brown slacks and knee-high boots. His shirt collar shone white beneath the well-worn leather jacket of a seasoned pilot. The man circled the plane, patting the Indian chief symbol of the Escadrille as only one preparing to mount for flight would do.

Cody started running, realizing what was about to happen, and knowing he'd never make it in time to stop the man from taking off in his plane.

The first rays of the sun touched the mechanic's blue scarf as it billowed above him. Cody watched in horror as the man slid into the cockpit. One end of midnight blue silk was tossed high in the wind like a flag of victory as the plane began to roll down the runway.

Blue, the color Sarah always wore. The same blue Bart had worn the day he'd crashed and burned years ago. Cody pieced the clues together in his mind.

Sarah's scream rang out in the dawn air as the engine roared. Cody fought hard to believe the man he saw was real and not a ghost who was taking his flight to certain death. Bart had been so close, and Cody had not recognized him. And now Bart would fly his mission.

Cody glanced back at the women. Sarah had fainted, and Katherine was kneeling beside her on the grass. Without hesitation, he ran to the other plane.

"I'm going up in yours, Cliff," he yelled as he jumped

into the cockpit and started the engine. "See after the women."

Before his words could register on the stunned pilot, Cody was heading down the runway a hundred yards behind Bart. Within minutes he was airborne and circling so he could see Bart's plane, *his* plane, crossing into no-man's-land between the trenches. Firepower brightened the sky without reaching Bart's plane. Puffs of man-made smoke drifted skyward to join the gathering thunderclouds.

Bart flew a mile over the line until he was no more than a dot. Cody stayed parallel to him on the other side and watched for a signal. He couldn't help but smile. There was no doubt in his mind the pilot was Bart. No man handled a plane the way he did. Even with the war below, it felt good to be in the air again with his old friend.

They flew with their backs to the sun the way the Red Baron liked to do. That way they'd be harder to spot coming out of the light. It wasn't much protection, but it was all Bart could count on.

Cody found himself talking to Bart as if his friend could somehow hear him. "Steady, now. No hurry. Keep an eye out. Watch your back." He thought of all the things that could go wrong with Bart's plane besides running out of gas. The engine could lock up, sending him into a dive. Oil could splatter over the body and catch fire. Most pilots claimed that fire was a frequent passenger on their flights. If one started, there was no way Bart could make it across no-man's-land before he went down.

The sun rose higher and still they flew. Cody knew fuel was too low to even bother checking now. "Come on back home!" he yelled at Bart as if his friend could hear him. "We'll refuel and go up again."

Only Cody knew Bart understood that wasn't in the plans. "Fly until you find them or you run out of fuel. Thousands of lives are at stake." Only when Bart reached the buildup, there'd be enough guns waiting to shoot a hundred planes down. So the orders should have read, "Fly until you die."

Suddenly the ground started popping as if someone had set off a long string of firecrackers. Cody saw several German planes scouting along the horizon heading north. A magnesium flare shot from Bart's plane, spotting the sky white with a starburst signal and pinpointing the buildup at the same time he gave away his position to the enemy planes.

Swearing loudly, Cody dived and searched for a place to land. He wanted desperately to cross the line and give Bart a hand in the dogfight, but he had to notify the troops on the ground of what Bart had found or it would have all been wasted.

Moments later he touched ground just behind the trenches with the jolt of a rookie and jumped from his plane. Several men crawled out of their foxholes and ran toward him.

"Wire your command office that we've found the buildup!" he yelled in French. "Wire them your location. You men are sitting right where they plan to come across."

It seemed as if he shouted the order a hundred times before the men finally heard and started running back to the trenches.

As soon as he knew the message would be sent, he climbed back in his plane. He'd be lucky if there was enough gas to get him off the ground, but he had to try to find Bart. He should have crossed over the line just behind Cody, unless he'd made one last circle to get more information.

By now the sun was too high to offer any protection. Thunder rumbled to the south, but it was drowned out by the roar of war. Cody took to the air in one expert sweep and headed back to where he'd last seen Bart's plane. He flew through thin, wet clouds as he crossed over the jagged veins of trench warfare and entered enemy skies.

About the time Cody reached the spot where he'd last seen Bart, he heard the roar of another plane coming in fast on his left. He maneuvered and prepared to fire just as he spotted his own plane clearing the mist.

Bart's blue scarf was flying as he circled Cody and waved toward safety. They flew side by side, wings almost touching as they had when they'd done shows. Turning west they headed toward home.

They crossed the German trenches with the help of cloud cover. Cody took his first deep breath since he'd been airborne and set his sights on the green land just beyond the Allied trenches.

But before he could exhale, his engine sputtered and locked. In near panic, he watched the propeller stop as if a giant hand had held it motionless.

He fought wildly at the controls as the nose of his plane pointed toward the earth. Pulling at the sticks did little good, for he had no control of the plane.

Cody watched the earth hurry toward him. He had crashed many times, had even jumped from the plane a few times before it hit the earth. But never in no-man's-land. The ground was barren and dead with constant firing across what had once been a pasture.

Without the engine the world was strangely silent as he went down. He could feel bullets hitting the sides of his plane, but no sound reached him. Air rushed past his ears as he headed down.

Pain suddenly sliced across his leg as a bullet went into his muscle. Another cut deep across his shoulder. His hands braced against the controls, fighting the pain, fighting the blackness that was trying to invade his mind. By instinct he released his belt. One more bullet, he thought, and I won't feel the pain of the crash.

The plane hit the battlefield like a broken toy. It bounced and tipped almost over before rocking to a stop, hurtling Cody from the craft.

Bullets and bombs were everywhere. He grabbed his useless left arm with his right hand and rolled away from the plane, which was taking all the gunfire. The ground was hard and uneven, bruising and scratching him as he rolled.

When he was several feet from the plane, he stopped rolling and raised his head an inch, realizing he'd lost all sense of direction. Even if he could keep from passing out, he had no idea which side was which. They both seemed to be firing at him and the plane.

Cody's mind darkened, and he thought he heard the roar of another plane. Suddenly, from nowhere, Bart flew in low and slow. He passed so close that if Cody had stood up, he could have touched the wings.

Blinking at the wind and dust, Cody turned his head an instant later to see Bart's plane crash in flames. Black smoke rose in the air, curtaining off the sight of the far trenches.

"Now's our chance!" Bart yelled from only a few feet away as he stood dusting himself off like some cowboy who'd just jumped from a bronco. "Let's run for it."

Cody tried to get up, but blood soaked his leg and shoulder. "Go on without me. You can make it before the smoke clears."

Bart grabbed Cody's good arm and slung him over one shoulder. "Hang on. I've got fifty bucks says we both make it."

He limped across the uneven ground toward the Allied trenches.

"Drop me!" Cody yelled.

"Like hell!" Bart shouted above the firing. "What'll I use for a shield?" His baritone laughter blended with the thunder and gunfire. "If I drop you, one of those crazy Frenchmen might shoot me for trying to act like one of them."

"You can make it alone!"

"Trust me, partner. I've already died a few times. I know how to do this." Bart's hold remained firm around his friend.

A huge explosion shook the earth as lightning split the sky. Nature had decided to join in the battle. Bart dived for a trench a few yards away. The world turned black in Cody's mind. In his last moment of consciousness, he saw Kat's face before him.

Thirty-one

SARAH BURROWED INTO her pillow and smiled before forcing her eyes to open. Slowly the room took form. The ever-moving tent walls, a lamp that never seemed to cast enough light, Kat sitting beside her.

"I had the strangest dream," Sarah began.

Kat stared at her with a mixture of worry and fear in her green eyes.

Sarah forced the world into focus. "It wasn't a dream! I did see Bart!" She could tell by Kat's reaction that her words were true. "He was wearing a blue scarf. He took Cody's plane." She lowered her voice to a whisper. "He took the death flight."

Katherine nodded. "I didn't know." Her fingers were laced so tightly together they were ghost white from lack of blood circulation. "I never dreamed the mechanic was Bart. I never got a clear view of his face, and he was so much thinner than Bart."

Sarah didn't understand Kat's reaction. "Of course you didn't know. I'd talked to him many times and didn't guess. How could we? We both thought Bart was dead."

Katherine closed her eyes and bit her lip until she tasted blood. "I knew he was still alive somewhere."

"But you told me—"

"Bart made me swear to tell you he died the day he was burned. After the accident the doctors told him he'd probably never walk again. He didn't want you to waste your life nursing him."

Sarah's hand covered Katherine's laced fingers. "And you went along with the lie? You allowed me to believe he died?"

Katherine nodded, wishing she could travel back in time and change one sentence. One lie. "Sarah, I—"

"No, Kat." Sarah pulled her hand away. "I don't want to talk about it now. My mind is flooded with worry. Until this morning I thought my Bart was dead. The moment I discovered he was alive I learned he had gone on a suicide mission. A mission I practically begged him to take for Cody. I can't handle any more pain, any more lies."

All the years of friendship were tumbling around Kat's feet. She would have given her life to go back and restore Sarah's trust, but she couldn't change history, only the future. "Will you forgive me?"

For the first time in her life Sarah's eyes were cold when she looked at Katherine. "I'm not sure I can forgive you or him. When he returns, if he returns, I may very well strangle him for what he's put me through."

Katherine couldn't help but smile. She'd never seen such anger in her friend. The anger would melt away the pain of feeling betrayed. Mild little Sarah was forging a strength amid the fires of her wrath. A power that when combined with her compassion would see her through any ordeal.

"Remember." Katherine stood and moved toward the door. "I'm here if you need me. I'm not perfect, but I'll always be your friend."

Sarah didn't answer for a long while. Finally she said, "You had no right to do what you did. I would have gone to Bart."

"I know," Katherine answered. She didn't have to explain. Sarah could figure out her reasons for lying. She stepped outside the tent to allow Sarah time alone, knowing she would have to abide by whatever Sarah decided.

Thirty-two

By the time Katherine and Sarah received word about their men, the sky had turned dark with rain. They were both working when Dr. Wells called them aside and gave them a message. The report simply stated that both planes had gone down in the no-man's-land between the two trenches. Both men were listed as missing.

"Bart's not dead," Sarah said soberly. "I believed it once, but not again." Her eyes were devoid of tears. She'd cried an ocean of tears for him already.

Sarah pivoted to return to her duties, but Katherine's hand on her sleeve stopped her.

"All I can say once more is I'm sorry." Katherine felt as though her world had come crashing down around her lie. With each hour that passed without Sarah speaking to her, she felt worse. "I wanted to tell you, but after Bart disappeared, there seemed no point. I've let that lie eat away at me for so long. Every time I looked at the scar on my palm, I wanted to confess, but Bart made us swear to be silent."

"Us?" Sarah looked straight into Kat's eyes. "Cody also knew, of course."

"He was there. He's the one who pulled Bart from the fire," Kat answered.

Sarah stared at Kat. "Neither of you thought I had a right to know Bart was alive."

"We were wrong." Kat could no longer face Sarah. All her bravery had vanished. "I see that now."

"We need to get back to work." But Sarah didn't move. Katherine nodded, but also stood motionless.

Then slowly Sarah placed an arm around Katherine's shoulder. As always, she felt Katherine's pain. She remembered the day they'd become blood sisters; she had felt both cuts as if they were both her own. "I should be really angry with you, but all I can think about is that my Bart was alive and was near me and I didn't even know it."

Katherine held Sarah tight, wishing she could make up for all the pain her lie had caused.

Finally Sarah tried to lighten the mood. "Stop worrying about the past. The anger I feel toward you and Cody is nothing compared to what I feel for Bart. If he isn't dead this time, he'll be returning to an angry woman, not some frightened girl. All those months he was in the shadows and never let me love him. He's got some making up to do."

Both women laughed, but the worry lines never left their faces. They worked and talked, trying to pass the time without allowing dread to consume them. After three days of waiting, vehicles of every description began to arrive from the south carrying wounded. The drivers told of a great battle in which men had fallen by the thousands.

Katherine and Sarah asked every driver and wounded man who could speak if he'd seen two planes go down at the same time in no-man's-land just before the battle. Every time the answer was the same: no.

Finally, almost four days after the men had flown off, a driver stepped into the hospital one night and motioned Katherine to him.

When she reached him, he whispered, "You know them two pilots you were looking for?" He smiled, happy with himself for what he'd discovered. "I got them both on my truck. They're shot up . . . ."

Katherine was too far away to listen to more. She lifted her skirt and ran for the tent.

The ambulance was parked outside in the rain. A huge black tarp draped over the back of it offered shelter but no warmth for the bunks with wounded inside.

Katherine didn't notice the mud or the rain. She climbed into the back of the truck and moved from cot to cot. "Cody?" she called, afraid to hope.

"Hi, Red," said a familiar voice, minus a French accent.

"Bart!" Katherine dropped to her knees beside his bunk. "You both made it back."

Bart coughed. "Plus a few bullet holes and minus a little blood. I had to bring him back to you. Sarah begged me to, and damned if I don't do whatever that little lady tells me."

"And did you come back to her?" His leg and arm were bandaged. Katherine could see the right side of his face now, all scarred and twisted flesh. But after what he'd done, he would never be anything but handsome in her eyes. "You've come back to Sarah?"

Bart remained silent until he realized she was prepared to wait all night for the answer. "If I could have gotten off this truck, I wouldn't have come back. They loaded us up before I knew the driver would head this direction. She can do a lot better than the likes of me for a husband. It's best I walk away. Tell her—"

"No!" Katherine answered before he could even begin his request. "I'm not telling her anything but the truth for as long as I live. If you have something to say to Sarah, you'll have to tell her yourself. But you're right. If you haven't got the sense to know how much she loves you, you don't deserve her."

"That's what I've been telling him for three days." Cody's voice was weak, but clear as it came from the bunk above Bart's.

Katherine cried out and reached for her husband, hugging him so hard he groaned in pain.

"Easy on the boy, Red," Bart grumbled. "I didn't save his hide to have you squeeze him to death."

When Katherine released Cody, he was laughing. "I've always wanted to die in your arms, but not this way."

The pain in his eyes brought forth all her nursing skills. Within an hour both he and Bart were settled into a corner of the hospital and their wounds had been cleaned and dressed. Bart's were mostly flesh wounds and bruises, but Cody's shoulder would take months to heal. Due to his blood loss, he had little more color than the sheet, but Dr. Wells wasn't worried. All the medicine Cody needed to recover stood beside him holding his hand as if she planned never to let go.

By dawn both men were resting quietly and Katherine sent one of the nurses to wake Sarah. Ten minutes later Sarah stormed into the hospital like a whirlwind in blue.

Dr. Wells blocked her path to Bart. "Now slow down, Nurse Sarah," he said in a voice that rang with laughter for the first time in a year. "I know you're mad at this man. Katherine told me all about it. But I'll have none of the wounded killed by my nurses."

Sarah replied with deceptive calmness. "Is Bart in any danger of dying from his wounds?"

The doctor relaxed. "No. He'll recover. Fact is, after he spends a day or two in here for observation, I'll probably kick him out."

"Thank you, Doctor. I have no intention of doing him bodily harm." Sarah smiled so innocently she could have melted steel. "I'm sure Katherine exaggerated when she told you about my anger."

The doctor nodded and took a step backward. He'd found it hard to believe gentle little Sarah could hold more than a pint of anger.

She stepped around him and moved with all the grace of a trained nurse to Bart's bed. Pulling up a stool, she sat staring at his sleeping face for several minutes. It was a face she'd loved years ago. She'd touched his cheek in the shadows only days ago and never known whose heart beat so near her own.

The scars on the right side of his face ran from his hairline down past his neck. For a moment she wanted to turn away, for she could almost smell the burned flesh and bloody skin that must have been fused together to create the mark. It must have been horrible living with the pain until the wounds eventually healed. She could imagine what it had been like watching the red, seeping, swollen flesh heal into the twisted scar. And then to look into people's eyes and see pity in those who were strong enough to look directly at his face.

With steadfast determination, she gently reached across the bed and pulled the restraints into place across his chest and arms. Her fingers brushed over his powerful chest as she checked the straps to make sure they were secure. He was far thinner, but the strength was still within him.

Bart slowly opened his eyes and stared at the ceiling of the tent in confusion before recognizing his surroundings. As he turned toward her, Sarah found herself lost in his smoky gray eyes. Eyes that were filled with love and longing at the sight of her. Eyes that stared at her as if God had granted him one more look at her before condemning him to a lifetime of blindness.

But before she could speak, he turned away, hiding the right side of his face from her. "I brought Cody back to Katherine," he said.

Sarah straightened slightly. "And you? Did you come back to me?" She fought to keep the tears from falling. She had to be strong now. Her future, her life, depended on it.

"No," he answered after hesitating. "You can do far better than the likes of me. As soon as I'm able, I'll be on my way."

Anger boiled in Sarah's gentle body as only Bart could make it do. She reached out and jerked his face toward her with both hands. "I could waste my time asking you if you love me, Bartholomew Rome, but I know you do, so there is no use lying to me."

"That doesn't matter."

"That is all that matters," she argued.

He tried to pull his head away, but her tiny hands held him forcefully. His powerful chest strained against the straps that bound him to the bed. "What the hell!"

"You're not running out on me again." She smiled like an angel who'd just caught the devil's tail. "It looks as if you came back to me one too many times."

Bart struggled against the restraints for several more minutes before he finally fell back in defeat against the pillows. He looked straight at her without hiding his scars. "You have to let me go, Sarah. I'm too old for you, I'm crippled, and I'm scarred all over, not just my face. I can't make you look at me every day for the rest of your life."

Sarah pressed her palm against his scar and stared directly at him. There was no pity in her voice or in her eyes, only anger blended with a touch of passion. "How could you have run out on me when I needed you the most? How could you have put me through so much pain just because of a few scars?"

"But look at me, Sarah."

"I am looking at you, Bart. I see a man with about as ugly a scar as I've ever seen." She leaned closer. "What makes you think you were all that great looking before the crash? If I'd been hoping to fall in love with a handsome man, I never would have gone riding with you that first night. It wasn't your face that attracted me; it was your heart. As far as I can tell it's still bigger than a barn, even if it is paired with a brainless head."

Sarah brushed his dark hair away from his eyes. "I fell in love with the man behind those gray eyes, not the wrapping."

She lowered her head slightly and kissed his lips. "I love

you," she whispered in her kiss. "Don't ever leave me again."

Bart strained now to break the restraints so he could pull her to him and never push her away. He felt as if his heart might explode with pleasure. Never in his wildest dreams did he think she'd want him.

"You could still love me like this?"

"I never stopped loving you." She brushed his cheek lightly, not even feeling the scar. "Just as I know you never stopped loving me."

A voice invaded their private heaven. "Pardon, mademoiselle. You sent for a chaplain?"

Sarah looked up at the hospital chaplain. Confusion filled his features. He'd already prepared himself to give last rites, but the man before him didn't seem to be near death.

"Yes." Sarah stood up and straightened her uniform. "I want you to marry me to this man."

"What? Here? Now?" The chaplain hadn't performed a wedding in so long he was uncertain he remembered the words.

Bart started shaking his head so violently he rocked the cot to which he was strapped. "Wait, Sarah. Give it some thought. You may want me now, but in a few months you'll change your mind."

"I think not, Mr. Rome." Steel reflected in her blue eyes.

The priest looked perturbed. "I'm not in the habit of marrying people in hospitals. And the groom doesn't look too willing. He is tied to his bed."

"That's damn—"

Sarah clamped her hand over Bart's mouth. "Please, Father," she pleaded with the priest in a voice that would have made angels comply. "He's the father of my children."

"What!" The priest's face turned red with anger. If there was one thing he couldn't tolerate, it was soldiers who left nice girls in a family way just because of the war. He pointed one long finger at Bart. "Is that true, sir?"

Sarah released Bart's mouth just long enough for him to say, "Yes, but—" before she smothered his protest.

That was all the priest needed to hear. He straightened like a gladiator preparing to battle sin and quickly married the couple before him. He didn't even bother to ask the man in bed to say "I do," for in his mind the man had already said it.

When the ceremony ended and the priest moved away, Sarah gave Bart a quick kiss on the cheek and disappeared to complete her duties. She could hear him swearing as she walked away, but she didn't turn around.

It took Bart until suppertime to persuade someone to untie him. He tried ranting and raving, swearing at everyone who passed, threatening, and finally pleading, but no one listened. Finally, when Katherine appeared to relieve Sarah, she came to his aid, thinking someone must have bound him by mistake.

"How's Cody?" Bart asked as he sat up in bed for the first time all day.

"He's very weak. He lost a great deal of blood. Even now the shoulder is still seeping some." Katherine sounded worried. "He told me how you saved his life. How you wouldn't leave him in the field."

"I knew you and Sarah would murder me if I came back alive without him."

Katherine hugged Bart. "Thank you," she whispered. "How can I ever thank you enough? Of course I understand that Sarah plans to murder you for lying to her."

"She picked an interesting weapon." Bart laughed. "She married me while I was tied down."

Katherine's laughter filled the tent.

Bart stretched his bandaged muscles. "Stop that, Red, and tell me where Sarah is. I have to talk to her."

"I have no idea." Katherine wondered why Sarah hadn't

talked to her new husband before she left the hospital. "She disappears almost every night about sunset, but I'm not sure where she goes. Wait and I'll ask someone to send for her."

Bart stood up, balancing himself carefully. He bit back the pain as he slid on his trousers and shirt. "Never mind. I'll find her."

"But you can't leave your bed," Katherine protested. "Now I see why they had you in restraints." She glanced around for an orderly to help her get this tall man back into bed.

"Nonsense." He stomped into his boots. "There aren't enough nurses or doctors in this war to stop me." He was past Katherine and out the side door of the tent before she could try to prove him wrong.

He knew where he'd find Sarah as he moved silently around to the back of the tent. The sun was down, but the light still glowed violet in the sky.

"Sarah?" he called softly, not wanting to startle her.

She turned to see her shadow man move toward her. "Are you still angry with me?" she asked.

Bart pulled her gently into his arms. "I love you more than I ever thought would be possible."

"Even though I made you marry me?"

Bart chuckled. "We've been married since the day we met. You just made it legal."

His fingers brushed the sides of her waist lightly loving the feel of her as always. "You're my wife," he murmured into her hair. "You've always been my reason for living."

"You don't mind sharing me?"

"With whom?"

"Your son. He owns half my heart."

Bart kissed her forehead. "I can't wait to see him." He searched for the right words. "Do you think I'll frighten him?"

Sarah shook her head. "He's a Rome, stubborn and

brave, but he has a gentle side also. In only a little time, he'll see you true.''

Bart's lips moved along her cheek, and he kissed her deeply. There was no need to hide his love for her in the shadows. She had come freely into his arms, and he never planned to let her go.

He slid his hand up to her breast as he'd longed to do for almost a year. "You've changed slightly." Even through the material he could tell she was fuller, far more woman than the girl she'd been when they'd made love.

Sarah ran her fingers over his chest. "So have you. I may have to learn to cook so I can put some fat back on you.''

His fingers circled over her, feeling the tips of her breasts even through the uniform. "You're perfect just the way you are.'' He lowered his mouth to kiss her lips as his grip tightened over her soft flesh.

Finally he gained enough control to pull away slightly. "Tell me, my wife, why'd you have to lie to the priest? You told him I was the father of your *children*.''

Sarah nuzzled his chest. "You might be, after tonight.''

Bart pulled at the buttons of her uniform. "I'll take you up on that challenge.'' He'd waited forever to touch her.

She pushed away from him and ran into the darkness. "Catch me, shadow man!'' she yelled.

He didn't have to run. He knew where she was going. Bart walked slowly toward his tent, smiling at what he knew would be waiting for him. The answer to his dreams. Sarah.

Thirty-three

KATHERINE SPENT ALL of her off-duty hours sitting beside Cody's bunk. As time passed, his wounds healed, but the fever remained. In his mind he slipped in and out of reality, making Katherine's fears mount.

More than a week had passed since he'd been brought to her. Finally one morning, with grateful prayers of relief, she looked into feverless brown eyes.

"Cody." She touched his forehead with a cloth. "How do you feel?"

"As if I'd been dragged by a plane around the world," he whispered. "I dreamed Bart Rome dropped me in a hole."

"He did. It saved your life." Katherine fought the urge to giggle. "Would you like some water?"

Cody nodded. After taking a long drink, he stared at her. "When I was about to crash, I saw you as clearly as I do right now."

Katherine covered his hand with her own. "You always said you feared you would."

"No." Cody shook his head slightly. "You don't understand. I saw you and knew I wasn't going to die."

Katherine reached for the cloth, fearing the fever had returned.

Cody stopped her hand. "I saw you with gray in your hair and my children all around you." He smiled as if he knew a great secret. "We're going to have a huge family. Blond sons and redheaded daughters. And''—he tightened his grip on her hand—"I'm afraid the house will always be a mess."

Katherine kissed his whiskery cheek. "I'll stay home and clean it."

Cody laughed at her lie. "Sure you will."

Dr. Wells interrupted them. "Well, young man, it's about time you got out of that bed and left it for someone who needs it."

Cody didn't release Katherine's hand. "I can move in with my wife."

"No, son." The doctor lifted a chart. "You're going home. The United States is going to need good pilots. As of yesterday, Uncle Sam joined in this fight. You boys will be flying under your own flag from now on."

"But—"

"Bart mustered you out of your unit. You're going home as soon as you're able to travel. I'm sending my head nurse back with you to see you get home safely. She's served more than her time here. From what I understand, we can use a few thousand pilots who know how to fly like you and Bart. They'll be telling stories of that last mission for years."

Katherine could hardly contain her joy at the thought of heading back to the States. "What about you, Dr. Wells? Are you going home?"

The doctor shook his head. "More Red Cross nurses are heading over every day. Someone has to stay here and tell them how to run a field hospital."

Katherine hugged him, realizing the man had finally found his calling.

"God protect you," she said.

"And God go with you," he answered.

Three weeks later Bart watched as Cody was carried toward a supply ship heading back to the States.

"I can walk!" Cody yelled.

"Sure you can." Bart shoved him none too gently back onto the stretcher. "You'll fall off the gangplank, and I'll have to jump in the water to save your hide one more time."

"I don't remember asking you to save my life!"

Bart laughed. "I don't remember you thanking me either, but I'll let that pass. I got to keep you alive long enough for you to father my future daughter-in-law."

"What makes you think any daughter of mine will want to marry a Rome?" Cody couldn't help but smile. "I was hoping to have brighter children than that."

"You might have if they inherit their brains from their mother." Bart tipped his hat at Katherine and Sarah, who were waiting at the railing. "I figure our children will marry because of those two. There's no separating them, you know."

"I know." Cody watched the women closely. "To love one is to love them both."

"That's a fact," Bart agreed. "Only I'll be stationed on the East Coast, and you'll be out west. Sarah and Kat will be separated by an entire country."

Cody shook his head as they boarded the ship. "They'll never be far from each other. If their friendship could survive knowing the two of us, it'll survive a few miles."

The men neared as Sarah raised her hand in the air and Katherine did the same. As the women's palms touched Sarah said, "We'll be friends forever and ever."

"Forever and ever," Katherine answered.

The ship's horn bellowed as Bart saluted Cody; his face and his life were no longer in shadows.

Cody pulled a French coin from his pocket. He pitched the copper five-cent piece at his old friend. "For my life, Bartholomew. Hang on to that," he yelled above all the racket. "If a Rome ever needs a Masters, send the coin and we'll be there."

Bart nodded and slipped the coin into his vest pocket. He

placed his arm around Sarah and they moved toward the cabins. When he leaned on her slightly, his limp was hardly noticeable.

Katherine moved to Cody's side. "I love you," she told him. "Think you can endure being grounded until this ship reaches harbor?"

"As long as I'm with you," he answered as he pressed her hand to his lips, "I'll always fly under the rainbow and touch the stars with you by my side."

442